*White Rose Rebel*

# White Rose Rebel

JANET PAISLEY

VIKING
*an imprint of*
PENGUIN BOOKS

VIKING

Published by the Penguin Group
Penguin Books Ltd, 80 Strand, London WC2R ORL, England
Penguin Group (USA) Inc., 375 Hudson Street, New York, New York 10014, USA
Penguin Group (Canada), 90 Eglinton Avenue East, Suite 700, Toronto, Ontario,
Canada M4P 2Y3 (a division of Pearson Penguin Canada Inc.)
Penguin Ireland, 25 St Stephen's Green, Dublin 2, Ireland (a division of Penguin Books Ltd)
Penguin Group (Australia), 250 Camberwell Road, Camberwell, Victoria 3124, Australia
(a division of Pearson Australia Group Pty Ltd)
Penguin Books India Pvt Ltd, 11 Community Centre, Panchsheel Park,
New Delhi – 110 017, India
Penguin Group (NZ), 67 Apollo Drive, Rosedale, North Shore 0632, New Zealand
(a division of Pearson New Zealand Ltd)
Penguin Books (South Africa) (Pty) Ltd, 24 Sturdee Avenue, Rosebank, Johannesburg 2196, South Africa

Penguin Books Ltd, Registered Offices: 80 Strand, London WC2R ORL, England

www.penguin.com

First published 2007
1

Grateful acknowledgement is made for permission to reproduce the following extracts:
*True Stories* copyright © Margaret Atwood, 1981, reproduced with permission of
Curtis Brown Group Ltd; 'The Little White Rose' from Hugh MacDiarmid's *Complete Poems*,
reproduced with permission of Carcanet Press Ltd.

Set in 12/14.75 pt Monotype Dante
Typeset by Palimpsest Book Production Limited, Grangemouth, Stirlingshire
Printed in England by Clays Ltd, St Ives plc

A CIP catalogue record for this book is available from the British Library

ISBN: 978-0-670-91718-1

www.greenpenguin.co.uk

Penguin Books is committed to a sustainable future
for our business, our readers and our planet.
The book in your hands is made from paper
certified by the Forest Stewardship Council.

For Sarah and Melanie, guid-dochters, with love

'There was a singular race of old Scotch ladies. They were a delightful set – strong-headed, warm-hearted, and high-spirited – merry even in solitude; very resolute; indifferent about the modes and habits of the modern world, and adhering to their own ways, so as to stand out like primitive rocks above ordinary society. Their prominent qualities of sense, humour, affection, and spirit, were embodied in curious outsides, for they all dressed, and spoke, and did exactly as they chose.'

*Lord Cockburn, 1779–1854*

# Acknowledgements

Thanks to the Scottish Arts Council for financial support, to Judy Moir for sound editorial advice, to Rennie McOwan, Maggie Craig and Pamela Fraser for research books, to Lucy Conan and Johanna Hall at BBC Radio for the experience in dramatizing history, to Kevin MacNeil for essential assistance with Gaelic, and to Eirwen Nicholson for checks on historical accuracy.

Don't ask for the true story;
why do you need it?

It's not what I set out with
or what I carry.

What I'm sailing with,
a knife, blue fire,

luck, a few good words
that still work, and the tide.

*Margaret Atwood*

I want for my part
only the little white rose of Scotland
that smells sharp and sweet – and breaks the heart.

*Hugh MacDiarmid*

# ONE

In the distance there was a drum beating and the faint skirl of slow pipes. It was a call to the clans, for a chief was dying. At such a time even bitter enemies forgot their grudges, laid their swords aside and set off to honour the call. Undisturbed by the distant beat, a roe deer grazed in the fading light of dusk among heather and rock on the foothills of the Cairngorms. A shot cracked off, then another, with barely a heartbeat between. The deer staggered, fell.

'*Trobhad!* Come on!' Calling out in Gaelic, a young girl, maybe twelve or thirteen years old, dashed from the thicket of nearby trees, her grubby face alert with joy as she ran barefoot towards the wounded beast, the musket in her hand still smoking. Her long dark hair was crazily tangled but her dress, though clearly Highland, was velvet and lace.

'Anne, *fuirich*! Wait!' An older youth in a chief's bonnet and kilted plaid emerged behind the girl, the second gun in his hand, the gleam of his red-gold hair still discernible in the gathering dark.

Anne did not heed or hesitate. She dropped the musket as she ran, drew a dirk from the belt at her waist and, to avoid its hooves, leapt over the injured deer, short sword poised. As she leapt, the terrified animal thrashed, trying to rise. Its flailing hooves smacked against her shin. Anne yelped, stumbling on to the heather. The youth, two steps behind, threw down his gun, drew his dirk, fell to his knees and yanked the deer's head back to finish it. Anne lunged forwards on to its chest to plunge her blade first into the animal's throat.

'I got him,' she said. There was challenge in her voice. The lad glanced at her across the shuddering carcass as the earthy stench of blood rose between them. 'All right, MacGillivray,' she conceded. 'We both got him.' Then she thrust her fingers into the slowing spurt from the deer's neck and, with the middle one, drew a bloodied line down the centre of her forehead. 'But it's my kill.'

I

Satisfied that her right was secured, she jumped to her feet. Pain twisted up through her body. The yelp was out before she could stop it. As she staggered, the young MacGillivray caught hold of her. Anne raised her long velvet skirt and looked down. Her right ankle had begun to swell. She tried again to put her weight on it, biting her lip so as not to squeal again with pain.

'I'll carry you,' MacGillivray offered.

'And what about the deer?'

'It'll have to wait.'

'*Gu dearbh, fhèin, chan fhuirich!* Indeed it won't!' She would not lose the kill. There were few deer left on the hills, and they'd been lucky to find this one. Hungry folk were not the only hunters. 'The wolves would have it before we were half-way home.'

'I'll put it in a tree.'

'You'll take it back to Invercauld. People won't arrive to an empty larder now.'

'They'll bring food, if they can. It's been a thin year for all of us.'

'But he will eat.' Her throat constricted. 'And get strength from it.' Her voice wavered. 'Maybe then they can all go home again.'

MacGillivray stared down at her. At nineteen, he was a full head taller. He could remind her that the dying chief couldn't eat, hadn't for days. Instead, he caught her round the waist, lifted and slung her over his shoulder.

'What are you doing?' She struggled.

'Putting you in the tree,' he said as he strode back to the thicket.

While she shimmied her backside into the fork of the tree he put her in, MacGillivray primed and loaded her musket before handing it up.

'But I still think it should be the deer.'

'Will you go, Alexander?'

He slung his own musket to lie across his chest and swung the deer carcass across his shoulders. He was not happy at the prospect of returning without her. They were not his clan. These were not his lands.

'MacGillivray,' she called as he set off. He turned, still ready to hoist the deer into the tree and her out of it. 'That way,' she pointed. 'Follow the drum.'

MacGillivray let his breath out, turned and headed the way she directed. The limp head of the deer banged against his back with every stride, blood still dripping.

'Tell them I shot it,' she yelled as he vanished out of sight.

Now she was alone. Among the rocks, two courting wildcats circled each other, yowling. A hunting owl hooted. The moon rose above the hills. Its light made the pool of deer blood gleam in the dark. From the valley beyond, a wolf bayed. Anne shifted in the tree. If the pack came this way, they'd pick up the blood-scent and be after it. MacGillivray had slung his musket first. To load it, he'd have to drop the deer. The wolves would dart in. They would be ravenous, their natural caution blunted. He'd get one shot in, and time to load and fire again as they dragged the deer away but, with only a dirk to use then, if there were more than two wolves, the kill could be lost. Anne looked around the tree, hung her musket on a short branch and drew the dirk from her belt.

By the time the moon reached eleven o'clock in the sky, the wolves had found the congealed puddle of blood. They could smell the sour stink of humans too, but hunger removes much reticence and the ribs of these three animals were visible through their scraggy pelts. One sniffed around the puddle. Another raised its head and yowled. The third picked up the trail of what to them was wounded prey and they all loped off, following it. The fork in the tree where Anne had been was empty. Near it, a jagged branch bore the pale white wood of a fresh cut.

Dribbles of deer blood shone on the rough track made by MacGillivray. Breathing hard, Anne hobbled across rock and heather, a crutch hacked from the tree under her left arm, the butt of her musket under the right, her swollen ankle roughly bandaged by cloth torn from her skirt. She had gone some way towards Inver-cauld but not enough. From behind her, further back on the trail, a wolf howled. She stopped, half-turned, listened, trying to gauge how far, how fast. The heather-clad ground and low trees were cut against dark shadows deepened by the high moon. The front of Anne's dress shone darkly in its light.

Leaning on the musket butt, she touched the bloodstain with her hand. It was still wet. Wolves would not normally have troubled her. They were shy of folk but starvation changed both man and beast. That was why she was on the hill when she would rather be at home, and why she'd left the safety of her tree. Without thinking, she'd gone after MacGillivray to protect her kill. But in the time she'd taken, he could have reached Invercauld and be half-way back to fetch her so now, as the wolves followed the blood-spoor, they would find her instead, reeking of the deer they tracked.

Heart thumping, Anne gripped the musket butt tight, swung round and lurched forwards, intending to travel faster. Instead, she slammed into something solid. Winded and disoriented at the sudden presence, it took her a few seconds to realize it was a man she'd walked into. He was dark-headed, long black hair to his shoulders, but old, maybe even thirty, and he was a stranger. Without speaking, he reached out and, though she ducked, clamped his hand on the top of her head and wiped the blood trophy from her forehead with his thumb.

'Seadh, a-nis,' he said. 'So, it's a warrior I've found.'

Anne was sure that the tone of his voice betrayed a smile she could see no evidence of on his face. The lilt of it confirmed he didn't belong in this glen.

'Are you a MacDonald?'

He seemed to find the question even more amusing than her kill mark and bent down, his face close to hers.

'And if I was?'

Using all the length and strength of her arm, Anne swung her musket hard. The barrel cracked across the man's shin. He let out a yell and curled forwards instinctively, but the force of the blow threw her off balance. She lost her grip of the musket and staggered, about to fall. The man caught her shoulders, propped her up again on the makeshift crutch.

'A warrior would know,' he said, and there was no smile in his voice this time. 'If you have a wounded leg, you attack with the opposite arm.'

Anne didn't need telling twice. She swung the wooden crutch. It, too, cracked across the man's shin. He yelled again, crumpling back a step from her. Anne swayed but, being ready for it this time, managed to keep her balance and stay upright. The man recovered quickly. His dark brows frowned over angry eyes. Furious, he grabbed the crutch from her grasp, broke it in two over his knee as if it were kindling and tossed it away into the heather. Then he snatched up her fallen musket, pointed it in her direction and, as she stared defiantly, wavering now without any support, he fired.

There was a loud yelp from behind her. Further down the trail, the lead wolf spun round as the ball bit into its shoulder. It whimpered and slunk off, limping. The other two halted and began to back away. Anne stared up at the man, her mouth open, impressed by his speed and accuracy. Her admiration came too late. The man glared back at her.

'Now for you,' he said.

At Invercauld, the pipes and drums played on, slow and steady. Torches flickered like fireflies on the hills. All around the chief's squat stone house small cooking fires flared in the dark. The air was heavy with expected sorrow and thick with murmurs. Beside the door of the house, the white rose of June bloomed, reflecting the moonlight from its ghostly perfumed flowers. Jean Forbes stood in the doorway watching the torch-bearing searchers return from the hills. She was on edge, irritated more than worried. The young girl who clung to her side sensed her mother's mood and seemed to be trying to hide among the folds of her skirts. MacGillivray hurried towards them.

'She was gone,' he said, his breath coming hard. 'We ran all the way, by the shortest path. But she wasn't there.'

'*Och*! Then where?'

MacGillivray spread puzzled hands. This was his responsibility and a heavy one at such a time.

'Some of the men followed other roads home. She had cut a crutch and a tracker found her trail, but that will be slow.'

Jean, the Lady Farquharson, was much younger than her dying husband – his fourth wife – and Anne was not her daughter. The girl could never do as she was told, and this was not a night when the clan's attention should be distracted by a wayward, foolish child.

'My husband will not hold on much longer,' she snapped at MacGillivray. 'She must be found!'

MacGillivray had no answer for her ire, but he tried to frame one. As the first word of apology reached his tongue, a musket shot sounded behind him and silenced it. Alarmed, people turned towards the sound. In the muttering that followed, names were uttered, 'M<sup>c</sup>Intosh', 'Aeneas', names spoken in recognition but with deference and respect. Then Aeneas M<sup>c</sup>Intosh strode into the light from the doorway, musket smoking in his hand, Anne perched on his shoulders.

Relieved, Anne's kinfolk crowded around. Lady Farquharson noticed the missing girl first but it was the man who carried her whose presence was the greater pleasure.

'Aeneas! *Fàilte.*'

'Lady Farquharson,' Aeneas responded. 'My uncle sends his regrets. In his poor health, the mountain pass defeats him.'

The woman nodded. The M<sup>c</sup>Intosh was the elected head of Clan Chatton, the clan of the cat, a federation to which all those present belonged. Farquharson's death would be dishonoured by his absence. But she and Aeneas were of similar age and maybe there were other benefits in his presence, so she hid her disappointment at his news.

'We're honoured to be in his thoughts,' she said. 'Will you take his place with the other Chatton chiefs?'

Aeneas was the nephew of a chief, not one of them. He'd come to pay his respects to a deserving warrior because he chose to, not simply to bring the M<sup>c</sup>Intosh's regards, and would have waited with the other kin outside. But he acquiesced, accepting the honour, and slid the now wriggling Anne from his shoulders to set her on the

6

ground. Lady Farquharson fixed the grubby bloodstained girl with a look of disdain.

'Your father's waiting,' she said, then turned and, taking the child clinging to her skirts with her, vanished into the house. Anne glared at MacGillivray, furious, fingers clenched at her sides.

'You didn't come back for me!'

'We couldn't find you.'

Anne leapt at him, punching, and the ferocity of her attack bowled them both over into the rose bush.

'We looked everywhere,' he protested, struggling to grab her flailing fists.

Anne was lifted into the air, a white rose tangled in her tumbling hair. Aeneas had her by the back of her dress.

'Is this what you do when your chief is dying?' he thundered.

'*Na can sin*, he is not,' Anne shouted back at him. 'He's sick, that's all!'

'So you hunt without his permission, drag MacGillivray with you, then get yourself hurt so those who bring respect to a brave man must turn away to save a silly girl?' Aeneas had not let go his hold of her, though even in his rage he was mindful of his shins. 'But you will behave now, before you go in, or I will give you the spanking you have earned right here!'

Anne was at her own door surrounded by her own tribe. He wouldn't dare. With all the icy sarcasm of superiority, she spat her answer at him.

'You certainly will not, sir. For you are not my father or a chief!'

Without a word, and in one easy move, Aeneas dropped to one knee, pulled her over the other and administered a resounding smack on her backside, quite hard enough to thoroughly dent her pride. When he stood her back on her feet, she hesitated, glaring at him. When none of the watchers spoke or moved to defend her, she tossed her head and hobbled off on her swollen ankle into the house.

Aeneas studied MacGillivray. The young chief stared, resolutely, at the ground. A scratch on his cheek from a rose thorn oozed tiny beads of blood.

'Maybe I should take over your training,' Aeneas suggested. The hint of teasing in his voice went unnoticed. The youth's head came up, eager.

'Would you?'

'I'll speak to McIntosh when we return,' Aeneas answered. His uncle was MacGillivray's guardian. He would approve.

'I would have waited for you,' the lad blurted out, 'but no one knew where you'd gone. I came yesterday –' now his pride was returning '– to represent my people.'

'As you should,' Aeneas agreed.

Inside Invercauld, the crowded main room glowed with candles. A peat fire smouldered in the hearth. All the Clan Chatton chiefs, male and female, were gathered round with their husbands or wives, standing or sitting, waiting. James Farquharson, a youth of sixteen, sobbed quietly next to the low bed on which his father lay. Lady Farquharson, her young daughter, Elizabeth, still holding on to her skirts, turned from beside the bed as Anne entered.

'Look at the state of you,' she hissed.

Unheeding, Anne brushed past to the bedside. As she looked down at her father, her rebellious demeanour changed and, for the first time that evening, became that of a frightened little girl.

'Daddy?'

The Farquharson's eyes flickered open. His head turned towards her and he half-rose, gripping her shoulders.

'I got a deer for you,' Anne said. 'A deer! Now you can eat well and get better.'

Just inside the doorway, Aeneas McIntosh stood beside the MacGillivray. He'd assumed the girl hunted for pleasure, indifferent to her father's impending death.

'No food,' Farquharson said. He was fading, and it seemed everyone but his elder daughter could see the shadow of death on him.

'Then I'll have someone mix the blood with ale. That'll strengthen you.' She turned to her half-sister, still hiding behind her mother. 'Elizabeth –' she began.

'No.' Her father tightened his grip on her shoulders. 'No, Anne.

It's you and James will need to be strong now. My time is finished.'

'*Chan eil! Chan eil idir!* I won't let you go.' Her voice broke, but she raised it, anguished, and glared at those standing around the bed, tears glittering in her eyes. 'Why do you all stand there? Do something!' No one moved or spoke, though there was some uncomfortable shuffling. Her stepmother put a hand on her shoulder. It might have been compassion, but Anne shook it away. 'Am I the only one?'

'*Isd, a ghràidh,*' her father said. 'Hush, lass.' But a faint smile lit his gaunt face. 'Your brother will be chief now, if the clan wishes it, but you, you'll always be my warrior.' With a trembling hand, he reached up and pulled the white rose from her hair. 'My Jacobite. When the Prince is man enough, he'll come,' his voice faded, 'in his father's place.'

The prince he spoke of was a boy of seventeen, living in exile. His grandfather had ruled the three independent nations of Scotland, England and Ireland but was deposed in 1689. When Scotland united with England in 1707, the Prince's father became the linchpin of revolt against that Union. Eight years later, Farquharson joined the rebellion of 1715, hoping to crown James Stuart as King of Scots and restore Scottish independence. The rising failed. King James returned to France. Now the cause invested hope of leadership in his young son.

'We'll fight,' his daughter promised. 'We'll fight for the Prince. You know we will.'

The Farquharson's breath shuddered in his chest.

'Fight,' he fell back on to the pillow, 'for your freedom.'

'We will. I promise.' Anne raised her head, grasping for the comfort of familiar words, and though she was half-blinded by tears, her voice rang strong. 'For prosperity, and no Union!'

And while her father could no longer hear the affirmation, people would remember that he died with the white rose symbol of their struggle in his hand as every person in the room repeated it.

'Prosperity and no Union!'

# TWO

Sunrise over the snow-covered peaks brought the first day of spring to the mountains. The light rippled like liquid down the rock gorges where the great waterfalls began to drip and thaw. On the lower green slopes near Braemar, black cattle grazed and a cluster of sheep scattered from a boy herding a few goats. Turf cotts crowded the overpopulated landscape. Reek from burning peat spiralled up through the central smoke holes in their roofs. In the yard at Invercauld, a cockerel crowed among the foraging hens, announcing the dawn, asserting his masculinity.

It was seven years since the old chief's death but little, and much, had changed. The wolves were gone, hunted to extinction to preserve deer and protect the hill sheep. Cleared woodland had released more land for crops and homes, the wood providing a stable and paddock for the house. The crowing cockerel was interrupted by the clatter of hooves as a horse trotted across the yard. The rider was taller and had lost that lean and gangly look of youth, but the long red-gold hair was still unmistakable.

'Anne!' he called as soon as he was within earshot of the house. 'Anne!'

A young woman turned from searching for eggs among the frosted tufts of grass that edged the coop. Slim as a reed inside the heavy tartan plaid around her shoulders, she had an easy, fluid grace. The tumbling wild hair was tamed, its rich chestnut brown sleek against her clear skin, loosely tied into a long plait down her back. She held two eggs in her hand and, seeing the rider was MacGillivray, a glorious smile spread across her face.

'Alexander!' She waved, and he rode over. 'I didn't think the pass was clear of snow yet.'

'I came the long way round.' He dismounted, wrapped his arms round her and kissed her, she mindful of the eggs. They'd become lovers, at least now and then, last spring. Among the clans, urges were satisfied as they arose. Casual couplings in the heather were common. Women often took a man to bed just for the winter.

Anne could have married, but no one else appealed to her. MacGillivray was in no position to. Marriage came late to Highland chiefs whose clans must provide for them and their children. His sporran pressed into Anne's belly. Either he was aroused or it was full of oats. She pushed him back, giggling.

'Will you stop? *Sguir dheth!* It's freezing and I have my hands full already.'

'*Ach*,' he groaned. 'It's been a long winter.'

'So that's all you're after,' she grinned, 'a bed-warmer.'

'No. Well, yes, that too. But I was sent. I've to bring you all to Moy.'

'Then McIntosh is dead.' She was immediately sombre. 'I thought I heard the lament, during the night, but so faint and far away I was sure I dreamt it.'

'Shaw's piper was sick and didn't pick it up. But he's fine now so you'll hear tonight. And wait till you hear this.' Now he was more excited. 'They have chosen their new chief, his nephew, Aeneas.'

'Aeneas McIntosh?' Anne's mouth fell open in disbelief. 'Are they mad?'

'But he's a great warrior.'

'Great at smacking children!'

'That was years ago.' MacGillivray laughed. 'Remind me never to cross you. Your memory is as long as waiting.'

'And yours is as short as butter-bread. No wonder he hasn't married, with you running after him like a catamite since the night my father died.'

'He's my cousin.' He flushed at the accusation. 'And he tutors me. Besides, he couldn't marry till the chief's heir was decided.'

'Well, he can now. I hope you'll both be very happy.' She headed for the house, furious. MacGillivray was easily impressed. No doubt Aeneas beat him to the sword!

'Anne,' he called. 'You have to go.'

She turned back to face him.

'The MᶜIntosh was not here when my father died.' Though she spoke defiantly, it covered a deep hurt. MacGillivray crossed the few steps to her, softened by her vulnerability, wanting to make things right.

'It's not just for the burial,' he reminded her, gently. She held his gaze for a moment, tender for that moment, then the spell broke.

'I know!' she snapped. 'Clan Chatton will also choose a new chief. So, will you lead the federation, Alexander? I think not. Maybe my brother, or MacBean, Macpherson, Davidson, Shaw, MacQueen? No! It will be none of them. MᶜIntosh will! Well, hear me now. That man will never be my chief! I won't vote. And I won't go!' She grabbed his hand. 'Here, you'll want breakfast.' She thrust the two eggs she held into his palm and marched off towards the woods. MacGillivray grimaced at the smashed eggs dripping thick white and yolk through his fingers.

'You forgot MᶜThomas!' he shouted after her.

Anne strode out of the trees across the open grassland towards the burn. She meant to follow its course up to the great falls, to the deep brackish pool where the fine mist from cascading water drifted against her face. But there would be little spray today from frozen falls, and that was where she first made love with MacGillivray, last year, on the morning after her nineteenth birthday, the day after the last wolf died.

A rainstorm on the night of her birthday had ended before dawn. Up at the falls, in spring sunshine, the damp grass had still steamed of it. Rainbows hung in the mist above the white froth of water. She waded into the pool, dress hauled up around her naked buttocks, after a slow salmon. It circled, lazy, brushing her calf. She slid her hand into the water, stroked its long, heavy body, gently, gently. There was a rustle on the bank, a footfall on the pebbles. She knew who it was, without turning. The way he'd looked at her down at the house, the way he'd be watching her now. Without turning, she knew. Her fingers stopped stroking the fish. The caress lost, it slid around her thigh and away. She turned to go to him, knowing what she'd see in his eyes and what she'd do about it.

So she wasn't going to the falls. Not in her present mood. Instead she turned downstream, towards the strident bleating of the lambing pens. Her cousin leant indolently against a post, watching. Most warriors were tall. Francis Farquharson of Monaltrie was taller than most, his silver-blond hair startling in the crisp light. Baron Bàn folk called him, for that hair. Ten years older than her brother, he had administered Invercauld and mentored James since their father died.

'Just late enough to be no help,' he said, glancing over his shoulder as she approached. He and her brother had worked the night through. 'The shepherds were back at first light.'

'I can lamb a ewe,' she snorted. 'Small hands, see.' She held them out. His were huge, useless for a difficult birth.

He laughed, amused by her indignation.

'Except you might want for practice again. We'd be as well rid of sheep, bar what we can eat. There'll be few sheared now the English have shut off our markets.'

Behind him, a suckling ewe trailed afterbirth from its stained rear. Beyond the pregnant and nursing beasts, her brother struggled to pull out a stuck lamb. The stink of birth and the stench of death mingled in the cold air. Shearing was a couple of months off. When the clan's need of wool was met, spare fleeces were normally baled then sent to Moy. From there, the collected Clan Chatton wool was transported on to Aberdeen for export to the Low Countries. It was vital trade which funded imports and financed cultural travel to strengthen bonds with France, Spain and Italy, countries that were Scotland's friends but England's enemies. This year, spare fleeces would stay on the sheep. Britain's parliament had banned Scottish wool exports to protect the English textile trade.

'So what high dudgeon brings you down here?' Francis asked. 'Is it my aunt, again?'

'McIntosh is dead. Alexander brought word.'

Francis nodded. A light breeze ruffled the blond hair round his shoulders. His blue eyes gazed steadily at her.

'Then it's MacGillivray who annoys you.'

'He is too patient,' she burst out.

'It will be years, Anne. He has no suit to press.'

'It's not that.' She grabbed his hand, pressed it against her breast, above her heart. 'When I want to marry I will know it here.' Still gripping his hand, she thrust it down into the folds of her skirts, between her thighs. 'And not just here.'

Her passion roused him to more amusement.

'Maybe it's here you should know it,' he said, tapping the forefinger of his other hand on the side of her head. 'Then you might have considered Louden.'

She slapped away his hand from between her thighs.

'As if I'd wed a government lackey!'

'Not even an earl?' Francis queried.

'Nor a baron either,' Anne retorted.

He had asked her on that birthday, the day the last wolf died, but only to mock her stepmother. Anne had gone to the window, put her face to the damp glass, listened to the drumming rain. It battered against the panes, stoated up from the cobbled yard outside.

'They say he'll come this year,' she said.

'Or next,' Lady Farquharson snorted behind her. 'It's a union of your own you should be thinking of. No good ever came of politics, not that I've noticed.'

The rain scythed down in the darkness, silver blades slicing through the yellow pool of light from the window. It was their custom for women to marry young. Children arrived without proper provision if they didn't. Men married late, free to start their own family only when younger siblings were grown.

'Nineteen,' Lady Farquharson grumbled. 'It's time you were out of the house.' Her suggestions of suitable husbands for her step-daughter were less than generous: an ancient widower, a twice-divorced brute, and the earl, Lord Louden. At forty, Louden was a suitable age, but he was also a staunch supporter of the Union.

'Countess would suit you better, Aunt,' Francis suggested,

straight-faced. 'He'd be wasted on Anne.' He took hold of Anne's hands then. 'I should propose to you myself,' he said, 'for your birthday.'

'And for my birthday,' Anne retorted, 'I would turn you down.' He was only tormenting Lady Farquharson, making a better suggestion than hers. At thirty-four, her cousin was still not ready for marriage.

The lamb James worked to save slithered, lifeless, out of its mother. Tethering the ewe to a nursing post, the shepherd went to pick the best of the orphans. On his knees, her brother already had his dirk out, skinning the steaming corpse. Its skin would be tied on a motherless beast to induce the childless ewe to suckle it. Its carcass would add to the sweet-smelling heap of bloated dead. Francis leant his weight on the post and considered her.

'Maybe it's time I explained about men and women,' he teased.

Anne snorted. Highland children witnessed copulation often, animal and human. As farming folk, they learned about mating early. And there was nothing she hadn't heard from her stepmother about making a good match.

'What do you know about women?' she challenged.

'Walk about a bit,' he suggested.

Tossing her head, Anne strutted back and forth in front of him, typically arrogant.

'Enough,' Francis sighed. 'I know enough.'

James came over then, bloodstained, tired but glad to have saved the ewe. He was slender and lithe, very like Anne with his brown hair, full mouth and wide eyes, but her opposite in temperament.

'Just in time,' Anne said. 'Francis is about to tell me how to breed.'

Living in a family of voluble women, James never spoke just to fill a silence, spending his words carefully. He glanced at his cousin.

'You haven't told me yet.'

Anne shrieked with laughter. Francis hooted. Pleased with

himself, James smiled. As they set off through the field, Anne repeated the news of M<sup>c</sup>Intosh's death to her brother. He accepted it solemnly, expressing no surprise that Aeneas was the new chief.

'But we don't have to choose him,' Anne added, insisting that Macpherson was a wiser choice to lead the Clan Chatton federation. 'At least he might try to influence parliament!'

Cluny Macpherson was certainly a persuasive talker, but the chiefs had lost their power in parliament at the Union. Demands for a federal arrangement were refused. Scotland was allowed only sixteen peers and, in the House of Commons, forty-five seats to more than five hundred held by England. Clan Chatton had ignored parliament since.

'We're outnumbered, Anne,' Francis said. 'However the Scots vote, it makes no difference. Only the English vote counts.'

'One country can't outnumber one other country,' she protested. 'There are only two in this United Kingdom of Great Britain. Size should not matter.'

Francis stopped walking. He stretched up to his full height, well over six feet.

'I think you'll find it does.'

Anne folded her arms and cocked her head at him.

'What matters is the size of our ideas,' she corrected, pointing back to the raucous sheep pens. 'You'd leave them to sweat through summer and waste a season's wool because England says we can't trade it.'

'What would you do, shear them and burn it?'

'Store it. Things can change, or be changed.'

'It would rot, Anne,' James said.

'Not if it was scoured first.'

'The moths would still have it,' Francis said.

Anne tucked her cold hands into the warmth of the thick woollen plaid. Soon, their winter clothes would be put away for summer.

'*Peighinn rìoghail,*' she said, triumphantly. 'Pack the wool in double linen sacks with dried pennyroyal leaves between the layers. That'll keep the moths out.'

There was a silence as the two men let the idea penetrate.

'We'd be ahead,' Francis looked thoughtfully at James, 'ready to trade whenever the chance came.'

'Without losing a year's wool,' James nodded.

'You clever woman,' Francis praised Anne. 'Promise you'll wait for me.'

'Convince me that size matters first,' she retorted, grinning.

They headed on home, discussing the storage of wool as they walked. Somewhere dry and cool would be needed, perhaps a barn sited among trees. With sacks to weave and wool to prepare, the clan's shearers, spinners and weavers need not be idle after all. As they crossed the yard towards the house, the memory of wolves returned to Anne, this time of her childhood encounter, on a moonlit night with a dark man, of fear, a single shot taken in the dark, her father dying. Wolves were pack animals, hunters, yet their howls, which she had not heard since then, ached of loneliness. Now there were none.

'Do you think it really was the last wolf?' she asked.

'Last year?' Francis shrugged. 'Who knows?' He looked down at her. 'What does it matter, even if there was one other left? It couldn't live on alone.'

The deceased M<sup>c</sup>Intosh had ordered that hunt. A baby had been taken and the cottars at Moy swore the creature responsible was a wolf. The day it died, before she knew it, was her birthday. That night, as rain battered the house, Anne stood before the long mirror in her bedroom. Naked in the guttering candlelight, her skin looked honey-smooth though, in daylight, it was buttermilk white. She shook out her hair so it drifted against her back, the length of it brushing her buttocks. Raising her hands, she cupped her breasts, feeling her own blood-heat in them. She stroked her palms down to the flatness of her stomach. Child-bearing let women create the future. But at a cost. She had cost her mother's life.

For the beasts it was simple. Fertility, desire and mating all came at the same time. For women too, though desire could rise without fertility – the torment she'd suffered in the last few days was a certain sign. Except in marriage, men were to be avoided at such times. Marriage meant childbirth. Maybe she avoided that too. But her skin was hot, fevered, heart thudding, her breath quick, her womb eager for seeding. She leant into the mirror, the glass cold on her cheek, on her breast, slid her fingers between her thighs, into the wetness there, gasping at the tremor that ran up through her belly.

'What are you doing?' her half-sister asked, sleepily, from the bed.

'Nothing. Go on back to sleep.'

But Elizabeth was awake, fair hair tumbling out of her nightcap, pushing herself up on to her elbows.

'I know what you're doing,' she said. 'I do it all the time. That's why I come to bed early.' Elizabeth was sixteen, and very annoying.

Anne pulled on her night shift, tucked her hair up into a cap, snuffed the candle and slid into bed.

'Go to sleep,' she snapped, turning her back abruptly, pulling the covers up to her chin. When she slept, she dreamt of wolves. When she woke, it was to an empty bed, to birdsong and the absence of rain. She had gone to the kitchen in her shift, her sleep-tousled hair tangled around her shoulders. MacGillivray was there, unexpectedly there. He'd come to stop their party leaving for the hunt. MacQueen's tracker had killed the beast the day before, her birthday, its head already presented to the old chief at Moy.

Apart from the cook, MacGillivray was alone in the kitchen, sitting by the table, not eating now, but gazing at her, that long, red hair knotted in the nape of his neck, shoulders tense. It was the first time she cared he was a man. She went to the falls later, knowing he would follow. Up at the pool, cool water swirling round her thighs, all she could think of was the heat rising in her, the way he had looked at her earlier, the same look she'd see in his eyes when she turned round.

He'd be waiting inside the house now, waiting for her. At sunset, her brother's piper would pick up the new lament from Shaw's, and they would be in mourning. Before then, she had some persuading to do. That would be why she remembered the wolf.

# THREE

The day after the Farquharsons departed for the funeral was a fine one, bright and dry with a mild west wind that promised warmth. As good as her word, Anne remained behind with Elizabeth until dawn spurred her into action. Cajoling her perplexed sister, she led the way over the mountain pass to Rothiemurchus. When night fell, they took shelter with a cottar's family. The law of hospitality meant doors were open to any traveller. It was a life-preserving law in wild terrain, where weather could turn rapidly from benign to deadly.

Next day, with the Cairngorms behind them, they walked on across heather moor dotted with the ever-present turf cotts towards the Caledonian forest that edged Loch Moy. Even at seventeen, Elizabeth had still not given up on childish whining.

'*Tha mi sgith*. If we'd gone with the others, we could have shared the horses.'

'Except we're not going,' Anne said.

Trailing a bit, Elizabeth made a face at her older sister's back.

'Is that why we're walking miles in that direction, so as not to get there?'

Anne sighed and stopped. She was fond of Elizabeth but often wished her half-sister had more of their shared father in her and less of her mother.

'The man's a rogue, Elizabeth. I wouldn't honour him by being at his adoption as McIntosh. But he might not lead Clan Chatton. James and Francis will vote against him, I asked them to, and MacGillivray. The Macphersons will vote for themselves, they always do. So maybe he'll not be elected. I want to see that happen. I want to see that man's face when it happens. Come on.' She took her sister's hand. 'It's not much further.'

*

19

At Moy Hall, thousands of Clan Chatton had gathered. Each clan had its own chief, usually chosen from the senior family, though no adoption was automatic. The person most fitted to the post, man or woman, was selected, and removed if they proved unfit. Distinguishable in the crowd by the twin feathers in their bonnets, the chiefs congregated around the doorway of the two-storey building, along with their husbands, wives, sons and daughters. By chieftain standards, Moy Hall was imposing – many of them still lived in turf cotts like their kinsfolk – but it was mortgaged to the hilt. New taxes levied since the Union had impoverished the clan. Aeneas would need his wits about him to keep the land for his tribe.

Lady Farquharson stood with Anne's brother, James. Until her stepson married, she had equal rights over clan decisions. One or two of the widowers and bachelors among the assembled chiefs had mulled over the possibility of an alliance with her. She might still bear more children and was a good-looking woman, if a bit sharp. Yet, despite her obvious relish for male company, she turned down all offers of remarriage. It was said she favoured Aeneas but wouldn't marry below the rank of chief. Today might see that settled too.

Throughout the crowd, deliberately positioned to encourage a positive vote in their favour, were dozens from Clan McIntosh. The door of Moy Hall opened and Lady Anne Duff, the Lady McIntosh, emerged. For the moment, she was the most powerful member of the federation, wife of their late chief, buried only the day before. In her hand she held his chief's bonnet with its two eagle feathers. Behind her, Aeneas was bareheaded, clearly uncomfortable with ceremony. MacGillivray took his place beside him, holding the third eagle feather that would mark one of the waiting chieftains as head of the federation. The widow spread her arms.

'Fàilte oirbh,' she welcomed them all. 'It is my duty,' her voice rose to reach the whole crowd, 'to pass on the chief's feathers.'

A roar for Aeneas went up from the McIntoshes, startling some ducks from the loch behind so that they rose in a flapping flutter that seemed like applause.

'But there is a third feather my husband wore,' Lady M<sup>c</sup>Intosh continued. 'Only the tribes of Clan Chatton can decide who will wear it now.'

Far behind the crowd, over the edge of the lake, Elizabeth hissed at Anne.

'This is stupid!'

They were up in a tree, next to each other, standing on one branch, holding on to a higher one, and spattered with water from the rising ducks.

'If you'd move out a bit, we'd see better,' Anne whispered, edging her sister along the branch and further out over the loch, as she craned to see what was happening over on the steps of Moy.

At the front of the crowd, Lady Farquharson caught Aeneas's eye. He nodded to acknowledge her and she dropped her gaze, a pleased smile flitting over her mouth. First husbands were about common sense. Second husbands could be for the pleasure of it. She'd always appreciated the way Aeneas looked, his skill and astuteness. Now he also had status, and she had worked on James to improve even that. The only person who might gainsay her, Anne, wasn't there.

Beside Aeneas, Lady M<sup>c</sup>Intosh looked out across the throng.

'Which chief will lead Clan Chatton?' she asked.

In the tree, the branch dipped alarmingly as Anne stretched to see and hear.

'I'm going to fall!' Elizabeth squeaked.

'*Isd!*' Anne snapped. 'Be quiet!' She saw the Macphersons raise their fists into the air. Under the ancient law of tanistry, every voice was equal but, in federation business, each clan was equal, with only one vote, regardless of size. Any members might dissent. A count then determined their tribe's vote for chieftainship of Clan Chatton.

'Macpherson!' they called in unison.

Ecstatic, Anne struck the branch in front with her own clenched fist.

'Yes!' she breathed. Now she had a clear view of Aeneas. It was the first time she'd seen him in daylight. His hair was raven-black, brows dark over darker eyes. It was silky, that hair, she remembered, at thirteen, astride those shoulders. In height he matched MacGillivray's six feet but, while Alexander stood relaxed, Aeneas was taut, poised. Like a storm about to break, he seemed to be brooding, discomfited by the call. There was jostling, and angry mutters from his clan. Good, she thought.

The MacBeans raised their fists and called their choice.

'M<sup>c</sup>Intosh!'

Anne watched Aeneas. There was a dangerous energy about him but, strangely, a mature authority, uneasy at the waiting, but easy in his own skin.

'M<sup>c</sup>Intosh!' The M<sup>c</sup>Thomases called.

Was it his age? He didn't seem such an old man now as she'd thought at thirteen. What would he be, thirty-six, seven? The same as her stepmother.

'M<sup>c</sup>Intosh!' The MacQueens, apart from Lady MacQueen who called for Macpherson and in doing so cancelled out her husband's vote. But no one expected different from her. Cluny's brother had been keeping her content for several years, whisky and age having cooled her own husband's ardour long ago.

Elizabeth frowned at Anne. Her sister seemed to have forgotten why they were there, perched in a tree over the loch. The shouts went on, turn by turn.

'M<sup>c</sup>Intosh!' From the Shaws.

Anne was engrossed in appraising the man she'd resented for so long. He was eminently watchable, a deepening image like a still loch with a racing sky reflected in it. An unexpected thrill rippled across her abdomen. If he'd been any other man, it would have pleased and excited her. But with this man, it was surely alarm.

'M<sup>c</sup>Intosh!' The Davidsons.

'Anne!' Elizabeth nudged her. It was their family next.

'Oh, no,' Anne gasped. James would speak as she'd suggested. Where was Francis? 'Do you see Francis?' What had she heard, four or five votes for M<sup>c</sup>Intosh? Her family would look foolish. She remembered that infuriating amusement Aeneas could demonstrate. He might know it was her influence, if he recollected her at all. Her brother and stepmother raised their fists with the rest of the Farquharsons.

'M<sup>c</sup>Intosh!' they shouted, not one voice at odds.

MacGillivray took a step forward, facing his people, fist raised. He, at least, would not let her down.

'M<sup>c</sup>Intosh!' he thundered as his clan echoed him. It was done. A great shout of affirmation went up. MacGillivray slid the third feather into the M<sup>c</sup>Intosh bonnet clasp beside the other two. Aeneas dropped to one knee so that his aunt could place the bonnet on his head.

'Aeneas! Aeneas! Aeneas!' chanted his ecstatic clan.

'Did you see that?' Shocked, Anne turned to Elizabeth, the spell broken. 'They voted for him!' The tree shook. 'James voted for him, and MacGillivray!' The branch under their feet dipped alarmingly.

'Anne, keep still!' Elizabeth shrieked. It was too late. Her grip was lost. Even as Anne tried to grab hold of her, she crashed out of the tree, yelling as she fell with a splash into the shallows of Loch Moy. Anne looked down, horrified, at her sister thrashing in the water. Then she remembered the gathering and looked over to the house, more horrified. Aeneas was on his feet. He and MacGillivray seemed to be staring right at her. Surely the leaves screened her? Both of them started to run towards the water. The last thing Anne wanted was to be caught, here, hiding in a tree like some misbegotten child. She stepped back along the quivering branch and slid behind the main trunk, pulling her dress tight round her so as not to be seen.

MacGillivray and Aeneas arrived, together, at the lochside. In the shallows, Elizabeth, dress ballooning, struggled to get upright. Aeneas had seen her once when she was barely ten years old and didn't recognize her, but MacGillivray knew who it was immediately.

'Elizabeth?' He was mystified, knowing she'd stayed behind at Invercauld with Anne, but he waded in to help her out.

Behind Aeneas, others hurried down to join them, curious about the interruption and concerned that it might be some breach by a rival clan. In minutes, Anne would be discovered, hiding like a thief from justice. There was only one thing she could do in the circumstances, brazen it out. Carefully, balancing herself so she would not collapse backwards into the water, she dropped out of the tree, landing lightly on her feet no more than a yard from a startled Aeneas. Three dirks around him were half-drawn in response. He simply stared at her, then waved away the protection.

'It seems we have a pair of nestlings,' he said, and there it was, that infuriating half-smile.

Behind her, Anne could hear Elizabeth's undignified spluttering and MacGillivray's shocked 'Both of you?' She kept her eyes coolly on Aeneas and strove to appear off-hand.

'We were just passing,' she said.

They were deep in McIntosh territory. Aeneas waved a disbelieving hand that took in loch, forest and the distant Cairngorms. A shout of laughter escaped him. Anne shot him a look that would have shrivelled most recipients and, in that second, saw the first flash of recognition in his eyes. A long moment passed before he got her name to his dumbstruck tongue.

'Well, Miss Farquharson. *Fàilte*,' he said, as he doffed his new chief's bonnet and nodded. Mocking her, she knew. Let him utter one word about how she'd grown and those dirks would be needed to protect him. He didn't. Lady Farquharson, pushing through the crowding guests, got there first. She was mightily embarrassed and even more annoyed.

'Elizabeth? Well!' she screeched. 'Anne? I don't believe the pair of you!'

'It was Anne's idea,' Elizabeth protested.

Any thought Anne had that Elizabeth would not betray her evaporated like spit off a hot stone.

'How could you ruin such a special moment?' Lady Farquharson snapped at her before turning to Aeneas, touching his arm in apology. '*Tha mi uamhasach duilich*. I'm so sorry, Aeneas.' Then she called furiously for James. MacGillivray moved to Anne's side.

'You didn't want to come,' he said. 'What are you doing here?'

'Being stabbed in the heart,' she said, glaring at Elizabeth.

With the excitement over, the crowd dispersed towards the food and drink. Anne's brother appeared from among them.

'James,' Lady Farquharson commanded. 'Get the horses and wagon ready. We're leaving.'

James took in the surprising sight of his sister and stepsister but decided questions could wait.

'Francis took our wagon on to Inverness,' he said, glancing at Anne, 'for linen.'

'Then ready our horses. The others can walk or wait for him.'

James hurried off towards the stable.

'Will you not stay?' Aeneas finally found his tongue. 'Your daughter will need dry clothes.'

'That's very accommodating of you, considering.' Lady Farquharson was not about to let her embarrassment lengthen. 'But she can dry out as she walks home.'

'*Och*, Mother!' Elizabeth wailed.

'Then at least let me lend you more horses,' Aeneas offered.

Reminded that he could now afford horses to lend, Lady Farquharson set her humiliation aside.

'Why, Aeneas,' she flirted. 'You're so kind. It really isn't easy schooling young people in responsibility without a husband's strength and wisdom.'

Anne glowered. Sometimes she wished she could vomit on demand. MacGillivray, knowing she would not want to be beholden to Aeneas, spoke into her ear.

'You can borrow my horse.'

Anne looked up at him, appreciating the offer, but her desire to preserve her dignity was stronger than any need for comfort.

'No, thank you,' she said and, louder, for Aeneas's benefit. 'I came out for a walk and I intend to continue it.' She wheeled around and strode off towards the mountains and home, head held high.

'You won't be half-way before dark,' MacGillivray protested.

'The others will soon catch her up,' Aeneas said, watching Anne's ramrod-straight back as she marched, determinedly, away.

MacGillivray shrugged. It was pointless trying to dissuade Anne from any course of action once she'd set her mind to it. But her pride would fade when she was beyond the cause of it. She wouldn't let her family ride past and leave her on the road.

His new chief clamped a brotherly hand on his shoulder.

'Time for a drink,' he said.

They headed for the house, following the fretful Elizabeth and her complaining mother. Aeneas grinned at MacGillivray and nodded to the two women in front.

'Yours looks a little wet,' he said.

# FOUR

At Invercauld, young voices shouted.

'Prosperity and no Union!' Two groups of children, wooden swords raised, rushed across the training field towards each other and met in a clash of wood against leather targes. One little girl cowered behind her targe, ineffectively trying to stab around it as the boy who'd engaged her thrashed the lights out of the leather shield.

'No, no,' Anne called, and stopped them. Crouching behind the girl, she slid one arm round her to slot through the straps of the targe and grasped the girl's sword arm at the wrist with the other. 'Like this, Catríona.' She pulled the targe across the girl's body to shield her torso while leaving her sword arm exposed, then she pushed the targe outwards and thrust forward with the sword. 'See?' She repeated the move. 'You push his sword away then thrust.' The girl sighed.

'Will the Prince ever come, Anne?'

'Of course he will.' She gave the child a reassuring squeeze. Nine years old and doubting already. Anne had been hearing and telling the story for twenty. Sometimes she, too, wondered if that was all it was, a fairy story for children. It had become indistinct in the telling, as if the Prince were a fiction and not someone made of flesh and blood. Was a false hope better than no hope? Not that it mattered for battle training. Everyone learned to fight as soon as they could hold a practice weapon, once a week after lessons.

The government had banned the bearing of arms in public, but a clan's status and security still lay in the number of broadswords it could field. There were always enemies. At any time some rival clan, pushed to the limits of its own land, might decide Invercauld, or parts of it, could be annexed to feed and house their folk.

'Besides,' she said to the girl. 'People who won't defend their home deserve to lose it.' She beckoned the boy forward and he swung his sword. Anne guided Catríona's targe, pushing the blow away. The boy's targe shielded his body. 'Good,' Anne said. 'Now hold it.' Moving the girl's sword arm, she pointed out the boy's weak spots. 'If you're quick, you might get him here.' She touched the sword tip against his exposed upper right arm. 'Then his sword arm is hurt and he'll submit. First blood is all you need draw. But the only way is around his targe. Think fast and move fast. Now, you try.'

She stood up, and the children set to again. A flicker of movement up on the mountain caught her attention. Her imagination must have conjured up intruders. There appeared to be a thin line of distant riders coming through the pass towards them.

'I got him! I got him!' Catríona squealed with excitement. Anne answered automatically, still watching the hillside.

'Well done!' There *were* riders up there, and people walking. Who were they? What did they want here? She turned to the children. Eventually, they'd become skilled, formidable fighters. Right now, they were messengers. She clapped her hands for attention. 'We have visitors. Will you put everything away and run home. Quickly, quickly.' As they ran to throw the practice weapons into their wooden box then scatter back to their various cotts, Anne scoured the slope, squinting to pick out some sign of identity.

High up on the mountain track, the front rider was resplendent in trews, velvet jacket and full chief's regalia. An illegal sword glittered at his side. Highlanders, and on serious business. Behind the chief, a clansman led a riderless white horse. Could that mean what it ought to? She scanned the rest of the column. Three black cattle followed, a few sheep and goats and a fat pig driven by a boy with a stick. Other clansfolk drove the animals along, keeping them in line. At the rear was another rider, a second chief. A chief with red-gold hair.

'Oh, dear life!' Anne turned and ran to her home. Inside the house, she charged past her stepmother, knocking a chair sideways in her hurry to get to the window, where she peered out towards the mountains.

'What on earth is going on?' Lady Farquharson righted the tumbled chair.

Anne turned to her stepmother just as Elizabeth ran in from outside.

'Mother! Mother! Oh, Anne, did you see?'

'Did she see what?' her mother demanded.

Elizabeth was almost delirious with excitement.

'M<sup>c</sup>Intosh. It's M<sup>c</sup>Intosh. And he's got . . .' She flapped her hands, unable to get out the words.

'Gifts.' Anne finished for her, cold now, matter of fact. 'He's bringing gifts.'

It was enough to restore Elizabeth's tongue.

'Marriage gifts, Mother! A bridal horse, cattle, sheep, oh, I don't know what else. James went to meet them. He's coming to propose, Mother!'

Lady Farquharson grabbed the back of the chair, her knuckles white.

'*O mo chreach*, my goodness. And look at the place!' She scooped up her embroidery and handed it to her daughter. 'Quickly, *greas ort*. *Och*, my hair. I must change. Oh dear.'

'You said he'd want a wife now he could afford one.' Elizabeth hopped up and down, hugging the tapestry to her chest. Calmly, Anne walked towards the back door.

'Where are you going?' her stepmother asked.

'Somewhere quiet. Out of the way.'

'What!' Elizabeth couldn't believe her ears. 'When Mother's about to receive a proposal?'

'She's not my mother,' Anne said, and slipped out.

Lady Farquharson stared at the shut door.

'Well, really!' Then, remembering. 'Oh, my goodness, my hair!'

Outside, Anne walked a well-trodden path through secluded trees. Behind them, a horse, cattle and people passed by, going the opposite way, towards her home. She caught glimpses through the dark trunks and low branches: Aeneas, the blue bonnet with its three feathers, long black hair to his shoulders, plaid sweeping down his back, his people, a fat pink pig, an unusually sombre MacGillivray.

Inside Invercauld, Lady Farquharson, in a hastily donned silk gown, silver jewellery flashing, hurriedly fastened herself up. Elizabeth set a tray with a crystal decanter and wine glasses on the table and arranged herself beside it. Food might often be reduced to oats and rabbit, but they could still put on a show when required.

James came in from the front door, about to announce their visitors, but Lady Farquharson, irritated by him spoiling Aeneas's view of her in all her finery, waved him aside. And there was Aeneas, silver basket-handled broadsword belted at his left side, a black-and-silver-handled dirk on his right.

'Fàilte, McIntosh,' Lady Farquharson embraced him. 'It's good to see you, Aeneas.'

He seemed nervous too, giving only a cursory nod while his eyes flitted about the room. Behind him, MacGillivray stopped just inside the doorway. He, too, wore his full chief's regalia. Elizabeth rearranged herself by the decanter and flashed him a flirtatious smile. After he'd fished her out the loch at Moy, she'd imagined a great deal more between them. That he was Anne's lover was neither here nor there. Her sister was obviously not wrapped up in him. She'd walked away from his company more than once recently. And, as far as Elizabeth was concerned, if she could seduce his attention away from Anne, that would make having him even more exciting.

Since neither man spoke, Lady Farquharson rushed into the gap.

'It's a few weeks longer than we expected.' She could hardly believe her tongue would make such a *faux pas*. 'I mean, before you came to collect your horses.'

'I had other things on my mind,' Aeneas said. He seemed somewhat clipped for a suitor.

'A new chief's duties, of course,' she excused him. 'A glass of wine?'

Elizabeth picked up the decanter. Aeneas could stand on ceremony no longer.

'Lady Farquharson,' he said. 'I'm here to propose marriage.'

The lady gasped at his directness, fluttering a lace handkerchief to fan her face.

In a clearing among the trees, Anne knelt by a headstone, brushing dust and moss off the words with her fingers. The writing on the stone read: 'John Farquharson of Invercauld. Died 1738.' Below was written 'Beloved wife, Margaret Murray, died in childbirth 1725'.

When she was very small, her father gave her a pony from Shetland. It was half the size of his horse but big for her. Once she could ride it, he said, she could do the estate round with him. Impatient to start, she tried to mount. Tried and failed, repeatedly, till furious with frustration, she threw herself on the ground, beating and kicking the dirt with her fists and feet. He'd lifted her in the air, at arm's length.

'You can't fight your own shadow,' he said. 'Learn to live with it.' When she stopped struggling, he dropped her into the saddle. After that, she rode with him every time. Her stepmother thought the pony a waste.

'She could have sat with you,' she complained. 'The size of her.'

'And what would she learn,' her father asked. 'How to be a passenger? She'll be out from under your feet.'

It was common enough for children to lose one, or even both, blood parents. To be raised by first, and sometimes second, stepparents. Yet she resented her stepmother, though she'd never known her own. Only her father's arms ever held her. It was his broad chest she cradled into, or beat her fists against. Her protector, teacher, comforter, he always forgave, always, always loved. She was still hollow from his loss. But it was a mother she wanted now, that tenderness, someone who might understand the need to walk without a shadow. Her fingers traced the date of her own birth, the day that was her mother's last. From the clump of grass beside the stone, a chicken clucked and scurried

31

off. Anne parted the clump to reveal a large brown egg, still warm.

Voices called her from around the estate. The new couple required her approval so that the celebrations could begin. Anne picked up the egg, its warmth filling her hand, and rose, resolute. She was a Farquharson, her mother and her father's daughter, and she would play her role.

Little Catríona, the girl who had finally mastered the targe earlier, ran down the path to the graves, calling for her.

'Anne, Anne, you're wanted up at the house,' she could hardly hold her excitement. 'The man says we might be roasting the pig.'

'Then she'll be out from under our feet,' Anne smiled and walked past the perplexed child towards the house.

Aeneas turned nervously as the door opened and Anne came in. The doorway crowded with clansfolk, MᶜIntosh and Farquharson. News travels fast by word of mouth. Anne stopped beside MacGillivray, flashed him her brightest smile, took hold of his hand and laid the still warm egg in his open palm.

'To keep it safe,' she said. Then she walked over to her step-mother and Aeneas, words of congratulations ready on her tongue. On the floor beside her half-sister's feet, the crystal decanter lay shattered in a pool of red wine. Elizabeth's expression appeared to be frozen, giving nothing away. Well-known faces peered in the window, scuffling for space to see. Lady Farquharson seemed waxen, and stiff as an over-starched apron. Anne stopped in front of her and waited, expectantly. The older woman gulped.

'Aeneas –' she stopped, then started again. 'Aeneas has something to say to you.'

Behind Anne, Elizabeth squeaked and grabbed the tray of glasses off the table. Anne looked round at her sister, who cradled the tray in her arms. Did she expect her to explode with rage? It would be good, at least, to have Invercauld to herself and James. She turned her full glittering gaze on Aeneas. But he only stared back at her. No words came.

'I presume you mean to say it out loud,' Anne prompted.

'Will you be my wife?' he said. It burst out of him, like a sneeze he'd been fighting to control for some time.

It was not what Anne expected to hear. But she had heard and did not need to ask him to repeat it. Everyone in the room had heard. They had heard it before, expected it. That was why the decanter lay broken, why her stepmother and sister stood frozen. Now they anticipated her response. Nobody breathed. The clansfolk in the doorway had heard and passed it on to those outside so it murmured round the house like the wind. Anne leant back on her heels, shocked and becoming more and more so. MacGillivray shifted the egg, still cupped in his hands, to safety behind his back. Elizabeth lifted a protective arm in front of the wine glasses and screwed her eyes shut. Anne let out her breath.

'Yes,' she answered. 'I will.'

The egg in MacGillivray's hands shattered. Elizabeth's tray tipped and the four wine glasses fell to the floor, breaking in turn like a peal of bells. Lady Farquharson's spine gave way and she folded like a rag doll into the chair behind her.

Aeneas, not knowing what else to do, moved towards Anne to kiss her. Then he realized his sword and dirk would get in the way and stopped to swing them both behind him. He took hold of her then, but realized he still had his bonnet on. Without letting her go, he whipped the hat off, tossed it on the table. But now he was about to kiss this woman who'd kept running through his mind since that day at the loch and whose deep blue eyes were now dark as flood water he might drown in, wanted to drown in, and she was waiting, and he knew if he didn't stop now he might never stop, so he stopped.

Anne gave up waiting. She put her hands on each side of his head and her mouth on his. A great cheer went up from outside.

Around the house, dozens from both clans leapt and cheered and hugged. Others, having further to come, were still running to be there. A woman pulled a small drawstring bag from inside her dress, opened it and took out the one coin it contained as if it were the greatest treasure in the world. She glanced at her husband.

Money was rare in the Highlands, where even chiefs made payment in kind. Proudly, the woman went to the doorway, to where a small wooden chest sat near the budding white rose. She propped the lid open and tossed the coin into it.

Inside, where the stillness was broken only by Lady Farquharson exclaiming her shock, the kiss came to an end.

'You surprise me, again,' Aeneas said. 'I thought you might say no.'

'I surprise myself,' Anne said.

Needing to do something physical, Aeneas turned to MacGillivray. He gripped the younger man's shoulder, offering his right hand. MacGillivray swallowed hard. Apart from Aeneas, there wasn't a person in the room or the mountains who wouldn't know his disappointment, but he took his mentor's hand and shook it warmly.

Aeneas frowned. He withdrew his hand and spread it out to look at the palm. It was smeared stickily with egg yolk and shell. Anne snorted with laughter. Aeneas looked at MacGillivray's horrified face, and he, too, began to laugh. The tension that strung the younger chief taut like a harp string was released. MacGillivray joined in, the three of them united by their laughter. All around the room the others chuckled and hooted, everyone except Lady Farquharson who was now bemoaning the waste of a good egg.

Out on the doorstep, where the Jacobite rose would soon spread its white, perfumed petals, the small wooden box filled with the coins being tossed in. Whisky and ale mysteriously appeared to toast the couple, the new clan union and, as always when toasts were made among them, the king across the water.

Far away, across that water, at the court of Louis XV, King of France, a much larger chest also filled with coin. Nearby, a tall, elegant young prince leant over an ornately carved table, poring over maps and charts with his naval commanders.

# FIVE

Across Raigbeg ford, the M<sup>c</sup>Intosh guard of honour waited: six warriors on foot, one on horseback, and the piper. Seeing them ahead, Anne drew Pibroch, the bridal pony Aeneas had gifted her on the day of his proposal, to a halt. Her kinsmen had wreathed the pony's halter with white roses, plaited them into its tail. Her kinswomen had sewn others on to her white lawn dress. Half-opened buds nestled in her hair. Every breath she took was filled with their perfume, a reminder of her Jacobite heritage and the memory of her father.

On the other side of the mountains, the fields and cotts of Invercauld she had left behind were near empty. All those fit to walk were determined to see her wed. The slow had set off days before, on foot or in carts. The warriors and those who could match the horses for pace marched behind the mounted party. At the bridge of Carr, where they'd broken the journey for the night, the people celebrated with a wild generosity they could ill afford. Even her stepmother, riding next to Elizabeth in the party behind, had finally thawed. She would have a more amenable household to run with Anne gone. It seemed every person in the Highlands wanted this wedding. All, but one.

As Anne hesitated at the ford, her cousin, Francis of Monaltrie, pulled up beside her. He would guess why she halted. Lord George Murray reined in at her other side. Her deceased mother's cousin and the Murrays' most notable warrior, he was there as custom demanded, to ensure Anne was doing as she wished and not bending to the will of others. Women did as they pleased in tribal society, and their menfolk made sure of it.

'Is it this far and no further, Anne?' he asked.

Behind them, her brother, James, the box with her wedding tocher strapped on his horse, had stopped the advance. Across the water, the stewards waited, the sun glinting on the one rider's red hair.

'It's MacGillivray,' she said.

She hadn't seen him since the day Aeneas proposed. But she should have expected this. It was Alexander's right, and his duty, to be at the right hand of Clan Chatton's chief. That duty included protecting his chief's bride. Yet surely Aeneas knew by now. Was he taunting or testing them?

'The choice is still yours,' George Murray reminded her.

Anne smiled at him. He was twice her age, wise and serious, yet would uphold her decision however temperamental or capricious.

'I've already made it,' she said, and urged Pibroch forward into the shallow Findhorn waters, through its clear wash to the other side.

After the greetings were made, the M<sup>c</sup>Intosh escort fell in at the side of the bridal party. It was unnecessary security. Their clan, whose lands they were now on, knew they were no raiding party. The cotts were empty, the people already at the house. Taking up his position at the front, the piper pumped his bagpipes and, with music skirling, set off to lead the way. MacGillivray swung his horse round behind the pipes. Careless of protocol, Anne spurred forward to ride at his side.

'I will arrive beside you,' she said. Surely he was still her friend and ally?

MacGillivray glanced at her, a look just long enough for her to see pain in his normally untroubled eyes.

'Does he not know?' she asked.

'He hasn't said. And what would I say when I don't understand?'

Anne didn't answer. He was, and always would be, dear as the world to her. The silence between them filled with the thud of walking hooves and the chatter from behind. Then MacGillivray said what was in his mind.

'We belong together, you and I.'

'This is my wedding day, Alexander.'

'That day by the falls.'

'I was nineteen,' she protested. The whole world changed in a year.

'You were in too deep. Skirts gathered round your middle, the water round your thighs. Trying to coax a fish.'

'He was mine. One flick of the wrist.'

'You knew I was there, watching. I saw your spine stiffen, your head lift. That's when I knew you would come to me.'

Anne wouldn't deny the desire that immobilized her.

'It seemed like hours, those minutes. I felt the length of that fish slip round my leg and slide away.'

Now he looked over at her again. His blue eyes burned with certainty.

'You want me still.'

She met his look with her own certainty.

'Yes, I do.' Then she laughed, letting the tension out of her. 'And if Aeneas doesn't please me, I shall come to you again.'

Frustrated, MacGillivray threw his arm wide to indicate his own clan lands at Dunmaglas, out of sight to the west.

'We'll have fat cattle by autumn and a harvest.' The crop swayed green and tall around them. 'Look how the barley grows.'

'With an English malt tax on every bushel, we can't profit by it.'

'When our larders are full, my clan will want me wed. A few good years.'

'It's settled.' Her tone was firm, but he could not leave it be.

'You wouldn't marry for fortune or favour,' he said. 'So why?'

It was a question she had not dared ask herself. Aeneas was a stranger, a closed book, yet from the moment she saw him on the steps of Moy at his adoption, she had wanted him and been shocked and angry with that wanting. He haunted her, an affecting presence that she longed for every wakeful moment. Aye, and no doubt in her sleep too. If a night spent tumbling the blankets with him would have cured her, she would have done that. But this went deeper than between her thighs, though she couldn't understand or explain.

'We can't know why we do things,' she said. 'I only know I must do this.'

Around Moy Hall, many hundreds of Highlanders had gathered. The white rose of June bloomed at the great front door and under windows, planted there so its perfume would fill the house. There was a buzz of activity. Men and women set food and drink on long tables: a roast pig, venison, game birds, rabbits, fish, oatcakes, barrels of ale. Hearing the distant skirl of pipes, they hurried to finish.

Inside the main hall, with its twin fireplaces on opposite walls and wide, sweeping staircase, an adolescent girl set out fish and meat delicacies beside brimming stoups of claret. From the open doors in the dining room, Aeneas frowned out at the frantic last-minute preparations. Then he, too, heard the faint skirl and his brow cleared. He was dressed in a fine kilted philabeg, woven specially for this day and made by the clan's best kiltmaker, plaid pinned over his shoulder with a silver brooch. His favourite silver-handled broadsword and dirk gleamed at his sides. Beside him, Forbes of Culloden, Scotland's elderly Law Lord, sounded off.

'The burial costs are not met. Fifteen hundred guests and your clan's mortgage debt for this hall not cleared. Now this! Hens and oats are not currency, Aeneas. The tax bill alone . . .'

'We deal in what the land provides,' Aeneas cut in. 'These taxes are your government's invention.'

'And fine words might well remove them,' Forbes agreed. 'But in parliament, not here, and not today.'

The girl had come in from the hall to set a tray on the already crowded table. Aeneas reached out as she passed and snatched up an oyster. The girl, every bit as quick, smacked his hand. Aeneas pointed across the room, indicating her attention was required. When she turned to look, he slid the oyster into his mouth and swallowed. As he slipped the empty shell back on to her tray, the girl realized the trick and glared at him. He grinned and winked.

'Too slow, Jessie,' he said, lifting a glass of wine.

'A wife will soon have you sorted,' she told him sternly. Then her excitement broke as a wide smile. 'I'm near gone with it all.' And she hurried off again.

'A wife might sort many things,' Forbes said, as he heard the approaching pipes. 'I hear she brings a healthy tocher. And in coin not corn.'

Aeneas threw back his head and laughed.

'I'm neither wedded nor bedded yet, Forbes,' he said. 'But I daresay the banks would have you feeling my pockets even if I were a corpse.'

'Which you could be if I report that weapon you're wearing,' Forbes nodded at the sword sheathed at Aeneas's side. 'In the current climate it would be judged as sedition.'

Aeneas smiled at him, unperturbed. In Europe, England warred with France. Last month, the British army had been defeated. Now there was talk that a French force led by the Jacobite Prince would soon invade England. Several clans had sworn to rise in support and secure Scotland. Forbes suspected M'Intosh might be one of them.

'My clan land is not public,' Aeneas corrected, giving nothing away. 'And I'll not be half-dressed at my wedding.' He raised his wine glass. 'Slàinte,' he said, and downed it.

Lady M'Intosh hurried in through the glass doors. This would be the last day she'd regard Moy Hall as her home, but she, too, was eager for this wedding.

'Aeneas,' she urged, unnecessarily. 'They're here!'

'We'll settle our business after I'm married,' Aeneas told Forbes before following his aunt outside.

'Not with promises, you won't,' Forbes retorted. 'Not this time.'

But promises were the order of the day. So that all could see, a low platform decked with heather, Jacobite roses and white ribbon had been erected for the ceremony. While her family found their positions fronting the large group of Farquharsons, Anne waited with her cousin beyond the edge of the crowd. Until her brother reached twenty-five, Francis was senior and would be her witness. They walked together on to the platform, to where Aeneas stood waiting, MacGillivray at his right side, before the minister. The three men made an imposing line-up in their different tartan plaids, chiefs' feathers fluttering, the banned silver-handled weapons glittering at their sides.

Between them, in her billowing white lawn and satin dress, Anne seemed fragile, delicate as a butterfly. It was the first of June, midday. The sun was high overhead. There were no shadows. Into the palpable silence of the crowd, her voice rang clear as she made her vows, the last committing her to his clan.

'Where you go, I will go. Your home will be my home, and your people will be my people.'

Aeneas was no less certain. He looked into her eyes, steadily, speaking solely to her. They might have been alone rather than surrounded by crowding Highlanders.

'And where you are, there I will be,' he said, his voice firm and sure. 'My sword and clan in your defence, for only death can part us now.' Then, as they were pronounced married, he cupped his bride's face with his hands and kissed her.

A great cheer went up from the assembled tribes. The air filled with tossed blue bonnets and whoops of celebration. As the wife of their chief, Anne Farquharson was now the Lady M<sup>c</sup>Intosh, bound to serve the clan and they her, to the death if necessary. She was a popular choice. Aeneas's aunt, now the Dowager Lady M<sup>c</sup>Intosh, was first to congratulate the new couple.

'You will stay on here with us, won't you?' Anne asked.

'That's kind of you, *a ghràidh*,' the Dowager replied. 'But I'm looking forward to town life in Inverness. It will be less work, more pleasure. Moy needs only one mistress. You'll do well.'

Determined to be next, Francis loomed forwards. Pushing his sword and dirk behind him, he bent down, kissed Anne thoroughly, then wrapped her in a bear-hug.

'You made a fine choice,' he approved. 'And Aeneas made a better one.'

With the rest of their two families clamouring to shake hands, it was some time before Anne could extricate herself to look for MacGillivray. He stood back from the well-wishers, at the edge of the platform, his six-foot frame and startling red hair preventing the invisibility he seemed to wish for. Anne put her hand on his arm.

'I don't love you any the less,' she said. 'And you know that Aeneas loves you like a brother.'

For a moment she thought he would walk away, an action that would forever put them at odds, but he stayed his ground, loyalty to Aeneas and love for her fighting his feeling of loss. He drew a deep breath.

'Co-dhiù,' he said. 'At least I don't have to cross mountains to see you now.'

The anxiety vanished from Anne's expression. A broad smile brightened her face. She laughed, put her arms round his neck, reaching up to kiss him.

'There's how fine you are to me,' she declared.

Behind them, among the folk crushing to congratulate him, Aeneas watched his right-hand chief lift his bride off her feet and swing her joyfully around, his expression contained, unreadable.

# SIX

Bagpipes droned, started up. Drinks were poured, the feasting began. Aeneas led Anne up to begin the dancing, his touch causing a shock of arousal, exciting her. He was strong and confident in his movements but light on his feet, and he wanted to be rocking their marriage bed not skipping the reel. She could see that in his eyes, as nakedly as he could read it in hers.

'So,' he said, half smiling. 'You mean to stay, and were not just passing after all.' He was teasing over her comment at the lakeside that day when Elizabeth fell in.

'A gentleman wouldn't remind a lady of her indiscretions,' she said.

His hand pressed into the small of her back pulling her against him as he bent forwards and put his mouth close to her ear, his breath warm against her neck.

'Except I am no gentleman, Lady McIntosh,' he said quietly, 'as you will surely find out before long.'

A tremor ran through her. How she longed to know his body, to touch his skin and feel his hands on her, and how afraid she felt at the same time. He leant back, looked into her eyes.

'Besides,' he said, 'it was your thrawnness that day made me realize I could marry no one else. A wife should have some fire in her.'

The dance changed at that point, into a progression. Aeneas spun her round and, when he should have let go, held on a second too long so she was late getting to her next partner, aroused, excited and laughing. Forbes took hold of her and, despite his years, skipped them back into step with the dance. The old judge was her step-mother's uncle but an infrequent visitor to Invercauld.

'It's a wise man you have married, Lady McIntosh,' he said, as they swung round, 'and a fine idea that you bring your own funds with you. You'll be putting them to good use, no doubt, keeping your new husband out of jail.'

Anne stopped dancing, the anticipation of bedding her husband draining from her.

'Jail?'

Aeneas and MacGillivray were immediately beside her. Aeneas grabbed Forbes by his shirtfront as, around them, the dancing halted and the music faltered into silence.

'Prison, is it?' Aeneas thundered into the older man's face. 'Whoever you send to fetch me would come back to you in a box!'

Dirks were being drawn. Bristling clansmen surrounded them; the short swords classed as working knives were as lethal in their practised hands as any broadsword. Sweat stood out on Forbes's face. He had misjudged the moment.

'Prison won't be necessary,' he squeaked.

Aeneas released his grip on the judge. Forbes smoothed the creases from his shirt before continuing.

'Your wife's money will do instead.'

The intake of breath all around was audible. Murmurs ran through the crowd, passing on the word. Farquharsons pushed through to the front. They hadn't impoverished themselves to benefit the McIntoshes. MacGillivray glared at Aeneas.

'So that was it.'

Anne stared at her husband. The tocher was her clan's gift to ensure she was well provided for in her married life. He had no claim on it.

'Aeneas, what is going on here?'

'Nothing I can't resolve,' he assured her.

Around them, the Farquharsons grew more voluble. Threats were issued, more dirks drawn.

'Of course, there is an alternative,' Forbes said, drawing out a piece of paper from inside his coat. 'Sign that land over to the bank.' He presented the paper to Aeneas.

'Our best farmland?' Aeneas was stunned. 'Without it, my clan will starve.'

'We can always rent it back to you.' Forbes shrugged.

'Then it will work for you,' Anne said, 'and the clan will still starve.'

'The court would grant it anyway,' Forbes said. 'Or there's always cash.'

'*Nous verrons,*' Aeneas said. 'We shall see.' He jumped back up on to the platform. 'We have a debt to pay,' he called to his clan. 'The bank wants our best land.' A roar of refusal rose from the crowd. 'Then would you pay with Farquharson money?'

'No!' his clan bellowed again. All around them, relieved Farquharsons slid their weapons back into belts.

'But we can pay,' Aeneas announced, 'with service in the Black Watch!'

Voices rose in disbelief. The Black Watch was a new regiment raised to prevent a second Jacobite rising in the Highlands. Forbes had lobbied parliament to get it. Now it was used against France. Only clans loyal to King George would think of joining it. People looked at each other in horror. A stocky M<sup>c</sup>Intosh cottar stepped forward.

'You ask us to fight for this government?'

His wife joined him. 'We'll not help the English rob and starve us,' she shouted.

'Or kill our allies!' another shouted.

From the rear, a fourth called out. 'What kind of chief would ask this?'

The atmosphere became volatile again.

'It's true,' Aeneas agreed with his clan. 'The Black Watch fights for the English against France. But while they're gone, companies are needed to police the Highlands. And who better to do that than our Jacobite clans?'

A scrawny old woman with a pitchfork pushed to the front of the crowd.

'We police ourselves,' she spat out.

'Then raise a company,' Aeneas said, 'and be paid for doing so.'

The clan was not convinced. It wasn't forty years since Scotland's parliament had been bribed into union with England. Resented from the beginning, it had proved an unequal marriage. The clans suffered most, their tribal way of life eroded by new laws and taxes, their customs threatened by the encroaching English culture. Thirty years earlier, they had raised arms, determined to put their own King James back on the throne and set Scotland free. That rising failed, but hope was not destroyed. Now, despite the rumours, it seemed their new chief did not share that hope. Anger and dissent grew among them.

'You might be a widow here before you're a wife,' Forbes whispered to Anne.

She gathered up her skirts and ran up the step to stand beside Aeneas.

'This government beats us down at every turn,' she called to the crowd. 'They tax our crops, our beasts and any money we make in trade. They tax us for making our own ale and stop us shearing our sheep so that English wool-traders can grow fat. Now they would take your land. But if you join the Watch, why, you can take from them for a change! And by doing no more than you already do, keeping the Highland peace!'

The mutters turned to murmurs as people began to appreciate the irony of this.

'Three meals a day, paid for by the English!' Aeneas shouted.

The crowd laughed.

'And a shilling each from the German Lairdie's brat they call king!' Anne added.

There was more laughter. The old woman waved her pitchfork.

'I'll go,' she cried.

'Only young men, Meg,' Aeneas explained. 'Fools that they are, they don't want women.'

'*Sasannaich!*' Old Meg spat in the dirt.

The wife of the clansman who'd first objected pushed her oldest son forward.

'Our Calum will go,' she said.

'And me.' Another lad stepped up.

'I will.'

'Me too.' Shouts came from everywhere.

Forbes was bemused. A M<sup>c</sup>Intosh contribution to the Black Watch was unexpected but acceptable, very acceptable given the prospect of rebellion. He could only declare himself satisfied. Aeneas grinned at Anne, swung her up into his arms, stepped down from the platform and, to enthusiastic roars of encouragement from their clans, carried her through the open doors into her new home.

It was the first time Anne had been inside Moy Hall, though she barely registered the long dining room or the wide square hall. What impressed her senses was the physical closeness of the man cradling her. In the swing of each step, his hard chest against her ribs, the back of his neck in the crook of her arm, the silkiness of that black hair brushing her fingers, the pressure of his arms on her back and thighs, how lightly he carried the weight of her.

'I should show you round,' he said, as he headed for the broad staircase, with no obvious intention of setting her down. From outside, the pipes picked up the interrupted reel, the dance resumed.

'It will wait.' She nuzzled into the curve of his neck to breathe the musky scent of him, brushing her lips against the smoothness of that skin, tasting the slight saltiness of it with her tongue.

'Woman,' he groaned, leaning his head into her a little, 'we'll never get beyond the stair.'

So he kissed her face, cheek, eyes, forehead, her hair, little kisses which she echoed, yet he never stumbled. At the top was a door, which he pushed open with his back, into a corridor with many doors. He carried her through the first to a wood-panelled bedroom bright with sunlight, threw his bonnet off, set her down. She had her mouth on his before her feet touched the ground, searching the warmth of his lips, for his tongue, arms round his neck, fingers tangled in his long hair, acutely conscious of his hands, one under her shoulder blades, the other in the small of her back, drawing her into him. It was a hungry kiss, fierce, their breath hot, exchanging, bodies clenched together, hands gripping and moving against clothes till the need for skin became irresistible. She tugged his belt loose and it thudded to the floor, dirk with it. Unlike the pleated great plaid which would have fallen away from his body without a belt to hold it, the kilt did not.

'Wait,' he said, chest rising in deep breaths, stepping back to remove his sword and unpin the brooch from his plaid.

She stood, dazed with desire, watching his fingers undo buckles, kilt and plaid drop in a heap, tartan hose pushed off his feet, till he stood in his long shirt, paused, about to reach for her again.

'I would see you without the shirt,' she said.

In one sweep, it was over his head and he was naked before her, taut, muscular, his body perfectly beautifully male, the smoothness of relaxed muscle, his cock jutting out, firm, ready. She put the palm of her hand against his chest. Her eyes wanted to close, her limbs to give way, limp with desire while he'd be stronger with than without it, nature ensuring its intention. But she wanted to know this body that would be joined with hers in marriage, before sensation removed perception, so she walked around him, close, tracing fingers and mouth across his skin, smelling the scent of him as she pressed a kiss between his strong shoulders, lightly, and felt the muscles in his back quiver, the same quiver in his buttocks.

As she came round in front of him again, her fingertips touched a scar on the shoulder of his left arm, an old scar, white with age, that had been deep.

'Before I learned not to drop my guard,' he said, looking into her eyes.

Brown, his eyes were, the colour of peat, and the look in them made her want his mouth again, want to take him into her. But he saw the urge rise in her and shook his head.

'Not yet,' he said, put his hands on her shoulders, turned her round so her back was to him and began to undo the hooks that fastened her dress.

White petals from the rosebuds stitched into it scattered to the floor and fluttered across the room as her dress slid down. When she stepped out of it, he swept it up, threw it on to a chair. The

47

stays over her shift fastened at the front, so he turned her to face him. Unlacing them, his knuckles brushed her breasts. Her breath, through parted lips, came in small gasps.

When the stays were gone, she expected him to push the thin straps from her shoulders, to let the shift fall from between them. But he put a hand round her back, slid his right hand down to raise the hem of it, reached under to stroke her thigh, the curve of her hip, over her belly, pushing his fingers down into that springy hair and on, into the wet heat of her sex.

'You're ready to fuck,' he murmured, thrusting in so that her knees buckled.

She pressed into him, gripping his shoulder to steady herself, reached for the weight of his erection with her other hand, but he stopped the touch, stepped back, his eyes blacker now, the light of the window behind him, the muted pipes changing smoothly from reel to strathspey, dancers whooping.

'I would see you without the shift,' he said, echoing her, his voice thick, and heavy without a smile in it.

A tremor ran through her belly. She slid the straps off her shoulders, shrugged off the silk, slithering, to the floor. Naked before his nakedness, her arms raised of their own accord, open for him. If he would not come to her now, the feeling banked in her would break into rage.

'Let your hair loose.'

'It will get in the way.'

'Not in mine.'

Now she was angry. She swept the long plait round, tugged the white ribbon from it, the last rosebuds falling, ran her fingers through the coils to loosen them, threw it over her shoulder and shook her head. The weight of hair swung, tumbling down her back, over her breast, falling to her hips. She glared at him but, paused in that stilled, watchful energy, he didn't seem to care. Then the heat of his skin was on hers, the strength of his arms holding, lifting as he put her and himself into their marriage bed, his body covering hers.

Even there, he seemed in no hurry to give himself to her, so there was nothing to deny and then nothing she would deny. He knew, as she had not, that the skin between her fingers, and in the palm of her hands, was more sensitive to touch than her breasts; that words murmured against hot skin aroused as much as stroking. So she let go, and went with him. All he prevented was when her hands, or mouth, or his own urgency might husband him too soon.

It was a long, slow coupling until, finally, he held her when she cried out for him to, as she shuddered in the dissolution of pleasure. It was only then, in the washing away, that he moved into her again, slow strokes changing quickly to deep, hard thrusting. Clenched to him, she was consumed, not by her own pleasure now but by his.

'*Mo ghaoil*, my love,' she whispered, when he groaned her name, juddering as his seed came out of him into her, lost in wonder. She felt tears come just holding him, vulnerable as he was, unguarded now, while stillness washed through the weight of him.

'Are you crying?' he asked, raising himself to look into her eyes.

'No.' And, in truth, she wasn't now, because her belly quivered, but with laughter.

He smiled, chuckled and rolled over on his back. They lay together, hearing the dancers call outside, the jig on the pipes, her head on his sweat-damp chest, fingers tracing the softer rise and fall of his abdomen, the smell of sex about them.

'How can you know all that?' she asked.

His head rose, looking at her, brows drawn together, then he grinned, broadly, threw his head back on the pillow laughing, a deep, throaty laugh which he would not explain though she pushed her fist into his ribs and threatened to fuck him again, but it was far too soon and they had to wait a while.

Reluctant to rejoin their guests, at least before morning or even the day after, they let the afternoon drift on to evening. They ate and drank from a tray the girl, Jessie, had left at the door. It was when dark fell, when pipes and celebrants grew silent, that the enormity of marriage struck Anne. She would sleep the night beside him, rise in this bed next day.

'And wake making love,' he smiled, though his eyes were shut, near sleep.

'In the morning?'

'I don't think the English have passed a law against it yet,' he said.

'Then they must mean to tax it,' she said. And they laughed again, together.

# SEVEN

A grey drizzle of rain hung over London, barely penetrated by the rising sun. In his chambers at Kensington House, the Duke of Cumberland splashed cold water into his face. At twenty-four, he already had the bulbous look of an English bulldog. His defeat at Fontenoy still smarted, the return home ignominious, leaving the French in victorious possession of Flanders. Behind him, a servant held his red coat ready. The Duke dried himself, threw the towel down beside the china bowl of water and slid his arms into the waiting sleeves.

'Cope! Hawley!' he called.

The door opened and General Hawley, a skinny ancient spider of a man meticulously dressed in black, came in.

'Your Highness,' he bowed. 'All's well with the king?'

'My father is –' Cumberland hesitated '– concerned. Where's Cope?'

'It's morning,' Hawley shrugged. It was well known in the army that General Cope liked his bed. From the hallway came the sound of clattering. The door burst open and Cope appeared, a rotund, red-faced man with his buttons half done and his wig askew, scarlet uniform spattered with rain. He flapped his hands, apologetically.

'Ah, I'm sorry, I was –'

'Late,' Cumberland snapped. His jowls quivered. He swept up a sheaf of papers and waved it at the two generals. 'Last week HMS *Lion* engaged two French frigates. The *Elisabeth* limped back to Brest. The *du Teillay* escaped. Now our intelligence reports my cousin has gone from France.'

'He wouldn't be such a damn fool as to land,' Cope said. 'Not with only one ship.'

'That we know of.' Cumberland sat down heavily and began to

write. 'You'll mobilize for Scotland. General Hawley, you'll join General Wade in Northumberland.'

'England's Jacobites won't start an insurrection,' Hawley objected. 'They only talk. A few gibbets swinging in the Highlands would ensure the peace.'

'Or one for a would-be king,' Cumberland corrected. He handed the paper he'd been writing to Cope. 'A letter of credit, Johnny. That should cover your payroll. Find him.'

Rain had battered down throughout the first two weeks of July, a hard, unceasing rain that cut like knives, drumming on roofs, puddling fields and flooding the burns into spate. When it stopped, it was suddenly summer, dry and hot as if no such rain could be imagined, far less fall. Only flooded fords, swollen lochs and fast-flowing rivers gave the lie to that, and the crops. Grim-faced, Anne and Aeneas sat on their horses side by side, staring at the devastation. The field of barley was flattened.

'The wheat will be the same,' Aeneas said, dismounting to check the standing height of broken stems.

'Can we harvest it now?'

'Aye,' he squinted up at her against the harsh sun. 'But for hay.' That would mean overwintering more cattle so the crop could return its worth fed through the beasts. It would be spring before any value derived from it.

'At least the oats are in.'

'Plenty of porridge,' he agreed, swinging back up into the saddle, 'and less to wash it down with.'

'So it's ale and *uisge beatha* you mourn,' she teased. 'Or that we'll miss our contribution to German Geordie's keep?'

He leant an arm on his horse's neck and studied her for a moment.

'There's another shame this is a barley field,' he said slowly, seriously, despite the light in his eyes. 'You'll not be wanting ears of that inside your skirts.'

The sudden twist of pleasure inside Anne, though familiar now, was always unexpected. Throughout June, they had tried walking through the estate so she could learn it but could barely pass a grassy patch among the heather or a copse of trees. Hand-holding was fatal to forward progress so, if she was to know the extent of Moy, they had to traverse it on horseback. Unlike Aeneas, she could not control her smile.

'I doubt they'd be a joy under the kilt either,' she said.

'*Ach*, I'm a man.' He grinned now. 'I can stand the itch.' Then he chuckled. 'At least till later.'

It took longer than it ought to reap and stook the half-ripe grain. Aeneas sent fifty cotter families over to help cut and stack at Dunmaglas, where MacGillivray, with more barley in exposed fields, would have suffered greater loss.

When the work was done, the boys who'd volunteered into the Black Watch assembled at Moy Hall. They'd been kept back for a harvest that would no longer come, their income from military service needed even more now. Lined up, fresh-faced and eager enough for adventure, they were mostly oldest sons of the poorest families. Cotters on the periphery of the estate were often exiles from other clans, banished for some transgression or voluntary exiles over some dispute, given the thinnest soil and most meagre grazing allowance until they proved themselves to their new chief.

Anne had dressed up specially to inspect the volunteers, walking the lines with Aeneas. A few, whose mothers refused permission, were sent home. In customary fashion, for welcome or to see men off to war, she kissed each one warmly on the mouth as Aeneas introduced them. They were tender boys, at the pretty age, sixteen or seventeen, not much younger than she was. This would be their first time away from home.

'Calum M<sup>c</sup>Cay,' Aeneas said.

She remembered Calum from their wedding day, the first one pushed forward.

'Duncan Shaw.' The elder of two brothers, his mother had allowed only one to go.

The next boy was gangly with a wide lop-sided grin.

'Shameless,' Aeneas said. 'He has no other name.'

'M<sup>c</sup>Intosh,' Shameless said proudly, mistaking his chief's meaning. 'I'm with Howling Robbie.' Certainly the two boys stood, fingers entwined, close together.

'*Howling* Robbie?' Anne queried, smiling.

'Do you not remember from the dancing,' Aeneas said in her ear, 'or him singing later in the night?'

Now she remembered; the hooching and hollering which owed more to energy than tunefulness. She kissed them both soundly.

'It's good you're going together.'

There were fifty volunteers, the last Lachlan Fraser, the black-smith's son. Anne questioned that one. A smith was an important asset, not one to be given away lightly and not into government forces when a rising could be imminent.

'The French never left port, Anne,' Aeneas reminded her. 'Only two ships escaped the blockade and the navy turned them back.'

'But they might try again, and if the Prince lands in England, these boys could be sent there, on the wrong side.'

'I won't let that happen.'

Anne turned back to Lachlan, who stood, head down, fretting. Like all the young men there, he was eager to go fully armed and become the warrior he had trained to be since childhood.

'You can go with my blessing,' she said, kissing him. 'But only for six months. Moy has more need than the Black Watch of a blacksmith in the making.'

Aeneas mounted up then, to deliver the boys to Fort George in Inverness. Anne stayed behind to make tokens for the next day's handfasting but she watched them go, uneasy. She'd supported Aeneas in recruiting them because it felt right at the time, but now, watching them march proudly away, kilted plaids swinging, it seemed as though they marched to join an enemy. The clan had instinctively been repelled by the idea of their sons supporting a government garrison. Perhaps that should have been heeded.

The following morning there were disputes to settle before the afternoon ceremonies. Moy Hall, like the land, belonged to the people, as did their chief. It was to him they brought problems they failed to resolve among themselves. The first two were simple, a boundary disagreement and some cattle put on to another's grazing. Aeneas resolved them equally simply. He knew precisely where the boundary fell. If transgressed again, twice the ground encroached would be given for use to the aggrieved family. He didn't accept the excuse that cattle wandered into a neighbour's field.

'It is for you to see they don't,' he told their owner, warning him that the neighbour would also gain an extra beast if it happened again, before addressing the need by allocating extra rights to the common grazing.

Anne listened carefully. It would take time before she knew Moy and its people well enough to make such clear-headed judgements. At Invercauld, she, too, had known every stone and tree, each name and person. She swallowed a surge of homesickness.

The third complaint was made with great anger. A crowd pushed into the hall, propelling a bruised cottar prodded on by an old woman with a pitchfork, and all of them speaking at once.

'Let one of you speak first,' Aeneas said, nodding to a stocky cottar. 'Ewan?'

'He has put a *torr-sgian* into his wife,' Ewan said. 'And she has the wounds in her back to show for it!'

'So it's no accident?' Aeneas questioned.

'They'd not be cutting peat this late,' Anne, staggered by the brutality, interrupted.

'Nor indoors either,' the old woman snorted. She poked the guilty man with the prongs of her fork.

'All right, Meg,' Aeneas said, frowning. 'Could none of you prevent this?'

'As soon as we knew,' Ewan drew himself up, proudly. 'But the harm was done.'

Aeneas ascertained the woman would recover, then listened, calmly, to the man's story, how it was an accident, how his wife was sharp-tongued and ungrateful, how he'd become enraged but meant no harm to her.

'And I'm right sorry now,' he said pitifully, clasping his bonnet to his chest.

'Your temper is yours to keep, Dùghall,' Aeneas said. 'You came to us needing a home when your own chief banished you. Is this why?'

'His wife said they ran from her family's anger.' Meg answered instead.

'Will she go with him a second time?' Aeneas asked.

'She says not,' Ewan answered.

'Says and does are different things.' Aeneas stood. 'I'll see to this outside.' As the cottars huckled the man out of doors, he called for Jessie to bring a binding cloth and turned to Anne when she rose to go with them. 'You needn't see this.'

'Aeneas,' she insisted. 'When you're not here, I must deal with these matters.'

'If I'm not here,' he said, buckling on his sword, 'MacGillivray would deal with the likes of this.'

'We haven't seen him since the wedding,' she reminded, following behind.

'He'll come when there's need,' he said, standing aside to let her go out first. Outside, he called Will, the stableboy, to fetch a tether. With it, he bound the now whimpering Dùghall's right hand to the tethering post at the door.

'Hold him,' he said unnecessarily to Ewan, who'd kept a good grip of the man to prevent him running off. To Dùghall, he said, 'you'll not do harm, nor find another home, so readily from here on.' Then he drew his sword, raised it and swung it down, hard, slicing through the man's wrist, the blow taking the tethered hand clean off.

The man fell back against Ewan, squealing. Blood oozed from the blunt end of his arm. As Aeneas sheathed his sword, Jessie went to bind the wound, Will to recover the tether and remove the severed hand.

'If you take him to the smith,' Aeneas told the cottars, 'Donald will sear the wound. Then see him off our lands.'

'He'll be an outcast now,' Anne said, as Aeneas came up the steps. The enormity of the wounding was greater than disfigurement. No chief would take the man in, his value as warrior or worker nullified, his untrustworthy nature evident. Hanging might have been kinder.

'His wife will be less inclined to follow him,' Aeneas said, 'when she hears.'

The men were already dancing at the far end of the loch where the handfasting feast was laid out by the summerhouse. Highland men danced often, alone, making their own mouth-music, or in groups. Fast or slow, the dances were complex, requiring skill. Dancers often risked injury if weapons were involved in the display. Now they danced exuberantly to the pipes, in celebration. Aeneas was immediately called to join them, which he did, taking his place at the front of the group.

Anne joined the women, talking and laughing with them as they watched the men, kilts and plaids swinging, feet flashing like knives. Handfasting was an old custom which many clans no longer observed, but the McIntoshes were descended from Celtic priests, their ancient ways dear to them. The men and women who took part committed themselves to live together as married for a year and a day. On that last day, if both chose it, they married. If either one chose not, the bond ended. It was a custom ignored rather than approved by their church. When marriage was refused, children conceived or born during handfasting were often given to the father's family after weaning, but the choice lay with the woman. Pregnant or nursing, she was more sought after by other suitors, her fertility assured.

When the dance ended, to much cheering, the couples lined up under the trees at the edge of the loch. Turn by turn, they joined hands, taking each other by the wrists, which Aeneas bound lightly together with plaited ribbon. Beside him, Anne gave each girl a corn dolly for luck. The ceremony was late that year, normally taking place after haymaking, delayed by the rains and the immediate need to salvage crops when the sun returned. When the dozen joinings were complete, the women sang an old Gaelic song of love, voices echoing across the water. Aeneas stood behind Anne, his arms wrapped around her waist, swaying together as she joined in the singing. When it ended, the couples scattered to private places already chosen among the trees. Sun and summer were to be enjoyed. Come rain and winter, most of them would take their pleasure in crowded single-roomed family cotts.

Watching them go, Anne leant back against Aeneas, resting her head under his chin. Her arms were folded over his, palms resting on the backs of his hands, fingers entwined. The crackle of feet through trees became distant. Excited voices faded away. They stood for some time, feeling the warmth of the air, the slight pressure of each other, listening to the drone of insects, the peep of birds, hearing the water lap gently behind them. Aeneas moved his chin against the top of her head, and she turned her face into him.

'We could do likewise,' she said.

A white sail slapped in the wind, straining against ropes and mast as the boom swung. Out from Moidart, the boat turned towards Loch nan Uamh, heading in for Borrowdale. As the prow rose, cutting through the swell, a white wash trailed out behind it. On the deck, boxes of munitions were stacked. Seven men travelled on the boat. In the prow, leaning forward, sat a prince. He was tall, lean, with fine, aristocratic features, deep brown eyes and clear skin. Dressed in courtly fashion, he wore blue silk breeches and jacket, white stockings, a fine lace jabot at his throat. An eagerness enlivened him as the land rose green and purple mountains reared before them. He turned to the man standing beside him.

'L'Écosse, O'Sullivan,' he announced. 'I am come home.'

Anne woke with a start. Disorientated in the early morning light, she looked around the wood-panelled room. Then she remembered and stretched sensuously in the empty bed, smoothing the rumpled sheets with her legs, the last night's lovemaking running over again in her mind. Beside her, the other pillow still bore the indentation of her husband's head. She pulled it towards her, buried her face in it, breathing in the scent of him. If he did not come back to bed soon, she would have to get up and find him or else pleasure herself. She wondered what he would do if he came back then. Would he take over or want to watch? The clash of metal on metal penetrated the room. Swords, and seriously engaged by the sound of it.

Instantly, she was off the bed, a robe pulled on, and over to the window. She pushed it up, leant out and looked down. Fear twisted her heart. It was Aeneas and MacGillivray in the yard below, broadswords flashing in the warm August sun. The fight was fast, vigorous and dangerous. Aeneas pushed MacGillivray away and the younger chief immediately swung at him again.

'I hope you're working up an appetite,' Anne called down.

The men broke off and looked up.

'Working against one,' Aeneas called back, making it obvious what he'd rather be doing. MacGillivray lunged again with his sword. Aeneas stopped it above his head with his own. Faces close, the two men's eyes met.

'Too slow,' Aeneas said. His dirk was drawn in his left hand, the point of it pressed just below MacGillivray's ribs. MacGillivray grinned. Both men laughed. MacGillivray disengaged and sheathed his sword.

'Every time,' he complained.

'Be glad you're on the same side,' Anne called.

Aeneas slid the dirk into his belt and sheathed his own sword. Then he put his arm round MacGillivray's shoulder.

'Never mind, little chief,' he said, warmly. 'One day.'

'Aye,' MacGillivray agreed. 'You'll be old first.' They laughed again. Anne smiled down at the pair of them. Life was hard enough without animosity between kinsmen.

'I thought you were home in Dunmaglas,' she called to MacGillivray.

'I was, until the MacDonalds raided my cattle last night.'

'We were warming up while we waited for your agreement to raid them in return,' Aeneas called up. 'Come down and join us while we eat.'

As she turned away to dress, Anne felt rich indeed. Both were skilled, MacGillivray brave and daring, Aeneas cool-headed, fast and deadly accurate. Together, they were invincible. They would have her permission for the raid. She snatched up the white pillow from her marriage bed and danced it around the room.

# EIGHT

Blood leaked from a fresh incision in a cow's throat, ran into a wooden dish. Old Meg held it. In her other hand, on the cow's back, she held the dirk with which she'd made the cut. Beside her, a pitchfork stood propped against her cott. Behind her, a baby cried. A young woman, carrying the crying baby swaddled against her in a tartan shawl, came up from the next cott, her top loosened.

'What can I do?' She put her hand against her empty breast. 'I'm dry of milk.'

'Fetch some oats, Cath,' Meg said, not turning from her task. 'I'll give you blood to mix with them.'

'He'll not manage that,' Cath answered.

'Not him. Yourself.' Then, as the young woman went off to fetch a dish of oats, she shouted, 'And drink water. Plenty water.' Her attention was on the bowl as it filled with the cow's blood, but she could see Anne walking over the rise towards her, following the path that led past the cotts, a covered basket heavy on her arm. Before the chief's new wife had covered half the distance, Cath was back with her dish of oats. Meg stopped the wound on her cow's neck, then carefully dribbled blood from her bowl into Cath's as the young woman stirred it into the cereal. The sound of hoof-beats disturbed the quiet. Both women looked up towards it.

A man on horseback had come from behind the cotts on the same path Anne walked but heading towards her. He was clearly a stranger, his dress foreign. A few yards behind him, a woman on foot led her own horse by its reins. Anne nodded as the man passed her by without a glance, but as she reached the perspiring woman, she stopped, drew a flask from her basket and held it out.

'Uisge?' she offered, then realizing that would not be understood, tried the Latin. 'Aqua?'

The exhausted woman grabbed the flask and, as the male rider halted, turning in his saddle towards her, she gulped the liquid.

'Helen!' The man commanded, his voice and language revealing he was English. 'Don't drink that filth!'

'It's only water,' Anne explained, using his tongue now she knew what it was.

The man swung his horse around, whip raised. Anne sat the basket at her feet, ready to protect herself. Back at the cotts, old Meg put the bowl of blood down on the grass and snatched up her pitchfork. The man swung his whip, aiming, not at Anne, but to knock the flask from his companion's hands.

'I said, Don't drink it!'

As the whip came down, Anne caught and held on to the end of it, preventing the striking of its target. Old Meg ran up the path towards her. Cath, the swaddled baby slowing her, hurried behind. Anne glared at the man on the horse above her.

'Servants are not whipped for drinking water,' she said.

'Servant?' the man spluttered, incredulous. 'She's my wife!'

Anne let go the whip, shocked that he had no shame for himself. Meg arrived beside her. The Englishwoman held the flask out to Anne.

'I've had enough,' she said. 'Thank you.'

Meg went to the woman's horse, running her hands expertly over its back leg. The man stirred in his saddle, clearly uncomfortable.

'Move, Helen,' he insisted. 'These northern tribes are savages.'

As Cath arrived beside them, Meg looked up from her examination of the horse. 'Tha e crùbach,' she said, in her own Gaelic tongue. 'It's lame.'

Anne grabbed hold of the bridle on the man's mount.

'Among savages,' she said, 'wives don't walk while husbands ride.'

'Release my horse,' the man ordered. 'I am a servant to His Majesty, King George.'

'Is that so?' Anne smiled, keeping hold of the reins.

The man went for his pistol. Too late. Before his hand touched the butt tucked into his waist, old Meg's pitchfork was aimed squarely at his middle. Anne was amused that he thought loyalty to the usurper would impress anyone this far north.

'And do you have a name, servant of King George?' she asked.

'James Ray,' he snapped. 'A name you'd do well to remember.'

His ugly manners did not dent Anne's courtesy or cheerfulness. She was curious. They were far travelled, the English rare in these parts.

'And you, my dear?' she asked the woman.

'Mistress James Ray,' the man butted in. 'Obviously!'

'You have the same name?' Anne frowned, still addressing the woman. 'Are you not mistaken for brother and sister?'

'Well, no. How else would a wife be known except by her husband's name?'

'I was sure he called you Helen.'

'He did,' Helen agreed. 'For that's who I am, but to be called Mistress Helen Ray I'd have to be widowed.'

'Then you must hope it comes soon,' Anne smiled, 'Helen whoever-you-are.' She translated the joke for Meg and Cath, and the three Highland women chuckled. But, whereas the English-woman quickly stifled a smile, her husband was incensed.

'I may call my wife what I choose,' he snarled, 'but you will address her as Mistress Ray.'

Anne considered him. He seemed barely aware of his situation, so intent was he on asserting himself. Meg's two-pronged pitchfork would aerate his gut with a flick of the old woman's wiry wrist.

'And you may address me as Anne Farquharson, the Lady M'Intosh,' she told him. 'A name you might rather forget.'

'Lady!' Ray snorted. 'I doubt it.'

Anne drew her dirk. Beside her, Cath shifted the baby into the curve of her left armpit and did likewise.

'While you're on our land, you'd do well to mind your manners,' she informed Ray. 'Now, would you care to dismount?'

The question was a politeness backed by cold steel. In moments, Ray was off his horse, his wife reluctant to mount it in his stead.

'I should obey my husband,' she said, glancing at him nervously.

'What on earth for?' Anne asked, amazed.

'Because I'm bound to. You must've made the same vow.'

'No Scottish wife would promise such a thing. Our men would think us daft.' Anne turned to the cottar women. 'Obedience to a husband?' she asked.

They shrugged, mystified, the idea too strange to contemplate.

Helen was prodded to mount the healthy horse at dirk point.

'Try to remember who you really are,' Anne told her, then she handed Ray the reins of the lame horse. 'Now your situation's in better order,' she said. 'You may go. But be warned, you'll be watched all the way to Inverness. Good day to you.'

Helen Ray clicked her husband's horse forward, her expression bemused but carefully controlled. Her husband followed, leading the lame mount. Anne, Meg and Cath watched them go.

'Sasannaich!' Cath said, disgusted by the intruders.

'Heathens!' Meg spat on to the path.

Anne grinned at them and stuck the dirk back in her belt. It was her first visit alone to these cotts, but she had won their approval. She picked up her basket.

'Some food we can't use,' she said as they walked towards the turf homes. 'The clan is more than generous.'

'Do the Farquharsons not care to honour their chief?' Meg snipped, the fragile camaraderie between them suddenly at risk.

Anne took in the tethered beast, the crusted scars on its neck, the bowl of blood tucked against a tussock of grass. These people were poor but they would be proud. A clan demonstrated status by its provision for the chief. Returning gifts could be taken as an insult.

'They do,' she said, carefully. 'And they, too, would go without to fulfil that honour.'

Meg nodded, satisfied with the compliment.

'Then you have no stomach for what is in the basket?'

'Oh, I do,' Anne smiled. 'We're so well provided for, there will soon be rumours I'm with child. But goodness shouldn't go to waste. The meat should be used before it turns.'

Both cottar women considered this, their own need less apparent to them than the need of others.

'Old Tom is sick, in the end cott,' Cath offered.

'And he has a wheen of grandchildren,' Meg added.

Hooves drummed on the path at their backs. All three turned fast, half-expecting a pistol-waving irate Englishman to be bearing down on them. It was MacGillivray who rode over the rise, a roped black cow lumbering behind him.

'So, this is a drove road for MacGillivrays now,' Anne teased, as he reined in. 'You've made thin pickings of your thieved beasts, Alexander, if one is all you've brought back.'

'The others are up at the house,' he explained. 'This one is by way of interest from MacDonald.' He tossed the cow's rope to Cath. 'Aeneas sent her down. You'll want the milk.'

As Cath's eyes lit up, Meg was already running expert hands over the animal. MacGillivray offered Anne a ride back to Moy.

'Go on,' Cath said, as Anne hesitated. 'I'll see the food goes where it's needed.' Anne handed her the basket, took hold of MacGillivray's outstretched arm and was hauled up behind him. MacGillivray looked down at Meg, still appraising the cow.

'Just the milk, mind,' he said, then he trotted the horse away, Anne's arms round his waist. Meg cast a knowing look at Cath.

'Away,' Cath rejected the suggestion. 'That was over when she married M<sup>c</sup>Intosh.'

'Over?' Meg cackled, enjoying the idea. 'It's under him I'd be.'

Over midday dinner in the dining room at Moy Hall, Aeneas and MacGillivray regaled Anne with the story of the raid.

'They were still celebrating stealing from Alexander, drunk with success,' Aeneas explained. He had enjoyed turning the tables. Cattle-raiding was a way of life. The shaggy, long-haired Highland beasts on the hills were native, but short-haired cattle were plundered from further south in Scotland or England, fattened in the glens then sold back to the Sassenach Lowlanders at their annual trysts. It was almost an arrangement. The prices paid by southerners for fattened clan beef reflected the extra weight but not the original beast. So it was hardly stealing to relieve a neighbour of some of their stock, though it was a matter of honour to fetch back what was taken.

'The guards were snoring in the heather,' MacGillivray said. 'Aeneas took us in under their noses and we drove the cattle out past them again.'

'It wasn't till we were well clear that we counted them,' Aeneas went on. 'And he,' he slapped MacGillivray's shoulder, 'he tells me then that only ten had been raided from Dunmaglas.'

'How many did you take back?' Anne asked.

'Twice that,' Aeneas laughed. 'MacDonald will be scratching his head when he sobers, wondering why his herd looks so thin after he'd just increased it.'

'He'll be a week working it out,' MacGillivray hooted. 'He can't count above ten before he runs out of fingers!'

Aeneas filled more ale into their tankards.

'So we're all better off,' he said. 'MacDonald's herd will have more grass to fatten on. Yours is increased, and we have five new beasts in our stock. A fine morning's work.' He raised his tankard. 'To MacDonald.'

Anne and MacGillivray responded to the toast.

'MacDonald!'

'There is something more we can do, that might offset the harvest losses,' Aeneas pondered. 'Trade some of our stored wool.' He paused. 'Quietly.'

When they heard the Farquharsons had sheared all their sheep, on Anne's suggestion for safe storage, they'd both followed suit.

'Smuggle it out to the boats?' MacGillivray said, catching on. 'You won't need to ask me twice.'

'And the Black Watch might look the other way now,' Anne said dryly.

'It's a fine thing to have,' Aeneas raised his glass to her, 'a wife with impressive ideas.'

The door from the kitchen clattered open and young Jessie rushed in.

'Aeneas, there's trouble,' she got out.

He was instantly on his feet, the chair scraping back.

'What, is it the MacDonalds?'

'No, no,' the girl said. 'It's the Dowager.'

From outside, Will, the stableboy, half carried the exhausted woman in through the front doors. Aeneas and MacGillivray rushed to help, relieving the young lad of his burden and carrying Aeneas's aunt to a chair.

'She's galloped that horse from Inverness,' Will complained.

'Would you see to it?' Aeneas asked, and the lad hurried back out.

Anne poured ale into a fresh tankard and held it to the Dowager's lips.

'Here,' she urged. 'Drink.'

The older woman gulped the liquid down.

'What on earth brings you in such haste?' Aeneas asked.

'The Prince,' the Dowager gasped.

'But his ships were turned back,' Aeneas said. 'Is he taken?'

'No.' The Dowager shook her head. 'He's come. He's here.'

'Here?' Anne said, beginning to look round, then stopping. 'Where?'

'Put in at Borrowdale and is heading for Glenfinnan now.'

'He's here?' MacGillivray frowned as if, surely, this couldn't be.

The Dowager nodded. 'Aye.' Now she had her breath back, her voice steady. 'He has come at last.'

There was stunned silence as the news sank in. MacGillivray was first to speak.

'Now we can free ourselves,' he shouted, lifting Anne off her feet to swing her round. 'And live how we please!'

As he let her go, Anne gripped his arms.

'He's come,' she squealed, then turned to her husband, alive with excitement. 'He's come, Aeneas. He's really here! Oh, Jessie,' she said to the wide-eyed girl. 'Would you fetch wine, and glasses? We must celebrate.'

As the girl rushed out, Aeneas pulled a chair over beside his aunt and sat down.

'And the French army, are they with him?'

The Dowager was slower to shake her head this time. 'Seven men, they say.'

'*Seachdnar!*' Aeneas repeated, appalled. 'Seven men!'

'Some guns and ammunition.'

Aeneas stood, throwing his chair back angrily so it toppled with a clatter on the wooden floor. 'The clans won't rise for seven men!'

'They'll rise for him,' Anne asserted.

'I very much fear they will,' the Dowager said.

'We'll give him an army,' MacGillivray affirmed. He was already impatient to go. 'We'd best move fast to bring Clan Chatton out, Aeneas, or Macpherson might seize the chance to steal command from you. He's not forgiven your chieftainship.'

Aeneas walked to the window and stood, looking out, his back to them. Anne's tremendous surge of joy was seeping away. She walked over, put a hand on his shoulder. There was tension in him.

'Aeneas?'

He turned then, but when his eyes met hers, they had no warmth or excitement in them, only cold certainty, and were strange to her.

'I'll not bring the clan out,' he said.

'Not fight?' She misunderstood. He couldn't mean that. 'But we must. We agreed, when he came, that we'd rise.'

'Words are easy said.'

'Like those that bind us?' Anne accused.

'No, of course not!'

'This is our cause he comes to lead.'

'Without the French, the government will crush this in its infancy. I will not risk our people for seven men. We'll wait to see what the other clans do.'

'We've waited long enough,' MacGillivray reminded him. 'Our people die of patience!'

'He's come alone,' Aeneas reiterated. 'And England won't easily give Scotland up. Make no mistake, Alexander, if this starts, we daren't lose.'

'It has started,' the Dowager said. 'Lochiel sent the fiery cross from Achnacarry. The Camerons are already marching. That's how I know.'

'You see?' Anne put her hand on Aeneas's arm, entreating him. 'We should all stand together.'

'With the Camerons?' Aeneas said. 'That we won't.' Their two clans had been at odds for centuries. 'Lochiel is a foolish old romantic.'

It was more than MacGillivray's hot temper could bear.

'But a loyal one,' he retorted, snatching up the short-bladed *sgian dhubh* he had been eating with. 'Man, is it water not blood in your veins!' And he stabbed the knife deep into the table.

Instantly, Aeneas pulled his dirk. 'We can settle that outside,' he challenged.

The Dowager leapt out of her chair and between them.

'It is settled,' she said forcefully, and while she might have meant their unspoken rivalry over Anne, it was his loyalty she called on to calm MacGillivray. 'When Clan Chatton chose Aeneas, we chose a warrior with a wise head not just a strong arm. You wanted that lead then, Alexander. Will you fail the first test of your own bond?'

MacGillivray could, with impunity, set his king before his chief, but he struggled with it. The Prince was still formless, King James a vague and distant notion. Aeneas was flesh and blood, and here, supporting and defending his own. That morning's adventure to benefit the MacGillivrays had been at his lead.

'Since I could walk, Aeneas,' he said, 'you have led. Lead now.'

Aeneas pushed the dirk back into his belt.

'As I'm trying to,' he said. 'Any fool can fight, but it takes wit to win. I'll speak to our other chiefs.'

MacGillivray, who would not have stood down to any other man, took his hand off the hilt of his dirk.

'Then I'll ride with you,' he said.

'Our chiefs will come out,' Anne said. 'They've wanted this for so long.'

Aeneas took hold of her, gently, asking for patience.

'I'll ask them to wait,' he said, 'until the French arrive.' He and MacGillivray left then. Joyless and uncertain, Anne watched them go, then she turned to the Dowager.

'But what if the French wait for us to declare?'

'A few more weeks will do no harm,' the Dowager assured her.

Jessie hurried back into the room bearing wine and glasses. Her excitement faltered as she saw the men had gone and the mood changed.

'Are we not celebrating now?' she asked.

'No matter.' The Dowager relieved the girl of the tray. 'We can always drink.'

# NINE

Deep inside Anne a fear had taken root, a fear she didn't want to admit to, not even to herself. She had married a man she didn't know. Now she discovered qualities in him she could not have guessed. Aeneas wasn't like MacGillivray, open and easy to read. She could always tell what MacGillivray would do. Sometimes, she even knew what he would say, often before he appeared to know himself. But Aeneas had unknown depths to him. What now surfaced did not bring delight with the surprise. She was uncertain about his loyalties or what he held dear, and that uncertainty threatened her.

To keep from dwelling on it, she resorted to brittle conviction. He would come back chastened, convinced, enthused. The other chiefs would talk him round. She had Will prepare the four crosses ready to be sent out to raise the clan and doubled the watch on the cattle in case MacDonald tried to take advantage of Aeneas's absence and steal back his beasts. She kept busy with estate business, dispensing extra grazing rights to an elderly couple who lived on the edge of Drumossie, and she heard more news. The Prince raised his standard at Glenfinnan, announcing his father's commitment to restore Scotland's independence with his crown. From Angus, the newly wed Margaret Johnstone and her husband, Lord Ogilvie, joined Lochiel for the cause. The MacDonald chiefs, cattle-thieving forgotten, took their people out.

All around, the land throbbed with talk. A government army was marching north to reinforce Inverness. Weapons that had not seen daylight for years were taken from their hiding places, sharpened and polished till they shone. Several chiefs lit the fiery cross and sent the runners out with it, calling their clan to arms. Many, like Aeneas, did not. Still he did not return. Anne entertained the Dowager, who had stayed on to keep her company. When she tired of the house, she showed Jessie how to mince the meat of a hare with onion and turnip to make a thick, nourishing broth. Next day, she set off with a flask of it to visit the north-western cotts. Even as their world spun into rebellion around them, the sick, old man, Tom, would still need good fresh food.

It was mid-morning as she came over the rise in sight of the cotts. Ahead, she saw Cath, baby wrapped against her in the tartan shawl, holding the gifted MacDonald cow while old Meg, on a stool beside its rump, drew milk from its swollen teats. She expected a welcome but, as soon as the women saw her coming, Cath tied the rope to the tethering post and hurried away through the cotts. Meg watched as she drew near, head tucked side-on against the cow's black hide, hands working rhythmically at its udders. Her expression was shuttered, suspicious.

'I brought some meat broth for the old man who's ill,' Anne said.

The hiss of milk spurting into the wooden pail stopped. Old Meg sat back on the stool, drying her hands on her rough skirts.

'Cath's gone to let him know you're coming.'

'You guessed my reason?'

Meg shrugged.

'No one else here wants charity.'

'It's not charity,' Anne corrected. 'We look out for each other.'

'That's as maybe.'

'The woman who was hurt with the peat-spade,' Anne asked, 'is she well?'

'Gone back to her own people, a week past.' The old woman turned again to her milking. 'It's the last one at the far end,' she said. 'They'll be expecting you now.'

Perplexed by the change in attitude, Anne walked down the row of turf dwellings. There seemed to be no one else about. Many of them would be in the fields, seeing to crops, beasts, turning peats or collecting wood for winter fire stocks, but she would have expected some women and children to be busy spinning wool, churning butter or making cheeses. Then, from the corner of her eye, she caught a flutter of movement crossing the gap between cotts. A woman's skirt, an ankle. Whoever it was, she was avoiding Anne, going in the opposite direction, and did not want to be seen.

Anne sighed. The trust she'd won from them last time had gone. While Aeneas hesitated, his people did not know where they stood. They would come out for the cause. That was not in doubt. But, just as the rising needed the leadership of the Prince, the people needed leadership from their chief. Maybe they thought Anne had influenced his decision to wait. Clearly, it would take longer than she thought to be accepted here.

Cath emerged from the last cott as Anne arrived. She nodded to indicate that Anne should go in but did not speak. Anne dipped her head to pass in under the low doorway, her spirit more depressed than when she'd set out.

As soon as she was out of sight, there was a flurry of activity. Meg jumped up from her milking and waved the unseen person out from behind the cotts. A woman emerged, her arm round a young lad. Shielding them with her body from sight of Anne's possible re-emergence, Meg ushered them into her own cott, closed the door tight then, with barely a pause in her movements, resumed her position on the milking stool and continued her task.

Inside the dim, smoky one-room interior of the old man's cott, Anne warmed the broth in a pot over the low peat fire. The old man lay propped up on a bracken pallet, coughing.

'I've brought you some hare soup, Tom,' Anne said. Behind his pallet, two small grubby children crouched, staring at her with wide, mesmerized eyes. Both were girls, though it was hard to tell at that age and in the gloom.

'It's a princess,' the bigger child informed the smaller.

Anne smiled and told them who she was, in the customary style, her own name followed by title and her husband's, just as she had with James Ray on her previous visit.

'Your chief's wife,' she explained as she spooned the steaming soup into a bowl. 'And perhaps there will be broth enough for three in this pot.' She knelt down, stirred the broth with the horn spoon, tested the temperature was not too hot, then held the spoon to the old man's trembling lips. He swallowed greedily. Nothing much was wrong with his appetite. Behind her, the door of the cott opened. A stocky, fair-headed man came in. She recognized him right away. He was the cottar who first challenged Aeneas's request that they send their sons to the Black Watch, the same man who'd held the brutish Dùghall while Aeneas took the hand off him.

'Ewan McCay, Lady McIntosh,' he introduced himself. 'This is my home and you're welcome in it. How is my father?'

'Alive,' Anne said. 'If you would send the older one,' she nodded at the children, 'up to the Hall every third day, Jessie will see to it there is always fresh broth for him.'

'I'll see she comes,' Ewan said. 'Thank you for your kindness.'

From outside, a horse whinnied. There were shouts of alarm, raised voices and squeals of fear. Ewan turned for the door. Anne planked the bowl into the hands of the bigger child.

'Feed this to your grandfather,' she said, and followed Ewan out.

Outside, the sudden brightness blinded her, but then she saw. Around Meg's cott was a group of the Black Watch. Two of them had a grip of a young boy, Ewan's oldest son, the volunteer. They dragged him towards the cattle-tethering stake where Meg bled her beast. The milking cow was freed and shooed away while other soldiers held Meg and the boy's mother, both of them struggling, the mother shrieking her son's name.

'Calum! Calum! Ewan, they have Calum!'

Ewan was well ahead of Anne, racing to save his son. The officer on horseback wheeled round, his horse neighing at the cruel jerk of the bit in its mouth.

'Stop that man,' he shouted, an English voice scything through the Gaelic cries.

Ewan launched himself through the circle of soldiers but was brought crashing to the ground by a blow to his head from a musket butt. Anne ran through the gap he'd made, leaping over his prostrate body. She reached the terrified lad and threw her arms round him, pushing away the soldiers' hands that held him.

'What are you doing?' she shouted. 'He's a boy. Leave him be!'

Calum wrapped his arms round her waist, gripping his own hands together so he could not be easily torn away. She was his chief's wife. While he was with her, he was safe. No one would dare lay hands on her.

'We ran away,' he whimpered. 'They would make us fight the Prince.'

'No, they won't. *Cha dèan iad sin*,' she soothed him, tightening her arms round his trembling shoulders, resting her chin on his head. 'Only your chief can say what you will do. He wouldn't ask that of you.'

They were surrounded by soldiers, most facing outwards, guns trained on the cottars appearing from their homes. The lieutenant on horseback guided his horse through into the circle. It was James Ray, the Englishman she had thwarted a few weeks before.

'Release the deserter,' he commanded Anne.

She tightened her grip.

'He's a frightened boy,' she said. 'And you have no authority here.'

Ray dismounted, drew a pistol from his saddle bow and walked towards her.

'His chief will deal with his disobedience,' Anne insisted.

Without a hesitation, Ray pushed the pistol against the boy's forehead and fired, deafeningly loud in Anne's ears. The back of the boy's head exploded. Blood and brain spurted over her face, neck and shoulder. His warm body went limp in her arms, the dead weight of him too heavy to hold. Cottars gasped and cried out with horror. The boy's mother screamed, breaking free of her restrainers. Griefstricken, she lurched across the grass to her dead son, now sliding down from Anne's grip to the ground.

Ray, back at his horse, drew the second pistol from his saddle bow, aimed and fired. The ball hit the bereaved woman full in the chest. She fell just as she reached her son, her body landing over his. Anne, immobilized with shock, stared open-mouthed at Ray, blood spattered across her cheeks, trickling between her breasts, her dress smeared with red.

'She would only breed more traitors,' Ray said, before turning his horse, calling to his men. 'Come, we're finished here. There are more to hunt down before dark.' He rode off, the soldiers running behind.

The dozen or so cottars who'd been invisible to Anne earlier surged forwards. Some issued low moans of shock and horror, others were in tears. Gently, they disentangled the bodies of mother and son. Carefully, they straightened their limbs and clothes. A man tended Ewan, who was beginning to come round from the blow to his head. Voices asked Anne if she was all right. She could barely make them out. Hands touched her, checking, cleaning away shattered flesh, offering care and concern. But she barely felt them. She had seen death before but not this brutal. Not a mother and child, the most valued, most treasured and protected people in any clan. She could neither speak nor feel nor move.

The arrival of more horses sounded like the distant tremor of drums beating in the air. Then Aeneas was in front of her, touching her hair, her face, her shoulders, her breast.

'Are you all right? Are you hurt? Anne, will you speak to me?' His voice was like an echo heard through water.

'I am fine,' she heard her own voice answer.

'You are very far from fine,' he said. 'But the blood on you is not yours, thank God.' Reassured she was alive, he shouted, anger rising out of him. '*Gonadh!* Damn them! Damn them to hell!' Then he was giving orders. To MacGillivray. 'Take my wife home.' To the cottars. 'Help her up.' To Ewan. 'Go easy, or we'll lose you too.'

Then Anne was in the saddle, MacGillivray wrapped around behind her, his strong arms holding her, taking the reins, trotting the horse away towards Moy. Behind her, she could still hear Aeneas, angry at the harm to his people, instructing the care of their bodies, alternating between swearing and soothing.

Back at Moy, the Dowager took over, helping Anne upstairs to change while Jessie fetched towels, a bowl, a jug of warm water. Stripped to her shift, Anne bent over the bowl. The water was sparkling. She splashed it up on her face. Now the water was red with blood. Again and again she threw the liquid in her face. The red only deepened.

'Enough now,' the Dowager said. 'Will stoked the fire, and the water is hot enough. Jessie has drawn a bath. We'll get you clean.'

But even as she sank into the deep warmth of the bath, letting her head fall back so it soaked her hair, the clear water round her turned blood-red. She had helped send young Calum to the Watch. She had failed to protect him at the cotts. Aeneas would bring the clan out now but she, she would never feel clean again.

At Fort George, Aeneas dismounted outside the commander's headquarters. He had a dozen young lads with him, all in Black Watch uniforms, all apprehensive. They had heard about Calum's execution. Now their chief might be leading them to theirs.

'All you need do is stay here,' Aeneas said. 'Can you do that this time?'

The boys nodded, but their fear and trepidation were obvious.

'Be strong,' Aeneas said. 'I'll tell you the price we'll pay when I come back, but it won't be your lives. That much I promise you.' It was a big promise. A new British force under English command had recently arrived in the fort. But the regular garrison was Scottish, including their commander, Lord Louden. The Earl of Louden was no fool. He would respect a chieftain's right to determine justice for his own clan.

Inside, Forbes was already making his case. As Scotland's supreme judge, peace was his business. He had persuaded several chiefs to stay neutral if the threatened conflict came. Never one to miss an opportunity to compel another, he had possession papers ready in his hand. The other man in the room was not Louden. He was a stranger, a general and English, red-faced, plump, a man who liked his food and port wine. He was also polite, standing to greet Aeneas and shake his hand.

'General Cope, Chief McIntosh,' he introduced himself. 'John Cope. I'm afraid Lord Louden is out of the fort. Perhaps I can help.'

Hearing the Englishman's name, Aeneas would have turned around. The commander of a force sent to quell the Jacobites would have no qualms about ordering the firing squad for Black Watch deserters. But an abrupt departure could mean fighting their way out, and his boys were no match for guards with muskets.

'Then I won't trouble you,' he said, easily as if he were untroubled. 'We'll return when Lord Louden is available.'

'Not at all, not at all,' Cope said. 'I'm sure we can settle this between us. You saved us a deal of trouble rounding up these lads.'

'They're my clansmen,' Aeneas said. 'Their desertion is my dishonour.'

'Well, very kind of you to take it like that,' Cope said. 'Now, the thing is, what to do about it.'

'I doubt more shootings will help,' Forbes butted in.

'Maybe not, maybe not,' Cope said, seating himself again. 'We don't want to push more support to this Pretender Prince. But desertion is a serious matter. Port?'

The question was to Aeneas. He nodded and sat down opposite. The more amenable the negotiation could be kept, the better. He had to buy time, the appearance of neutrality, but not with young blood. While Cope poured, he decided how to play it.

'Maybe it's the words rather than the deed which give us a problem,' he suggested. 'The death penalty for desertion is just. I have no quarrel with it.'

'Very glad to hear it.' Cope pushed a generous glass of rich wine over to him.

'But these boys were not on the battlefield,' Aeneas went on. 'They are not cowards who ran under fire.'

'That's true,' Cope nodded. 'Absent without leave is a different matter, a different matter entirely. Is that what you claim?'

'Isn't that what it is?' Aeneas asked. 'They were confused. The country is rife with rumour. They simply went home to find out what they should do.'

'In the king's army,' Cope corrected, 'we are told what to do by our superiors.'

'Sir, with your pardon, these are voluntary recruits, and Highland. They're bound first to their clan and, there, I'm their superior.

Their service in the Black Watch is in lieu of our clan dues. I have the right to rescind it.'

'On payment of your debt,' Forbes reminded him, waving the papers he held. 'Your undertaking is in default again, your commitment insecure.' He changed tack. 'But perhaps we can settle the matter like gentlemen. The land settlement, I'm sure you'll see that's the best solution now.' He put the papers on Cope's desk, in front of Aeneas. 'A signature, and this nasty problem will be resolved.'

Aeneas glanced at the papers.

'This is twice the land you asked for before.'

'It buys you twelve lives too, this time.'

'Do not threaten me, Forbes,' Aeneas warned.

'But they would all be released from their service, all fifty of them,' Forbes blustered. 'I'm sure you may have other needs for them now.'

Aeneas drew him an icy look. Instinctively, his hand fell to his sword.

'These are dangerous times to be making inferences.'

Cope had been watching both men closely as he sipped his port. Now he put the glass down and leant forward over the desk.

'Perhaps none of us should issue threats, Chief McIntosh,' he suggested. 'Or I might assume that weapon at your side wasn't on the king's business in pursuit of deserters and have you charged.'

'I can't sign away this land,' Aeneas told him. 'I'd save a dozen lives now at the cost of dozens more in the future. My clan could not survive without it.'

'Then put your own offer on the table.' Cope sat back.

'I have lost one boy,' Aeneas said, playing for time. 'And his mother killed.'

'That was regrettable,' Cope said.

'Most regrettable,' Forbes agreed.

Aeneas did not doubt the judge meant it. He made money from Highlanders. Deaths meant financial losses. He was also a Scot and, despite his disagreeable government stance, at least understood the clans and their culture.

'You have my apology,' Cope added, 'that an officer would forget himself and shoot a defenceless woman. But, as you said, these are dangerous times. It's good you have an eye to the future. From what I'm hearing, some of your fellow chiefs are less circumspect. Maybe they're unaware we have made our peace with the French?'

Aeneas did not let the shock surface in his expression. While he digested the news, he returned Cope's gaze with apparent calm and revised his first impression of the general. The man may look overindulgent, but he understood diplomacy. The warning was clear. The French might encourage the rebellion to harry England but would be unlikely, now, to send real support. Freed from their overseas engagements, the full force of the British army could soon be unleashed against the budding Jacobite forces.

'No doubt you recall the outcome of 1715?' Cope prompted.

Aeneas had been seven years old when the first rising happened. His own father died in it. One battle saw the Jacobites defeated. By the time King James arrived from France, again without that promised army, it was already over. Many chiefs who supported it lost control of their clan lands, with vast tracts ceded to those who'd sided with the government.

'I guarantee these young men will remain in the Watch, whatever happens,' he offered.

'Even if we call it unofficial absence, desertion can't be seen to go unpunished,' Cope countered. 'We need trustworthy troops under loyal leaders.'

'Then I'll raise their number to a full company. Captain them as you will.'

Cope smiled, leaning forward to make his point.

'Absentee commanders only confuse loyalties,' he said. 'And a fence very quickly makes an uncomfortable seat.'

He had stated his price: twelve young lives for MᶜIntosh commitment to the government. Like Forbes, he suspected Aeneas was hedging his bets and might go to the other side. The judge did not betray the Highlander's Jacobite sympathies to Cope, but he saw the chance to take the game and lifted the papers from the desk.

'There is more than one way to skin a cat,' he said, holding them out. The words were carefully chosen to leave Cope in the dark. Clan Chatton was the clan of the cat.

'There is,' Aeneas agreed. Forbes was offering the chance to stay on that fence, at a price. The Chatton federation chiefs were bound to him by oath on pain of death. As their chief, he could deliver a guarantee that none would join the rising, or he could sign. Signing the papers removed his obligation to the Black Watch. It also removed the possibility of future prosperity from his clan. He did the only thing left to do – bluff. Get off the fence himself and hope that Forbes would not reveal how much more they could have gained. 'My lads outside will stay in the Watch,' he told Cope.

'Did you not hear?' Forbes pushed. 'That won't serve.'

'No.' Aeneas gazed steadily at Cope. 'I will serve,' he turned to look up at Forbes, 'with them, and a full company, as their captain.'

'You don't offer much, McIntosh,' Forbes scoffed. 'One sword, a hundred youths and your principles.'

Aeneas jumped to his feet, drawing his broadsword.

'This sword,' he said.

Before either of the other men could move or draw breath to protest, he sliced the candle on the desk neatly down the middle, swung the broadsword round past the hat-stand which held General Cope's hat and sliced the front legs off a small wooden table. As the table tilted, he spun the sword to click every handle off a chest of drawers in one downstroke and completed his turn by slicing horizontally through the sheets of paper in Forbes hand.

'I'm glad you spared the hat-stand,' Cope said.

Without turning to look at it, Aeneas stretched his arm and touched the nearest top hook of the stand with his forefinger. Stem and top parted company where it had been sliced through. He caught Cope's hat as it fell, sitting it on the desk as the top of the hat-stand clattered to the floor.

'Well, I'm impressed, I must say,' Cope said. He picked up the half-sheets of Forbes's papers which had fluttered on to his desk and tore them through. 'You, your lands, and these young men outside are safe. You have a command, Captain. I trust you'll keep it.' He rang the handbell on his desk.

'You're a man to watch,' Forbes glowered. 'And I will be watching.'

That was enough for Aeneas. Clan Chatton remained uncommitted. His chiefs could make their own choices. The judge was not going to reveal how much more he could have given. Behind them, a soldier came in the door.

'Captain M<sup>c</sup>Intosh,' Cope said. 'This is your lieutenant.' As Aeneas turned to the soldier, a stranger to him, Cope went on. 'Lieutenant Ray, Captain M<sup>c</sup>Intosh will take charge of your troops forthwith.'

James Ray clicked his heels and saluted.

# TEN

'*Taigh na Galla ort!*' Anne swore, rising from her seat at the midday dinner table. 'I don't believe this!' It was later than usual, early afternoon. They had waited for Aeneas, the table richly set with food and wine for the last expected meal before they committed to war. 'You've joined the government against us?'

'I'm not against you,' Aeneas said. 'We're together.'

'Not in this.' Anne paced the room. 'Not in this.'

'It's a ploy, surely.' MacGillivray was mystified.

'No,' Aeneas said. 'The French will not come.'

'They'll come when we put our own army in the field,' Anne raged. 'When they see our strength, when they know we're united and will win, then they will come!'

'You believe this English general speaks the truth?' the Dowager asked, trying to calm things.

Aeneas nodded, but it was Anne he answered.

'It's the British army that will come now. You've just washed away the blood of one of our children. Will you wash away the blood of thousands?'

Anne stopped pacing.

'Two of our people died, Aeneas. A boy and his mother. Does her death mean nothing?'

'Of course not. I only meant . . .'

Anne cut him off. 'You meant to use guilt against me. I tried to stop the Englishman. He wouldn't listen. I was of no account to him, like Calum's mother, a woman. By his custom, I have no authority.'

'English laws are different. He'll learn our ways.'

'Will he, or are we learning theirs? You decided what we'd do without asking me!' Furious, she marched out of the room then, calling for Jessie as she went.

'Anne!' Aeneas would have gone after her, but the Dowager caught his arm.

'Let her calm down,' she urged. 'Nothing will be gained while she feels so insecure. You should have consulted her.'

'There was no time. I can explain.'

'Everything you say will sound like a further threat. Let her come back in her own time, when she's restored.'

MacGillivray had remained seated, trying to get his head around his chief's unfathomable actions. Now he stood, scraping his chair back and facing Aeneas.

'Can you explain to me?' he asked.

Upstairs, Anne threw off her clothes, letting them land where they fell. Her body was rigid with fury. The wardrobe door flung open so hard it crashed against the wall.

'My blue riding habit,' she told Jessie. It was an outfit she felt good in, confident of her appearance and strengths, the velvet trimmed with tartan. Jessie held it while she slipped it on. Her hair was dressed quickly but carefully. She would do, she would do very well, and he would see that.

'There's a matching bonnet somewhere,' she said. As Jessie searched the drawers for it, Anne opened the lid of the box which contained her tocher and took out handfuls of coins. She put some into the velvet drawstring bag which would be tied to her waist. Others went into a leather pouch which would go in her saddle bag. Aeneas had made his choice. Now she had made hers.

Downstairs, MacGillivray was arriving at his own.

'I won't join you in this,' he told Aeneas.

'I don't ask you to,' Aeneas answered. 'It was myself I committed, not you or our other chiefs. But I still ask that you hold back from rising. Nothing can be gained from haste.'

'For a few months, Alexander,' the Dowager added, 'until the situation is clear.'

'My people will want leadership,' MacGillivray said, struggling with the idea of prudence. 'They won't come out without my word.'

'Then you need only hold your tongue,' Aeneas said.

'If I can.' MacGillivray smiled ruefully. 'I'll return to Dunmaglas.' He held out his hand to his chief. 'But the next time we meet, we may be enemies.'

Aeneas took a firm grip of the younger chief's hand.

'Then at least we part as friends,' he said, embracing him.

Behind them, the dining-room door opened. Anne strode in. She was pale, deathly calm now, her jaw set with determination. The blue of her riding habit deepened the blue of her eyes to a summer midnight.

'Will you wait, Alexander?' she asked.

In her hand, she carried the blue bonnet. At her right side, the velvet purse of coins hung. The dirk beside it was standard for travel. The silver basket-handled sword slung at her left side was not. Behind her, Jessie carried a pair of silver pistols.

'Have Will mount those on Pibroch's saddle,' Anne told her.

As Jessie left the room, Aeneas found his tongue.

'You're going out?'

There was a moment as Anne set her shoulders, lifted her head, looked him straight in the eye.

'I'm going to bring the clan out,' she said.

His answer was quick, too quick.

'I said no!'

'And I'm no English wife to be owned and ordered,' she corrected him. 'You spoke for yourself. I speak for me.' She put on the bonnet, dressed, in the absence of roses, with a white ribbon cockade, and turned to MacGillivray. 'What do you say, Alexander, will you follow my lead?'

It took less than a blink for MacGillivray's face to break into a wide grin.

'I will, Colonel,' he said, automatically crediting her with the rank that Aeneas would have held with the clans in wartime. 'And so will our warriors, to the ends of the earth if you ask it.'

'It might be to the end of your lives,' Aeneas snapped.

Anne whipped round to him again.

'Our lives,' she said. 'And our choice how they will be lived or lost.' With that, she turned for the door and left, MacGillivray following her.

Aeneas did not move, nor did he speak. The Dowager watched him but she, too, kept silent. They heard the horses' hooves clop outside the front door as they were mounted, then the clatter as they were ridden away. As the sound faded, the silence grew into an unbearable emptiness.

'It will be all right,' the Dowager whispered. 'If we're represented on both sides, we surely cannot lose.'

Aeneas drew his sword and, with a bellowing roar, like a bull caught in the slaughtering trap, cleared food, wine, dishes, glassware from the table in one wild, ranging sweep, sending them all crashing and clattering to the floor as his rage broke.

Anne and MacGillivray rode east first, collecting volunteers from that side of the estate before swinging north and west. The request for one adult male from each family was easily met. Wives and older children, when possible, joined the march. They were as valuable to Highland troops as the men.

'You'll want a blacksmith,' Donald Fraser said, folding his leather apron.

'So will Moy while we're gone,' Anne reminded him. The estate must continue to run for their return.

'Then my son can be fetched back from the Black Watch,' Donald said, and went in to douse the fire in his forge.

On the edge of Drumossie moor, the elderly couple Anne had given extra grazing to waited outside their cott.

'Go on then, if you must,' the old woman said to her husband, handing him an ancient sword recently sharpened. 'I will only slow you down.'

MacBean took the sword. He was seventy, a big man with a good swing still.

'I'll write to you,' he said.

'And have me running in and out of Inverness to check?'

'You can ask the post-boy when he passes.'

Anne leant forward on her horse.

'You're not obliged,' she told him. 'Not when you're needed here.'

'I am obliged to myself,' MacBean said, drawing himself upright. 'Death should come with honour.'

'He's only under my feet anyhow,' his wife assured Anne, then busied herself tucking MacBean's plaid better around him. 'You be sure and keep your chest warm.'

'Don't fash, woman.' The old man stopped her. 'I'll be back to your botherations before you know it.'

By the time they reached the north-west cotts, it was early evening and word was ahead of them. The cottars stood around the freshly dug grave which would hold the wrapped bodies of mother and son that lay waiting on the grass beside it. Ewan stepped forward to speak first, a V-shaped scar on his forehead from the musket butt red and puckered in the lessening light.

'I've a wife and child to put in the ground, then I'm yours,' he said to Anne.

She shook her head.

'I won't ask you, Ewan. Your father and other children need you here.'

'Cath will see to them,' he said. Beside him, Cath clutched her baby to her side.

'As my own,' she said.

Old Meg stepped forward and spat.

'I should've let daylight into that *Sasannaich's* innards first time,' she said, raising her pitchfork. 'He's overdue it now. I'll fight.'

The lands of Moy delivered a warrior force of almost three hundred, with half as many women and children in support. Anne's bag of coin was lighter by the shillings paid to the families who stayed behind. Now they would head for Dunmaglas, to add the MacGillivrays, before criss-crossing the countryside to collect those who would fight from the other Chatton tribes. Anne halted Pibroch on the ridge that bounded Drumossie moor as her troops marched past, a great long line of men, women and children, carrying only a little food, weapons and extra clothing. Far below, Moy Hall was lit by the setting sun, shining gold as the waters of the loch beside it turned brilliant orange.

MacGillivray rode up beside her.

'He'll join us,' he said, 'when he sees what his people want.'

'While he disregards me?' It was inconceivable that a husband would act on such a matter without consulting his wife. Yet Aeneas had done so. 'Come,' she said, turning Pibroch. 'We want to make Dunmaglas before it's pitch dark.' She rode off towards the front of her forces to lead the way. As the swollen, vermillion sun tipped the horizon, the sky above the moor turned blood-red.

At Moy Hall, Aeneas was packed up, ready to leave. Will, the stableboy, held his horse ready at the front door. The Dowager saw him to it.

'Must you go now? Anne might leave the troops with Alexander at Dunmaglas. She could be back tomorrow. You should talk this out.'

'I tried. She wouldn't listen.' He put his foot in the stirrup and pulled himself up into the saddle. 'Louden will be back in the fort. He'll have heard my clan is marching. If I don't show face tonight, he'll think my word is broken before it's kept.' He took the reins, thanked Will and was about to ride off.

'You won't be among friends, Aeneas,' his aunt said. 'Be careful of your anger.'

'I will,' he said. Enmity was all he expected of an enemy. From a wife, he had expected support. He slapped the reins and rode off, skirting the loch, taking the shortest route across Moy to Inverness and Fort George. As he rode, an empty space rode beside him. MacGillivray was like a second self, always there when adventure called, closer than a brother. Yet he had not struggled with divided loyalty. Anne only had to ask, and he was at her side. Aeneas couldn't have said which betrayal cut deepest, Anne's or MacGillivray's. He would not contemplate the one that might yet come. They would be together for two weeks, maybe more, gathering volunteers, taking them to Glenfinnan.

Once she had delivered them, Anne's honour would be satisfied. Married women marched only with their husbands in Highland armies. Lacking hers, she would not stay. She would pass command to MacGillivray and return to Moy. Two weeks. In two weeks, he would settle this with her. By the time he clattered into the cobbled yard of the fort, his control was restored. He would need his wits about him here.

Lord Louden did not trouble to hide his relief. The M<sup>c</sup>Intosh company was hostage to their chief's return. He had not relished ordering out a firing squad if Aeneas failed to show.

'Good to know you're with us, M<sup>c</sup>Intosh,' he said. 'Though I suspect General Cope thought your commission secured your tribe too.'

'I've delivered what I promised,' Aeneas said.

'More than you think,' Louden agreed. 'MacDonald of Skye and MacLeod have followed your lead. We have companies from both.' Tactfully, he didn't add that, like Aeneas, other chiefs who declared for the government had clansmen and kinfolk who did not follow suit. 'Your orders.' He handed Aeneas the papers. 'Your billet is in the south block officers' quarters. Your men are drilling in the square.'

'A punishment?' It was late, near dark.

'I thought them better occupied.' He opened the door. 'You can relieve them now, Captain.'

Cope was on his way in as Aeneas went out. He paused on the step to let the Highlander pass, greeting him with a nod that was returned. Cope let the lack of salute pass. He was learning a little about Highland ways.

'Every inch a chief,' he said to Louden, watching Aeneas stride away. 'Fine-looking, well-made and no manners.'

'Different manners,' Louden corrected. 'I can't decide if he's a brave man or a coward but I wouldn't want his marriage bed, not now.'

'Would you have wanted it before?' Cope asked.

'Oh, aye,' Louden laughed. 'Anne Farquharson could rouse most men between the sheets. And out of them, as we're hearing. Have you come for a nightcap?'

89

'With news,' Cope said. 'But it will slip down easier with a drop of port behind it.' Louden ushered him inside, followed and shut the door.

The company engaged in musket drill in the square recognized Aeneas as soon as he turned the corner towards them. Relief wrote itself on all their young faces. They had not been issued shot and they knew why. They might have defended themselves if their chief had failed them. Now he was here there was no need for fear. They were safe. Lieutenant Ray stopped barking orders and turned to salute Aeneas.

'Captain,' he clicked his heels.

'Lieutenant,' Aeneas sighed. 'Maybe we could forgo the formalities till I'm in uniform?'

'Sorry, Captain,' Ray saluted again. 'They say troop ships are coming with more reinforcements. Do you think we'll see action soon?'

'Let's hope not.'

'I ask because I'm eager, not because I'm afraid,' Ray said indignantly.

'Then you're a fool,' Aeneas told him. 'Men will die in this, Ray. And every one will be someone I know. Men I've fought. Men I've hunted with. Men whose cattle I've stolen and whose wives or daughters I've bedded. But I don't relish the death of a single one. So let's hope, instead, that a show of strength is all it takes and this insurrection melts away without a shot fired. Killing is a duty, but men should get their pleasure from women.'

A loud round of applause and cheers rose from the company. Ray spun round and they leapt back to attention.

'Will you stand the men down?' Aeneas smiled.

'Captain.' Ray snapped out a salute, missing Aeneas's wince as he turned to the company again and called out, 'Stand easy!'

Aeneas walked away to his quarters, grinning now he had his back to the over-eager Englishman. When he found his room, it was adequate. A bunk, table, chairs and a decanter of whisky courtesy of King George. Troop ships. It was early days. If the reinforcements were generous, the Jacobite chiefs would withdraw.

Life was hard won in the clans and not spent where it would profit none. A few days could see the end of this. He was pouring a second glassful when the last post sounded and his door was knocked. It was Ray who came in.

'All settled, sir,' he said.

Aeneas raised a finger, forestalling the salute.

'Fine,' he said, lifting an empty glass. *'Uisge beatha?'*

'Oh, whisky. Yes, thank you.' He watched Aeneas pour a generous measure. 'You know, I met a madwoman on my way up to Inverness. She was with a tribe of savages. Forced me off my horse and put my wife on it. She spoke the Irish too.'

Aeneas recognized the story. Meg and Cath would be pleased to have grown to a tribe. He handed Ray his drink and went over to the window. Outside, the night was lit by a bright waxing moon.

'A madwoman, indeed,' he said.

# ELEVEN

Charles Edward Stuart stood outside his tent at the Glenfinnan encampment. Like his cousin, the Duke of Cumberland, he was twenty-four years old, the son of a king. There the resemblance ended. Charles might have stepped straight from a child's fairy story, elegant, tall and handsome, his face fine-boned, his body lean. Dressed now in red-tartan philabeg and plaid topped with a scarlet jacket, he wore a white powdered wig, a blue sash slung over his shoulder. Before Scotland united its parliament with England, when the Scots king sat on both thrones and ruled Ireland, his grandfather was deposed by the English, who put a Dutchman in his place. When that line died without heir, his father waited to be called, but again the English chose a foreigner, a German from Hanover, whose son, George, now ruled. Prince Charles had come to win back his father's throne.

'*La victoire est certaine*, O'Sullivan,' he said to the Irish adjutant-general beside him. There were a million Scots. More than half lived in the Highlands. 'There are six hundred thousand people in these hills, at least fifty thousand trained warriors.'

'They won't all come out, sir.' It was Lord George Murray who answered. 'And Cope's troop ships arrive at Aberdeen. As soon as those reinforcements join him in Inverness, he'll want to engage us.'

'With a paltry few thousand?' The Prince was scathing. Born and raised in Italy, he spoke French to his Scottish commanders, a language they shared. 'Cumberland must think we are easily frightened. We will have *deux armées*, Lord George. Five, ten armies!'

Cheering from the east side of the camp interrupted the boast. All three men turned towards the interruption. A woman, dressed in blue and riding a white horse, rode down the slope towards them. It was Anne Farquharson, the Lady McIntosh. MacGillivray rode beside her. Behind them marched several hundred troops, cheering as they came in sight of the already assembled clans, those with pistols firing in the air.

'You see?' The Prince smiled at Lord George.

As the Clan Chatton troops veered off to spare ground, Anne and MacGillivray rode on towards the standard to present themselves. Lord George was beside Anne as she dismounted. He had brought her mother's clan, the Murrays.

'You must be saddle-sore,' he said. 'But it's a pleasure to see you. I was in two minds about the wisdom of this. Word of your action decided me.' He led her over to the Prince. 'My cousin, sir. Colonel Anne Farquharson, the Lady M<sup>c</sup>Intosh.'

The Prince immediately took her hand and, much to Anne's amusement, kissed it.

*'La belle rebelle,'* he exclaimed. 'We hear you have inflamed the countryside. Now I see why.'

'No, sir, *vous êtes trop généreux,*' Anne said, 'that was yourself.' She presented MacGillivray as colonel-in-chief of her troops. He would lead them on the field. Wine was brought as the other chiefs crowded round to congratulate her: Lochiel, Keppoch, Glengary, Ranald, M<sup>c</sup>Gregor, Lords Elcho, Tullibardine and the Ogilvies. Anne raised her glass.

'Prosperity and no Union,' she toasted. It was a declaration she had not made since her father's death but one she relished now. The response resounded around the camp, falling like an echo as those further out took it up.

'Prosperity and no Union!'

O'Sullivan waved MacGillivray over to register his force on the roll.

'Six hundred warriors,' MacGillivray told him. 'Two hundred women and children in support.'

Nearby, the Prince spoke into Lord George's ear.

'Must they bring so many women?'

'It's the other way round, sir,' Lord George told him. 'The wives and mothers who bear them, and will bury them, decide when clans will fight. It's the women who bring the men.'

Margaret Johnstone, the Lady Ogilvie, stole Anne away to meet some of the others.

'I didn't expect so many,' Anne said, looking round as they walked through the camp. Everywhere, groups were settled round fires, cooking. Swords and dirks were sharpened, pistols cleaned and polished.

'What else can we do? If we don't end this Union, our way of life will soon be gone.' She slipped an arm through Anne's. 'What do you think of our Prince?'

'Oh, he's fine-looking, with his clothes on,' Anne joked. 'If he leads as well as he charms, we've already won.'

Margaret stopped to introduce her to Margaret Fergusson, the Lady Broughton, a stunning woman wearing a feather-plumed hat and fur-trimmed outfit, whose equally dapper husband, Sir John Murray of Broughton, was sharpening her sword.

'Call me Greta,' she said. 'I'm dealing with recruitment and supplies.'

'Sir John is the Prince's secretary,' Margaret said.

'But when we engage,' Greta boasted, 'he'll ride with Lord Elcho's cavalry.'

'Do we have enough horses?' Anne asked.

'Not yet,' Greta grinned. 'But we'll solve that soon. You can help.'

'I'd be pleased to,' Anne said, 'but I mean to go home.'

'You've been very brave,' Margaret said. 'I couldn't have left David.' Like Anne, she was twenty, the same age as her young husband, a wealthy lord who could afford early marriage. 'I had to persuade him, you know,' she said. 'Men don't always understand what we're losing. If English attitudes finally overwhelm us, men would have rights and power. We'd have none.' She squeezed Anne's arm supportively. 'But you'll convince Aeneas. You've inspired so many.' She pointed to a trouser-clad woman busy directing the erection of tents. 'That's Jenny Cameron. She heard what you were doing, rode out and raised three hundred for the cause. Oh, and Isabel forced Ardshiel out because of you. He'll arrive soon.'

94

'Forced him out?'

'Yes,' Margaret laughed. 'Said she'd raise and command their people herself if he'd stay home and keep house. Handed him an apron!'

Both of them giggled at the thought of burly Ardshiel in an apron, poring over household accounts, supervising the dusting or baking of bread. But Anne's mood wasn't lightened by it. Ardshiel had come out. Aeneas had gone to the other side. If he'd done nothing, if he'd waited, as he first said, that might have been bearable. This was not.

As soon as she could escape the energy and excitement of the camp, she wandered off alone to the edge of it. A massive full moon was rising, cut across by thin purple cloud. It was like the wound in her heart, splitting her in two, she in one place, Aeneas in another. Her husband had joined the enemy. There was no greater hurt he could do.

When MacGillivray found her, sitting on a rock, she was staring at the risen moon.

'Your tent's ready,' he said, coming up behind her. 'And supper is about to be served.' When she did not respond, he turned her to him. Her eyes were luminous in the dark, bright with unshed tears. 'Hey.' He pulled her close, wrapping the warmth of his arms around her.

'I can't be this alone,' she sobbed. 'Not now, not here. He should be with us. He should be beside me.'

'I know.' MacGillivray pulled her tighter to him, his anger at Aeneas, the man he considered a brother, suddenly fierce. They stood a long time, holding each other, until Anne's tears ran dry, until their bodies began to remember fitting into the shape and warmth of each other, of being this close, and it seemed as if no time at all had passed since then, as if nothing had changed.

'I'm not as strong as I thought,' she said, looking up at him.

She would kiss him now, he could see that. And if she did, they would stay together, at least that night, rocking each other into old familiar ecstasies. And it would do nothing to lessen the wrench he'd feel when she left in the morning, which is what she would do, for she wanted him now only to fill the emptiness of Aeneas's absence and not for himself. He put his hands on her shoulders, stepped back from her.

'You're stronger than you know,' he said. 'You'll persuade him. Aeneas is no government lackey. Here is where he wants to be.'

'He told you that?'

'As good as. He only went to protect the lads in the Watch.'

'He could have brought them here.'

'But he believes we'll fail.'

'And we will, if we divide against ourselves.' Anne would not be mollified. 'That's what I'll tell him, when I get back to Moy.'

At dinner, MacGillivray sat with Margaret and Greta on either side of him, flirting outrageously. Anne sat opposite, next to Lord George. The Prince had appointed her cousin commander-in-chief. His head was full of tactics.

'We'll break camp tomorrow,' he said. 'Our numbers can't be sustained in this area for much longer.'

'Do you go to engage Cope?' Anne asked.

'No, I think we'll do better for the time being to go around him. Let him scurry about the Highlands. I have other plans.' He looked at her seriously, sympathetically. 'What of you? Margaret says you'll return to Moy.'

Anne nodded.

'In the morning. I've done what I had to do.'

'But you'll need protection there.'

'Aeneas won't let harm come to his own house.'

'I'm sure he won't, or at least he'll try to prevent it. But you're perilously close to Ruthven barracks. The government army is assembling there. Some officer might seek his spurs by arresting the rebel Lady McIntosh.'

'No, George!' Anne was shocked. Her marriage had proved insecure, now the safety of her home was in doubt? 'But I must see Aeneas.'

'Let him bring himself, if he will. Your absence will surely weigh on his conscience. Come with us, at least for a time. I'll draw Cope away from Inverness. Then, if you must, you can return home with impunity.'

'It will work, *vous verrez*,' Anne insisted. 'No one will be hurt.'

'I think it's a great plan.' Beside her, Greta backed her up.

'Me too,' Margaret agreed. 'Wish I'd thought of it.'

They were in the state room at the palace of Holyrood, at the foot of Edinburgh's Royal Mile. They had been camped there for a week, the capital city's gates shut against them. The Prince had forbidden storming the walls, unwilling to lose lives or alienate his father's subjects inside those gates. Every day, more and more sympathizers climbed or bribed their way out to meet him, to pledge their loyalty before sneaking back into the city for the ten o'clock curfew.

'*Mais oui*, if I hold a ball,' the Prince said. 'The music will distract the guards and provide cover.'

'A fine idea, sir, to be sure,' O'Sullivan agreed. 'Very fine.'

'As long as my men go in first,' Lochiel insisted.

'No one would deprive you of that right,' Lord George assured him. 'Anne, we'll leave it to you to persuade MacGillivray.'

The three women set to work, Margaret and Greta with their needles, Anne with her charm.

'One rope and I'd be over,' MacGillivray protested.

'And the whole city alerted,' Anne said.

'Then pass me off as a lawyer.'

'Did you ever see a six-foot lawyer with thighs such as yours?' Anne smiled. 'Besides, this will amuse everyone and take the sting out.'

'Not out of me, it won't,' MacGillivray railed. 'I'll be a laughing stock.'

'Only among your own,' Anne giggled. 'The Edinburgh folk wouldn't dare. Green silk,' she couldn't resist adding. 'It will go wonderfully with your hair.'

'No ringlets,' MacGillivray insisted. 'I would go to my grave first.'

She had won.

'A very pretty bonnet,' she promised. 'And a fan.'

Later that night, Duff peered out from the guardhouse in the city walls. He was a squat, thick-set man, a shoemaker, more at home bent over his cobbler's last than manning Netherbow Port with a musket in his hand. In the dark, he could see little outside the window beyond the first few buildings. From further down the Canongate, he could hear music from Holyrood. The Jacobites played the rebel song, 'The Auld Stuarts back Again'. All night, they'd treated Edinburgh ears to jigs, strathspeys and reels. Now, it sounded like the party was coming to an end. Above him, in the tower, the bell would soon toll the night curfew.

His fellow guard had gone down below to usher in a group of women, pocketing their bribes. They worked it between them, twice the usual fee for entry and exit, half to the guards, half to the city. Duff took the payments on their way out. Men were rarely admitted, as a precaution, and were rigorously checked but, with none in this group, his companion was quickly finished. Duff heard him climbing back up the turnpike stair.

'Hoi,' a voice called from outside the gate, 'you forgot me.'

Duff threw open the window and peered down. A woman stood below, hands on her hips, wealthy by the look of her, with a feather-plumed hat and fur-trimmed outfit.

'Name yersell,' he called back. He wasn't sure why he asked. One woman couldn't be a danger, even if she gave a Highland name or had an unfamiliar accent.

'You dare ask my name?' The woman was indignant. 'Name yourself.'

'Duff,' he called back, equally indignant. 'Duff, the shoe-maker.'

'Then I'm your wife, idiot,' she yelled up at him.

Duff was triumphant. He didn't have a wife! She tried to trick him. His fellow militiaman reached the top of the stair. Duff turned to him.

'I dinnae hae a wife,' he said. A dirk pointed at his throat. It wasn't the other guard who'd stepped into the guardroom. It was a woman in a green silk gown, a very tall woman in a bonnet, the dirk in her hand.

'That's a pity,' she said. Her voice was deep and rich with a Highland lilt to it. 'But if you keep quiet while we let her in, you might live long enough to get one.'

Duff was in no danger of making a sound. The point of the dirk pressed sharply against his Adam's apple. Now that he'd turned, he could see, through the side window, that down below, inside the gate, the other guard lay motionless on the ground beside it while a third woman unbolted the footgate, a young, slender woman with dark hair. She was one of the group which had just entered, the others having vanished up the King's High Street.

Down on the Canongate, as the footgate opened again, Lochiel's men emerged from the shadows of deserted buildings, racing past Greta into the city. Inside, a few took over from Anne to unbolt the great metal cart gates, pushing them wide so the rest of the Jacobites could flood in behind them. As the Netherbow bell sounded the curfew hour, the rest hurried to the other three ports to relieve the guards there of their posts. In the castle at the top of the hill, the garrison drew up the drawbridge when they realized what was happening. By the time Lord George rode up to the gates, Edinburgh was taken. The only casualty was a guard with a sore head.

'It did work, George,' Anne said as he arrived. She was seated by the gate, sharing a flagon of ale with Greta. In the doorway to the guardhouse, sharing a similar flagon with the bemused Duff, was MacGillivray, bonnet thrown off, his red hair dull gold in the moonlight.

'I like the dress,' Lord George called up. 'Green suits you.'

# TWELVE

The following morning, Anne watched the Prince make his triumphal entry into Scotland's capital. He'd waited for daylight so the people could enjoy the spectacle. In full Highland dress, with an array of pipers marching before him and the Netherbow bell announcing his arrival, he rode up from Holyrood with his entourage. Waiting to introduce the provost, Anne felt triumphant too. On the way south, they'd taken Perth. Now, they had Edinburgh. The streets were lined with folk, all wanting to see Prince Charles.

The city had lost much of its wealth since parliament removed to London, the country's lords and ladies a rare sight on its streets since then. The new elite were merchants, lawyers and scholars from the university, altogether less generous with the poor, more sparing with their coin. Still, their women fronted the crowds of fleshers, baxters, coopers and shopkeepers, dressed in their finest and fluttering fans as the Prince passed by. He nodded left then right to them as he went.

Arriving at the City Chambers, he leant over to O'Sullivan, who rode beside him.

'Is Edinburgh stuffed with simpering giglets?' he asked.

'If you wouldn't mind humouring the ladies, sir,' O'Sullivan replied. 'They might well have a bob or two we could be making good use of.'

When they dismounted, the Prince offered Anne his hand to be kissed.

'*Ma belle rebelle,*' he said, 'you are worth ten men.' He glanced at Provost Stewart. The man was terrified, his powdered periwig askew under his hat. 'It is most kind of you to welcome me to your fair city,' he said.

Unsure if this was warmth or sarcasm, the provost almost forgot his fear for his neck. He had locked the city gates against the rebels, but neither the Union nor the Whig government was popular here and while their forces still garrisoned the castle behind him, it was Jacobite swords that swung in his streets.

'But ye're maist welcome, sir,' he said, bowing and bobbing. 'It's just, we havenae much here and you've a sizeable army.'

'*Ma foi!*' the Prince exclaimed. 'We are not common thieves come to rob you. We will billet where there is space. What provisions we need will be paid for. Now, *mon ami,* if you lead the way, I will address your council.'

Anne watched them go. The Prince, with his instant charm and regal air, was strangely out of place here. The city was a crowded, filthy place, smelling of human waste. Its buildings towered above narrow streets and dark closes. Only where she stood, on the wide King's High Street, did daylight have any hope of penetrating. MacGillivray, having shed his silk gown, organized provisions for their own regiment. Lochiel's men were stationed around the castle perimeter, in case the small government force voluntarily locked inside should suddenly be afflicted by foolhardy courage and emerge to do their duty. A hand tugged at her skirt.

'Missus, missus, yer ladyship.'

Anne looked round. A grubby young girl, maybe twelve years old, had a hold of the cloth. The child's hair was lank, her feet bare, her clothes made of sacking. Having got Anne's attention, she let go.

'Ma faither will fecht for ye, if ye gie us a penny for breid.'

The girl's Scots tongue was unfamiliar. Anne understood the Doric Scots of Aberdeenshire but had rarely heard the southern form except when city beggars overwintered with poor cottars, abusing the law of hospitality afforded to any in need. Like most chiefs, she spoke Gaelic, French and English. Only cattle-rieving Highlanders had a grasp of Lowland Scots. But what she deciphered, she doubted. If the girl's build and health were any guide, the man, if there was such a person, would hardly be fit to hold a weapon, far less swing it.

'What's your name?' she asked.

'Clementina. Please, missus lady. We're stervin enough tae die of it.'

That might well be true. Anne dug into her drawstring purse, taking out two pennies. No doubt she'd be surrounded by urchins and beggars as a result, but this child was sore in need of a decent meal. A wash would not have gone amiss either. She handed the girl the coins.

'Here,' she said. 'Get yourself some broth to dip your bread into.' The girl had the coins from her hand and was gone, melting quickly into the crowd. She could easily have been a ghost, with her pale, grey skin. This city was bound to be haunted by many. Five women crossed the road towards her. No ghosts these, Anne smiled. They were too vibrant, full of life. It was Greta, with Margaret and three others from their army.

'One diversion deserves another,' Greta said. 'Will you help me now?'

They made their way to the city stables. While the two grooms goggled at so many glamorous women, the farrier was delighted to do business, until he heard what it was.

'But I cannae sell ye the horses,' he protested. 'They're stabled here and arenae mine tae sell.'

'You have some for hire,' Greta insisted. 'The rest you can deal for your customers. How you share the profit is for you to decide.'

The man would not have it, proclaiming he'd be out of business without horses.

'How sad,' Greta said. 'Don't you think that's sad, ladies?' They all agreed it was, indeed, extremely sad. Greta drew her sword. 'Bloodshed on such a happy day would be even more sad,' she said.

The farrier grabbed a hot iron from the forge. He turned with it in his hand to find the tip of Greta's sword against his chest. Anne's pistol pointed at his head. The other women had their swords covering the grooms.

'Are we supposed to do this?' Anne asked Greta.

'What, shoot the farrier?' Greta queried. 'Only if he supports German Geordie and the Whig government.'

'I dinnae, I dinnae,' the man protested.

'Or if he attacks the forces of his rightful king,' Margaret added.

'I wouldnae,' the man said, dropping the iron back into the fire, shouting, 'Prosperity and no Union,' as he did so and adding, for good measure, 'Long live King James!'

'Well,' Greta smiled. 'It seems we have a good patriot here, ladies. Prince Charles will hear of you, my man,' she told the nerveless farrier. 'Now, if you and your grooms would just saddle up the stock.'

Before long, they rode five new mounts down the Canongate, leading another twenty horses behind them. At Holyrood, Sir John Murray of Broughton was delighted with his cavalry.

'Twenty-five new steeds,' he crowed. 'Greta, you're amazing.' Dapper as he was, instead of swinging his wife around and ruffling her feathers, he took her hands and they danced a few steps of a jig.

Anne had to turn away. The neat little man's exuberance over his wife's exploits distressed her. If only she could expect similar joy from Aeneas. She would return to him soon. There was no reason to stay longer. Cope had re-embarked his troops at Aberdeen to sail for Edinburgh when he discovered Lord George avoided him by marching south. It would be safe at Moy again, safe from Cope's army but not her husband's ire. She went up to her room in the palace. It was glorious, tastefully furnished with an ornate carved ceiling and rich drapes at the windows. But it wasn't home.

Outside the window, she could see the high grassy mound of King Arthur's Seat, where many of the troops had chosen to camp in the open air they were used to. Turning her head, she could also see right up the Canongate, its dilapidated, once-grand houses also taken over as billets, to the Netherbow port, its metal gates open wide now and guarded by Jacobites. A rider rode out through them, coming down the hill at speed. He was excited, she could tell, shouting news she could not hear at this distance to everyone he passed. She could see it catch them and spread, their heads turning, groups forming, the word shared. The rider was MacGillivray.

By the time Anne got herself down the wide stairs and out to the front of the palace, he was off his horse, tying it. All around, people rushed, their lingering ended as a sense of purpose energized them all.

'Anne!' MacGillivray called as he saw her. 'Cope has arrived at Dunbar. George sent me down to say we leave to engage him soon.'

'Then he thinks we'll win?'

'He must do. But, win or lose, we have to fight sometime. That time has come. Will you stay to see us off?'

Anne hesitated. Win or lose? If they lost, she would arrive home like a beaten dog. But if they won?

'No, I won't see you off,' she said. 'I'll come with you.' More than Perth or Edinburgh, a triumph on the field would prove the justness of her actions. A victory would show Aeneas how wrong he was.

Cope had chosen the flat ground of Prestonpans as his battlefield. In the bright September sunshine, more than two thousand troops were ranked behind cannon. They were in a strong position. The sea behind protected their rear. A great boggy marsh made their left flank inaccessible to Highland warriors who charged on foot. The only approach was head on or on their right, where the artillery was formed up.

'Look at their guns, Alexander.' Anne was mounted on Pibroch, beside MacGillivray, on a rise to the west overlooking the battlefield. 'We can't match cannon.'

'We'll be past before they can fire more than once,' he said.

It was bravado and she knew it. Neither of them had seen a battle, but anyone could tell a head-on charge on foot would see dozens cut down before they reached the enemy lines. MacGillivray, like other Highland chiefs, led from the front, never asking any man to do what they would not face themselves. He would be charging, with her people, into hell-fire.

Further along the ridge, she could see Lord George wrestling with the problem. He was deep in discussion with the Prince,

O'Sullivan, the Duke of Perth and the recently arrived Earl of Kilmarnock. Their army was now three thousand strong, greater than the one they faced but not so well equipped. It would be suicide to fight them here.

'I'm going to tell George we won't fight.' Anne tugged at Pibroch's reins. MacGillivray still scoured the enemy. He threw out his arm, pointed towards them.

'No, Anne. Look!'

At first, all she could see were English redcoats and dragoons, then her eyes picked out the dark tartan in their midst. It was the Black Watch, and from the pennant that flew above their command centre, Lord Louden's regiment from Inverness. Her heart became a stone in her chest. Would they have them fight their own people? A movement at the front of their lines drew her attention. An officer and his lieutenant walked along the row, pausing now and again to speak to the men. Despite the dark tartan of his unfamiliar uniform, she'd know that stride anywhere. It was Aeneas.

Aeneas stopped beside Lachlan Fraser. The boy was just seventeen. Though it wasn't cold, he seemed frozen, trembling with it.

'Hold your nerve, lad,' he said, kindly. 'They can't assemble before dark. You'll have a night's sleep first and, when they do come, the guns are between you and them.'

'My father's with them,' the boy said.

Aeneas squeezed the lad's shoulder. There was no answer to that.

'Maybe not,' he said. 'We're well placed. They might turn round and go home, and no shame in it.' He was fooling no one, least of all himself. The Jacobite force had grown as it marched. They might choose not to fight here, but someday soon they would. If it was here, the government would have the victory he expected. It was sufferable. One quick, sharp shock to rout the rising and they could all go home, licking their wounds.

'Captain M<sup>c</sup>Intosh.' Ray saluted beside him. Would the man never learn? 'we have more company.' He nodded towards the rise.

Aeneas scanned it. He had already spotted Charles Edward Stuart, with his commanders, and George Murray, whom he knew well. In other circumstances he would have been with them, and would be yet, if the French defied the government's belief and came. Like young Lachlan Fraser, he was also torn in two.

'The woman,' Ray said, pointing. 'Do you not see the woman, sir?'

It was Anne, distant, but unmistakable. Anne mounted on the bridal horse he'd given her, and next to her, MacGillivray. Rage rose in him, the same anguished rage he'd felt when she left, only greater. A month had passed since then. She had not come home when he expected she would, after delivering her troops to Glenfinnan. She had not gone home when he hoped she would, after the government army left Inverness. It was not enough she shamed him by acting independently of her husband. She had stayed on without him, as no other woman would. Stayed with an army her husband opposed, stayed with MacGillivray.

'That's the witch I told you about, Captain,' Ray explained. 'Twice now I have nearly put a shot in her. This time, I will make sure!'

Aeneas spun, grabbed him by the collar and raised the lieutenant up on to his toes until their faces were level.

'On the contrary,' he spat out. 'You will see that no harm comes to her, or answer to me. She's mine, you understand? Mine!'

Anne dismounted and paced about the ridge.

'What is he doing here, MacGillivray?' she railed. 'And with the man who shot Calum and his mother. This is not what he said. This is not what you said!'

'I don't know. He won't raise arms against his own.'

'He's about to,' Anne snapped. 'He's about to watch them slaughtered under those guns. Does he hope to humiliate us into turning around? Is he so determined to have his way he'll kill his own people to achieve it?'

Lord George began directing troops down on to the battlefield, placing them carefully. But still they would be funnelled to the guns. The Prince rode back over the rise to address the Highland chiefs before they, too, took the field. She could hear him below.

'Follow me, gentlemen, and by the assistance of God, I will, on this day, make you a free and happy people.'

If only, Anne prayed. Oh, if only. How could Aeneas do this? Did he care nothing for his people, for her? A hand tugged at her skirts. It was a grubby young girl, the beggar child she'd given tuppence to in Edinburgh.

'Clementina!' Anne exclaimed. 'What are you doing here?'

'Ma faither came tae fecht, like I said he would,' the girl explained. 'He said I'm tae bide wi the wummin.'

'They're over there,' Anne pointed. She didn't have time for this. A decision was needed. MacGillivray would have to take her troops down soon.

'I ken,' Clementina said. 'I was wi them but yin lady said the man ower there,' she pointed at Lord George, 'was askin if there was a road through the bog.'

'Bog?' Anne looked back over the field. The marsh was on the government's left side. Between it and them, there were enough fields of firm ground to line up on but no way to get there. The bog was clearly treacherous, puddled with stagnant water. She turned back to Clementina.

'What do you know of the marsh?'

'We yaist tae live ower there, oan the ither side,' the girl said. 'Tae ma mammie died and ma faither thocht we'd dae better in Edinburgh. We couldnae get work and we couldnae pay the gate fee tae get back oot again, no tae you came and opened thaim.'

The M<sup>c</sup>Intoshes were being called.

'I have to go, Anne,' MacGillivray said, dismounting to leave his horse in her keeping.

'No, wait,' Anne said, before turning back to Clementina. The girl's Scots speech was a struggle for her. 'So what do you know of the marsh?'

'I ken the way,' the girl said. 'I ken the way through it.'

# THIRTEEN

When night fell, the two armies settled for sleep, out of range, facing each other. Pleased with his preparations, Cope retired to a tavern near Musselburgh to spend the night. Aeneas was restless. Come morning, MacGillivray would be centre field, in Clan Chatton's traditional battle position, directly opposite him. If Lord George sent the MacDonalds first, to attack the left flank, the guns would fire diagonally across the battlefield, catching the centre-attacking clan as they did. The same was true if the Camerons charged the right flank first. The guns would swing in their direction but would still mow down any attack in the centre of the field. The only way to open up the centre was to send Keppoch and Lochiel simultaneously. Would Lord George do that, or would he send the M<sup>c</sup>Intosh regiment first to draw fire away from his wings?

Aeneas knew what he would do. In MacGillivray's shoes, where he'd have been if Anne had her way, he would refuse to charge. MacGillivray would not. The man was brave to the point of fool-hardy. He would charge when ordered. He would charge, believing speed and ferocity would take him down the field and through the guns before his casualties mounted high enough to stop them.

'Good speed, Alexander,' Aeneas prayed. 'Good speed.' It was a foolish hope. If his cousin made it through the cannon fire, he would be into Aeneas's lines, among the terrified sons of his own Clan Chatton forces, cutting them down, uncle against nephew, brother against brother, father against son. And if MacGillivray made it down that field, Aeneas would have to stop him. In his life, he had slept under the stars more often than under a roof, in heather, on rock, in trees, in kind weather and cruel, but he had never slept in a harder, more inhospitable bed than this. He drew his plaid tight round him and tried to stop his racing mind.

★

There were no stars that night. A mist rolled in from the sea, blotting out the landscape. The Jacobites doused their fires, removing any possibility the guards on the government lines could see their movement. They were under silent orders. Every weapon, every scrap of metal, was tied down, tight to their bodies. The fully armed had dirks and broadswords either side, twin pistols in their belts, some had a Lochaber axe or two-handed claymore slung at their back where all stowed their targes, a few carried muskets and, as a last resort for close fighting, inside their shirts, the short, sharp *sgian dhubh* was tucked. In front of them all, a bare-foot twelve-year-old girl led the way. Burly, rough Highlanders, bristling with blades, stepped carefully, in single file, from tuft to tuft of rough marsh grass, winding through pools of mud and water, past clumps of reed, following a child.

On the government's left flank, two gunners lay asleep under their cannon. A hand slid over the mouth of one. His eyes flickered open. A dirk sliced across his throat. Simultaneously, his companion met the same fate. Pushing the bodies back between the wheels, the two Camerons responsible lay down with their plaids wrapped around them to sleep. The next two pairs of gunners up the line were similarly, soundlessly dispatched.

One by one, the rest of the Jacobites reached firm ground, lined up and then lay down among the stubble of recently cut wheat, to sleep in their plaids. The later ranks were armed with what they had, billhooks, staves or pitchforks, whatever they could find. They would be the last wave on the field, and might find better arms among the fallen. It took several hours for the last man to come safely across. When all were in place, Clementina, by then asleep, curled up at the edge of the marsh, was wakened and sent back to the women behind the ridge.

In the grey, early morning mist, among the government infantry, a soldier stumbled from his blanket, staggered a few steps south to the edge of his line, fumbled in his clothes and began to relieve his bladder, yawning as he did. The yawn froze, half-complete. Across the flat field in front of him, wreathed in fog and barely visible, stood an array of ghosts, blocked rank on rank, it looked like, ready to do battle. Mouth open as fear stood his hair on end, the soldier turned slowly, unable to comprehend the meaning of this ghastly long line. His urine splattered over the sleeping bundle at his feet. The infantryman inside it woke and yelled a curse.

Further back, among the Black Watch, Aeneas, only half asleep, jumped to his feet and looked towards the shout, straining to see. In the milky, drifting air, deep lines of Jacobites stood, ghostly, immobile, waiting for day. He turned to the west, to where they had been last night but could see nothing, only swirling grey. He glanced south again. They were still there, ethereal in the fog but real enough. He bent and shook Ray awake, telling him to get their men roused and ready, while he ran back to wake Lord Louden. On the left flank, soldiers were waking now, standing, struggling to comprehend the fearsome sight to their left. There were more shouts.

'Jacobites!'

'Arm yourselves.'

'On our flank.'

'Sound the alarm!'

'Wake yourselves. On your feet!'

Hearing them, watching the flickers of movement through the mist, MacGillivray stood in front of Clan Chatton, unmoving, breathing deep, as the government army across the stubbled field woke up.

Up on the ridge, the Prince and Lord George, both mounted, waited side by side. They could see nothing below, the sun had not yet risen above the horizon, but they could hear the shouts of alarm. Prince Charles Edward Stuart smiled to his commander-in-chief.

'A rough rising, indeed, Lord George.'

Beyond the command party, further back, Anne sat motionless on Pibroch. Beside her, Margaret and Greta were also mounted. All three had swords at their sides and pistols at their saddle bows. On Anne's other side, she had put Clementina on MacGillivray's horse so the girl could see. It was the least she could do. Behind them, stilled with fear and poised with anticipation, stood the women and children. Revered among tribes, they were not risked in battle. A few had chosen to risk themselves. The rest would have work to do, when it was over. The sun tipped the horizon, putting a glow on all their faces. Down on the battlefield, the mist began to thin and lift.

Shaken rudely awake by Aeneas, Louden was out of his tent.

'We're outflanked,' Aeneas said, pointing. 'Where's the general?'

'He stayed the night at the inn.'

'Then you'd better take command. It will soon be light.'

Louden grabbed young Lord Boyd, the Earl of Kilmarnock's son. 'Order the dragoons mounted.' Then, to Aeneas, 'Have the guns turned and bring your company round. Cover that flank.'

'That's not possible,' Aeneas frowned.

'Try,' Louden barked.

Aeneas ran back to his company. The light was growing, the mist thin threads now, revealing patches of the enemy. As he arrived back at his men, he saw Duncan Shaw, on his feet but staring down at them.

'What is it you can't look at, lad?' Aeneas asked.

'My brother, sir. He's over there. I haven't fought him since he bled my nose when I was ten.'

'Then you can bloody his in revenge today.' Aeneas hurried on to James Ray. 'Lieutenant, will you order the guns turned?'

'To fire across us?' Ray was incredulous.

'Do it!' Aeneas snapped. Small wonder the English barked orders. Requests did not work with them.

Ray ran off towards the nearest cannon.

'Turn the guns!' he called as soon as he was in earshot. The huddled gunners round the cannon did not respond. Ray ran on.

Across the field, MacGillivray turned from scouring the enemy lines when the fog allowed him glimpses, to speak with Donald Fraser in his front line.

'Is that not your son over there?'

''S e,' Fraser said proudly. 'My eldest, the only boy.'

Opposite, behind the redcoat lines, the young Black Watch soldier had turned to face them.

'Then go on back with Ewan,' MacGillivray ordered.

'It's my place to be in the front line,' Fraser said stubbornly.

'I'll not have father and son kill each other under my command,' MacGillivray insisted. 'Now get on back.'

Rankled at the loss of place, Fraser fell out and moved back through the lines, his position filled by the man behind.

James Ray had reached the gunners. He stopped running and stood four-square, furious that they seemed so oblivious to their army's predicament.

'Are you all asleep still?' he yelled. 'Turn the guns!'

At the nearest cannon, the two huddled gunners rose and threw off their plaids, revealing themselves already armed, flintlocks aimed at Ray. In turn, the other two pairs of gunners down the line did likewise. All twelve pistols pointed at Ray. His mouth fell open, his arms flapped. He about-turned and ran, hell for leather, back the way he'd come.

Aeneas, trying to order the guddle of Black Watch into lines facing south, saw three of their six cannon were captured. The clansmen who'd taken them began to turn the guns round to face the government troops. Beside Aeneas, a soldier crossed himself. Ray went running past without stopping.

'Retreat,' Aeneas muttered. 'We have to sound retreat.'

He left his sergeant to sort the men out and hurried back to find Louden.

On the rise, Anne leant forward over Pibroch's neck, craning to see Cope, to see what he would do now the tables were turned. Locals and folk from Edinburgh began arriving on the slopes and other vantage points to watch the battle.

'Whit are we waitin for?' Clementina asked.

'Enough light,' Anne answered. 'So we know our own.' A movement among the enemy caught her attention. It was Aeneas, running back through the ranks. He seemed to be chasing his own lieutenant. She wondered where he was going that he would leave his men without command. Aeneas reached a group of officers, Louden among them, and gesticulated, pointing. His lieutenant ran on. Anne could see nothing of significance in the direction Aeneas pointed, except a drummer boy. A drum! She trotted Pibroch over to Lord George.

'George,' she said. 'They're going to retreat.'

'A minute more,' Lord George said. 'Let them see each other first.'

'*Mais non,*' the Prince objected. 'Shouldn't we allow them to retire?'

'We won't have this advantage another day,' Lord George said.

The Prince had been scouring the scene too.

'I do not see General Cope.'

'He's not there,' Anne told him.

'*Pas ici?* Then this retreat might be a ploy,' the Prince said. 'He might mean to bring a force in behind us. We'd be caught between them.'

'With respect, sir,' Lord George assured him, 'he hasn't the troops.'

'Then where is he?'

In the Musselburgh tavern, a red, tasselled nightcap was all that could be seen from below the covers when the landlady went into the guestroom.

'Sir,' she said, tentatively. 'General Cope?'

The heaving bump in the bed snored.

'General, sir,' the landlady tried again. 'You wanted wakened early.'

There was a snort, a gasp and one eye peered out of the covers.

'What time is it?'

'Dawn, sir. Your retainers left a half-hour ago.'

Cope threw off the covers and leapt out of bed. The landlady averted her eyes from his short white nightshift and went out.

Downstairs, she set his breakfast on the table. In minutes, he was clattering down the stairs, his uniform buttoned askew, trying and failing to straighten his wig and fasten on his sword at the same time.

'You'll want tae eat, sir,' the landlady waved at the steaming-hot plate of food. 'Ye cannae die on an empty stomach.'

'No time, no time,' Cope headed for the door.

'But they'll no start withoot you.' The door banged behind him. 'Will they?'

# FOURTEEN

On the flats, MacGillivray watched Lord George on the rise. The sun was half up now, the mist almost clear. He could see well enough to charge and wanted the order. On the ridge, Lord George's sword was raised, held aloft and then chopped down. MacGillivray tugged his blue bonnet forward, reached behind his head to draw his two-handed great-sword and raised it high above him.

'Claymore!' he roared.

The same cry rose from all the chiefs, from Lochiel on the left to Keppoch on the right. All those in the front line scrugged their bonnets and drew their pistols. As the other chiefs shrieked their war cries, MacGillivray thrust his sword forward.

'Loch Moy!' he bellowed.

The war cry howled from Clan Chatton behind him, and they erupted across the field in the Highland charge. MacGillivray set a cracking pace. The inexperienced conscripts at the front of the government army had never witnessed such a sight. Terrified, they fired off their muskets, too soon. Every shot expired uselessly before it reached the Highlanders rushing towards them. Now in range, MacGillivray stopped abruptly, his warriors halting with him.

'Aim,' he shouted. 'Fire!'

The pistols were discharged. As the redcoats who took the fire fell, the Highlanders dropped the guns at their feet, lifted their targes off their backs and, in one searing slash of steel, all their swords were drawn and raised.

'Loch Moy!' MacGillivray screamed again, the cry echoed by his men. They raced on towards the enemy. The redcoats still standing among the dead and wounded in the front government line stared in horror as the wild, bladed tribes rushed at them. Back on the Jacobite lines, the second line scrugged bonnets. In front of her men, having refused to place them under another command, Jenny Cameron drew her sword.

'Claymore!' she shouted. The men behind echoed it, drawing pistols.

All along the line, the roar sounded.

'Claymore!' Ewan M<sup>c</sup>Cay shouted for Clan Chatton. There was a beat, then the war cry, each clan with its own.

'Loch Moy!' The M<sup>c</sup>Intosh cry roared again and they rushed down the field.

The straggled front line of redcoats waited with bayonets poised as the first wave of Jacobites thundered down on them. Mac-Gillivray, leading his men, arrived first. He brought his claymore down, hard and fast, across the nearest soldier. The man's neck and throat split open, his head tilted, blunt white bone exposed. Blood pumped out as he toppled. MacGillivray was already past and on to the next.

Up on the ridge, Anne saw and turned away, her stomach heaving.

'Mibbe we shouldnae watch,' Clementina suggested, her face greyer than before. Her father was down there.

'I must,' Anne said. 'I brought them here. But you go back to the M<sup>c</sup>Intosh women. Say I sent you and you've to stay with them.'

The girl didn't need telling twice. She turned MacGillivray's horse and rode over the brow of the rise to where they waited. Anne turned her attention back to the field.

Aeneas had heard the attack begin and ran back to his own men. The redcoat lines between his Black Watch and the Highland charge wavered, breaking up. The Camerons cut a swathe through the infantry to set about the dragoons. Nearest the sea, the MacDonalds butchered their way deep into the enemy lines. MacGillivray and his men were through the front line, cutting down soldiers as they came. Bayonets, targes and swords clashed. The men in the depleted front lines dithered about whether to attack them from behind or turn to face the second line of Highlanders now charging towards them. Instead of doing either, they took to their heels, running through the fighting, back through their own forces, leaving the field.

Aeneas, running forward, drew his sword, pushed a young soldier out of his way and swung at the Highlander about to engage him. Nearby, the two Shaw brothers squared up to each other, beating the lights out of each other's targes.

At the rear, Louden tried in vain to deploy the cavalry.

'Fall back! Fall back!' He shouted to the infantry, desperate for clear space to let the horses through. Redcoats from the front lines ran through them, escaping the battlefield. Turn by turn, each of the three captured cannon fired off shot. Horses screamed and went down. The cavalry broke up, the dragoons turned and galloped in retreat. Louden grabbed the drummer boy.

'Sound the retreat,' he ordered. 'Now!' Then he held him by his jacket while he did, in case he, too, ran away.

As the retreat sounded over the field, Aeneas dropped the M<sup>c</sup>Gregor he'd engaged with a blow to the head and strode over to where the Shaw brothers wrestled on the ground, weapons abandoned. He yanked the younger one off.

'I did it,' Duncan shrieked. *'Rinn mi a' chùis!'*

On the ground, his brother's nose streamed blood.

'And it will do you,' Aeneas said. 'Go!' He turned the boy by his collar, pushing him in the direction of the retreat. As he did so, a clansman ran the boy through, his sword plunging into Duncan's stomach, through him and out of his back. The weight of the boy's body took him to his knees. Aeneas roared and, before the clansman could withdraw his claymore, he thrust his own sword through the man's neck, pulling it back sharply as the man fell. Aeneas lowered Duncan to the ground, bent over and ripped the claymore from the dead boy's twitching corpse. In front of him, the older lad was on his feet, blood streaming from his nose, staring in horror at his brother.

'Duncan?' he said, as if he expected a response.

Enraged, Aeneas, sword in each hand, raised the captured

weapon and yelling as if he might strike the boy in two, brought it down, sweeping past him, to thrust it deep into the ground.

'Take your brother home,' he said. As the boy struggled to get the dead weight on his back, Aeneas looked around the battlefield. The fighting had thinned out. Highlanders chased after the retreating troops. Some way from him, he saw MacGillivray, still in the thick of it, slash a Black Watch soldier, taking his arm off through the shoulder and, without pausing, engage two redcoats. Behind MacGillivray, an injured redcoat struggled on the ground. Aeneas tightened his grip on his broadsword and headed towards his cousin.

On the rise, Anne drew her pistol and kicked her horse off down the slope, weaving between the spectators, towards the battle. Margaret tried to call her back but the call went unheard or unheeded. Anne galloped on.

The third charge of Highlanders drew their swords, shrieked their war cry and set off towards the disarray. The second wave had reached the isolated Black Watch lines. Most of them ran past, seeking Englishmen to kill, not fellow Scots. The Black Watch were barely holding. Their lines broke now, running to join the retreat. Ewan saw Lachlan Fraser, the blacksmith's son, cut down from behind with a single stroke.

Anne, riding hard through the cannon line, had her eye fixed on the injured redcoat behind MacGillivray. He struggled to his feet, a Lochaber axe from a nearby fallen Highlander in his hand. She spurred Pibroch on. The redcoat staggered, swung the axe up to sink it into MacGillivray's back. Anne pulled Pibroch up, raised her pistol, aimed. The axe swung down. A pistol shot cracked off. Blood spattered over Anne's skirts. The man fell, the axe landing harmlessly on the bloodied grass. Above him, smoke drifted away. Behind it, Aeneas stood, the smoking pistol in his extended left hand now pointing at Anne. She, on Pibroch, her pistol now aimed directly at him.

MacGillivray turned at the shot, saw Anne, the falling redcoat, Aeneas. The remaining soldier he was fighting made his escape.

Anne and Aeneas stared at each other. Men fled the field around them. Highlanders ran past in pursuit. Corpses lay everywhere. Horses shrieked. The wounded moaned and howled with pain. The field was thick with blood and severed limbs. The air smelt sickly-sweet. Anne had no words to speak. Aeneas broke the spell, stuck the pistol in his belt, raised the broadsword in his right hand and looked at MacGillivray. The look was a question. For answer, MacGillivray lowered his claymore. His chief turned his back and walked away.

'Aeneas!' Anne called.

Her husband kept walking. The Prince galloped between them, shouting uselessly to the Gaelic-speaking Highlanders pursuing the enemy.

'*Cessez de tuer!* Stop the killing! *Ceux-ci sont les sujets de mon père.* They are my father's subjects!'

Anne holstered her pistol on the saddle bow, swung Pibroch round and rode back to the ridge.

The third wave of Highlanders reached the front line and slowed, stumbling to avoid the fallen. Some ran on after the fleeing government troops. Meg, pitchfork in hand, led the way. She was mightily displeased not to have been in the front line and wanted a live one who still had some fight in him. The others stopped. There was no one left to fight. Government troops that couldn't get away dropped their weapons, raising their hands in surrender. Less than fifteen minutes after it began, the battle was over.

As Anne rode back up the rise, women and children streamed down it. Some of the children went to collect pistols and muskets dropped by the Highlanders as they charged. The others, the oldest, picked whatever weapons could be found from among the dead and dying. It was the women's job to tend the wounded, their own and the enemy's, patching them up on the field, then carrying them to the doctors from Edinburgh who waited over the ridge. Their own dead they took off the field for burial. The enemy dead, they robbed.

Donald Fraser also searched among the fallen, stopping at body after body, turning them over, looking for his son. Those killed with broadswords or dirks were often unrecognizable, with limbs and sections of faces missing. Claymores, usually swung in a circle, took a head off or cut the torso in two. The Lochaber axe did the same to a man's skull, splitting bone and brain. It was grizzly work trying to find someone in the slippery red mire. Fraser ignored the English, concentrating on bodies in dark tartan. He had almost given up when he turned over a body with a deep slash wound in its back, to see the unmarked familiar young face.

He knelt beside his son, knees sinking into the sludge of blood and flesh that once was men and grass. His love for his son weakened him with grief. In this torn body was the baby who had crawled around his feet in the forge, the child who'd strained manfully to blow the bellows, the young man who strove to beat as sure a horseshoe as his father. His eyes pricked with the start of tears as he stroked his son's pale face. The boy's arm twitched. Instantly, old Meg loomed over them, pitchfork poised.

'Mind for his *sgian dhubh*,' she warned, raising her pitchfork to strike.

'No, Meg!' Fraser shouted, sending her scurrying huffily away.

The boy's chest heaved, his eyes flickered open.

'You're alive,' Fraser choked, and glanced around to see who was near. 'Help me,' he shouted. 'He's alive. He's alive!'

# FIFTEEN

Three hundred English troops had died. The Jacobites lost thirty men, with seventy wounded, but took fifteen hundred prisoners, a third of them injured. Few of the enemy escaped. On the road back to Edinburgh, Anne and MacGillivray, both bloodstained, rode side by side. Anne's horse drew a pallet behind it on which Fraser's injured son was strapped. Immediately behind walked Fraser, Ewan, old Meg and MacBean, with Clementina and her father, reunited after the battle, following on with the rest of the troops straggling along the road from Prestonpans. They had left the Prince railing that no one would bury the English.

'I could have killed a man,' Anne said grimly.

'Maybe,' MacGillivray was not sure what had happened between them and Aeneas on the battlefield. 'Maybe you saved one, or two.'

A rider in a red uniform galloped towards them, bent forwards, head down, hand holding on his cocked hat, but recognizing the bloodied, battle-worn people on the road, he pulled himself erect and slowed to a walk. He was a portly man, jacket buttoned askew, the braid and style giving his rank away. As he clopped in stately fashion past MacGillivray, the chief tipped his bonnet.

'Fine morning for a dip, General,' he said.

It was Cope, hurrying to the battlefield. He guided his horse past the pallet.

'Shouldn't we take him prisoner?' Anne asked.

MacGillivray shrugged.

'Somebody should tell the English they lost,' he said, and screwed round in his saddle. 'If you ride fast, General,' he called, 'you'll be in Berwick in an hour!'

Cope spurred his horse on and galloped rapidly away down the road towards England. Anne grinned at MacGillivray. He smiled back. They both began to laugh. Behind them, the others joined in. It was over. They had won.

In the Duke of Cumberland's hand was a rough sketch of a massive, ugly, Amazonian woman with bulging biceps and monstrous thighs, her face twisted in a snarl, sword raised in her great fist as she rode a white horse down a slope to do battle against cowering English redcoats. He thrust the picture at Cope.

'Beaten by a woman leading bare-arsed banditti!' he raged.

Cope said nothing. He hadn't seen any woman like this. He hadn't seen the battle.

'Anne Farquharson,' he read, 'the Lady M'Intosh.'

General Hawley, his rejected request that he be sent to deal with the Scots now vindicated by Cope's ineptitude, leant over his rival's shoulder. He smiled thinly.

'Not much of a lady.'

Cumberland slapped the caricature portrait. 'These –' he was apoplectic, eyes bulging '– these are all over London. We are a laughing stock! Do you hear that noise, Johnny? It is the French breaking out. Breaking out in fits of laughter!'

'It's a fiction,' Cope ventured. 'There is no such woman.' He put the drawing down. It made him feel nauseous.

'That's to be hoped,' Hawley said.

Cumberland thumped the table.

'A few loutish Scots?' he railed. 'I want my cousin stopped. I want *her* stopped!'

'To be fair –' Cope started.

Hawley laughed. From his skinny frame, the noise sounded like breaking glass.

'Fair, to the first commander in history who arrived home without troops to announce his own defeat?'

'The vigour and prowess of their army,' Cope went on, undeterred, 'is such that the next commander who goes against it will suffer a similar defeat.'

'I wouldn't bet on it,' Hawley sneered.

'I would,' Cope said. Through the window, across the table, he could see the spires of London. Outside, barges sailed lazily up the Thames. The September sun was still warm and the world seemed a peaceable place to be. But he had seen the terrified remnants of his army and heard their tales. He knew the devastation that had been wrought and his losses compared to theirs. 'In fact, I'd bet £10,000 on it.'

'You must think highly of these half-naked savages,' Cumberland said. The sum was massive, comparable with the caricatured harridan's thighs.

'I do,' Cope admitted. 'And even more highly of their command.'

'What!' Cumberland shouted. A tremor rippled his jowls.

'Lord George knows his force's capabilities well.' Cope stuck to his guns. 'But he also knows his ground and how to use it to advantage.'

'I will take that bet,' Cumberland said. 'You will regret making it. Hawley, I'm dispatching you to Fort George, to take command there.' He sat down and began to draw up the orders. 'You will move to engage the enemy when your army is fully assembled. With what forces are available there and these commissioned here –' he handed Hawley the paper '– you will have seven thousand troops. Will that do it?'

Hawley snatched the order paper greedily.

'It will, Your Highness.' He turned to Cope. 'Unless you want to retract, Johnny, I'll take your bet too.'

Cope considered him. He loathed this evil, half-starved, poisonous spider of a man. At the same time, he would never lay off £20,000. It could ruin him to accept.

'Changed your tune?' Cumberland asked, smiling.

Hawley leered and sucked his cheeks in. It was meant to demonstrate his superiority but did more to expose the poverty of his soul.

'Not at all,' Cope said. That size of force would, like his, have many untrained conscripts. He glanced at the picture on the table in front of him. He rather hoped there was such a woman and that Hawley would meet her. But he recognized what it represented, the power and fear of what had come against them. 'You're on, Henry. May I wish you the best of luck.'

Back in Edinburgh, the city bells rung for days in celebration, varying their peals and order so as not to drive the residents mad. Anti-Unionists declared themselves openly. Waverers abandoned doubt. Hardline Hanoverians began to waver. At the Mercat Cross in the centre of the city, the Prince had the Glenfinnan Manifesto, written by his father, James Stuart, read again to eager crowds:

'We see a nation always famous for valour, and highly esteemed by the greatest of Foreign potentates, reduced to the condition of a province, under the specious pretence of an union with a more powerful neighbour.' The consequences of that pretended union with England were detailed. Severe taxation resulting in dire poverty, Highlanders prevented from bearing arms, garrisons installed and military government introduced as if in a conquered country. And it promised pardons for enemies, freedom of worship, the protection of fishing and clothing industries, and to call a free parliament, 'so the nation may be restored to that honour, liberty, and independency, which it formerly enjoyed'.

The Prince then proclaimed his father, James VIII, the rightful King of Scots and announced the Act of Union repealed. Apart from the isolated garrisons trapped in Edinburgh and Stirling castles and in the three Highland forts, Scotland belonged to the Jacobites. The nation was free.

Braziers were lit in the dingy city streets. Pockets of music sprang up wherever there was room to dance. Pipes and drums competed with fiddlers. A Jacobite farmer from Haddington had already penned a song now being heartily sung:

> Hey, Johnnie Cope, are ye waukin yet?
> Or are your drums a-beatin yet?
> If you were waukin, I wad wait
> Tae gang tae the coals i' the mornin.

A spout of ale poured into Donald Fraser's mouth, him on his back, a city woman bending over with the flask. His son was in hospital, recovering. Nearby, old MacBean and Ewan M<sup>c</sup>Cay sword-danced to the bagpipes to the delight of residents more used to righteous floggings than sinful pleasures for entertainment. Old Meg propped her pitchfork in a doorway and leered at a stocky Edinburgh trader, beckoning him to dance. It was Duff, the shoe-maker, who had failed, miserably, to guard the Netherbow gate.

'Eh, naw,' he declined. 'Ma shoes nip.'

Meg's bony hand shot out. Duff screeched. She had him by the balls.

'*Nì sinn dannsa, a Shasannaich,*' she said, dragging him by the testicles into the whirling group. Duff got the message.

Walking past, Anne and MacGillivray stopped to watch. The excitement of survival was contagious. Greta, skipping out from her husband in a pass, bent down and twirled a crippled beggar on his wheelie board. At the far edge of the dancing, Jenny Cameron arm-wrestled Provost Stewart over a barrel. He made a good showing until she leant over, put her mouth against his, parting his lips with her tongue. Then she slammed his hand down, broke off the kiss and grinned. Those watching cheered. Several men leapt forward to volunteer for the next bout.

Duff stumbled out of the dance, bumping against MacGillivray, who put a companionable arm round him.

'Duff, old friend,' he grinned, 'did you not hear the Prince? The dead were his father's subjects too. No celebrating, he said.' Then he pushed the escaping shoemaker back towards the waiting Meg, who clacked her heels and drew him, again, into the dance.

Anne took MacGillivray's hand.

'Maybe it's time we didn't celebrate too,' she said.

They joined the dancers, stamping and turning to the beat. They swung each other out and back, then turned around one another, all the time gazing into each other's eyes. The glow from the brazier lit red fire in MacGillivray's hair, his eyes shone, his lips parted in a slow smile. Anne's heart thudded, her breath caught. She reached out, gripped his belt, drew him towards her until her breasts pressed against the hardness of his chest and his hips were against her. He hooked his arms behind her back, drawing her tighter to him, and they turned and turned and turned. She didn't realize they had spun out of the dance until they were into the shadows and a wall pressed against her back. She reached up, pushing her fingers into his long, tangled hair and, as his head came down to hers, parted her lips for his kiss. She wanted him now, how she wanted him.

She eased them sideways a step or two, into the dark shelter of a close mouth, still kissing, tongue seeking tongue, tasting, touching as a desperate desire built in them both. It was she who loosened the front of her dress, pushing his plaid aside, his linen shirt up, so that her naked breasts rubbed against his skin. It was she who tugged the front of his kilt up to his waist, reaching under it to take his erection in her hands as he raised her skirts, put his hand between her thighs, into the wetness of her, pushing his fingers inside her, stroking and caressing her as she with him until they were both lost in the daze of feeling, until they were half-crazed with it. It was she who put her arm round his neck to help as he put both his hands under her buttocks and lifted her up till her hips were at the height of his own. And it was she who remembered the way Aeneas had looked at her, over the body of the shot redcoat, on the battlefield at Prestonpans.

MacGillivray felt the change in her as soon as it happened, his breath hot against her ear as he spoke.

'What is it?' he asked, his voice deeper and thick with arousal.

She moved her hands to his biceps, letting them rest there. He let her go till her feet were on the ground again, though their bodies still pressed close, skin against skin, flesh against flesh. He looked at her, head tilted, his eyes darker than shadows.

'I didn't fire my pistol,' she said. 'It was Aeneas. He saved your life, not me.'

MacGillivray bent his head down so his brow rested on hers.

'But you would have,' he said.

'Yes, I would have,' she agreed. 'But I didn't. It was Aeneas.'

He tipped his head back, gazing up at the starless, black roof of the close above them. Then he raised his arms, pressing his palms, one on either side of her, against the rough stone, and looked down at her again.

'I have never loved a woman in a city street before,' he said. 'Maybe this is not a good time to start.' He pushed against the wall, straightening his arms so his body moved out from against her. His kilt and her skirts fell back down between them.

# SIXTEEN

The sun had just gone down when Aeneas reached Fort George with the remnants of his war-torn company. It had been a harrowing week-long march through some unfriendly parts of the country. There had been many times, too many, when they were spat on, harangued, pelted with excrement, human or beast, and other, harder, missiles. Jacobite sympathizers abused them because they were government troops. Government supporters abused them because they'd been defeated. Among random acts of kindness from strangers who gave food, ale, bandages, the rare instances of pity and succour came equally from those of either camp or none. Friends were thin on the ground.

Even in Inverness, there was scorn, cat-calling and dark threats muttered against them by locals. As they stepped out the last few weary streets to the fort gates, they heard the pipes calling them home. Now those gates swung open, the drums beat out a roll. A guard of honour presented arms, slapping their muskets to their chests. Two straight, perfectly formed lines of Scottish soldiers paid their respects to comrades returning from war.

Behind Aeneas, sobs and sniffles began as the boys broke down. His own eyes started with tears. It would not do. He turned, halted the rag-bag company.

'You're not mothers' boys now, lads,' he said. 'You're warriors. Brave men I am proud to lead.' He had set out with a hundred of them, eager young lads, barely whelped boys a kitten could have shaved with its tongue. Thirty-nine were left, some bandaged, some limping, their numbers swollen by stragglers from other units picked up on the road and one horseless English dragoon with an ear missing. All of them were shocked by what they'd seen, their faces hollow-eyed and haunted. 'You left here with pride you hadn't earned. Now you have the right to it. So let's put some ramrod in those spines. Attention!'

They tried, all but the half-carried wounded jerking upright.

'Aye, Chief!' they shouted back.

'Now let's try that again,' Aeneas said, more kindly, with the flicker of a smile. 'Atten-shun!'

'Aye, Captain!' The salutes were snapped out, almost in unison.

'Better,' he approved. They'd do. He turned around and marched ahead of them, through the two lines of honour guards, past the drums and piper, into the fort, sixty-one men short. Dead, wounded, captured, or simply run away. Tomorrow, he'd sit down with them, do a reckoning. Who they saw fall, with what injury, which wounded were alive when they left the field. Tonight, he was just getting them home.

He marched them straight to the mess and banged on the hatch for the cooks. It slammed open, something smelled good. One of the cooks poked his head out.

'Supper's in an hour, sir.'

'Supper is now,' Aeneas said, quietly. 'They'll eat what you have, ready or not.' He had no notion of how crazed he himself looked, blood crusted on his plaid, face expressionless, his eyes bleak.

'Aye, sir,' the cook nodded. 'We'll move it up.'

He left them banging pots about, serving soup.

It was a relief to reach his quarters. But even there, he couldn't be alone. Forbes waited inside. He had a lantern lit. In its light, the old judge's eyes looked more rheumy than usual.

'I wasn't sure you'd be back, McIntosh,' he said. 'Since you are, you might want this.' He pushed a fresh decanter of whisky across the table.

'What are you doing here, Forbes?'

'I noticed you'd emptied the last one.'

'What is it you want?'

The old man got up. There was a definite wateriness in his eyes.

'I believe in this Union, McIntosh,' he said, his voice breaking. 'It's not perfect, but it is the only way forward.'

'Tell that to the Jacobites.' Aeneas poured himself a drink. 'We were defeated.'

'And now you must think! There is a world beyond here that has much to offer. Colonies are opening up. Who knows what Britain might achieve? But Scotland by itself? England on its own? France or Spain will simply gobble us up and spit out the pips.'

'So you came to talk politics?'

'We can do more together than apart.'

Aeneas swallowed a mouthful of whisky. Whatever the old fox was after, he was talking to the wrong man. The fate of nations was not his immediate concern. His wife had aimed a loaded pistol at him, in defence of MacGillivray.

'Right at the moment, Forbes,' he said. 'I'm a stranger to togetherness. *Tha mi sgìth,* and tomorrow I must sit down with my company and try to make a listing of our dead. So, if you'll excuse me.' He held open the door.

'My apologies.' The judge picked up his hat. 'You'll want sleep.' On his way out, he drew an envelope from his pocket. 'I brought this for you.' He gave it to the chief and went out. In the doorway, he turned. 'I'm sorry, Aeneas.' He put his hat on and walked away into the night.

Aeneas shut the door. There was no point speculating. At the table he sat down and drew the lantern nearer so he could see. He took the *sgian dhubh* from inside his shirt, slit open the envelope and withdrew the papers. Half-way down the top sheet, he had to start again, unsure if he'd read it right. It was the full deed and title to Moy Hall and, he turned the page, all the land currently held. It was the release from the clan's obligation, debt discharged, mortgage clear. It was cause for celebration, at quite the wrong time, and no one to share it with. Tomorrow, instead of writing to the mothers of their dead, he could march the living out of here, back to their families. He could speak to the bereaved, if he chose to leave. He could return to being their chief.

Was that why Forbes was sorry? Sorry to see him go or, and to his credit, for the price paid in young blood, a futile loss that could have been avoided? Or was he sorry for what this action had cost

Aeneas, the respect of his people, the fidelity of his wife? Carefully, he folded the papers and put them back into the envelope. Then he doubled it into his sporran, tossed back his drink, lay down on his bunk and went to sleep.

In the morning, he gathered the remains of his troop, and they went over the action, dredging their memories. He could vouch for Duncan Shaw's death himself, no doubt buried now at Prestonpans despite his order to the lad's brother that his body be taken home.

'Lachlan Fraser got it in the back,' one of the boys said. 'I was looking to see if he was following after me when it happened.'

'How bad?' The blacksmith's son would be the whole clan's loss.

'Split from shoulder to hip, Chief.'

Aeneas let the slip pass. The list went on. M\<sup>c</sup>Thomas shot in the face, Howling Robbie with an arm taken off, the M\<sup>c</sup>Intosh lad called Shameless running the wrong way from the field, Macpherson run through the gut. When they'd exhausted what they could recall for certain, the list stood at nineteen, and some of those might be captive injured. Of the other missing forty-two, they knew nothing. He would do two forms of letter. Injured during action, presumed killed. Those could be done that evening. The missing in action, unaccounted for, would keep.

In the afternoon, he requisitioned a horse and rode to Moy. The land spread out before him as he came over Drumossie, heather- and forest-clad, with the turf cott fires smoking through their roofs, the burns splashing over rocks, roaring as they foamed down waterfalls, the loch sparkling in the autumn sun. He would have more stone cottages built, clear some of the bracken and heather, put the best farmers among the clan into them. Self-sufficiency, that was the way forward. Dependency was in no one's best interests. He was making plans for the future, a future that Anne had no part in.

He rode past the blacksmith's stone-built forge. If Donald had been there, he would have stopped, offered his condolences on the loss of their son. But the forge was cold, the blacksmith gone. Donald was in Edinburgh, if he'd survived the battle, and Aeneas couldn't face Màiri and the younger children yet, not without the letter, not without something for her to hold on to.

At Moy Hall, Will and Jessie ran out to greet him.

'It's good to have you home,' Will said.

'And all of a piece,' Jessie added.

'It's good to be home,' he told them, and it was, if he ignored what was missing – Anne calling from the bedroom window or rushing out to meet him.

His aunt was relieved to see him, relieved he was unhurt, amazed by the papers from Forbes.

'By all that's blest,' she said. 'Then you're free.'

He nodded. The word itself was a gift, like the sun in the sky, the wind sweeping rain down from the hills or the snow that frosted the mountains. Gifts that were kind and cutting, that brought good out of bad, growth from destruction, peace out of pain.

'So you brought the boys home?' the Dowager asked.

'No.' He knew now why Forbes expressed his sorrow. Free of debt did not mean free to choose. The old judge was a peacemaker, but he'd known Aeneas couldn't profit then sit this out. He'd guessed Aeneas would join the Jacobites. He was wrong.

'But they needn't stay in the Watch.' His aunt was perplexed. 'The debt is paid.'

'They chose to stay, with me.' Forbes was wrong, too, about the Union. It was not the best choice Scotland had ever made. Power had to be equally shared, nation to nation, not given over to the greater population, the louder voice. Whether by intent or not, England swamped Scotland with its different ways. Too much that was good was being lost, crushed or thrown away. The people grew ashamed. That had to change. Somehow, someday, and in some other way, that change would be made. But Charles Edward Stuart didn't offer it. Aeneas had heard him on the field, shouting at Anne not to shoot, screaming at all the Jacobites to stop killing his subjects. He would use the Scots to take England, if he could. Whatever he promised, he wanted the Union intact. The face on the coin was all the difference he would make.

'One defeat doesn't finish this,' he went on. 'The debt we pay now is to ourselves, to keep Moy for the clan. I won't jeopardize their future.'

'If you won't join the rising, you could stay out of it.'

'Neutrality would look like I colluded with my wife.'

'Then we're at odds now too, Aeneas,' his aunt said. 'You've chosen like a man without a woman to give you balance. Did you not see Anne?'

'I did. We didn't speak. She made her point with a loaded pistol. Our differences are clear. We've nothing to say to each other.'

'Then you both lose.'

'Aunt –' his temper was rising '– she's chosen MacGillivray.'

'For goodness' sake, Aeneas. She's a young woman with a healthy appetite. What difference does that make? She'll come home again. Where else would she go?'

'If she thinks to make a MacQueen of me in my own house, she should think better of it and can make her home at Dunmaglas!'

'You'd put her out? You can't do that. She leads the clan now. It will be their choice. You don't have the right.'

'Then maybe I'm learning something from the English.' It was his last word. He gave her the deeds to secure, called Will to bring his horse and rode away.


While Aeneas was out of the fort, Louden had returned, his forces even more pitifully reduced. There was a considerable to-ing and fro-ing, a lot of new English uniforms about the place. Aeneas took himself off to his quarters and set about the painful task of writing the official letters to the next of kin. By the time he signed off the last one, his lantern was lit and the braziers were burning outside. The guttering light from the tallow cast strange shadows in his room. Night came early, now October was almost here.

His door was knocked and thrown open. The dark silhouette of a thin man in a black frock-coat and three-cornered hat was framed in the opening against the bluish back-lit smoke outside, skinny arms spread to grip the jambs, like some giant spider in its web. Death, Aeneas thought, death had come to visit. The man-spider put its forearms behind its back and stalked into the room. Louden followed it in, substantial as ever. The thing was a man then, not a supernatural, and looked about, not speaking, ignoring Aeneas seated at the table.

'Do intrude,' Aeneas said, putting his quill down.

'Sorry, Aeneas,' Louden said. 'This is General Hawley.'

'I'm not sure I like Scotch manners, Captain M<sup>c</sup>Intosh,' Hawley said. The rank was sneered out, meant to put down.

'No more than I like English timekeeping,' Aeneas said. 'We lost at least five hundred men, fifteen hundred taken prisoner.'

'Yet left the Jacobites barely scratched,' Hawley taunted.

'General Hawley is to replace General Cope,' Louden told Aeneas.

'Then you're two hundred miles too far north, General,' Aeneas said. 'Cope rode to England.'

'This woman the rebels have with them . . .' Hawley drew a copy of the caricature sketch from inside his jacket and laid it on the table, sliding it over to Aeneas.

The drawing told Aeneas nothing, but the name under it jolted him. So that was why the general graced his quarters. Covering his shock, he looked up and considered Hawley.

'I've never seen such a woman,' he said.

Hawley lifted the caricature, carefully, with his fingertips, as if it might contaminate him, and handed it to Louden, an eyebrow raised in question.

'Anne Farquharson,' Louden read out. Before he finished, Hawley cut in.

'Is she the Pretender's plaything?'

Louden cleared his throat, visibly nervous. 'Colonel Anne is, as it says –'

'Colonel?' Hawley interrupted again. 'The rebels rank their tarts rather highly.'

Louden winced. Aeneas pushed his chair back and stood.

'Colonel Anne is the Lady M<sup>c</sup>Intosh,' he said, tightly. 'My wife, General.'

Hawley did not appear surprised. Instead, he had the air of a man about to lay down the winning hand.

'Wife or no –' he smiled a sly, thin smile '– your loyalty to the government won't save her from the rope.'

'We don't hang our adversaries.' Louden was shocked at the idea.

'Not even in defeat,' Aeneas added, 'if defeat occurs.'

'Traitors,' Hawley said, 'we hang traitors.'

It was too much for Louden. The earl was a soldier, well used to brutality and death but he baulked at the thought of hanging a defeated enemy, and a woman to boot. He put an arm round Aeneas's shoulder.

'Come,' he said, changing the subject. 'We're dining in my quarters.'

Hawley leant against the table, crossed his ankles and waited till Louden had the door open and Aeneas was in the doorway.

'I expect the rebels celebrate more wantonly,' he sneered.

Aeneas tensed. Rage, that familiar burning jealous rage, welled up in his chest. Now it had a target. His fingers gripped the door jamb ready to propel him round on to this obnoxious man. He imagined snapping him over his knee, throwing the broken pieces, clattering, into the corner.

'Don't be a fool,' Louden said, under his breath.

Carefully, Aeneas let go the door frame and turned to face Hawley.

'No doubt they do,' he said, with apparent calmness. 'They have cause to.'

He went out then, Louden with him, leaving Hawley to prowl about his quarters and rifle his few possessions, if he cared to.

Outside, Louden fell into step with him.

'Sorry about that,' he apologized. 'They must be scraping the barrel.'

'I have to warn my wife,' Aeneas said. He had hoped he would no longer care. Obviously, he did, at least for her life.

'Amazing how deaf one becomes,' Louden responded, 'must be from riding behind the piper.' At forty, he couldn't yet claim advancing years. 'Aeneas, if you're chasing two hares, with a foot in each scrape, I don't want to know. But Hawley has ordered all

135

letters in or out intercepted for scrutiny. Don't risk the firing squad.' They were passing the cells. 'Which reminds me,' he stopped and had the guard open one. 'We picked up this man on our way back. Deserter, I think. Didn't want to come with us, but then he said you could vouch for him.'

It was Lieutenant Ray the guard hauled out into the brazier light. Aeneas considered him. The man trembled, his eyes pleading. He had left the field before retreat sounded.

'He's my lieutenant,' he told Louden then, knowing he lied, 'and no deserter.'

Relieved, Ray stepped forward to Aeneas and snapped off a salute.

'Thank you, Captain. You won't regret it, sir.'

Aeneas was not done. The night before the battle, Ray said he'd met Anne twice, had twice almost put a shot in her. He'd realized then this was the man who shot Calum McCay in Anne's arms at the cotts. The night before a battle had not been the time to deal with it. He clenched his fist. Late was better than never. Now would do.

'This is for Calum,' he said. He drew his fist back and punched Ray full in the face.

The lieutenant fell back, arms flailing, on to the ground.

Aeneas bent, took his arm, helping him up, brushing him down. 'Are you fit, Lieutenant?' he asked.

'Aye, sir,' Ray spluttered, dribbling blood from nose and mouth.

'Good,' Aeneas said. Then he drew his fist back again. 'And this is for Seonag, his mother.' He hit the man square, full force, on the chin.

Ray stayed down this time, the world reeling too much for him to rise. Louden checked him over. He would live. He had the guard take him to the infirmary, then he turned to Aeneas.

'Would you like him reassigned to another company?'

'No.' Aeneas shook his head. Enemies were best kept close. 'I think we'll understand each other now.'

# SEVENTEEN

City life began when the post-rider arrived at daybreak. Slops thrown out at the ten o'clock drum the night before had been cleared by the scaffies while folk slept. Doctors and lawyers made their way through cleaner streets than they'd gone home in, to the underground taverns to breakfast and see their clients. Traders buttoned back the shutters on the shops. Pigs that slept inside were ushered out to forage in the gutters. Edinburgh was becoming used to Highlanders. The government's baggage train had been captured during the battle by a detail of Camerons, enriching Jacobite funds by £40,000. The troops had been paid. Business was brisk.

Anne was also dispensing some of those funds. For weeks she had spent the days in a small room at the Tolbooth, dealing with the captured prisoners. The euphoria had faded as the consequences of victory trailed before her. On the rough wooden table, she had a pile of papers, an inkwell and quill and a small wooden chest of coin. One by one, the defeated were brought in. Most were without injury, some were still bandaged.

She gave each one the same choice. They could join up for the Prince or sign a parole bond binding them never to raise arms against the Jacobites again, on pain of death. Many of the Scots among them chose to join the rebels. Those paroled were provided with enough meal money for their journey home. Occasionally, one would resist signing, usually an English redcoat who feared censure from the army if he did. They'd be put in a sleep cell then, for a few days, and eventually changed their minds.

Robert Nairn, the paymaster, sat with her, noting names, details, choice made and money paid. He was a fine-boned, gentle man, about twenty, with a preference for men in his bed, and a favourite of the Prince. Habitually, he winced at every evidence of wounding but, as he'd got to know her, would whisper risqué comments in Anne's ear about the charms of those he found attractive. A lover rather than a warrior, he seldom wore a weapon. Anne wondered what, apart from the prevalence of male flesh, brought him to war.

They were reaching the end of a long task, fifteen hundred men bar those still in hospital. In other rooms, Margaret and Greta carried out the same work. MacGillivray put his head around the door.

'Two more,' he said, 'then we're done.'

Anne leant back and stretched the stiffness from her spine.

'Not a one today worth having the trousers off,' Robert said.

'*Sguir dheth!*' Anne tapped her forefinger on the table. 'Mind on the job.'

'Oh, it is, it is,' he smiled.

She laughed. A Black Watch soldier was ushered in.

'Shameless!' Anne cried.

'Not me,' Robert protested.

'No, not you,' Anne said. 'Him.' She knew the lad from Moy, when she inspected the volunteers with Aeneas before they left to join the Watch.

The young soldier's face broke into a beatific grin.

'Lady Anne!' He was surprised, delighted. 'I knew we'd won. Well, blow me.'

'Given half a chance,' Robert whispered.

Anne dunted him in the ribs.

'Behave yourself,' she said, 'at least till we're finished.' She explained the true situation to Shameless, and his options: fight for the Prince or take parole.

'Don't mind who I fight for,' he said, 'if Howling Robbie can come.' The pair went everywhere together, had done since they could walk.

'Robbie,' Anne asked, 'is he next?'

'In the hospital yet,' Shameless said. 'He has an arm off. Left one. No, right. One or the other, it is.'

'Then he won't be able to fight,' Anne told him, gently.

'Always said he'd take me on one day –' he looked over at Robert Nairn '– arm behind his back.'

She had him sign a parole bond instead, two copies, one for him to prove he could not rejoin his unit. Shameless, of McIntosh, he wrote. Laws made by the old parliament insisted all the young had some schooling. The Clan Chatton chiefs supported it. Aeneas ensured that continued. Aeneas, Aeneas, Aeneas. She pulled over a second bond.

'We'll do one for Howling Robbie,' she said. 'Then you can take him home.'

'Robbie must put his own name or mark,' Robert corrected. 'But as we've just one more to do, if Shameless will wait outside –' he smiled at the soldier '– I'll go with him to the hospital and complete it there.'

With that agreed Anne gave Shameless his parole copy, handed over enough coin for the week's walk and called for the next, the last. One of the awkward squad, as he was bound to be, the government foot-soldier, like most of the English, had no schooling, so could neither read nor write and was certain it was his own death warrant they wanted him to sign. Robert Nairn rephrased Anne's words, explaining patiently. From St Giles Cathedral, they heard the gill bell ring, calling the city's citizens to their meridian drink in the taverns. The man was too afraid to lift the quill. Anne explained again. Robert grew fretful. Finally, he reached over and drew Anne's sword from its sheath.

'Sign it now,' he snapped. 'Or I'll have your head off!'

Anne looked at him in amazement. The soldier grabbed the pen, scratched out his mark on both bonds, then screwed up his face in case the blow would still fall. With an apologetic shrug, Robert returned Anne's sword, lifted one paper, packed it into his case with the others and left. Anne put some coins in front of the soldier and shook his wrist to make him open his eyes again.

'Take the money,' she said, 'and go.' The job was done. She blotted the ink from the quill, flipped the lid over the inkwell. Howling Robbie with an arm off. Why had Aeneas not brought them out for the Prince? She fastened shut the coin-box and took it out to MacGillivray. He would return it to their treasury while she attended the war council the Prince had called for midday. They walked down the Tolbooth steps together. At the foot, old MacBean sat, reading a letter from his wife.

'Is she managing without you?' Anne enquired.

'Managing to chide me still,' MacBean replied. 'I'm to be sure and rub my chest with goose grease for the cold and to heat my whisky with a spot of sugar in it of a night, and –' he checked the lines '– not to be chasing after young women.' His old eyes twinkled. 'At what age are women not young?' he asked. 'I could chase after those.'

'When they're older than your wife?' Anne suggested.

'So, if they're nearly seventy, I have my pick,' MacBean chuckled, getting to his feet. Only five years older than his wife, he was spry enough, despite her obvious concern for his health, his pleasure in the letter plain. He tucked it carefully in his sporran and headed off for the nearest tavern.

'There is only one woman MacBean wants.' MacGillivray looked at her. They both ignored the uncomfortable distance they kept between them now. 'He's been with her for forty years.' It was a long time in a world where death ensured few marriages lasted more than ten, a long time with one spouse when most people married several times.

A shiver ran down Anne's spine. She could still see Aeneas, on that dreadful field, the look on his face. No love or understanding there, nothing she recognized. Was it anger, or despair? Every day she hoped he would arrive. Every day she was disappointed. Being wrong must be hard for him, climbing down harder still. Perhaps she should write.

'MacBean will be home soon,' she answered MacGillivray. 'We all will.' The victory had won over many doubters. New support arrived daily. They had enough troops now to secure Scotland. Cluny's six hundred Macphersons, recently arrived, swelled the Clan Chatton contingent. They could stay in the south. She would take her people home, rid Inverness of its weakened garrison, bring her husband round.

They walked on up the Canongate. No one was about, the shops shuttered, the traders in the taverns. Ahead of them, at one of the close mouths, there were raised voices. A struggle ensued. One of the town militia pointed a musket at Robert Nairn. Another had Shameless by the scruff, dragging him to the whipping posts beside the Mercat Cross. A minister of the dour Edinburgh kirk sounded off. Anne and MacGillivray ran the last few steps.

'Stop!' Anne cried. 'What are you doing?'

'Godless, they were involved in godless pursuits!' The minister rounded on her. Seeing he spoke to Jacobites, he poked a finger shaking with rage at Robert. 'Your man is yer ain concern. Take him tae yer Prince.' He spat that out, obviously a Whig but, even in extremis, capable of careful politics. 'But that,' he pointed at Shameless, now being bound, yelling and kicking, between the posts. 'That yin, we shall deal wi.'

'Anne,' Robert appealed, 'we were only kissing.'

'Fifty lashes!' Spittle frothed at the dour minister's mouth. 'And if he's conscious, fifty mair!'

Anne drew her sword, pinned the point at the man's throat. MacGillivray slammed the coin-box against the musketeer's head and, as the militiaman went down, drew his own blade. Robert took up the fallen musket.

'Anne, will you next time notice the gun?' MacGillivray said.

'I knew you'd see to it,' she said.

The militiaman tying Shameless saw the tables turned and put his hands up.

'I dinnae mind what they were doin,' he said.

'Why do you?' Anne prodded the minister. 'Did either of them do you harm?'

'They're an offence tae ma sicht,' the man spat out.

'Then you should have averted your eyes,' Anne said. 'Their pleasure is not your business. It was not you they kissed.'

MacGillivray cut Shameless free.

'Ye'll aw burn in hellfire,' the minister raged. 'Before God, sin will be punished!'

'Before God is where you'll be,' Anne warned, 'if you dinnae haud your wheesht.' She was pleased with the way that sounded. A few weeks more in the city and she'd have mastered the Lowland tongue.

The minister kept quiet. Anne's sword had nicked his throat as she spoke.

'Go back to your church,' she said.

He scurried off, possibly to find more militia. Like most inhabitants, they'd be in taverns drinking till the midday hour past. Wanting the situation settled before it escalated, Anne ordered the militiaman to see to his stunned comrade, and asked MacGillivray to take Shameless to Howling Robbie in the hospital, then get them both out of town.

'And you,' she said to Robert, 'had best come with me.'

He collected his own case and the coin-box, trotting after her up the street.

'I'm glad you came by, Anne,' he said. '*Tapadh leat*. Thanks for that.'

'Kissing,' she fumed. 'You just met. What were you thinking of?'

'You can't guess?'

'Robert,' she suggested, 'while we're down here, you had better wear a sword.'

In the city chambers, runes were cast on to a map spread across a table. O'Sullivan studied them. The Prince thumped the table, pleased.

'*Oui!*' He looked round for his commander-in-chief. 'You see, Lord George? Fortune favours us.'

Margaret Johnstone exchanged a glance with her husband, uncertain of this predictive campaign method. Anne and Robert hurried in and stood beside her.

'Now that we are all here . . .' the Prince said, pointedly. 'We have heard my cousin, the Duke of Cumberland, has set a price of £30,000 for my capture.' He paused, smiling. 'I have reciprocated, with an identical sum for my cousin's arrest.'

Laughter erupted from the assembled commanders. When it

ended, the Prince introduced the new arrivals beside him, the Countess of Erroll, who, as High Constable of Scotland, was a powerful ally, Lady Nithsdale, her sisters, Lords Lovat and Balmerino.

Jolted, Anne stared at Lovat. He was loathed by her mother's family, the Murrays. Before Anne was born, he'd tried to steal the Lovat title by forcibly marrying the Dowager, Amelia Murray, after failing to find and force her daughter. Afterwards, he fled to France to escape the Scottish court's sentence of death. In the last rising, he had fought for England. As a reward, King George pardoned the rape and granted the title. What was he doing here? The Prince should jail him and return the title to its owner. She barely followed what was being said.

'Lady Nairne and Lady Lude have also sent troops. *Mes amis –*' the Prince paused for effect '– we have won Scotland.' Those around the table cheered. The Prince waited, smiling, for silence. 'We are now ready,' he announced, 'to invade England.'

'England?' Lord George had not expected this. 'We should secure the border.'

'And the coastline?' O'Sullivan said. 'The Royal Navy doesn't travel overland.'

'Highlanders do,' Lochiel pointed out. 'And we have no designs on England.' He turned to the Prince. 'You're tilting at the moon, laddie. Our men won't cross the border.'

'Except to steal cattle,' Lord Kilmarnock snorted.

Mutterings rose around the council. Anne dragged her attention away from the despised Lovat back to what was happening. The Prince waved the dissenters down.

'Gentlemen,' he said grandly, 'I have come to restore my father to his three kingdoms.'

'Then the Irish and the English must win theirs for you,' Lord George replied.

O'Sullivan pointed out that his Irish mercenary Wild Geese, recently sent by King Louis, would fight with them. The Prince assured them England's Jacobites would flock to his standard, given the opportunity. He held up a sheath of papers, their written promises.

'Their politics are their business,' Margaret said.

The Prince smiled, disarmingly, with not the slightest hint of annoyance.

'To aid our king,' he said, 'is that not the business of us all?'

Everyone agreed it was. There were shouts of affirmation. Sensing the detractors were wavering, O'Sullivan picked up a letter, bearing seals.

'King Louis's after agreeing with you,' he said. 'This guarantees the French army will be helping us take London.'

'I gave you Scotland,' the Prince said. 'Will you not help me take England?'

Several of the council nodded. It was a fair request. Lord Lovat spoke in favour. England under King James would make a peaceable neighbour. Others backed him up. Anne was bemused by the turn of events.

'We fought to be free,' she protested. '*Pour être libre!* Our own parliament here again is all we need.'

The Prince turned to her, as he might to a rebellious child.

'And how long will you keep it, Colonel Anne,' he asked, 'with my cousin always knocking at the door?'

# EIGHTEEN

'Nothing ails me but the wanting of you,' MacBean wrote. He was seated on a grassy mound beside the river Esk, the sheet of paper balanced on his knee, writing to his wife. All around, on the Dumfries and Galloway hills, troops milled about. Some, like him, wrote final letters home. Some queued for the use of ink and quill. Others already marched in long lines streaming over the border into England, heading for Carlisle. Drummer boys marched at intervals alongside, beating time. Pipers led the clan regiments. The air thrummed. Even the Lowland volunteers, who now made up a third of the force, were in Highland dress. The Prince had ordered it, for effect. He also ordered women and children to stay behind in Scotland but, for the most part, that was ignored. Five thousand men would cross the border. Few wives would let them go alone.

Anne sought out Ewan McCay, a clutch of official dispatches in her hand. He, too, was seated, writing.

'Tell them yourself, Ewan,' she said. 'There's a horse ready. I said you'd ride home with the post.'

He jumped to his feet, the ink spilling as the next man in line reached for it.

'I came to pay the English,' he said, 'for my wife and son.'

'You've done that, with great honour,' Anne said. 'We need someone trusted for this mail.' She held out the dispatches. 'You must be needed at home.'

'Winter without a man will be hard for them,' he agreed. He took the bundle but stared down at it.

Anne touched his arm. He was a good man, who'd suffered enough loss and clung to duty because he was bereft. She didn't want him to die in England.

'Let the dead go,' she said, gently. 'Your father and daughters need you –' she paused, not sure of his feelings in this '– maybe even as much as Cath.'

His head came up. His eyes met hers, quizzical.

'Babies wear their father's looks,' she explained. 'How else would we know?'

'Seonag and Calum were all my life,' he said slowly. '*Ach*, but Cath . . .' He stopped, then began again. 'You think she cares for me?'

'I saw how she looked at you. More than any tumble in the heather merits.' Anne smiled. 'You have a new son, now, to raise. So, will you ride with the post?'

'I will.' The grimness that had determined him since that awful day at the cotts lifted. '*Tapadh leat*. It'll be good to go home.'

'The runners will bring the men's letters to you.' She held out her own. 'And there's this, if you can get it to him.' The paper, folded and sealed, was addressed to Aeneas. Even yet, when so many rallied to the cause, he had not come to join them, nor sent a single message of support.

'I'll see he gets it,' Ewan beamed, 'or die trying.'

Anne walked back to where MacGillivray held Pibroch and his own horse. She was leaving too, going home to raise reinforcements. With half their forces committed to invasion, more were needed to protect Scotland. She'd stop at Invercauld on the way. Her brother's Farquharsons had not mobilized yet. There had been no need for more Clan Chatton forces, till now. It would be good to see him, and Elizabeth, her sister. Her stepmother, she'd cope with. She hardly dared think about Aeneas, or MacGillivray. He would lead her troops south.

As she reached him, he nodded towards a couple who wandered past, hand in hand. The woman carried a pitchfork. It was old Meg, with Duff, the shoemaker, now decked out in tartan plaid.

'Edinburgh and ale have a lot to answer for,' MacGillivray joked.

'I'm not happy, Alexander,' Anne confessed. 'I agreed to accept the majority. It was one vote. We're half-hearted in this, and that won't do.'

'If I don't go, Macpherson will claim leadership of Clan Chatton, and that won't do either.' Cluny had an eye to the Prince's favour, had not come out until it seemed certain Aeneas wouldn't, and insisted on keeping separate command of his own clan.

'But England holds nothing for us,' Anne exclaimed, frustrated. 'They'll only be more annoyed.'

'Then maybe they'll chase us back home.'

'Don't joke.'

'Look, if they beg the Prince to relieve them, they've no more love for this government than we have. We go to rouse them, not compel.'

'So we're an inspiration, not an invasion?' She put her foot in Pibroch's stirrup. 'I wish I could believe that.'

'Believe.' He grinned. 'But fetch reinforcements.' He helped her up into the saddle, let his hands rest on her thighs, became serious. 'You'll see Aeneas.'

'I have to.' She couldn't explain the way her husband had looked at her. Yet he'd saved MacGillivray's life. 'I wrote to say I was coming home.'

'I'd be a liar if I wished you well in this.'

'Don't.' She leant forward, cupped her hand round his cheek. 'Don't make it harder than it is.'

He covered her hand with his own, pressed her palm against his face then, moving it down to his mouth, put a kiss in the centre of it, his lips warm, his breath hot against her skin.

'There are only so many times I can lose you,' he said, wryly. He let her hand go and leapt up on his own horse.

Greta Fergusson rode by, all feathers and fur, with Sir John Murray, her neat, little husband.

'You should come, Anne,' she called. 'The shops in London will be a treat!'

Anne waved. The couple's closeness, their mutual support, again deepened her sense of loss. Further down the slope, Margaret and David Ogilvie, together as always, led their Angus troops across the Esk. A little girl ran up and tugged her skirts.

'We're awa, Anne,' she said. It was Clementina. 'Ma faither and me are goin tae see the king!'

'Something like that,' Anne agreed. She met MacGillivray's eyes. He looked at her with a kind of desperation, as if they might not meet again. 'Look after my people,' she said, 'and yourself.'

Pulling Pibroch round, she walked the horse over to the three hundred troops who would travel with her, some women and children, many in tears, enough men to make a bodyguard while travelling and protect her at Moy from Louden's Black Watch. They fell in behind. She would not turn round, not look back, not see him watching until she was out of sight. She would keep going forward. There was nothing else to be done.

When she called camp that night, there were at least forty miles between her and MacGillivray, he marching the opposite way, she twenty miles closer to home, twenty fewer miles between her and Aeneas. She kept busy, helped collect firewood, fetched water from the burn. Neither took long. She had picked the stopping place sensibly, with woodland and river near to hand. November nights were cold out in the open, fires a necessity. She occupied her mind checking the children had everything they needed, talking with the women.

Most were going home to take care of things there, younger children left behind, older parents, beasts to be seen to before winter set in. They sat around the glowing fire, sometimes singing Gaelic songs, mostly silent. All had left a husband to go alone into a foreign land, knowing their man might not return. She couldn't give false assurances, their dread was the same as her own, and resorted to simply squeezing an arm or hand, listening, nodding, saying little.

Only the wives of the men she'd chosen as bodyguard were cheerful, they and their husbands, knowing they wouldn't die far from home. Speaking with them did even less to comfort her. She gave up, wrapped herself in an *arasaid* and lay down. The border hills were comforting, like rounded heavy breasts, but they seemed to raise the land up nearer to the sky, unlike the craggy mountains of Braemar, which sheltered and enclosed it. Above, a massive sky shone with sharp stars, the moon stared down. She felt exposed.

England. That had not been their purpose. The Prince. Winning Scotland back did not seem as great a triumph to him. Lord Lovat. Her father always said you could tell a man by the company he kept.

'Keep good company, lass,' he'd told her, 'whatever pickle you're in.'

Aeneas. His most constant companion was MacGillivray, until she had come between. The black sky arched above her, full of holes. The moon mocked. Emptiness ached inside her. What did she want, who did she want, where was she going, what doing, why? By the time she woke, the camp was already up, bannocks cooked and being eaten. The road waited. It would take nine or ten days to reach Braemar. If she'd ridden alone, like Ewan, the journey would have taken less than half that. Invercauld, family, her sister. She would hold on to that.

When the snow-capped mountains came in sight, the shape of the land began to speak to her memory. That peak, this loch, that hill, this river, they never changed. Woodland hugged the slopes, blazing red and yellow. Then it was this tree, that hummock, this rock, like old friends, the easy intimacy of the familiar, loved ones reaching to enfold her. She kicked Pibroch into a gallop. Half the guard would follow at their own pace. The other half would go on, taking the women and children to their various homes, before meeting at Moy. But she, she was where she belonged. She galloped into the yard at Invercauld and pulled Pibroch up in front of the house, that reassuring, unchanged home where she had grown.

The door was flung open and Elizabeth ran out.

'Anne, Anne,' she shrieked.

And Anne was off the horse, arms round her sister, hugging, crying, embracing, kissing, stroking her hair, breathing her in.

'Let me look at you. Can you really have grown? Has it been that long?' It had been six months since she left here. It felt like years.

Then it was James, her quiet brother, not sure if a handshake was quite the thing. Anne wrapped her arms round him, pressed her cheek against his. She wouldn't embarrass him with kisses. His joy in seeing her had a different expression, he'd always been restrained, but he held her tight as he could and for the longest time.

'So,' a voice grumbled from the doorway, 'are we living out in the cold now or do you mean to come in so we can shut the door?' It was Lady Farquharson.

Anne skelped up the steps and flung her arms round her.

'Oh,' she cried. 'It is so good to see you!'

'Well, indeed,' Lady Farquharson said. 'I see your manners haven't much improved. And what is that you're wearing?' The arch comment was on Anne's *arasaid*, the common tartan plaid cottar women wore draped over their shoulders and belted round the waist.

Anne burst out laughing. The *arasaid* kept out the cold and made a blanket for sleeping out in, just as the men's kilted plaids.

'I love you,' she shouted. 'You don't change.'

'No, but you should,' her stepmother complained, 'into something more feminine and in keeping with your station.' If she was pleased, she kept it to herself.

Inside, she had the kitchen prepare some food and mulled wine. Anne threw herself down into a chair, feet jutting out, looking round the room with affection she never felt while living there. It was good to be home. Lady Farquharson slapped her knee.

'Sit properly,' she snapped. 'Anyone would think you were a sailor.'

'Have you ever seen a sailor, Mother?' Elizabeth asked, eyebrows innocently arched.

'*Isd, no!* Don't be silly. Of course I have. I haven't lived my whole life here, you know. I've been around.'

Elizabeth and Anne burst into peals of laughter while Lady Farquharson huffed that she didn't know what was so funny. They only laughed more, clutching their sides, beating the floor. James fetched the wine, a quiet smile lighting his serious face.

Her cousin, Francis, joined them for supper. They sat up late, making plans. Following Prestonpans, the government troops at

Fort George had been replenished. The Farquharsons would raise two battalions, from Invercauld and Monaltrie, ready to take Inverness when the forces there moved off. Anne expected them to be called south when England divided in rebellion.

'They have several thousand troops at Ruthven,' Francis said.

'Doing what?' she asked.

'Resting,' James answered. 'Word is they mean to re-take Edinburgh.'

'I think they hoped the Prince would still be there,' Francis added.

'If he'd any sense, he would be,' Lady Farquharson piped up. She sat by the fire, stitching embroidery, commenting every now and then.

Anne was perturbed that they were in such close agreement.

'Maybe,' she said, 'if the only land we can hold is the ground we walk on.' Crossing the border had lost them control of the campaign. Success now depended on English support.

'We can hold Scotland,' Francis said, 'but if we take London, the government will fall. Without paymasters, this army they've assembled will just melt away.'

'So we do need England, the Prince was right?'

'This is when size matters.' He smiled at her, spread-eagled in the chair, taking up half the room as always. 'There are seven million English. They might want new government but not from Scotland. Either they rise for King James, or we will need the French.'

Aeneas, too, had insisted a French army was their only guarantee. Now she was home, the past made him present at every turn. It was on Invercauld hills they first met, she as a suspicious, raging child, he the stranger-warrior whose authority calmed the wild terror of grief in her. It was here, in this room, he proposed, calming her fears again, making order in the chaos of her emotions. On the battlefield, with every reason to kill him, he had saved MacGillivray's life. Maybe he saw deeper and further ahead than she did. The knot of dread in her gut unwound. He was only a day's ride away.

Going to bed with Elizabeth was like being a girl again. They undressed to their shifts, quickly because of the cold, but joking and laughing. It was good to snuggle into the shared warmth of another body. As soon as the candle was snuffed, her sister only wanted to talk about men, men as lovers not warriors.

'Are you fucking MacGillivray again?'

'No.'

'Oh, come on, Anne. You've been away for months. How do you manage?'

'We've been busy.'

'Is there someone else?'

'No.'

'*Och*, tell me. You must be fucking with somebody.'

'Nobody, honest.'

'I am.'

'Really? Who's this?'

'You won't laugh?'

'Of course not. If some man is mounting my baby sister, I want to know who it is.'

'It's the other way round. I took his belt off in the woods one day and, well, he looked quite interesting without his plaid. So I made him lie down and took him.'

'Just as it should be,' Anne giggled.

'You're laughing.'

'I'm not. Who is he?'

'You'll laugh.'

'I won't.'

'Dauvit.'

'Dauvit, the diviner?' Anne's voice rose.

'*Isd!*' Elizabeth hushed her. 'Yes.'

Anne started to chuckle, then she laughed. She writhed in the bed, turned over, beat the bolster with her fists. Elizabeth couldn't help but join in.

'Dauvit,' Anne yelped. 'Dauvit, the diviner.'

'You said you wouldn't laugh,' Elizabeth giggled. 'Mother will be through in a minute.'

'She wouldn't find it funny.' Anne hollered more. 'He's beneath you.' She buried her face in the pillows, squealing.

'He's good-looking,' Elizabeth protested.

'He is,' Anne chuckled. 'He's also slow.'

'Well, he's only for practice,' Elizabeth defended herself. 'And slow is fine. He does everything I tell him to and he's quite good at it.'

'I'll say he is,' Anne hooted again, 'and maybe not so slow.' She bit the bolster this time to control herself. 'Nearly every woman in the clan has had him, at least once.'

'Have they?'

Anne nodded. 'There's something about the way he stands, just watching, and his hands being so sensitive. Most women want to get the plaid off him, especially for a first time.'

'Did you?'

'Not saying.' Anne put her head under the bolster, snorting. Her body heaved. She squealed, laughing. The bed shook.

Elizabeth started to giggle too, shrieking and holding her stomach.

Sharp knocking rattled the bedroom door.

'Are you two wasting candles in there?' Lady Farquharson's muffled voice demanded from behind it.

The two young women only laughed the harder.

# NINETEEN

'Nothing ails me but the wanting of you,' the writing on the white page read. It was held under the nose of a nervous aide-de-camp who read it out.

'Romantic fool,' Hawley snorted. He threw the letter down on to the pile spilling from the postbag on the table. Next to it lay the Jacobite dispatches, opened and read. A whip cracked, rhythmically, into flesh. The cat-o'-nine-tails had cord thongs. This one had wire barbs added to the tips. With each stroke came a yelp of pain followed by a low moan. 'But this –' Hawley picked up a letter that interested him, the seal broken. It was addressed to Captain Aeneas M<sup>c</sup>Intosh, Fort George, Inverness.

In the bleak stone cell of Inverness jail, Ewan was bent forward, head hanging down, stripped naked and strapped between two wooden posts. His body jerked as the cat cut again into his bleeding back. The cries and groans stopped. Hawley stalked over to the limp prisoner, Anne's letter dangling in his left hand as if it was a bad smell. He could not read it himself. The aide who read it to him was now nursing a sore head from the clip with Hawley's pistol he'd received for vocalizing the unhelpful contents. It gave little detail, only that she would be back soon and hoped to talk.

Hawley waved the whip to stop, gripped Ewan by the hair and jerked his drooping head back. He was unconscious. The jailer threw a cup of water in his face. Hawley waited. The post-rider had been captured by a detail out from Stirling castle. The idiots there had kept him several days while they read the dispatches, worried for their own sorry necks, before they had sent their captive on, under guard.

Ewan's eyes flickered open, dull with pain. Hawley bent down close to the side of his head; his thin snake-lips brushed the tormented cottar's ear.

'The Jacobite whore,' he hissed. 'Where is she?'

Ewan's mouth moved. No sound emerged. Hawley bent closer.

'Say it again, man.'

'*Pòg,*' Ewan muttered, coughed, '*mo thòn.*'

'In English!' Hawley shook the cottar by the hair.

'Go,' Ewan gasped.

'Yes,' he encouraged. 'Go, go where?'

'To hell.'

Hawley let go the man's hair. The jailer raised the whip. Hawley stayed his hand.

'Rub some salt in his back,' he said. 'We don't want to kill him, not yet. He'll talk. It's just a matter of time.'

Anne held out a small silver box to Lady Farquharson.

'A present,' she said. 'The ladies in Edinburgh use it all the time.'

Lady Farquharson flipped the lid and stared at the brown powder.

'*Ciod e?* What is it, gunpowder?'

'Snuff. You take a pinch –' she showed her '– then you sniff it up your nose.'

'Really?' Her stepmother was not convinced. Anne had brushed it back into the box, not put it in her own nose.

'Go on,' Anne urged. 'Try it.'

Lady Farquharson took a pinch, sprinkled it into the V-shaped depression on her thumb as Anne had demonstrated, and sniffed.

'Oh,' Anne reached out and snapped the box shut, 'and you'll need a handkerchief.'

'What for?' Lady Farquharson sneezed.

'That's what for,' Anne said.

Lady Farquharson sneezed again, and again. Her eyes streamed.

'They do this for pleasure?' she asked.

'They do. You'll see in a minute.' They were outside at the door of Invercauld, Anne's horse saddled and waiting. She'd sent her remaining guard on ahead and had dallied long enough. It was early, first light, but in winter the Lairig Ghru was impassable so she must take the longer route around the mountains. She turned to her sister.

'I have to go.'

'Let me come with you, at least to Moy,' Elizabeth begged.

'Not this time.' She gave her a hug. 'Keep practising with Dauvit,' she whispered, grinning, in her sister's ear. 'You'll learn a lot.' Then she took her leave of James, smiled at her stepmother, now staggering about a little, still sneezing, mounted Pibroch and rode off.

'Well, my goodness,' Lady Farquharson kept repeating, clutching her forehead. 'My goodness me.'

Four hundred miles away, MacGillivray strode into the war council with Lochiel. They were in Derby, a few days from London, and should have been celebrating. The march down, thanks to George Murray's skill in outmanoeuvring General Wade's army, had been uneventful. Their spies reported London was in uproar, militias that would be no match for armed Highlanders were being raised. King George had his personal belongings packed on a Thames barge, ready to escape. They *should* have been celebrating, yet the faces round the council were tense. Runes lay scattered across the map on the table top. The Prince almost wept.

'You heard that man,' Balmerino thundered. 'Cumberland has his veterans back from the continent. Ten thousand seasoned troops, advancing on us as we speak.'

'The informer is a spy,' the Prince said, 'a government agent. He lies.'

'Somebody lies,' Margaret Johnstone, the Lady Ogilvie, spoke quietly but her voice carried more approbation for it. 'What happened to the promises of English support?'

'Only a handful at Preston,' MacGillivray backed her up, 'two hundred in Manchester.' The people of England had responded in various ways, fearful, curious or friendly, but they had not joined the march.

'Pitiful,' David Ogilvie agreed.

'We don't fight England's battles.' Lochiel thumped the table with his fist.

'If indeed they have one, except against us,' Kilmarnock added.

'*Mon dieu*, the good people of England will not fight against their true Prince.' The Prince slapped his forehead.

'They don't fight for you, either,' Jenny Cameron pointed out.

'The French army's after assembling at Dunkirk.' O'Sullivan came to the rescue. 'Ready to embark, so it is.'

'Show me,' George Murray asked.

'What?'

'The letters from the French.'

'Ah, well –' O'Sullivan was caught out '– I wasn't thinking to bring them.'

'Sir John?' Lord George turned to the Prince's secretary.

'We only have earlier communications,' the dapper man stared down at his feet. 'The confirmation hasn't come yet.'

MacGillivray leant forwards.

'Show me the promises from England's Jacobites,' he said.

Sir John continued to stare at the floor. Greta Fergusson, his wife, put an arm round him. A feather fluttered from her outfit to the floor.

'There are none,' she said.

George Murray stared at the Prince.

'You deluded us.'

'You would not have come else,' the Prince declared. 'Yet now we can take London. *Fait accompli*. Tomorrow, it will be ours!'

'No English support,' Balmerino growled, 'and nothing from King Louis but empty words.'

'The French army is coming,' the Prince shrieked. 'Trust me.'

'We trusted you about the English support,' MacGillivray pointed out.

'Louis will not let me down,' the Prince waved his hand in panic at the table. 'The runes never lie!'

Lochiel snatched up the runes and ground them in his fist.

'George, George.' The Prince grabbed Lord George by his coat. 'We can take London, you know we can. Tell them.'

'We're going home,' George Murray said. 'We'll wait there for the French to come. Those for?'

Every hand rose except from Prince Charles and O'Sullivan. Lochiel blew the dust out of his palm across the map. In a body, the Scottish commanders left the room. The Prince threw his chair across it.

*J'ai promis mon père,'* he shouted. 'You are fools, fools! I will never, never consult with you again!'

With every stride, Pibroch carried Anne over the route her wedding party had taken. Then it had been a sedate trot, with an overnight stop, a slow, celebratory advance through lush, green countryside. Now it was a brisk canter, the horse's hooves drumming on road, splashing through fords, thudding across open land, past forests of naked trees. Twice they stopped to rest, drink water and walk for a bit. It was cold, but winter would not grip till the year turned.

The December light was already failing when they arrived at Moy. Anne's trepidation returned. She was glad of the dark here. It wrapped around like a comforter, blotting out sights she couldn't bear to see: the tree she'd hidden in by the loch; the space where the platform was for her wedding; the bedroom window behind which she had first known her husband, that she had leant out of, afraid that Aeneas and MacGillivray were fighting to the death.

When Will, the stable-boy, ran to take her horse, he was wordless with surprise at seeing her. Inside, the Dowager sat beside the fire reading her *Scots Magazine*, attempting to look unperturbed, though she must have heard the horse arrive. When it was Anne who entered the hall, she threw the publication aside.

'Anne!' she exclaimed with relief. 'I thought, when I heard the one horse, it would be Aeneas.'

'And that worried you?'

'After your troops arrived, yes. But we had words last time he came, and he stays at the fort now.' She took hold of Anne's hands.

'All that can wait. It's so good to see you.' She called Jessie in and asked the excited girl to fetch ale.

'Not ale,' Anne said. 'I've got something better.' She put the small box she'd carried in with her on the table and opened the lid. 'Tea.'

'I've heard of tea,' the Dowager said, frowning at the black dry flakes in the tin. '*Ciod e?* Is it food?'

'Or seasoning?' Jessie put a bit on her tongue, then spat it out. 'It's got no taste.'

'You make it into a drink,' Anne said. 'The Edinburgh ladies have it for their four hours now instead of ale.'

'They drink for four hours?' The Dowager was impressed.

'From four o'clock till eight, when they socialize in their parlours, before dining. Their ministers preach against tea-drinking to make them go back to ale, but they won't. I thought, if it annoys that dour kirk, it must be a fine drink.'

The three women peered at the tea leaves. Anne, having only a vague idea of how it was prepared, gave Jessie instructions. The tea duly arrived, in a steaming kettle, with three tankards, a dish of sugar and a jug of cream.

'I arranged for a teaset to be sent,' Anne said, 'but this will do for now.'

Jessie was not convinced. She set down a flagon of ale.

'I brought this too,' she said. 'In case.'

The tea was not a great success. The taste was pleasant enough, though bland, but the black leaves floating in it stuck in their mouths and put them off. They resorted to ale.

'Now that we are as grand as ladies in Edinburgh,' the Dowager said, spitting out yet another tea leaf, 'you must tell us all about your adventure.'

Jessie brought steaming plates of minced collops and mealy potatoes through to the fireside. Knowing there was a story in the offing, Will came in from the stable to join them. With Anne and the Dowager settled in the big chairs, him on the hearth and Jessie on the footstool, it began. She told them about meeting the Prince and, since they'd yet to see him, was urged for detail. What did he wear, what colour were his eyes, hair, how tall was he, was he as good-looking as everyone said? Similar detail was asked of the arrival in Perth, the capture of Edinburgh, Prestonpans, the crossing of the border. It was a long story, almost four months of adventure, a story they would retell, that would be passed around the clan, a story for the long cold winter nights.

'Will they be in London now?' Will asked when she finished, his eyes shining, one side of his face red with the heat.

'They should be.' Anne nodded. 'Maybe the Prince sits on the throne tonight.' That news would travel fast, but, even with fresh riders and mounts relaying it, would still take a few days to arrive.

'Tell us again about putting MacGillivray in a dress,' Jessie giggled.

The Dowager chased them off to their beds. It was late enough for those with daylight rises. But, instead of laying a wet peat on to damp down the fire for the night, she stirred it up, added a log and poured more ale for herself and Anne.

'There is a bit of the story you missed,' she said, 'on the battlefield, you and Aeneas.'

'How do you know?' Anne was puzzled, then it dawned. 'Did he tell you?'

'He did.' The Dowager nodded. 'But I want to hear it from you.'

So Anne told her what had happened, about MacGillivray's danger, the redcoat with the axe, the pistol shot, and her frozen, unable to speak, at the shock of seeing Aeneas, so close, close enough to leap off her horse and embrace, except for the way he looked at her, close enough to speak, until he walked away without a word.

'Why did you leave that part out?'

'I didn't want them to know –' her eyes filled with tears '– that their chief thinks so little of me, to save MacGillivray but treat his wife with such contempt.'

'Oh, Anne, *a ghràidh* –' the Dowager got out of her chair and down on her knees in front of Anne's seat '– you've been so strong.

Don't cry. Here.' She handed her the handkerchief tucked in her waist. 'Dry your eyes.'

'I can't bear it that he hates me so much.'

'That's because you love him.'

'No.' Anne blew her nose. 'I don't know that I do.'

'Why else would you care what he thinks?'

'I don't know what he thinks. He won't talk to me.'

The Dowager took and held both her hands, looking earnestly into her eyes.

'He thinks you came on to the battlefield to shoot him.'

'What?'

'Because you thought he would kill MacGillivray.'

'No!'

'Your pistol pointed at him.'

'Because the redcoat fell before I could fire. I didn't see Aeneas till then.' It had only been seconds. She replayed it in her head. The smoke, seeing him there. Her finger on the trigger. The look on his face. The look on his face.

# TWENTY

Birdsong, a tangle of sound. Chirps, cheeps, the low burbles, a caw. Anne woke, disorientated, in the wood-panelled room. Bright winter sunlight crept in through the shutters. She stretched, arching back against the bulk behind her. Aeneas? Then she hadn't only imagined him coming home in the night. She spun round but, no, it was only the pillow, dragged under the cover during sleep to fill the empty space. Memory fed her another sound, the clash of steel. She got up then. It had all happened. She wasn't there but here, and alone.

Downstairs, Jessie had fires blazing and served hot porridge in the dining room.

'I've a pair of kippers or some salt herring, if you want,' she said when Anne came in. 'There's not much brought in by the clan, with so many being away and just the Dowager here.'

The Dowager was already seated, salting her breakfast, the table strewn with her papers. The *Caledonian Mercury* was standard fare and she filled the gaps left by its three weekly editions with the *Edinburgh Courant*. Now that war justified the expense, the *Spectator* and *London Evening Post* had joined them, more pertinent now despite the delay of their journey. She liked to read while eating.

'The English papers seem amazed our army behaves on the way south,' she said.

'Porridge is fine,' Anne told Jessie. 'The fish will keep.' She sat down at the table. 'What does "behave" mean?'

'I think they expected rape and pillage,' the Dowager considered, 'with us being barbarians.' But she could not keep a straight face. They both laughed.

'We pay for everything,' Anne said. 'It's friends we seek, not enemies.'

The Dowager indicated the steaming kettle on the hearth.

'We thought you might like some of your tea.'

Anne shook her head. 'I'll stick with ale, at least until the tea service arrives.'

'The Edinburgh kirk will love you for it,' the Dowager said, dryly.

'I doubt I'll ever redeem myself,' Anne said, 'after rescuing Shameless from that sour minister's notion of justice.'

While they ate, the Dowager gave her the estate news. The Shaws had lost one son, the body brought home by his older brother, stitched into his Black Watch plaid by some kind Lowlander. The journey took him two weeks, what with dragging the pallet he'd made from branches to carry the corpse. There were several dead, or believed dead, a few that Anne knew from Moy.

'And Màiri had the word from Aeneas, her Lachlan fell.'

'The blacksmith's son? But he's with us,' Anne said. 'His father got him off the field. It was only flesh that was cut, and he is so proud of the scar. All the way down his back, it goes. But he's alive, and doing well.'

'By all that's wonderful.' The Dowager beamed. 'Will can run over to Màiri's when he gets back from Inverness. I sent him to light the fires for me, take the chill off. It won't do, a house being empty in winter.'

Anne had more good news. Most of the young McIntosh captives from the Black Watch, missing after Prestonpans, had joined the Jacobite army, fifty of them. She couldn't remember all their names but had kept count. The Dowager knew of some who'd written from Edinburgh, but not that many. Anne frowned. The rest should have written home before crossing the border. She'd insisted on it.

'Did Shameless get himself safe home?' she asked.

He and Howling Robbie both, Robbie without a parole as well as short of an arm, the right one, and him right-handed, or was. The parole stipulated the holder would not fight the Jacobites again, on pain of death. Robert Nairn had meant to issue Robbie's at the hospital in Edinburgh but that was forgotten in the kerfuffle with the incensed minister at the Mercat Cross. Without one to show the terms of his release, Robbie might be considered a deserter. So Shameless had crossed out his own name on the one he had, inserted Robbie's instead and went off back to the fort again.

'He can't do that,' Anne objected. 'We'll have him on our records.'

'If he's ever taken, we'll plead for him,' the Dowager said. 'He surely can't die of stupidity.'

The rest of the news was of ordinary things. Meg's cow looked fit to survive the winter now she wasn't around to drain its blood. Old Tom was much the same, despite, or because of, the regular broth. Cath's baby was crawling.

'Did she stay with Ewan?'

'Ewan went with you,' the Dowager said.

'Yes, but I sent him home, at the border, with the mail.'

'*Och*, well, there's your answer,' the Dowager said. 'He'll be delivering every bit and piece himself. Do you know Cath's baby is his?'

Anne nodded, distracted. She was trying to count the days, how many? Too many, she was sure.

'So did Seonag,' the Dowager rambled on. 'Loved the baby, of course. The living are to be treasured. But she dusted Ewan down. Funny creatures, us women. We expect men not to mind sharing us, but if they do it, that's a different story. But, then, I suppose we're made for it and no man ever was. It's all they can do to keep one woman satisfied, if that.'

'That's too long,' Anne interrupted. 'Ewan, he should've been home. That's far too long.'

The door from the kitchens flung open. Will rushed in, Jessie close behind him.

'They're coming back,' he yelled. 'Our army, they're coming back!'

'*Dè bha siud?*' The Dowager spun round to him.

'What!' Anne was on her feet. 'From London?'

'They didn't go to London. They stopped at . . . at –' he couldn't recall '– some place near it. Lord George told the Prince they were coming home.'

Anne and the Dowager stared at one another, as if the answers to all the questions that raced through their minds could be found in each other's eyes.

'George will have his reasons,' the Dowager got out.

'That's not all –' Will was fair to bursting with it '– the government army is leaving Ruthven barracks! Going to Edinburgh, everybody says.'

'Going to head them off,' Anne conjectured. 'Going to engage us.'

'I would think,' the Dowager agreed. 'Oh dear, this is not good. There will be General Wade's army behind them now. Then they'll march into this one.'

Anne grabbed hold of Will.

'Would you ride round Moy? Tell the guards we're moving and I need every other warrior who'll come out. We'll gather at Invercauld.'

'I will.' The lad nodded frantically. 'Soon as you let go my plaid.'

She did, and he rushed out, the door clattering behind him.

'*Ach* –' Anne remembered. Too late. 'There's Dunmaglas.'

'I'll do that,' Jessie volunteered. 'And I'll send some runners from the first place I pass to the other clans.'

'Good girl, good thinking.'

And Jessie, too, was gone. Anne ran into the kitchen and came back with the *arasaid* Jessie had taken from her the previous night, throwing it round her shoulders and belting it at the waist.

'You'll be off back to Braemar, then?' the Dowager guessed.

'No, my brother's clan is already gathering. He'll know our plans have changed. I came to see Aeneas and there's more reason now than I thought, so I'm not leaving till I do. I'm going to Inverness.'

'But they're looking for you. You'll be recognized. See.' She lifted a London broadsheet from the table to show her.

'Not from that, I won't.' Anne stared at the caricatured sketch. Surely it was a joke? She glanced at a second drawing beside it. 'Jenny Cameron? They have her like a man.'

The Dowager would not be put off. 'Folk round here can put the right face to your name. It's dangerous.'

Anne flipped the loose fold of tartan that hung down her back up over her head. The hood effectively hid her face.

'Most women will be hooded against the cold now,' she said, 'and I look like a cottar in this.'

'But how will you get in the fort?'

'I'll worry about that when I get there.'

Then she, too, was gone.

'Jessie!' the Dowager called then, tutting at herself, went back to the dining room and poured herself another tankard of ale. 'Well, dear house,' she said, raising her drink in a toast, 'seems you're stuck with me again. *Slàinte!*' She drank it down.

On the edge of Inverness, Anne stabled Pibroch with a woman she could trust, getting the horse into her kitchen so the neighbours wouldn't talk. She left her sword and dirk, feeling naked without them, but wearing weapons was as good as declaring who she was.

'Be careful,' the woman said, as she made to leave on foot. 'They're hanging spies in the square. Struan Davidson it was, the other day.'

'The signwriter?' Davidson had collected funds for Jacobite troops. One of the dispatches sent with Ewan had been for him.

Anne pushed a pistol deep into the folds of her *arasaid*, in case. That alone would get her arrested, if it was seen, but at least she would not go without a fight. When she reached the square, there was a buzz around the gallows on the far side. It was market day, the square crowded with stalls, and folk were there to buy, see the troops off or watch another hanging. The crowds made good cover. Behind the gibbet, redcoat troops assembled, leaving the fort to join those at Ruthven further down the road. The gates were open, Lord Louden's pennant flying from the mast. The Black Watch was still there, though perhaps not for long.

Anne kept her head down and worked her way around, perusing the stalls like any other cottar wife. At one of them, she bought a flask of ale. That would do. She'd hurry to the gates, pretend she was a trader sent with a gift for Aeneas, no, for Louden, to wish him victory. That would get her in. Other women came and went, wives, sweethearts, those on business. In all the clatter of bodies, droning pipes, soldiers rushing about, those lining up, she'd never be noticed.

She turned to cross the thronging square, walking purposefully as suited being on an errand. High up on the gallows platform, some poor half-dead soul was lifted up by the armpits, head drooping on to his chest, towards the noose. Anne turned her gaze resolutely towards the fort, and froze. On the cobbles, at the foot of the gibbet, a captain in Black Watch uniform walked forward and stopped, looking up at the prisoner above. It was Aeneas.

Aeneas glanced up at the bruised and bloodied face of the man with the noose around his neck. Now he stared. Beside him, James Ray also stopped walking, and waited, his wife trailing behind. He looked idly around the square. Behind the breathless, waiting crowd, a hooded cottar woman, strangely familiar, stood transfixed, staring back, apparently at him rather than the hanging. Behind him, the trap of the gibbet clattered open. The condemned man dropped, the noose jerked tight around his neck, throttling, strangling. His legs kicked wildly. Aeneas saw who it was and grabbed Ray.

'Weight that man down!' he ordered, forcibly, pointing.

Ray leapt forwards, wrapped his arms round the dying man's thrashing limbs, and jumped, bending his legs so he dropped with all his body weight jerking the struggling man downwards. The man's neck broke, his legs twitched, the kicking ceased.

Anne automatically looked where Aeneas pointed. Her whole body chilled. She stared up at the hanged man, the hood of tartan falling back off her face. The man who swung on the gibbet was Ewan. Hardly able to comprehend, she gazed at the stocky warrior's bruised, dead face. Aeneas had hanged Ewan. She had sent the cottar home, to start a new life. She had sent him with a letter for

Aeneas, a letter asking that they talk, and this was her husband's answer. To Ewan, of all people, he would do this?

A skinny general dressed in black leapt in front of Aeneas, prancing like a demented stick-insect. Anne could hear his high, thin voice screaming.

'What have you done? I wanted that man alive!'

A hand touched her shoulder, another on her back, turning her round.

'You'll catch your death, dear,' a woman said, drawing Anne's hood back over. It was Helen, James Ray's wife. 'You shouldn't be out.' She propelled Anne, arm round her waist, in the direction she'd turned her, back across the square, away from the gallows, towards the other side.

Beside the gibbet, Hawley was apoplectic, screeching at Aeneas and Ray.

'You'll pay for this!' He whirled round to yell at the hangman. 'Cut him down! Cut him down!'

Ewan's body slammed, face down, to the ground beneath the trap.

'I wasn't finished with him,' Hawley raged. 'I wanted him drawn. The sight of his own gut might've loosened his tongue.'

Aeneas looked at the dead cottar's flayed back. Deep gouges gaped open, black with crusted blood. Exposed bone showed through.

'I doubt it,' he said, grimly. 'He's a cottar. He would have nothing to tell.'

'Do you think I'm a fool, McIntosh?' Spittle frothed at the side of Hawley's skinny mouth. 'He knew where your wife is!'

Ray looked round for his own wife, wondering where she'd gone. His eyes searched the crowd, the square. Across the far side, he caught a movement, the flutter of Helen's dress, two women vanishing between the stalls. He headed off after her, pushing through the crowd around the gibbet.

'Cross me again, McIntosh,' Hawley ranted, 'and you will dance on the gallows next!'

Aeneas drew a deep, hurting breath. Peace was all he'd been able to give Ewan. Anne had even more to answer for now; her whereabouts had led the clansman to this tormented death. Hawley was just a disease, a symptom, of what they'd done to themselves, but the sick love of torture and the rope was all his own. Icy calm, Aeneas stared contemptuously into the general's furious eyes.

'Every man should dance,' he said, 'before he dies.'

Reaching the other side of the square, Helen gave Anne's waist a quick squeeze.

'We, the officers' wives, we all think you're wonderful.' She pushed Anne into an alley. 'Now go, go quickly,' she urged.

Anne gave her a look of gratitude, thrust the flagon of ale into Helen's hands and hurried away through the close.

'And stay alive,' Helen whispered. She drew a deep breath, balanced the flagon on her arm, smoothed down her dress and turned out of the alley. Her husband stepped in front of her.

'You came in here with a woman,' Ray accused.

'Indeed not,' she held the flagon out. 'You were busy. I came over to buy ale. Then I was caught short.'

'A woman I think I recognized,' he corrected, pushing her aside to glance down the close.

Fearfully, Helen squinted around him. The alley was empty. Anne was gone.

'I didn't see any woman, dear,' Helen smiled. 'I was relieving myself.'

# TWENTY-ONE

MacGillivray stood on the carse looking up at Stirling Castle. He'd seen it before, while on a cattle raid in his youth. It was the gateway between Lowlands and Highlands, a fine castle, seeming to grow naturally out of the high rocky crag on which it stood. The flat carse-land all around meant it had a fine view of the land below. Like Edinburgh Castle and the three Highland forts, it had been garrisoned by British troops since the Union, as if the Scots were a subjugated people. When the rising began, those garrisons retreated behind their defences and stayed, immovable. The Prince was determined to remove this one. A company of the *Écossais Royaux*, sent by King Louis to support the Jacobite forces left in Scotland when the main body invaded England, had arrived from Perth. With them, they brought battering cannon, now being positioned to assault the castle. Every now and then, the garrison inside fired off a shot or two, but the Jacobites were well out of range.

'You think they would've run out by now,' Donald Fraser said. The blacksmith stood at MacGillivray's elbow. They'd begun the siege after taking Glasgow on the way home from England. It was a strange city, Glasgow, small compared to Edinburgh. Its people had rioted twice against the Union, in 1707 and again twenty years ago. Now it grew wealthy. Its merchant ships, no longer hounded by the English navy, plied the New World colonies. Trading in tobacco and sugar, it was the only part of Scotland to benefit from the bastard marriage of their nation. Few of its citizens still opposed the Union. The Jacobite army re-provisioned and left. Now they were mired in a siege at Stirling.

'I think they're cutting shot out of the rock,' MacGillivray answered. 'If we wait long enough, one day, the castle will collapse into the hole they've dug.' He turned to smile wryly at Fraser. 'Then we can all go home.'

It was early morning, the middle of January, but an unusually mild, wet spell. He hadn't heard from Anne since November, when she left him at the border. He could guess where she was, settled with Aeneas in Moy for the winter, peat fire blazing, mulled wine to hand, re-acquainting themselves with married life. Aeneas was a lucky, lucky man. No doubt he knew that now.

'Anne would have found a way in,' he told the blacksmith.

'Or winkled them out,' Fraser grinned.

The exercise was futile. At the Prince's insistence, wanting to keep a toe-hold in England, a Jacobite force had stayed to hold Carlisle. Cumberland's army, smaller than they'd been told, ceased pursuit to besiege it. Two weeks ago, Carlisle had fallen. The siege here was tit-for-tat time-wasting. Hunger and thirst were not weapons for warriors to wield. A man should act, or atrophy. Only twenty-five miles east, Hawley's army now occupied Edinburgh. Cumberland closed behind them. Either they should turn and face him or return home, as planned, to mount a fresh offensive in spring.

Instead, the Prince kept them here. When he wasn't consulting the French engineer about siege engines, he sulked in his quarters with O'Sullivan, drinking. The *Écossais Royaux* had also brought the information that their army *had* been assembled at Dunkirk but dispersed when the Scots turned back from taking London. Lord George now seemed unwilling to confront the Prince with demands for progress. Jacobite numbers were high, increasing all the time, but the Lowlanders were restless, old scores rose among the clans. Soon, they'd be fighting among themselves.

MacGillivray picked up a rock and hurtled it towards the fortress. It rattled into the naked branches of a tree.

'If the Prince wants this castle, he can wait for it,' he said. 'I'm going to ask our regiment if they will pack and go home.'

'You'll only get yes for answer,' Fraser said. 'They're all wanting back to their families, before the worst of the weather breaks.'

They began to walk back to camp. North of them, among trees, was movement, massed ranks. The two men stopped, straining to make out who, or what, came their way.

'Hawley's force from Edinburgh?' Fraser suggested.

'Not from that direction.' MacGillivray shook his head. 'Besides, the scouts would have given us warning.'

The marchers were out of the trees, on to the open carse. The strains of the pipes drifted over the distance. The tune was 'The Auld Stuarts back Again'. Jacobites, then, marching to the rebel song, men and women swathed in tartan, children running along-side. Behind the piper, three riders led them, blue bonnets on each. A tall blond man, wearing feathers, sat on one mount and, opposite, another, less imposing chief. Between them, on a white horse, was it, could it be?

'Anne!' MacGillivray ran, the soft pampooties on his feet scud-ding over the rough grassland, towards her. Before he had covered half the distance, Anne was galloping towards him. She pulled Pibroch up, slid off the horse and into his arms, kissing him, holding him, murmuring his name.

'Are you back to stay?' he asked, leaning back to look into her eyes.

'There is nowhere else I want to be.'

He kissed her again, her mouth, her face, her throat, her hair, holding her tight up against him, feeling the warmth of her body penetrate through his plaid.

When the others reached them, he swung her back up into Pibroch's saddle. She patted the horse's rump, inviting him to ride behind her. He leapt up and wrapped his arms round her like an unskilled rider who needed to hold on.

'Why didn't you send word you were coming?' he asked in her ear.

'George sent a runner. He wanted nothing to leak out.'

They rode into camp between her cousin and brother, seven hundred Farquharsons, McIntoshes and others of Clan Chatton marching behind. George Murray was waiting.

'Perfect timing, Anne,' he smiled.

'Your message was very precise.'

He held back the flap of the campaign tent, ushering them in. The other commanders waited inside – even O'Sullivan languished in a corner – all except the Prince.

172

'Hawley left Edinburgh with his army some days ago,' Lord George explained. 'He's camped at Falkirk, twelve miles away, and means to engage us here, tomorrow or the next day. I have a different plan.'

Joining the Prince's siege had been a feint, designed to seduce Hawley out of the capital on to terrain suitable for Highland warriors. Lord George intended to clear their way home. So far, the hated English general had unwittingly played along. Scotland had its own double agents at work.

After the briefing, MacGillivray walked with Anne to Pibroch.

'I wish you hadn't suggested this,' he said, bending on one knee so that she could use his thigh to step up into the saddle.

'It will help,' she said. 'And I want to see this man close up.' Hawley's reputation as a brute had grown. Edinburgh offered no resistance to his entry, yet he set up gallows in several parts of the city, imprisoned the provost and hanged a number of citizens just for show. As vicious as their commander, his forces smashed every window not lit to celebrate their arrival. The homes of suspected Jacobites had been ransacked for supplies.

'Then be careful, he might know you.'

'He thinks I'm an Amazon,' Anne laughed. Then, seriously, 'I know what I'm doing. It's you that must take care. Don't die now, Alexander.'

'If you're with me, I'm invincible.'

'Just watch your back this time.' She slapped the reins and rode away.

MacGillivray watched her go. All he had to do was survive. As had she, as had she. He walked back to his mobilizing troops.

It was a ten-mile ride eastwards from the Stirling encampment to Falkirk. The market town lay midway between the cities of Edinburgh and Glasgow, twenty-five miles from each. Following Lord Kilmarnock's instructions, Anne skirted the southern edge of it, high up on moorland. Down below, she could see Hawley's tents, his army camped on a flat plain between the rising ground and the town beyond. When she reached the burn the earl had described, she followed its course downhill through forest to the edge of Callendar estate, on the town's east side. Among the trees, she tied Pibroch in a clearing, comfortably loose so he could crop and reach the stream. Walking on down through the wood, she soon found the path that led to the rear of Callendar House and the door to its kitchens. Kitchens were safe entry points; people came and went all the time, nobody noticed. Even the cook, sitting with his feet up on the hearth, barely glanced at her. The housekeeper was another matter.

'What kin we dae for you?' she snipped, the minute she clapped eyes on Anne.

'I've a message from the earl,' Anne said, quietly, putting a finger to her lips to forestall the woman's shriek. 'Could you find some excuse to fetch your mistress down?'

'I'll gang and tell her there's a worry in the kitchen I cannae deal wi,' the woman fluttered.

While she was gone, Anne crossed her fingers and stood near the door, in case. It was only minutes till the countess appeared, pale with alarm, rushing over the stone floor, to grab Anne's arm.

'What dae you ken of my husband?'

'It's all right,' Anne said, quickly. 'Lord Kilmarnock is well and sends his regards. I'm to ask you to prepare a very special meal, a generous one, and it needs to be done now.'

'But we ay eat frugally at midday,' the countess puzzled, frowning. 'And, lassie, you're Highland. Dae ye no ken the danger ye're in?'

'You have General Hawley and his aides lodging here,' Anne said. 'So, yes, I know the danger. That's why I've come.'

'And you are?'

'Anne Farquharson, the Lady M<sup>c</sup>Intosh.'

The countess gaped. Her nervous housekeeper flushed, immediately embarrassed at mistaking their intruder's status, then her mouth fell open as the name registered. Even the cook, who'd been listening with little interest, jumped to his feet, sending the kettle clattering on the hearth.

'Then you maun be Colonel Anne!' the countess exclaimed. 'And in mair danger. The general and his aides are just up yon stair.'

'But he'll no ken it's me,' Anne said, trying out the local brogue she had learned from wee Clementina and the folk of Edinburgh. Now was as good a time as any to practise it. The countess shook her head.

'Lassie, that'll no pass.'

'It would with an Englishman,' Anne grinned. 'We likely aw sound the same tae him.' She became serious. 'I'd like to have a look at your guest and would serve or stay in the kitchens,' she said. 'But I'll go if it endangers you.'

'You'll gang naewhaur,' the countess said. 'It'll take baith oor wits tae get this dinner thegither.'

The kitchen was poorly stocked, the impoverishment of the estate one reason why the Kilmarnocks supported the rebellion. The housekeeper, kitchen girl and upstairs maid were all sent out to the grounds, running, to raid the gardens, dovecot, loch and home farm for ingredients. The boot-boy ran into town to beg, borrow and, as a last resort, buy. As the cook banged his pots and rattled out instructions, Anne rolled up her sleeves to help skin, chop, slice, stuff, flour and stir. Even the countess joined in. When it was done, she splashed her face with cold water to cool it, then bid Anne do the same.

'Efter aw that,' she said, 'ye deserve yer dinner.' And she led Anne up the servants' stair to her own rooms to prepare.

Lady Anne Livingstone was Countess of Kilmarnock through her marriage and, in her own right, Countess of Linlithgow, and of Callandar. Her aunt, the Countess of Erroll, was chief of Clan Hay and, as Lord High Constable, held the highest status in Scotland, supreme officer of the Scottish army, second only to the Crown. Lady Livingstone was her heir and, like her powerful, elderly aunt who had sent troops to support the cause, she was a staunch Jacobite who persuaded her husband to join the rebels. Reluctantly, she had accepted her oldest son should take the careful precaution of joining the government troops. Now she was beginning to enjoy herself.

'When we gang doon, say as little as ye kin help,' she instructed as she dressed Anne's hair. 'That Highland lilt will gie ye awa for sure if ye talk ower much.'

In the dining room, aides milled about, waiting. The general stood with his back to the women as they entered, studying Kilmarnock's portrait on the wall. Anne recognized him at once as the same general who'd been enraged that Aeneas had hanged Ewan. Hawley's reaction to the cottar's death didn't fit with the stories she'd heard of him since, a man fond of using the gallows. Aeneas wasn't just *with* the enemy now, he *was* the enemy, uncaring, brutal, inhumane. The two of them clearly deserved each other.

'Your husband is with the rebels,' Hawley said, addressing his hostess without turning.

'He is,' the countess answered, 'and my son is with you.'

Lord Boyd had turned to greet his mother as she came in. He was now looking at Anne.

'Lady Forbes,' the countess lied, using Anne's stepmother's name to introduce her to the company. 'Jean. She's come new tae the toon. My son, James.'

Lord Boyd bowed. He was not fooled, not for a moment, but he couldn't guess what his mother was up to or who their guest really was, and took his seat. The other aides were English and even less likely to suspect anything was unusual. Hawley barely looked at Anne. Instead, he studied the food. The table was laden with dishes: crowdie and cockaleekie soups, brown trout with shallots baked in butter, salmon with cream and parsley sauce, thick venison stew, grouse with rowan jelly, stovies, glazed swedes, steamed beets, pickled artichokes, onions stuffed with duck liver, thin barley bread, oatcakes, soft cottage cheeses, baked syrup apples with wild almonds, fruit jams and jellies, gingerbread, seed cake and a variety of sweet tarts.

'You eat well in Falkirk,' Hawley said, seating himself.

'We dae,' the countess agreed. 'Though no often wi an army oan the doorstep.'

Anne dipped her head, hiding her smile with a pretended interest in her soup.

'We'll leave soon,' Hawley said, 'to relieve Stirling. The rebels besiege the castle. It will be their final act.'

The meal continued. Anne said little, though every time she spoke, young Lord Boyd glanced at her and blushed. She flashed him a smile when he did, which only caused him to blush more. One day he would be High Constable of Scotland, inheriting three earldoms through his mother and one from his father. She wondered if he genuinely supported the government or if father and son simply hedged each other's bets. It might not be too long before she found that out.

For a skinny man, Hawley ate greedily, tearing at meat with his teeth, chewing audibly, gulping ale. His mean spirit must prevent fat settling on his bones, Anne decided. The man had no conversation, mostly grunts, and she daren't lighten the company. That was left to the countess and Hawley's aides. Eventually, they rose. They had been at table for two hours, more than long enough. Idly, Anne took her glass of sweet wine to the window and gazed out. The sky had grown dull and heavy with dark rain clouds. Wind buffeted the glass. Spots began to spit on it, multiplying rapidly.

'Thae soldiers oan the brae will be yours then,' she said.

'What?' Hawley asked.

'I didnae ken ye had so many in plaids.'

She had said too much. Lord Boyd excused himself and headed outside. It only mattered now if he returned to denounce her.

'My army is camped on Bantaskin flats,' Hawley sneered, 'as it would be. Artillery isn't drawn up and down hills without cause.' He glanced briefly out of the window. A hard rain scudded along, skelped by wind. 'Those will be estate workers.'

'Would ye care for a drink of tea, General?' the countess asked. 'I'm telt it's a particular like of London.'

'Not of mine,' Hawley said. 'A glass of brandy, if you have any.'

As the countess obliged, Lord Boyd came hurrying back in.

'General, sir, you'd better come quickly,' he said, glancing at Anne, too much a gentleman to betray her, too much a caring son to reveal his mother's part in this. 'The Jacobite army is up on the moor.'

The other aides rushed outside. Hawley became angry at the fuss.

'You've seen the same workers as this woman.' He waved rudely at Anne. 'The rebels won't advance. Not on a superior force.' He took his brandy from the countess. 'Your son should learn the art of war.'

'You'll hae much tae teach him,' she smiled.

One of the aides rushed back in, his uniform wet, his face chalk-white.

'General,' he reported, 'the rebels are indeed up on the hill, lining up for battle, and above our troops! Can't you hear?'

Anne threw the casement window open. Above the battering wind and rain, the sound of the pipes skirled in.

# TWENTY-TWO

Hawley galloped into his camp, his aides beside him, a napkin from the meal still at his throat. He ordered the artillery up on to the moor, but the rain had softened the ground at the hillfoot. The big guns became mired and stuck, wheels churning in the mud. Screaming orders at his troops, Hawley urged the dragoons and infantry up the slope. In possession of the high ground above them, the rebels waited, lined and blocked.

The redcoats struggled up the hill against the blustering storm, forming their lines east of the enemy, on lower ground. The two armies faced each other, neither with artillery. The Jacobites' few pieces maintained the siege at Stirling. Hawley's lay at the bottom of the slope, a slope that still favoured the Jacobites. Wind and rain squalled at their backs, blasting down into the government soldiers' faces.

Hawley grabbed a telescope from an aide and scanned the enemy lines: the barbaric tribes to the front; Lord George commanding the right flank; no command on the left; far in the rear, with the Irish Piquets and *Écossais Royaux* as reserves, the Pretender Prince. There was no sign, anywhere, of a wild warrior woman riding a white horse. His supreme confidence in himself, rattled by the enemy's unexpected advance, returned. His force outnumbered the rebels by about a thousand regular troops. He could easily negate the disadvantage of the incline. The Highlanders who fronted Lord George's formation could not face horses. One charge would dispel them. He brought the cavalry up front.

Seeing the enemy horse move forward, Lord George sent out the order to hold steady. His numbers were less than he'd hoped. The Prince had insisted two thousand stay at Stirling to maintain the siege. O'Sullivan had not yet appeared to command the left wing, leaving those chiefs without direction. Volleys of musket fire began from the enemy lines. Out of range, it was pointless, could only be intended to deter a charge before the cavalry were fully positioned.

'Hold fast! Hold fast!' Lord George shouted. Even over the buffeting wind, he could hear the click of misfires, due to the rain, among the government guns. The storm was with the Jacobites, their pistols shielded from the wet by their bodies.

The order to hold fast repeated along the lines. Tense with frustration, the Highlanders stood.

'Why do we not go?' Fraser asked MacGillivray. They were ready, eager for it.

'George knows what he's doing.' MacGillivray was grim, taut. He watched the government horse line up. Dragoons had the advantage of slashing down. The upward stroke of a broadsword to a mounted opponent had far less force. They were also close-ranked, without space to walk between them. If they came up like that, there would be no room among them to swing a sword.

Lord George drew his pistol. The Highlanders scrugged bonnets and drew theirs.

'Forward together, march!' Lord George yelled.

This was different. He wanted them in tight formation, no wild charge. MacGillivray was puzzled. Roaring Highlanders rushing at them might have spooked the animals into kicking or running off. If he was to risk being ridden down, he'd rather have a claymore than a pistol in his hand and take the chance he could behead the beast then stake its fallen rider. But he obeyed the order, setting the required marching speed, aware of the nervous tension in his warriors, a step behind him. Their whole front line marched forward *en masse* towards the waiting horse. Seeing the clans come down the hill, the dragoons below spurred forward, riding up towards them, keeping their tight formation and very quickly at full trot.

Marching beside MacGillivray, MacBean tucked his plaid tighter round his girth.

'Here they come,' he muttered.

As the gap closed, Lord George ordered halt, aim, fire. The pistols were discharged. The volley took almost half the dragoons off their horses. Some, the wounded or frightened, broke away, cantering off the field. Riderless animals followed. The others kept coming, picking up the pace to a gallop.

'Dirks,' MacGillivray shouted, drawing his own and holding it up so those behind could see in the pelting rain. 'Down!' he yelled, throwing himself on to his side on the sodden ground. From MacDonalds to Murrays, the whole front line dropped, curled, foetus-like. The ground shook with the thunder of hooves.

As the horses reached the row of human obstacles, they leaped to clear them. Twisting round, MacGillivray thrust his dirk up into the belly of the beast above him, rolling out from underneath as it squealed and staggered. All around, the other clansmen followed suit. Blood spurted, animals shrieked then toppled. The Highlanders strove to avoid flailing hooves and falling beasts, rising, if they still could, to deal with downed riders. Upright again, MacGillivray grabbed the dragoon he'd unseated and slit his throat. A weight thumped against his back, bringing him down, hard, a struggling horse on top of him, the breath forced out of his lungs. He gasped, but no air filled his chest. With one arm trapped, he couldn't rise enough. Legs scrabbling, he tried to bring his knees up to push. His back refused to arch under the heavy weight. His lungs burned.

The Jacobite second line had swung into action, slashing at any animal still standing, dispatching dragoons. Horses screamed and whinnied, kicking out. Donald Fraser ran to his chief and, with old MacBean's help, dragged him from under the dying beast. On his knees, MacGillivray drew in sweet, deep breaths. While he recovered, Fraser and MacBean stood guard. It was unnecessary. The cavalry charge was over. The surviving dragoons turned and fled on foot. Now the Jacobites could use their swords. MacGillivray got to his feet.

'Claymore!' The cry went up. Blades flashed. War cries roared. The Highland charge rushed forwards.

Lord George had hoped to keep good order but, without a

commander on the left flank, that was impossible. The MacDonalds, Camerons, McIntoshes and Farquharsons were off, tearing into the ranks of foot. Some chased fleeing dragoons down the hill past groups of locals who sheltered under trees, watching the battle.

Fighting in the centre, Clan Chatton parried bayonets with targes, cutting and slashing their way through the English infantry. As tight together as they dared for fear of wounding each other, they chopped and hacked, while bodies fell before them. In the thick of it, Duff, the Edinburgh shoemaker, wondered how he came to be here. A bayonet thrust towards him. He ducked aside. From behind him, a pitchfork speared the hapless redcoat. It was Meg, grinning with gap-toothed glee. The government lines broke. Whole companies ran from the field. Jacobites chased after them. With his right wing still battling those companies that held fast, the disorder of the left wing was exactly what Lord George had feared. Without O'Sullivan to constrain them, clan after clan broke away to pursue the deserters.

'Stop pursuit!' Lord George ordered.

Kilmarnock rode out from the rear, galloping after the scattered Highlanders to relay the order.

'We should sound the retreat, sir,' Lord Boyd prompted, for the second time. They had retired from the hill when the dragoons fled. 'The Highlanders won't stop fighting till we do.'

Hawley would not give the order. He sat on his black horse, telescope abandoned across his lap, grimly watching the rout of his forces. The battle was over, lost in twenty minutes. Cope would enjoy hearing of this. Cope would be laughing now. Cope would be a rich man, calling in their bet. He, Henry Hawley, would be ruined and disgraced. His only comfort was that no woman had a hand in his defeat. At least he could not be taunted with that.

In deepest misery, he led his officers back to camp to fire their tents before making their escape. While hundreds of his soldiers surrendered to Lord George, only one prisoner was brought before him. Dishevelled, his hat lost, after falling when his horse stumbled as he galloped to constrain exuberant Jacobites, long hair tumbling over his face. Hawley knew that face from the portrait that hung in Callendar House. It was the Earl of Kilmarnock.

'I hope you enjoyed the hospitality of my home, General,' Kilmarnock said.

Hawley glared down at him. The man seemed amused, despite his situation, as if he was aware that the extensive dinner had prevented the earlier discovery of the Jacobite army.

'Your wife might have some explaining to do,' he spat.

'The countess is generous,' Kilmarnock smiled, 'particularly to guests such as yourself and Anne Farquharson.'

'Farquharson?' Hawley frowned, the name rang a bell but not the right one. 'Forbes, she said.'

Kilmarnock shook his head.

'You must have misheard. It was Lady M<sup>c</sup>Intosh, *Colonel Anne* Farquharson.'

A titter ran round the surrounding aides, quickly stifled. A dark flush spread over Hawley's pallid face. He snatched up the telescope and swung it. It cracked into two pieces across the side of the earl's head, bruising his cheekbone and splitting the skin at his eyebrow. Kilmarnock staggered. Blood trickled into his eye.

'Bring the prisoner,' Hawley snarled, wheeling around towards the road for Edinburgh.

Lord Boyd slid off his horse, took off his hat and walked over to the captive.

'Father,' he nodded. He pushed the older man's blood-spattered hair back and covered his parent's bare head with his own hat.

MacGillivray was chest deep in the waters of Callendar loch, scrubbing blood and bits of other men's flesh off himself. The sky had cleared hours ago, blowing away the rain, the winter sun low on the horizon. Behind him, on the bank, lay his discarded shirt, plaid and weapons. To the west, the sky glowed pink and gold. The cold water eased his cuts and grazes, a bayonet had nicked his forearm, the fallen horse had bruised his ribs. As he doused his head and scrubbed, he sang:

'Up and scour awa, Hawley, up and scour awa.'

Lord George had ridden on into the town, taking the Prince to safe lodging. There were small pockets of lost government troops to be flushed out, groups of their own roving Highlanders to be brought back under command, but Falkirk was theirs. Hawley's attempt to fire his tents was defeated by the rain. His guns, baggage and supply wagons were captured. MacGillivray had gathered his own warriors, directing them to shelter. Now he was alone, exuberant, adrenalin still coursing through his veins. The words he'd heard the Lowlanders singing on the hill birled in his brain.

'The Hielan dirk is at your doup and that's the Hielan law,' he sang, splashing noisily and ducking below the water again.

Behind him, from the bank, the shining tip of a sword, lethal and menacing, thrust out over the water towards him. As he straightened up, it paused behind his shoulder.

'Hielan Geordie's at your tail, wi Drummond, Perth and aw.' He sang on, oblivious.

The sword tip rose, level to his shoulder, at the side of his neck.

'Had you but stayed wi ladies maid an hour or maybe twa . . .'

The sword tapped him on the shoulder. He turned his head, looking down, saw the blade, spun round. The sword tipped under his chin. Anne was on the bank, arm stretched out, wielding it. The range was useless. All he had to do was step backwards. But she'd made her point. A speared Lochaber axe could have run him through.

'Is that you watching your back?' she asked.

'Washing it,' he grinned. 'Come on in. Give me a hand.'

'I will not. It must be freezing.'

'Not where I am.' He grinned wider. 'Hotter'n hell.'

Anne smiled, plunged the blade into the banking, unbelted the *arasaid* she had over her dress and let it fall. She bent, patted it.

'*Trobhad,*' she invited. 'You come out.'

He took two steps towards her. The water level dropped to his navel. He stopped.

'Will you hold out my plaid?'

'I'm not touching that,' she said. 'It will be bloody.'

'It's fresh and dry,' he protested. 'I got it clean from supplies.'

'And did you also get shy?' she asked. She held her hand out, not the plaid. '*Trobhad!* Come on, out.'

He gripped her hand, firmly, and winked. Then he pulled, using his other hand to push her at the waist so she flew on past him and splashed into the deeper water behind. Laughing, he turned round.

'Let that be a lesson to you,' he chuckled.

Her dress ballooned on the surface. He waded over, caught the material to help her upright, but all he gripped was wet cloth. He searched the sodden folds for firm limbs. The dress was empty. He pulled it up, dropped it, spun round, looking. Under the water, bubbles rose at his back. He felt teeth nip his buttocks. A laugh burst from him, but then his knee was kicked from behind and he went down. Anne broke the surface, naked, looking for him. He rose a few feet away and spouted water at her from his mouth.

'It *is* freezing,' she giggled, sweeping water back at him. He slid under the surface again, coming up behind her.

'A back worth watching,' he said, reaching out, running his fingers down her spine. She turned round, her wet breasts brushing his bare chest. The game was over. Their eyes met and held. She slid her arms round his neck. In the chest-deep water, their bodies pressed together. Their mouths met and kissed, and kissed.

He swung her up, still kissing, carried her to the bank. Keeping her tight to him, he laid them both down on her *arasaid*, reached out and pulled his plaid over them, rolling them over twice so they were bundled together. Inside the warm tartan, they kissed each other's chilled skin, mouths, faces, throats, until heat grew in them. Words of desire and love murmured between them as hands and tongues explored every part of each other they could reach. The world blotted out. There was only sensation, overpowering, her parted thighs astride him, his hands on her buttocks, her hips raised, guiding him, the thrust down. A hundred times he might have spoken her name but never did it cry from him like this. In the steamy dampness of hot, wet skin, blanketed together, bound the length of them, arms, legs, hearts, hopes and lives, when he finally rolled them over, driving for release, it was him she cried out for, his name she spoke.

'Alexander,' she moaned. '*Mo chridhe*, my love.'

Bells rang out all over Edinburgh, celebrating the victory. Whose victory, no one was certain. The first rider, a terrified dragoon, declared for the Jacobites, the second for the government, a third that it was indecisive, a fourth hailed the rebels. The citizens had suffered under Hangman Hawley before he and his ruffians departed to give battle. Now they were determined to be seen, and heard, siding with the winner. Prince or general, one or other would surely arrive soon, triumphant, to reclaim the capital. Provost Stewart remained a prisoner in the Tolbooth, where Hawley had consigned him, and could not be released till then. City business was conducted from his cell. It was stuffed to the gunnels with the bailies, all of them fussing.

'Weel, if it's the Jacobites hae won,' one of them said, 'you'll be let oot and we kin get back tae the city chambers.'

'If it's the government,' Provost Stewart said, 'Hawley will hear hoo pleased we are tae be free fae the rebels and maybe let me oot anyroad.'

'Mair important,' grumbled another, 'his lot might no break the windaes this time.'

'We'll ken soon enough,' the provost reassured them. 'The victors will come here tae announce theirsells.'

'And if it's the Prince –' a third bailie rubbed his hands, counting the profit that would come from royal favour '– we've made a better showin in support of him than Glasgow ever did.'

The door of the cell was flung back with a clang against the stone wall. General Hawley, despite his lack of stature, filled the doorway.

'Who ordered the bells rung?' he roared.

A dozen faces fell. Twelve bulky bailies endeavoured to melt into the walls. Trembling, Provost Stewart got to his feet.

'We wantit tae commend yer triumph, sir,' his voice wavered. Hawley did not have the look of a conquering hero about him. 'Maybe we are a bit previous . . .'

Hawley grabbed him by the throat.

'Previous?' he snarled.

'If it's the noise ye dinnae like –' the provost was turning purple '– Bailie Jamieson there'll have it stopped.'

Bailie Jamieson slid round the door and vanished. Whether he was heading for the bells or making his escape was debatable. Hawley let go of the provost's collar.

'Get out,' he said. 'All of you. Get out.'

The members of Edinburgh council did not have to be told twice. As fast as their portly bulks and the small cell door would allow, they were out, and scurrying up the High Street.

'What happened there, ye think?' asked one.

'Did they win or no?' asked another.

'Wha cares?' the provost said. 'We're oot, and withoot oor necks stretched.'

One by one the city bells fell silent. Hawley consigned Kilmarnock to the castle dungeon, put a guard on the provost to make sure he didn't escape the town and filled the Tolbooth with other men, his own. Any deserters he could identify, and the junior officers who'd failed to keep control on the field, were court-martialled and sentenced to hang. For the next two weeks, the gallows he'd erected on his last visit were kept busy. Sixty were dispatched before he was interrupted.

# TWENTY-THREE

William Augustus, Duke of Cumberland, rode into Edinburgh looking every inch the conquering hero he intended to become. Fifes and drums, immaculate cavalry, scarlet coats and gold braid accompanied him. The city bells rang out again, with expedient fervour. Folk lined the streets to see this younger son of King George. Comparisons with the bonnier Prince Charlie were passed in whispers. The Duke nodded to the crowds, but he had little time for the backwater of Scotland or its whining inhabitants. His father had ordered him to crush the Scots.

'If none remain,' Pelham, the government leader, had added, 'it will be no loss.'

Cumberland had come to stamp out the rebellion. His princely cousin had made a first mistake, turning back from London at Derby. His second was returning to besiege Stirling after Falkirk, when he could have routed Hawley's army, taken the capital and held Scotland. Instead, he left his enemy a foothold. The Jacobite command, so far invincible, had its weaknesses. They could be exploited, a third mistake encouraged.

'You let me down, Henry,' Cumberland said, carefully controlling his temper. Hawley was a favourite of the king. 'And I'm hearing rumours I do not like the sound of.'

They were in the state room at Holyrood Palace. Hawley paced about. Cope sat to one side, wealthier by £20,000, vindicated, calm, playing with a folded-paper caricature of Colonel Anne. He was the only man who'd have dared repeat the gossip to the Duke.

'That woman, that bloody rebel, had nothing to do with it!' Hawley lied. 'We had the bitch of a storm in our faces. The guns stuck and couldn't be put in use, and they had the advantage of the ground.'

'So, if I order up a storm at my back,' Cumberland mocked,

'and turn the ground to my advantage, these half-naked barbarians can be beaten?'

Cope leant forward, benignly. He could afford to be generous.

'Personally, I'd put my money on artillery,' he said, 'though suitable ground wouldn't hurt.'

'We'll leave betting aside.' Cumberland's purse was also lighter by this defeat. 'Defeating them is required. Severe miscalculations have been made. These loutish savages can fight. They're well-organized, daring, audacious.'

'And ill-disciplined,' Hawley burst out.

'The way they took down your horse?' Cumberland corrected. 'I think not.' It was said Hawley was a by-blow of the king. That being so, the Duke would have wished for a brighter half-brother. His viciousness was all Hawley had to commend him, if it was directed to the right foe. 'I want to know their strengths and their failings. I want to know who commands, who can be bought, who ignored. This time, we will take our time. So –' he paused, leant back and considered both generals '– bearing in mind there is more than one way to skin a cat, I want a plan.'

In the clearing among the trees, Anne knelt by a headstone, brushing ice and moss off the words with her fingers. 'John Farquharson of Invercauld. Died 1738', it read, and below, 'Beloved wife, Margaret Murray, died in childbirth 1725'. She had brought a white cockade to put on the grave.

'We're winning,' she whispered. 'I wish you could know. I'm doing all I can.'

Doubts had haunted her last visit home, over Aeneas, over the venture into England. Now they were gone. A chicken scurried off from the clump of grass beside the stone, clucking. Anne parted the icy blades to reveal a large brown egg, still warm. Chickens, like people, were creatures of habit. She smiled, picked up the egg and stood.

As she crossed the yard, a horse clattered into it, MacGillivray on its back. Seeing her by the trees, he rode over, slid off and wrapped her in his arms.

'The pass is too risky,' he said. 'We should go round, and soon. Before the snow comes.'

'We'll go now.' She looked at him, thoughtfully. Doubt never troubled Alexander. She'd never known him hesitate, as if the light of clear reason always lit the path he should take. 'Why do you fight?'

'How else can we survive?'

'I wondered if you chase your own hopes and dreams, or those of others.'

'You think I fight because you asked me to?'

'Because we grew up with it. Would we think, and do, the same if we hadn't?'

'We would. Our ancestors put freedom above life, above god and king. The men who sold us into the Union dishonoured them. But, if we choose to stay enslaved, the shame is ours.'

'Others don't think so.'

'Aeneas, you mean?'

'No.' She put her hand over his mouth. 'Don't speak his name. That's finished.'

He kissed her fingertips, moved her hand to lie on his chest, above his heart.

'If you mean the Scots who're still against us, they fear what they might lose. Their lives, land, trade.' He shrugged. 'What England gives, it can take away.'

She would never understand. There was no pride, no dignity, in subjugation. Without self-respect, both nation and people were poor things, and the poor had nothing but poverty to lose. Did they have no faith in themselves?

'The Kirk threatens their immortal souls, if they join us.' She could feel his heart beat against her palm and moved her hand inside his plaid, against his shirt, to feel it better. When she was this close, this close to the pulse of life and vigour in him, the loneliness went away.

'Then they deserve immortality,' he said. 'They pay dearly for it. No song, dance or coupling.' He pulled her tight. 'I would rather this life, however short.'

'I have an egg in my hand,' she warned.

He nuzzled her neck.

'Let's see if you can hold it without breaking.'

'So that's why you fight,' she teased. 'To sing, dance and fuck.'

'To spend my male urges between your thighs –' he nipped the lobe of her ear with his teeth '– is this not why the world was made? Can you think of a better cause?'

'It's cold. Be serious.'

'Anne,' he leant back and looked into her eyes. 'If it wasn't cold, this would be serious indeed. Ice is forming under my kilt. And that is no state for a man to be in when his passion is aroused.'

They were still laughing when they fell in the door of Invercauld together. Lady Farquharson glared at the pair of them.

'Can't you two grow up?'

'We will, we will,' Anne promised.

'We just won't grow old,' MacGillivray grinned, turning his back to the fire and raising his kilt to heat his naked backside. Anne giggled.

'I don't know if I should let Elizabeth go with you,' her step-mother grumbled.

'But she begged to come, last time I was home.' Anne said. 'Where is she now?'

'Out the back, putting every piece she possesses on the cart.'

'Good. We need to get away before the cloud breaks.'

'I don't know.' Lady Farquharson sighed. 'You're just here and you're off again.'

'We only stopped to pick up Elizabeth.'

'And will Francis and your brother be home soon?'

'They will,' Anne assured her, 'with the rest of our troops.'

The Prince had been persuaded to give up besieging Stirling and come north when Cumberland reached Edinburgh. Anne had left earlier, a week after the battle, when all the prisoners had been paroled. She brought half her own company with her as bodyguards but had sent them on ahead to Auchterblair. She and MacGillivray would spend the night with them there. It would be the next day or soon after, at Moy, that she could expect trouble. Lord Louden still held Inverness. Hawley had not taken the Black Watch companies south with him. That meant the Jacobites would have Louden to contend with when they returned and, along with his forces, Aeneas.

Lady Farquharson stopped stitching the white ribbon into yet another cockade and considered Anne. 'I don't suppose you brought any of that snuff back with you?'

'No, I'm sorry.' Anne bit her lip, trying not to laugh. 'I didn't get to Edinburgh this time.'

'My little box is quite empty.' Her stepmother turned back to her sewing, hiding her disappointment.

'Next time, I promise.'

'It really is rather good for clearing the head.' She glanced at MacGillivray, then at Anne again. 'You should try it,' she said.

As they slept, a few inches of snow fell. The world changed overnight into its quiet winter shroud. In the morning, Anne and her party set out early from Auchterblair. Wrapped against the chill, Elizabeth begged to ride behind MacGillivray rather than in the wagon.

'He'll keep the cold off,' she pointed out, clambering up behind him from the wagon step when he nodded yes. Her space in the cart was taken by a woman with a young child, who could now sit on her lap. Elizabeth tucked herself tight in at MacGillivray's back, arms round his waist, head rested on his back. She was pleased he'd arrived home with Anne this time. Now she could make sure he noticed her. She'd never quite got over the desire for him she experienced after he fished her out of Moy loch. He was one of the more marriageable chiefs, and it was time she had a home of her own to run. Surely, by now, he would be looking for a wife.

They set off, white smoky breath puffing damp clouds into the crisp, clear air. The horses' hooves crunched in the snow, the wagon wheels creaked through it and, behind, the march of several hundred feet crump-crumped along. Every now and then, they'd stop, scrape snow out of the horses' hooves, clear the wagon wheels, kick ice off their shoe soles and go on again. It was very boring. Elizabeth cuddled into MacGillivray. She wondered how long it was since he'd had sex. Probably not long. He was the kind of man to inspire lust in women.

She thought about Dauvit and all she'd learned about how to please a man and how to please herself. Anne was right. The diviner was a good teacher. However many *Sasannach* women had lain down with MacGillivray, she knew she could surprise him. She pressed her cheek into his plaid, between his shoulder blades. He was broad-shouldered, strong. She could feel his muscles moving under the cloth as he guided the horse. His taut abdomen shifted against her gloved hands with every stride.

He and Anne, riding side by side, talked about war and troops and arrangements. Elizabeth thought of love, warm skin and rumpled sheets, white like the snow-laden landscape but infinitely more fun. She hitched her hips closer and tighter against Mac-Gillivray's buttocks and felt him tense. Even though his plaid was tucked around and beneath him, he was aware. She moved her upper body, enough so he would know it was her breasts that shifted against his back. They were not far from Moy. Flat white flakes of snow began to fall. Her breath, hotter, came faster. She shifted her gloved hands higher, drawing them back to his waist. Perhaps, if she removed the gloves, she could warm her hands inside his plaid.

'Snow stop!' MacGillivray called, pulling the horse up.

It didn't seem that long since the last one. Snowflakes drifted against Elizabeth's hot cheek, melting instantly. MacGillivray jumped down, drew his dirk and picked out Anne's horse's hooves quickly and efficiently. Then he turned to his own but, instead of bending to lift the horse's foot, he plunged his dirk into the ground and reached up. His hands gripped Elizabeth by the waist. With one quick swing he had her down off the horse. Was he going to kiss her? His head tipped forwards, his hands tightened round her waist, he let his knees bend and, with another quick swing, hoisted her up, up behind Anne.

'Your sister's on heat,' he said to Anne, by way of explanation. 'You go ahead, we'll catch up.'

Anne urged Pibroch forwards. She seemed to be trembling. Elizabeth pressed against her, mouth close to Anne's ear so she would hear.

'What's wrong with him? And why are you shaking?'

'Oh, Elizabeth,' Anne spluttered, laughing. 'Can't you behave?'

'You sound like Mother. Does he like men now, is that it?'

'*Isd, no!* Can't you guess? He's with me.'

'What does that mean?' Elizabeth sat back, shocked. '*Na can sin!*' She thumped her fist against her sister's back. 'You told me you weren't!'

'When was that?'

'Last time you were home.' Elizabeth was furious. 'I asked. You said not.'

'That was then,' Anne chuckled. 'Things change.'

'So he was in your bed last night, at Auchterblair?'

'Yes.'

Elizabeth slumped. It wasn't fair. Anne had a husband.

'Then I hope it's just for fun,' she grumbled.

'Now who sounds like mother?'

They crumped into the snowy yard at Moy, and were off the horse, kicking their boots at the door before Will realized he was needed and appeared, running from the kitchen, stumbling through the drifts.

'It's all right, Will.' Anne stopped his apology. 'Who's at home?'

'Just the Dowager,' the lad said. 'Just like last time.'

MacGillivray and the others were only a few yards behind.

'You're still a married woman,' Elizabeth hissed at Anne as they went inside. 'You have to realize that makes him fair game.'

Anne grinned, as if it was a joke.

'I think you'd be wasting your time,' she said. 'But don't let me stop you.'

Elizabeth grabbed her sister's cloak, stopping her in the hall. 'You mean that?'

'Look,' Anne smiled. 'If Alexander wanted you, how could I be in the way? I'd be happy for you both.' She took her cloak off and hung it up. 'I just don't think he will, that's all.'

The Dowager was coming down the stairs. She stopped with surprise to see them, then hurried down. 'Anne, *a ghràidh!*' she cried.

Elizabeth took her own cloak off, a slow smile spreading on her face. So he wasn't forbidden. He would just need persuading, that was all.

# TWENTY-FOUR

The Dowager was certain Moy was safe. Military duties kept Aeneas busy at Fort George. Louden's troops harassed known Jacobites but would not raid Moy, not with the M<sup>c</sup>Intosh chief among their commanders. Anne's bodyguards returned to their homes or billeted themselves with friends or family in the surrounding cotts. The night was set aside for storytelling. This time there were six around the fire and two storytellers, Anne and MacGillivray. Outside, the snow had stopped. Inside, logs sparked in the grate. Plates of food steamed on the low table by the fire. Tankards of ale were topped up. There was the journey to Derby and a second battle to hear about, but the beginning was the place to start. For MacGillivray, that was just across the border, when they first tried to befriend the English. He had sent Donald Fraser to billet with a Carlisle blacksmith, thinking they'd have much in common.

'So Donald goes in the house, dirk in hand in case there's any opposition waiting for him. But the smith has fled. There's only the wife and her grown daughter, cowering in a corner, shrieking fit to burst. He tries talking to them but, of course, he only has the Gaelic.'

'Which they wouldn't understand,' Anne added.

'Not a word of it. So, to show he means no harm, he stabs his dirk into the table, out of harm's way. This only has the two women squealing louder.'

'What does Donald do then?' Jessie's eyes shone with eagerness.

'He did the friendliest thing he could think of.' MacGillivray laughed. 'And, seeing it had worked in Edinburgh, was bound to work again. He danced.'

'Danced?' The Dowager snorted.

'*Seadh*. He starts diddling, puts his hands up, and he does the Highland fling all around the room.'

'Did that do the trick?' Will asked, expectantly.

'Not a bit of it,' MacGillivray chuckled. 'The mother fell to her knees and started to pray, crying to God as hard and as loud as she could. The daughter wept, sobbing and shrieking.'

'So did he stop?' Elizabeth asked.

MacGillivray shook his head, near convulsed with laughter.

'No, he diddled all the louder, thinking he just wasn't getting through to them, and he grabs the girl's hand, trying to get her to join in.' He drew a deep breath, holding his chest to still his humour. 'We were still outside, allocating the others to different houses. The noise was woeful. I had to go in and drag him out, still dancing.'

He broke down then, laughing till tears ran, the others likewise, hanging on to their stomachs, roaring themselves helpless with laughter.

'They must have thought,' Anne hooted, 'that it was some kind of tribal ritual. What with his dirk in the table.'

'And him dancing round it,' Elizabeth shrieked.

'That he was about to carve them up,' Jessie laughed.

'And have them for supper!' Will hollered.

'Oh, dear.' The Dowager dried her eyes. 'I need more ale.'

The night wore on. Not all of the stories were funny. There were some losses, and the Prince's petulance and lack of heroism disappointed the listeners. But it ended with a victory. They all toasted Falkirk and the cause.

'I didn't see Clementina there.' Anne frowned at MacGillivray. 'The beggar girl from Edinburgh?' He still looked blank. 'The one who showed us the way through the marsh at Prestonpans?'

MacGillivray recalled her now.

'She didn't come back, stayed behind with her father at Carlisle. He'd turned his ankle and couldn't march home. But I fancy the truth of it was he'd grown sweet on the widow woman he was billeted with.'

'Then Cumberland has captured them.' Anne was distressed. It was because she'd given them money that the girl was there.

'If an act of kindness can be blamed.' MacGillivray took her hand and squeezed it. 'Cumberland won't detain children, or women either, for that matter. They might even parole most of the men.'

'So she could be safe home by now?'

'Or with a new mother and still in Carlisle.'

Anne wanted to kiss him for the comfort he offered, but she refrained. The Dowager was watching and Anne did not feel ready to state her rejection of Aeneas yet, not with so many for company. She let go of MacGillivray's hand and lifted her ale tankard. There seemed to be an awkward moment before anyone else spoke.

'The loss of Kilmarnock will be a sore one,' the Dowager said.

'He's alive and unhurt,' Anne leapt to reassure her. 'They took him to Edinburgh Castle, is all.'

'When we defeat them next time,' MacGillivray said, filling his tankard from the flagon, 'he'll be a free man again.'

'Next time?' the Dowager asked.

'In the spring. We're home to recoup and rest. Now that Cumberland commands, they risk everything in one throw. If we win, they'll have nothing left.'

'Will we get the chance to see the Prince then?' Jessie asked.

'I've invited him,' Anne answered, 'when the rest of the army arrives back, to dine here.'

'I'll cook for the Prince?' Jessie shrieked.

'With whatever help you need. But tell no one yet. Louden's troops in Inverness would be forewarned if they had word of that.'

Elizabeth was leaning back in her seat, watching the firelight gleam like gold in MacGillivray's hair. Now she leant forwards, pushing her tankard over to be filled. He looked into her eyes as he did so.

'Is the heat getting to you?' he grinned.

She lowered her eyelashes, then looked up at him again.

'Not at all,' she smiled back. 'I'm enjoying it.'

'Tell us about Meg's shoemaker again,' Will asked. 'I liked the bit where he said sorry to the redcoat after Meg pitchforked him.'

The Dowager was already at her porridge and the newspapers when Anne came down next morning.

'Your tea service came while you were away.' She didn't look up from her reading. 'Jessie would have brought you up a pot but you weren't in your room.'

'No.' Anne looked through the window at the clean, white world outside. All the edges were blurred, everything smooth, calm and settled. 'It wouldn't feel right, using the master bedroom. I can't stay married to Aeneas, not now.'

The Dowager considered her. 'Don't rush, *a ghràidh*. That's a big step. Let time help you take it.'

Anne sat down, glad that was out of the way. The Dowager had old-fashioned views, believing women, married or not, should just please themselves if they wanted another man. The old Celtic ways carried no disapprobation against a friendship of the thighs. It made things simpler. Their ancestors divorced husbands with ease, for failing to provide or be respectful, if he snored, gossiped, was impotent or just repelled. Divorce was rare now, a matter for the courts, but it was the only answer here. Aeneas had abandoned her. She had turned to someone else. Her choice was made.

MacGillivray came in then, greeting everyone cheerily and winking to Jessie who'd brought Anne's porridge. The Dowager slapped the pages of her *London Post* in annoyance.

'Would you look at this! They have us all as papists, led by the church of Rome.'

'What, because the Prince is Catholic?' Anne asked. 'He guaranteed religious freedom, and our parliament will be secular, as it always was.'

As with both nations, most of their force was Protestant, though many clans were Episcopalian rather than Presbyterian, the dour, national kirk that dominated further south. The Kirk was against the rising, the Catholic church for it, but Scotland's Episcopal church stayed silent. Jacobite supporters came equally from all three. But religion was a crucial issue for England, where the monarch headed the Anglican Episcopal church and their king could belong to no other faith.

'The Hanoverians will say anything to turn folk against us,' MacGillivray added. 'Even that we eat babies.' He made a growling rush at Jessie. 'So you better watch out,' he warned.

'Jessie?' Anne puzzled, looking round at the girl.

'She's been outside, being sick, every morning for a week,' the Dowager said.

'It's only first thing,' Jessie protested. 'I'm fine.'

'But with child.' Anne was delighted. 'Why, Jessie, I never noticed, and your waist has quite gone. Who is it?' She paused. 'Will, it's never Will?'

Jessie nodded, embarrassed to be the centre of attention.

'Two is warmer in bed in the winter,' she said, flashing a look at MacGillivray.

'Indeed it is,' he grinned. 'Will's a lucky lad.'

'Are you wanting to wed?' Anne asked.

'No,' Jessie got out, quickly. 'I'm a long ways off that. He's pestering me to handfast come haymaking. I said maybe.' Handfasting committed lovers to live together for a year and a day before deciding if they'd marry. Anne wished she had chosen that route now. In June, she could simply have unmade her bed without fault on either side. Instead, while she'd please herself who shared that bed, until she was divorced or widowed, her responsibility was here.

'So will the baby go to Will's people when it's weaned, or will you keep it?'

'I don't know yet.' Jessie became flustered. 'I'll get the rest of the porridge.'

She scurried out. MacGillivray drew his *sgian dhubh* and carved himself a slice of duck breast while he waited.

'A baby would be nice about the place,' Anne said.

'Aeneas doesn't know,' the Dowager reminded her.

'Well, I'm sure he'd –' She stopped. She couldn't speak for Aeneas. His opinion hardly mattered anyway. By the time Jessie's baby was born, Moy might have a new chief.

Jessie came back with MacGillivray's porridge.

'Will says he's getting your horse ready,' she told the Dowager. 'He'll put what he can in panniers and bring the rest of your things on by himself another time.'

'You're going home in that?' Anne asked.

'The road won't be too bad,' MacGillivray said. 'No more snow fell through the night.'

'But more will come,' the Dowager added. 'And I'd rather be back in my own house, now I can. If the Prince does take Inverness, he can stay with me. I should make ready, in case.'

'Will can take my horse,' MacGillivray offered. 'See you safe home.'

'You're a good man, Alexander.' The Dowager stood. 'I'll take my leave then.'

Anne went with her to the hall, helped her on with her cloak.

'You're not leaving because of us?' she asked, though she knew the reason.

The Dowager patted her cheek.

'My dear Anne, I said why I'm going. I speak my mind when I have mind to speak. Alexander *is* a good man. I'm sure he's also an exciting one. Pleasures are few and fleeting. They should be enjoyed.' She tied on her hat and was at the door before she spoke again. 'I don't think you've done choosing yet,' she said. 'Aeneas is also a good man.'

'No, *na can sin*, he's not.' Anne shook her head. 'He hanged Ewan. I saw him do it in the square, that day I went to see him.'

'Ewan?' The Dowager was puzzled. 'I never heard Aeneas had a hand in that. It doesn't sound like him.'

'Did you tell him I had no desire to shoot him at Prestonpans?'

'How could I? I've been here. He's been busy.'

'Then don't, because I would shoot him now.'

'Anne, if Aeneas ordered Ewan's death, he must've had good reason. I'll ask when I see him.'

They heard Will bring the horses round. The Dowager kissed Anne on both cheeks and left. Good reason? Anne watched them

201

plod off into the everlasting white, broken only by the stark, black bones of half-trees. To reject his wife, that was his reason, to cast their marriage aside. He'd taken his anger out on Ewan and, by doing so, confirmed himself her enemy. Now he guarded Inverness with a small force while an army of ten thousand Jacobites marched his way. Nothing except the landscape was black and white here. The Dowager would warn him. That's why she went so suddenly. Anne had given the information on purpose. She wanted Aeneas to know his days were numbered.

When Will returned from Inverness that afternoon, he plodded through a blizzard. White flakes whirled in the air. White earth, white air, white sky, blinding, blinding white. The knowledge of trees kept him on the route, knowing each copse, each individual trunk, the spread of branches whose stark-black multi-fingered hands cupped to catch the snow falling down. His knowledge of horses kept the trust between him and MacGillivray's beast, never the sudden trip over a blind edge, the slip into a snow-filled crevice, always firm ground under foot. He was seventeen, born to life in the stables, and let the animal go on a light rein as he talked softly to it or crooned a Gaelic lullaby into its flicking ears.

Sometimes the horse talked back, a gentle snicker, the gulp of a breath, turning its nose to the side. It wanted to stop, under the trees, did not like this blasting, blinding whiteness or the snow-balling in its feet. He dropped down then, knee-deep in the cold white-powdery drift, to pick out its hooves then walk beside its head, holding the bridle, breathing close to its nose, telling the horse about snow, about man, about war, about love and Jessie and babies, talking it home, talking them both home.

It snickered again as they plodded the last few yards to the stable at Moy. When he led it into its stall, its soft damp muzzle nuzzled him, pushing at his cheek, under his chin, nudging his shoulder. He stripped off the tackle, rubbed it down, put fresh feed out, and ploughed his way through the high drifts against the house, into the kitchens. Jessie had seen him come the last yards, the snow hand-cleared off that window. She was bent over a roaring hot stove, face flushed, a pot of broth bubbling on the top.

'You took your time,' she complained, barely glancing round as he came in, stamping the snow off his feet.

'Aye,' he said. 'It's snowing out.' She'd been worried. That was something. He sat and supped his soup in silence, listening to the fire crackle in the grate, watching Jessie move about, cooking supper for the house.

Snow brought peace. The land locked down. Nothing moved for weeks. On the first day after Will returned, Elizabeth looked out her bedroom window to see a snow-made Highland warrior, blue bonnet perched on a fat, round head, standing beyond the edge of the yard. MacGillivray was putting the finishing touch; a twig for a sword. Anne, caped and hooded, ran out to him, laughing. Though Elizabeth couldn't hear what was said, the white puffs of breath, the way her sister shook and moved told her if it was laughter or talk. MacGillivray spotted her at the window and waved her down. Watching him excited her. Anne wouldn't always be in the way. Then he'd be hers, indebted to her, and not just flirting. Anticipation sharpened her desire. She began to change into warmer outdoor clothes.

Out in the crisp air, Anne inspected her new fighter.

'Kiss me,' MacGillivray said, his breath condensing in water droplets on her flushed cheeks, 'before your sister comes out.'

'You can kiss me in front of her,' Anne said.

'Then she'd think I preferred you, and what would that do for my reputation as a blade?'

'I'll do something for your reputation.' Anne grinned, scooping up a handful of snow which she showered him with. 'Now you're a greyhead,' she giggled.

'Then we'll grow old together,' he retaliated, showering her.

Anne grabbed another handful, packing some in her fist and chucking the rest as he dodged it.

'Hey, *trobhad an-seo*, kiss first,' she said, when he packed a huge snowball to throw back, holding her arms out. He leapt over to her, jumping through the snow, put his arms round her waist, his mouth on hers. She looped her arms round his neck and dropped the snow she'd kept in her hand down inside his plaid, inside his shirt. That did it. As he wriggled against the melting chill at his spine, he wrestled her down into the snow.

'You can have me out here,' he threatened. 'And be frozen to me for ever.'

'Am I scared?' she laughed. 'Do I look scared?' And she stuffed more snow down his back.

A snowball skelped against the side of MacGillivray's head. He looked round. Elizabeth. He jumped up to arm himself. Elizabeth already had her second but missed. MacGillivray didn't. The soft snow thumped against her chest. Anne rolled over and got up to join in, the two young women taking on the warrior. Squeals and laughs and shouts erupted in the still, white air. Eventually, exhausted, they walked back to the house, MacGillivray with an arm around each of them.

'Thanks for the snow-warrior,' Anne said, giving him a peck as they kicked and scraped their shoes clear. 'We'll be safe while he's out there.'

'My lady,' MacGillivray promised, 'I'll give you an army to guard you.'

The next day, there were three snowy Highlanders, the next, five. Finally, there were seven.

'The number of mystical things,' he said. 'You'll never need more protection than that.'

'*Tapadh leibh*, my lord,' Anne smiled. 'Thank you.'

'I would protect you for ever,' he said, seriously.

She knew that. He would always be there when she needed him. The hurt part of her was buried deep when he was near. She was glad of him, glad of the snow, the peace and rest it brought. All their tomorrows should be this good, this right. The white-out was surely an omen, as their troops came home, that turned the world Jacobite.

# TWENTY-FIVE

The ice that had formed inside the stone walls began to melt. Drips ran down, harder to catch on the tongue. They collected where a cup-shaped hollow in one block of stone held them. A queue formed. Ragged, hungry and crowded together, the prisoners were desperate with thirst. The freezing stone dungeon of Carlisle Castle might have held fifty. Three hundred were crammed into it, men, women and children.

Clementina huddled into her father for warmth as they edged along the line towards the only water supply. High above, through the bars of the small stone window, she could see snow still falling, the flakes like black rain against the grey-white sky. Sometimes food came through that window, a loaf of bread pushed between the bars, a risky gift given by some compassionate Carlisle citizen. Very little came through the rough thick door. The guards were redcoat soldiers under orders to keep their captives on short rations. Hunger wasn't new to Clementina but, in Edinburgh, there had always been ways to get some food. Not here. Not inside these hard, chill walls crammed with bodies and limbs and empty mouths.

Even through his plaid she could feel her father's bones, sharp, angular. He shivered, coughing. She squeezed tighter to him as they shuffled forward another step to the tiny well in the stone wall.

'Colonel Anne will come fur us,' she said. 'I ken she will.'

'Aye, lassie,' her father coughed. 'Aye.'

A woman in the far corner, giving birth, moaned and screamed. Those nearest tried to give her space where there was none. A wet rag was passed across, hand to hand, till it reached the labouring woman. One of those attending held it to her mouth to suck. Another woman began to hum softly, then sang quiet words in her foreign Gaelic tongue.

*Bheir me ò, horo bhan o;*
*Bheir me ò, horo bhan i.*

Others began to join in, even the English recruits. The song had become an anthem, the words translated and learned over the weeks they'd been imprisoned.

Thou'rt the music of my heart;
Harp of joy, *o cruit mo chridh'*;
Moon of guidance by night;
Strength and light thou'rt to me.

Despite the soft, black snow seen falling above, there was a thaw coming and a baby being born among them. Clementina and her father edged closer to the small pool of water welling in the stone groove.

*Bheir me ò, o horo ho;*
Sad am I, without thee.

Lightning slashed across the night sky, searing the underbelly of stormclouds. Thunder growled, boomed and cracked among them. Rain battered on the cobbles, bouncing high, flooding the gutters. Aeneas stared out at it from the window of his quarters in Fort George. The sudden thaw had been quickly followed by this wild weather. Opposite, a horse stood, dripping miserably, tied outside Lord Louden's offices. It had arrived a moment ago, Aeneas just too late to the window to see who rode in on it.

The Jacobite army camped at Ruthven barracks. Cumberland's army marched north to Aberdeen. The next battle would be here, in the north, as soon as winter lifted. Even without the French army, all bets were on the Jacobites, unbeaten in every engagement. Here, on their home ground, they outnumbered everything the government could produce. Cumberland, despite his Dutch and Hessian auxiliaries, had only mustered eight thousand men. The

Prince, if he pulled in all his scattered troops from the areas they held, could command fifteen thousand.

There was scant hope for Scotland either way. If he believed his nation would grasp its freedom with maturity, he'd take his men to Ruthven and join the insurgency. But the Prince, victorious, would soon enforce a reunited kingdom. He wanted a throne and subjects, not free peoples running their own affairs. Aeneas spread his hands to grip the window frame, rested his forehead against the glass. Maybe he was fooling himself. Maybe he wasn't here to protect Moy for his clan. Maybe it was just pride, and he wasn't man enough to admit being wrong. Maybe he couldn't face Anne, humbled, and back down. Not to the woman he loved, not to a wife who loved another man.

A shaft of light from Lord Louden's quarters cut across the rain-washed cobbles, illuminating the driving rain as the door opened. A caped and hooded woman slipped out, hurriedly mounting the waiting horse. An assignation, in this weather? There was something faintly familiar about the figure, the way she moved, known but beyond recall. Aeneas slid the window up to peer out. Rain pelted into his face. Louden stood in the doorway of his offices. The woman jerked the reins, ready to ride off.

'The reward is yours,' she shouted. 'MacGillivray's mine.' Her voice was half-heard over the blustering wind. Lightning flashed, thunder rolled, and she was gone, kicking the horse away, fast. Was it Anne, did he not know his own wife, or did he imagine what was said? Aeneas closed the window.

He was towelling his face dry when his door clattered open, letting in the squall and, with it, James Ray.

'We've to muster at once,' the lieutenant gasped. 'Their Prince is unprotected, and we know where he is!'

In the master bedroom at Moy Hall, Anne sat in front of the glass fixing her hair, straightening the bodice of her white dress, fingers working fast. Lightning lit up the room, a flicker of brightness. Thunder cracked then grumbled, momentarily blotting out the music in the background. She had been away long enough and would be missed. Standing up, she flounced her wide skirts, smoothed the blue sash at her waist and turned to go. The tidy, unslept-in double bed stopped her in her tracks, her marriage bed, the memory of it a sudden, painful loss. As fast as it cut her, she shook it off as foolishness. The past was done with. MacGillivray did not give her grief.

She left, closing the door, and crossed the lobby to the large reception room. It was alive with noise, music, chatter. MacGillivray waited just inside the door.

'It's going well,' he said. 'He's almost cheered up.'

'Mmm.' Anne glanced around the room, checking. Jessie and Will, dressed up for the occasion, moved around with trays, serving titbits and drink. After the rigours of battle, the hard march home, everyone was enjoying the opportunity to relax, pleasurably. Silks, satin and lace swished around the room. Robert Nairn flirted with a musician. Margaret danced with Lord George, her husband with Greta. Sir John chatted with O'Sullivan and the Prince. He did look happier. His regal face had lost its petulance.

'Where's Elizabeth?' she asked.

'She went to lie down after supper,' MacGillivray said. 'Headache.'

'I thought she'd be in her element, dancing and flirting with all these young bloods. I should see if she's all right.'

MacGillivray caught her arm as she turned, drawing her close.

'Dance with me first.'

Across the room, the Prince waved and called. 'Anne!'

'Too late.' She raised her eyebrows at MacGillivray, then swept over to the group.

The Highlander leant back against the panelling, foot tapping to the rhythm. Jessie passed, on her way out, the spanking white apron tight over her gently swelling belly.

'Dance with me, Jessie,' he winked.

'Can't,' she blushed. 'I have to get more food. You'd think they were never fed.'

MacGillivray swung the door open for her with a flourish, making her giggle.

Across the room, the Prince was all compliments.

'You are the only bearable thing about our retreat, *ma chère* Anne,' he said. 'If you'd been with me at Derby, London would have opened its gates.'

'Better to be champion of Scotland,' Anne smiled, 'than Lord in the Tower.'

'Not while Cumberland takes back everything we gained.' His sulk was in danger of returning.

'*Au contraire*, it only seems that way. He can't win now.' Anne tried to mollify him. 'The English people won't fear our victory quite so much when it's won here.'

'They might even rejoice,' he pondered.

'Of course they will, *cela va sans dire*. Especially when you achieve it without French help. Their old enemy would have caused alarm. Resistance, even. Your tactics will be lauded.' Anne was tired of humouring this arrogant and petty man. Surely he must see through her?

He didn't. He nodded in appreciation of his own imagined talents.

'When the storm is over,' he mused, 'I'll bring the army out of Ruthven to capture Inverness.'

Anne raised her glass, toasting the idea.

'Now, I like the sound of that,' she said. Aeneas might sleep his last night in the enemy's bed. Tomorrow, he could be forced to surrender.

Beside the door, MacGillivray watched, impressed. Even across the room he could tell Anne wound the Prince around her little finger. He wondered how she could be bothered. The man was a liability, not an asset, having to be cajoled instead of providing authoritative command. His youthful good looks and charm, when he applied them, brought money and support, but a leader needed more than that.

At his side, the door swung open. Elizabeth came in. MacGillivray peeled himself off the wall.

'I thought you'd retired for the night,' he said.

'A wonder you even noticed,' Elizabeth retorted. 'Your eyes never leave my sister.'

'Well, you have my undivided attention now,' he grinned. 'You've changed your dress.' She wore a very low-cut hooped gown with a tight bodice that thrust her breasts up and out. 'If my heart wasn't taken, Elizabeth, you'd have it.' Then he frowned and laid the back of his hand against her forehead. 'You must have a fever. Your hair.' He took hold of one damp curl, played it between his fingers.

'I went out for some air,' Elizabeth said, looking away from him.

MacGillivray glanced at the window. Rain battered against it, lit up by another flash of light.

'In that?'

'Why, Alexander –' Elizabeth looked up, meeting his eyes '– are you afraid of a storm?'

Jessie rushed into the room, almost knocking Elizabeth down, her face alarmed.

'Anne,' she called. 'Come quick!'

MacGillivray vanished out of the door. Anne hurried over to it, reassuring her guests as she did.

'An accident in the kitchen, no doubt. Please, continue, enjoy yourselves.' At the door, she saw Elizabeth. 'Keep them happy,' she said as she went past.

MacGillivray was already downstairs. Anne ran to join him. In the hall, Donald Fraser carried in a soaked, hooded rider. Mac-Gillivray helped him get the storm-exhausted woman to a seat. Anne pushed the sodden hood off the rider's face. It was the Dowager, grey-faced, gasping.

'Louden's coming,' she got out. 'He knows the Prince is here.'

Anne turned to MacGillivray, speechless. Then she whirled round and ran back half-way up the stairs.

'George! Margaret!' she shouted.

The two of them appeared, with Lord Ogilvie, at the top.

'You have to get the Prince away,' Anne yelled at their startled faces. 'Now!'

All three vanished back into the room.

'Jessie, get the room cleared. All of them, out!' Anne turned and ran back to MacGillivray.

Before Jessie could move, the Prince bounded out of the door, O'Sullivan beside him.

'*Mon dieu!* Out of the way, girl.' The Prince pushed Jessie aside, running on down as the others followed. The strains of music fell away and died.

'Get them round the loch,' Anne urged MacGillivray, 'to the summerhouse. They can shelter there.'

'I'm going nowhere,' he said. 'Better they take him than you!'

'We need him,' Anne snapped. 'A body with no head soon dies. You're the only one who knows the way. Get out of here, through the kitchens. Go, go!'

Musicians clattered their instruments down the stairs. MacGillivray ushered the alarmed guests through the dining room. Anne spun round to Fraser.

'Muskets, Donald. Fetch what we have. Jessie, help him.' They dashed to fetch them. 'Elizabeth –' Anne turned to her sister, standing alone at the top of the stairs '– fetch my pistols down.'

'You can't take on an army by yourself.'

'Move, don't talk!' Anne shouted.

Will stood, bemused, at the foot of the stair. As Fraser and Jessie dropped muskets, pistols and bags of powder and shot on the hall table, Anne whipped up a gun and tossed it to him. He looked at it, bewildered, as if he'd no idea what it was for.

'Can you load, Will?'

'Load?'

'Watch Donald, do what he does.' Anne started to tip powder into the breach of another.

The Dowager coughed, leant forward.

'I can load,' she said, and began to do just that.

'Is there anybody else, Donald?' Anne asked.

'Meg and that Duff were in the stables. They're coming in. And I shouted my Lachlan out the forge.'

Elizabeth came down the stairs with Anne's pistols.

'Six, that's good,' Anne said, grabbing the pistols to load them.

'Seven,' Jessie corrected, loading a musket.

Anne hesitated, but the girl drew her a look that brooked no argument.

'Seven's better,' Anne agreed.

'You must be mad,' Elizabeth worried. 'Louden has two thousand men.'

'Magic number, seven,' Anne said, watching Will fumble with his musket. 'Can you shoot, Will?'

'At somebody?' Will looked up, horrified. His musket pointed at Anne.

'We want delay, not engagement,' Anne said, pushing his gun barrel up. 'Fire into the air.'

Will pressed the trigger. The shot exploded into the ceiling.

'Not now, idiot!' Jessie screamed at him.

'Look after him, Jessie,' Anne said, looping bags of powder and shot around their necks. 'Right, let's go. We'll get the others outside.'

They all ran to the front door, the storm blustering in as they opened it.

'Not you.' The Dowager caught hold of Elizabeth's wrist as she followed them.

Elizabeth looked down at her. The woman had a grip like iron.

'I was only going to close the door behind them,' she said. 'I don't suppose they'll be back soon, do you?'

Outside, the group of seven ran, bent against rain and wind, towards the road from Inverness. Anne squinted around as she ran, the downpour soaking her hair and face. If they could make Louden pause or hesitate, vital minutes could be won. Lightning flared, lit up the scene. The peat stacks near the road loomed up, great rectangular shadows in the dark.

'The peat stacks!' she shouted. 'Use the peat stacks!'

Donald and his son ran to one nearest the roadside. Anne took the next one up. The others placed themselves, peering round.

'Keep behind them,' Anne shouted. 'Will, you hear?'

'Aye,' he shouted back, cowering near Jessie.

'When they come after us,' Anne yelled, pausing to let a roll of thunder die away, 'drop the guns and get out of here. You know the ground, they don't!' Their wet tartan would help them vanish quickly in the grey-black night. She gritted her teeth. In a white dress, even rain-soaked, one spark of light would have her stand out like a beacon. As if to mock, a great bolt of lightning lit up the glowering clouds.

Back in Moy Hall, the Dowager had her breath back. Elizabeth watched the older woman peel off her sodden cloak and hang it to dry.

'You shouldn't be out on such a night, at your age.'

'Why not?' The Dowager looked round at her. 'You were.'

'Me?'

'It was you who compelled me to come. No one else knows that road like I do. No one I might have sent would have the authority to deal with you.' She lifted down a cloak already on the hook, but damp. 'You told Louden the Prince was here,' she accused, throwing it at Elizabeth.

'No!'

'At least show some honour.' The Dowager spoke harshly, scornful. 'Aeneas saw you.'

'All right, yes!' Elizabeth wailed. 'And now you've ruined every-thing.'

'You informed on the Prince! What kind of woman are you?'

'He's a *poseur*,' she tried to explain. 'As soon as he's captured, this war is finished. Things will be normal again.'

'So you betray your own sister.'

'Look how she is with MacGillivray. She should be with Aeneas!'

'And you think she should hang for that?'

Thunder cracked and boomed like cannon directly above the house.

'No, *cha dèan iad sin!*' Elizabeth protested. 'They won't do that!

Nobody would hurt Anne. Louden said they'd lock her up and let her go when it's all over.'

'You really are a foolish child.' The Dowager was scathing. 'These are not honourable people we fight. Your scheming might well have brought her death.'

Elizabeth bit her lip, her face crumpled. She had been terrified when it went wrong, when Anne called for guns and ran out into the night.

'I didn't know she'd do something this stupid, did I?'

# TWENTY-SIX

Anne strained to hear above another peal of thunder. It rippled on, the rain drumming. No, it was pipes, and marching feet. Uncertainty was all she hoped to create. Louden might halt his advance, maybe even form up.

'Wait, wait,' she breathed, deep and fast. Timing would be everything. They had to be close enough to hear but not to be sure of what they could see.

'Anne,' Fraser hissed from behind the next stack. 'Do you hear?'

Nothing was visible up the road, nothing except blackness. Lightning flashed. Way ahead, a patch of shadow moved, coming round the bend. Had she left it too late? She raised her arm.

'Now!' she yelled.

Donald Fraser fired first, the flash from his musket slicing the dark.

'Loch Moy!' he roared.

'Lochiel! Lochiel!' his son, Lachlan, bellowed, and fired.

Sporadic shots followed from the others, with random shouts and battle cries.

Riding behind the piper, Louden saw flashes of musket fire from down the road, and heard shouts.

'Hold up, MᶜCrimmon,' he ordered and, as the pipes wailed to silence, shouted over his shoulder, 'Aeneas, what can you see?'

Aeneas strained, peering forward in the teeming rain, seeing nothing except the scattered discharge of muskets in the dark, hearing shouts, commands. Beside him, James Ray strained too.

'Is it the Jacobites?' Ray asked.

Behind them, the nearest marchers caught the word. Jacobites. It ran back the ranks like wildfire.

★

Among the peat stacks, Anne's band of seven roared, fired off their guns and pelted from stack to stack to load, bellow and fire again.

'Come round, Macpherson!' Fraser bawled, fired, ran.

'Move up, Drummond,' Jessie shouted, fired and ran, bent low, to the next stack.

'MacBean! A MacBean,' Will bawled, screwing his eyes shut before squeezing the trigger of his musket.

'*Creag Dhubh!*' Anne yelled Cluny's war cry, fired one pistol, ran to another stack, fired the other, then reloaded.

Two stacks away, Duff fired, then remembered to shout.

'Come in ahint!' he roared, jumping over to the next stack beside Meg.

She fired her musket off and ran to the place he'd vacated.

Feet stopped marching among the government troops. They could be walking into an ambush. Fighting in the dark, unable to tell friend from foe, was a fearful prospect. Lightning shot a bolt across the night. The ground before them lit up. Shadowy groups of men lined the road ahead, hundreds of them, muskets firing in their direction. Further back, more shadows. Rank on rank of Highlanders, blocked for battle, waiting for them. The Black Watch hesitated, the front turning to fall back, the rear pushing on.

'Steady up, steady up!' Louden called. Thunder boomed around them. 'Play something, piper!' The pipes squealed back to life.

'But it's the Jacobite army, sir,' Ray shouted back in the pelting rain. 'We're outnumbered. It's a trap!'

That did it for most of those in earshot. Men turned and ran back the way they'd come, giving word of the ambush to those further back as they went past.

'A MacLeod!' the cry came from the shadows ahead. Aeneas frowned. A shot fired off. The piper groaned, staggered. The pipes wailed to a squeaking stop, the bag wheezed. Aeneas kicked his horse forward, caught the man as he slumped.

'*Och*, McCrimmon.' He pulled the shot piper on to his horse, blood running from his throat, a bigger hole in the back of his neck. The man was dead. Guilt coursed through Aeneas, like the rain running in rivers through his hair and down his face.

Inside Moy Hall, the sound of the storm receded. Elizabeth paced about. They could hear splashing feet running towards the house.

'If you know how to pray, child,' the Dowager said, 'you better do it.' She was seated by the fire, with a tankard of ale.

'Is that what you're doing?'

'I deal with the gods in my own way.'

The front door was flung open. Anne, Fraser, Lachlan, Jessie, Will, Meg and Duff came in, laughing, hugging, euphoric and dripping wet. The Dowager leapt to her feet.

'You're all right, all of you!'

'They ran away!' Anne announced, amazed, as if she still could not quite grasp it. 'They've gone!'

'Oh, Anne,' Elizabeth gasped. 'I was so afraid.'

'Mistook the peat stacks for troops,' old Meg chuckled.

'Thought we were an ambush,' Donald Fraser explained.

Elizabeth's jaw dropped. The Dowager glanced at her, grimly pleased.

'*Rinn mi a' chùis!*' Will shouted. 'I did it! We fired and ran about shouting war cries.' Still excited, he demonstrated. 'M<sup>c</sup>Intosh! Fraser! MacLeod!'

'The MacLeods are with the government,' Anne said, amiably.

Jessie turned on Will.

'Then it was you shot M<sup>c</sup>Crimmon!'

'Oh no,' the Dowager groaned. 'Such a fine piper, and Jacobite no matter what his chief says.'

'Whoever cried MacLeod killed him,' Jessie insisted. 'The shot went right by my ear, near took the skin off!'

'I wouldn't, Jessie,' Will protested. 'I wouldn't do that. I had my eyes shut!' He tried to take hold of her, to convince her, but she pushed him away and grabbed the musket off him.

'Get away, you're not safe to be out!' She stomped off to the kitchens.

'I could fight,' Will insisted. 'I could.'

'It's all right, Will,' Anne reassured him. 'It was an accident, and you all did well, better than I could have hoped. Away to the kitchen, all of you, and get out of your wet clothes. Jessie'll make some hot toddies.'

As they went, Fraser and Lachlan collected all the muskets and shot bags. Elizabeth took hold of Anne's arm.

'You'd better change too,' she said. 'You're soaked through. Come, I'll help.'

The Dowager had returned to her seat by the fire, and her ale.

'Before you go –' she paused. 'Was no one else hurt?'

Anne spun round, instantly angry. 'Would I have cared to notice!'

'Anne, please. It was Aeneas sent me to warn you.'

Anne gripped Elizabeth's arm for support. 'Why would he save a prince he will not fight for?'

'I think he was saving you.' The Dowager glanced at Elizabeth. The girl stared back at her with frightened eyes, silently begging her not to tell.

Anne laughed, without humour.

'Saving me for a hanging, like Ewan?'

The Dowager shook her head, sat her ale down and looked at Anne with a serious, steady gaze.

'He didn't hang Ewan. Hawley already had him in the noose with the intention of cutting him down, half-strangled, to be drawn while still alive. All Aeneas could do was end Ewan's suffering. That's what you saw.'

Anne blinked drops of rain off her lashes, wiped a drip from her nose with the back of her hand. She was beginning to steam by the fire. Aeneas had pointed to the struggling cottar. Ray leapt to break his neck. Hawley shouted he'd wanted the man alive. What the Dowager just said was true.

'No one else was hurt,' Anne said, quietly. Being in the wrong was not a comfortable place to be. 'Did you tell him I wasn't going to shoot him?'

The Dowager nodded. 'Truth is hard enough to deal with.' Her eyes flicked up to Elizabeth, but Anne's sister stared into the fire. 'You need to change.' She sat back. 'Look at the puddles.'

Next day, cheering crowds lined the streets of Inverness. The hated army garrison had vanished overnight. The Prince, with his entourage, rode into town, half the Jacobite army following behind. The story of the rout of Moy, how Colonel Anne had put Lord Louden's force to flight with a handful of serving folk, was all anyone could talk about. She was the toast of the town.

'La Heroïne has given me Inverness,' the Prince beamed at O'Sullivan.

'Without a shot fired, or a man lost, to be sure,' O'Sullivan agreed.

The Prince screwed round in the saddle to glare at his commander-in-chief.

'You see what a little faith can do, Lord George?'

MacGillivray cantered up, reigning in to match their slow, celebratory pace.

'The fort is abandoned. The townsfolk are tearing it down,' he reported. 'There's no sign of Louden, but hundreds of his deserters have joined us.'

The Prince nodded, waving regally to the enthusiastic crowds.

'Send out scouting parties,' Lord George answered for him. 'Make sure the area is secured.'

Not to be outdone, the Prince glanced round.

'And if you find any of their cowardly commanders,' he smiled, 'bring them to me. We shall be generous in victory.' Spotting Robert Nairn waiting at the entrance to a large house, he pulled his horse up in front of it.

The Dowager had ridden home at first light. She stood with Robert in front of her open doors, waiting for the Prince to dismount. When he did, she stepped forward.

'My home is yours, sir.'

He held out his hand to be kissed, then swept past, inside.

*

Aeneas knelt by the riverbank, bent forward and scooped water up to drink. It was icy, freezing his raw fingers. After delivering the dead M<sup>c</sup>Crimmon to the undertaker, he'd sent a message to MacLeod, the piper's chief, then set out to find however many of his scattered company he could. Two dozen of them lay about on the bank, dishevelled, exhausted, wondering what they'd do next. For a week they'd lived like outlaws, sheltering in barns and woodland, avoiding Jacobite patrols. Louden had fled to meet up with Cumberland, but joining the English advance didn't appeal to Aeneas. He splashed cold water on his face, and shook it off. His troop was tired, hungry, the weather wild and wet. It was time to give up, swallow his pride and take them home. The sound of a sword being drawn made him glance round.

A company of Jacobites surrounded his group, muskets and pistols primed and aimed at each of them. A few feet away from him, MacGillivray stood, broadsword in hand. Aeneas sprang to his feet, going for his own sword.

'I wouldn't,' MacGillivray said.

'I would,' Aeneas answered, drawing it free of the sheath. Without a pause, he swung at MacGillivray, who blocked the blow with his targe.

A few of the Jacobite guns came round.

'Don't shoot,' MacGillivray ordered.

Aeneas slashed, roaring as he did. Again, MacGillivray fended it.

'Don't be a fool, Aeneas,' he grunted. 'You're surrounded.'

Aeneas swung. Again MacGillivray stopped the blade.

'Will you fight back!' Aeneas shouted.

'Will you surrender?' MacGillivray fended yet another swing.

'Not to you,' Aeneas snarled. 'Not while I've breath.'

'Surrender to MacBean then,' MacGillivray suggested as he stepped back, dodging the next stroke.

A few guns swung again towards Aeneas but none fired, their loyalties seriously tested. He was their chief.

'Cover the Watch!' MacGillivray snapped.

The guns were turned back to cover their captives. They, too, were all from Clan Chatton. Old MacBean nodded a greeting here and there as he collected their weapons.

Aeneas rushed, played a feint to MacGillivray's targe, then swung his sword high and down. MacGillivray stopped the chop to his throat with his own blade.

'Please surrender,' he tried, as they pushed against each other.

'When you're dead,' Aeneas said. 'After I kill you.' He pushed MacGillivray back, then swung again and again. MacGillivray fended every blow.

'I won't fight you,' he shouted.

'Then you'll die,' Aeneas roared back. He rushed again, swinging his sword round to hack into the targe, then on the other side, where MacGillivray stopped it with his blade, then swinging it down.

Again MacGillivray blocked it, throwing off his targe as broad-swords crossed above their heads, faces close, looking into each other's eyes. Aeneas raised an eyebrow.

'You've improved.'

'Practice,' MacGillivray smiled. The point of his dirk, drawn in his left hand as their swords clashed, pressed just below Aeneas's ribs. One thrust and it was over.

'You'll have to do it,' Aeneas said. 'She'll never be yours while I live.'

MacGillivray flinched, his gaze wavered. He drew breath deep into his lungs, then thrust his dirk back into his belt and pushed Aeneas away from him. Aeneas slashed his sword crosswise. MacGillivray yelled. His left arm was cut, the wound bleeding. He stared at Aeneas, poised, glaring back at him, then sheathed his sword.

'You have first blood,' he said. 'If your honour isn't satisfied, then kill me.'

Aeneas let out a roar, raised his sword to shoulder height and thrust it straight forward at MacGillivray's throat with all the force of his anguish. He stopped the blade just short of nicking the skin, his muscles and the sword shuddering with the effort of not following through.

'Did I teach you nothing?' he raged.

'Didn't work, then?' MacGillivray gave a wry shrug. His surrender hadn't been a ploy, but he couldn't resist the joke. Aeneas didn't laugh.

'You tell them to shoot my men,' he bellowed.

The group of Black Watch stirred from watching the fight, looking worried. Their Jacobite guards frowned, puzzled. MacGillivray glanced around them.

'You heard the chief,' he told them. 'Shoot.'

'No!' Aeneas roared. 'You threaten to. Then I'd surrender.' He plunged his broadsword angrily into the ground next to his feet. 'But you don't invite a man to kill you when he most wants to see you dead!'

'I see,' MacGillivray said, and punched Aeneas full and hard in the face.

Aeneas staggered back, releasing his grip on the sword hilt. MacGillivray pulled it out of the ground.

'That's a good trick,' he said. 'I'll remember that.'

# TWENTY-SEVEN

'For the third time,' Cumberland railed, 'we are the butt of jokes orchestrated by this woman's hand!'

'She's a witch,' Hawley sneered.

'Your Royal Highness, sir –' Louden, circumspect, ignored Hawley '– Colonel Anne is barely twenty-one years old, hardly experienced, and was in her home at the time.'

'Casting spells, no doubt,' Hawley snapped.

'Maybe she sent your informer,' Cumberland suggested.

'That was her sister,' Louden admitted. 'But she seemed genuine enough.'

'Genuine enough to spring a trap!' Hawley screeched.

The grey northern city of Aberdeen which hosted the Duke and his troops was a bitterly cold and inhospitable place to spend the winter. While it saw little of the snow and ice which shut off the inland mountains and glens, gale-force north-easterlies whipped an iron sea into frenzied lashings of the port and its granite buildings. The Duke and his generals had taken up residence in a past provost's house on Guestrow, safe enough from spume and spray but not, it seemed, from bad news.

'Young or not,' Cope said. 'She's a commander to be reckoned with –' he was genuinely impressed – 'to rout an army two-thousand strong with only a handful of men.'

'A handful that were seen,' Louden protested. 'There must have been a hundred times that many.'

'Even so.' Cope smiled.

'Nonsense,' Hawley snapped. 'If our own informers can be trusted, there were five of them at most, and servants not soldiers!'

'It's the same thing in the Highland clans,' Louden corrected. 'Even the women and children can fight.'

Cumberland glared at all of them.

'This country is so much our enemy that what intelligence we get is deliberately contrived and contradictory to keep us uncertain how to proceed. But proceed we will, gentlemen. One day I will settle with this damn rebel bitch.'

February drew to a close, vicious with storms. The wind uprooted trees, brought rock and scree birling off the mountains. Rain poured down, filling lochs and tumbling burns in spate. There had been no news in or out of Moy and little hope of travelling the flooded roads to Inverness for supplies until the water subsided. When the sky finally cleared, it was mirror-sharp, the day cold, frosty. Anne carried the box with the remains of her tocher in it down to the hall table and opened the lid. It was half empty. In winter it was hard for the land to sustain its normal population. Now, all over the estate, there were extra billeted troops to feed.

'King Louis sent funds,' she said, 'but the ship was captured.'

'How interesting,' Elizabeth said, with complete indifference. 'Why don't you send them all home to be fed.' She was seated by the fire, stitching white-ribbon cockades for the troops. Jessie brought logs in for the fire.

'Some went home,' Anne said, 'but the Lowlanders can't.' She frowned at Jessie, busy stacking the bundle of wood in the hearth. 'Jessie, Will could do that.'

'I wouldn't trust him near anything that sparks.' Jessie pushed a fresh log into the fireplace. 'Is there something I can fetch you, a pot of your tea?'

Elizabeth shook her head.

'No,' Anne said. 'Thanks. Go put your feet up.'

Jessie left. Elizabeth looked up from her stitching. 'Is she all right? She looks a bit pale, and I'm sure I heard her being sick earlier.'

'She's fine,' Anne grinned. 'Just a little something she got from Will.'

'I'm glad you're all right,' Elizabeth burst out.

'It's not catching.'

'Not that, the other week. With the troops.'

Anne had never been so wet, not with her clothes on, but their nerve-wracking adventure that stormy night had delivered Inverness. Everyone called her a heroine. Yet she did not want to talk about that evening. Too much had changed during it, her certainties shaken.

'Forget it, Elizabeth,' she said. 'We were lucky, all of us.' She closed the tocher box. 'I'll do this later. You need a hand with those.'

'I can't forget. I've been very silly.'

'Don't tell me,' Anne said, teasing. 'You've stitched that to your skirt?'

The front door opened and closed, bringing a cold blast and MacGillivray with it, into the hall. Anne was never more pleased to see him. She ran to him, threw her arms round his neck.

'Oh, I've missed you,' she said, covering his chilled mouth and icy cheeks with kisses. 'Where've you been?'

He grabbed hold of her, put his mouth on hers and kissed her, hard, desperately and long, but as she returned it and the kiss grew gentle, he broke it off and held her tight to him, murmuring her name into her hair as if he had been gone for ever.

'What's wrong?' she asked but got no answer. 'Look, you're frozen.' She tugged his arm. 'Come over by the fire.'

He winced in pain, his right hand going to the arm she'd touched.

'You're hurt.'

'No, I'm fine,' he denied. He straightened up, as if something in him shut off, looking past, not at her. 'I've come with an order from the Prince.'

'An order?'

Elizabeth had ducked her head down over her stitching to avoid seeing them embrace, but his sudden formal tone drew her full attention.

'Last week, we captured a troop of Black Watch. They all chose to join us, except their officer. He also refused parole. I'm to place him in your custody.' He held out a document. Anne didn't take it. He laid it on the table.

'*Ciod e?* What is this, Alexander?' She smiled. 'Are you playing a joke?'

He looked at her then, his eyes bleak.

'The Prince believes you're best suited to have charge of him.' He took a step back and called over his shoulder. 'Bring in the prisoner!'

'Prisoner?' Elizabeth perked up as MacBean opened the door and nodded his charge to step inside.

Aeneas walked in through the door. The sight of him punched into Anne's heart, knocking the breath out of her. She stared in disbelief as he came towards her and stopped level with MacGillivray, flesh and blood, solid, the same easy, muscular swing, hair black as ever, brows furrowed. He stood, looking at her, his gaze steady and unwavering, the strangest of looks, cold as the ice that had frozen the loch hard during the snow weeks, but with anger burning in it. He said nothing. It was her place to speak.

Anne's wits scattered. Behind her, Elizabeth had gasped when she saw who it was. Fixated by the trio, she could only gawp. Anne's spine was rigid. MacGillivray was unreadable, his eyes still fixed on the wall behind Elizabeth's head.

Like a front-line volley, a thousand thoughts and feelings shot through Anne. She had not seen him since the day Ewan hanged, eleven weeks in which her life had turned around. She hadn't spoken to him since the day she left to raise the clan, six months and so much played out without him. Now he stood before her, distant, cold but angry, not wanting to be here, rebellious. He was her prisoner. She tilted her head to one side, the slightest of smiles curving her mouth. When all else failed, there was always manners.

'Your servant, Captain,' she said.

The brief flare in his eyes was rewarding, though quickly extinguished, before he nodded, curtly, in response.

'Your servant, Colonel,' he replied.

A moment long enough for the intake of breath passed, then MacGillivray turned abruptly and strode for the door.

'Alexander, *fuirich!* Wait!' Anne called.

He didn't stop. In two strides he would be out and gone. She gathered up her skirts, brushed past Aeneas, and ran after him, pulling the great double doors open again at his back, following him outside.

As soon as she was out of earshot, Elizabeth hurried over to Aeneas.

'Please don't tell Anne, about Louden. She doesn't know it was me.'

He looked at her with something like distaste.

'Then she should, when she can't trust those closest to her.'

'I was stupid, I didn't think.' She had to convince him. 'All I wanted was MacGillivray and for that silly Prince to be captured. We're on the same side, you and I.'

'Are we, indeed?'

In the yard, MacGillivray was already on his horse when Anne reached him.

'Where are you going?' she demanded. 'You can't leave like this.'

'I can't stay now,' he said. His eyes were bright, too bright.

'Then I'll come with you.' The defiance in her voice was meant to compel him, but they both knew he would go and she would stay.

'If you need me, I'll be around Inverness.' He tugged the horse's head round.

'What am I to do with him?' she wailed.

MacGillivray shook his head, slapped the reins and rode off, his troop of warriors falling in behind. Anne wanted to drag him back, furious that he could leave her, and that he'd done so in front of Aeneas. Her eyes stung with the prickle of tears. She watched him go, down the avenue, over the rise, even after he was just a dark speck vanishing out of sight. The lump in her throat was hard, painful. So he loved her, without condition, but he was gone just the same.

Aeneas had only to appear and MacGillivray deferred to him. The man she turned to, the man she clung to when everything else proved false, the man who'd always been at her side, had ridden away from her when she needed him most, and Aeneas was the cause. Neutered, defeated and a prisoner, he could still cause her pain.

She turned abruptly and hurried back inside.

Elizabeth served mulled wine and looked pleased with herself. Aeneas stood by the fire, glass in hand, a wary look on his face. No doubt warned by Will about their guest, Jessie had brought food in and was just leaving for the kitchens again, beaming.

'The chief's home,' she said, superfluously, to Anne as she passed.

'What is going on?' Anne demanded of Elizabeth. 'He's a prisoner, not a guest!'

'I'm only being hospitable,' Elizabeth protested.

'Then don't,' Anne snapped. She glared at Aeneas. He seemed almost amused now, that quirky smile she had near forgotten playing on his mouth. 'I want an explanation. You sent your aunt here with a warning. Why did you do that?'

'Does it trouble you?'

She had also forgotten how his voice sounded, that deep, throaty lilt like a caress. 'If I'm beholden to an enemy, yes.'

'I doubt you accept debt to an adversary,' his eyes glittered, hard and angry, 'when you owe nothing to a husband.'

'Anne,' Elizabeth butted in, hastily, 'he was trying to be helpful.'

'To help himself,' Anne snorted, 'by currying favour with the Prince before it's too late!'

Aeneas flinched at that, a muscle twitching in his jaw.

'Nothing so devious,' he said, tersely. 'I protected my home.'

So it wasn't to save her. Why on earth had she hoped it would be?

'And now it's your prison,' she said, drawing a deep breath to ease the ache in her chest. It was her own weakness she must guard against. 'Confine yourself to your study and sleep in the boxroom.' She consigned him to the smallest room in the house. 'Jessie will bring up your meals.'

'Anne, you can't do that,' Elizabeth interjected. 'He's your husband.'

'No,' Anne snapped. 'He's my prisoner, and I can do as I please.'

'That arrangement suits me fine,' Aeneas snapped back.

'Then get out of my sight,' she ordered, turning her back as he put down his wine glass and left the room.

There was silence between the sisters until he'd vanished up the stairs and the door at the top shut behind him.

'What are you playing at?' Elizabeth asked.

'I don't want him here.'

'But it's his house, his place is here.'

'The house belongs to the clan, who are with me,' Anne corrected. 'And his place is in the wrong. It's time he learned that.'

'I'm sure he'll love you for it.'

'I don't want his love. But I will have his respect.'

'Not if you belittle him, you won't,' Elizabeth sighed. She poured a glass of the warm wine and handed it to her sister. 'You should be magnanimous.'

'He dishonoured me,' Anne snorted, 'before everyone. He joined the enemy without even asking my advice.'

'If he was anyone else, you'd be gracious.' Elizabeth sat, leant back, and made herself appear relaxed. 'You'd know, if you win and rub your opponent's face in it, then you haven't won.'

'Except this isn't a game.' Anne sat down too, leaning forward earnestly. 'We're at war, and I'm the only woman without my husband by my side. He shames me.'

'All the more reason to treat him well. He will have shamed himself then. Besides, you can't be disdainful of him while he's shut away.'

'Then what should I do with him?'

Elizabeth bent to pour more wine and fought to keep the smile from her face.

'Let him eat with us?' she suggested, as if she'd had to think about it.

'Not a chance,' Anne said. 'I can't bear to look at him.'

'He'll think you don't dare to.'

''S coma leam. I don't care.'

Elizabeth considered. Aeneas was an unexpected reward for her betrayal of the Prince. Already he had separated MacGillivray from Anne just by being here. There had to be some way to ensure husband and wife couldn't completely ignore each other.

'He'll be cramped in those rooms. The boxroom is a cupboard and six paces is all anyone can take in the study.' She shrugged. 'You could allow him a walk outside every day.'

'So he can escape?'

'Oh, come on. He won't dishonour a favour, and you have guards out now.' Another pause. 'Tell you what, I'll go with him.' She giggled. 'How would that do, your little sister having to walk with your husband, as if he was a naughty child?'

'But you hate walking.'

'I don't mind if it makes you look good. It would be better than sewing these interminable cockades.'

Once she had Aeneas out of the house, Elizabeth worked on him.

'You could be kinder to my sister,' she began. They were walking round the loch, the early March air crisp and dry. A frosting of ice coated the fallen leaves so they crunched underfoot.

'Are you meant to persuade me?' he asked.

'You're so suspicious, Aeneas,' Elizabeth smiled. 'It's boring without company, that's all. If you two were speaking, Anne might let you join us in the evenings.'

'I'm perfectly happy in the study,' he said. 'I doubt if I could keep my temper otherwise.'

Elizabeth stopped walking and put her hand on his arm, sympathetically.

'I understand that, I do. You must feel she let you down.'

'Let down is the smallest part of what I feel.'

Elizabeth patted his arm and walked on.

'It would be easier,' she said, casually, 'if you didn't care so much for each other.'

'I've seen how Anne cares for me. My opinions are discounted, my reasons not sought. She makes war against my wishes and a public mockery of my manhood. She assumes I'm foolish and vindictive, then uses that as excuse to go against me. An enemy couldn't care less well than she does!'

Elizabeth let the tirade wash over her. He hadn't denied that he cared for Anne and his anger was better out than in. Greylag geese paddled about in the water, fewer of them every night. In a month or so, those that hadn't been shot and eaten would be gone back to Iceland. Winter would be over. War would return. She had to move this on.

'Anne's such a proud person,' she said. 'Could never say sorry, even when we were small. Broke my finger on the training field once, said it was my fault.'

'I remember a crack on the shins she gave me, the day your father died, when I was trying to help.'

'Didn't appreciate it?'

'Not one bit. I ended up having to spank her.'

'And she appreciated that?'

He chuckled, he actually chuckled.

'Got even angrier,' he said. 'I think she expected the clan to rush to her defence.'

Elizabeth skirted that one quickly, before he noticed how that situation had reversed and returned to anger.

'Probably wanted you carved up and fed to the dogs,' she smiled. 'Fight and she'll fight back. But apologize and she's struck with remorse. Acquiesce and she falls over herself to do you favours. Cajole and she's eating out of your hand in no time.'

'Really?' Aeneas smiled.

'Really,' Elizabeth agreed. He was taking the bait better than she'd hoped. 'The light's going, shall we go back?'

# TWENTY-EIGHT

If Anne noticed that her sister always returned with Aeneas just as she'd settled down in the hall to do some paperwork, she didn't comment. At first, she studiously ignored them coming in, Aeneas helping Elizabeth divest her cloak and gloves, him walking past without a word, each footstep on the stair returning to his rooms. She kept her head down, answered letters from Margaret, Greta, George Murray. The news was not always good. Jenny Cameron was captured while visiting her wounded from Falkirk and taken to Edinburgh. Anne hoped Provost Stewart and their other friends there would keep her spirits up until they could secure her release. She dealt with the estate, kept the household accounts up to date and let Elizabeth and Aeneas proceed with their daily walks.

During the day, she checked on the troops billeted around, dispensed payments or visited Donald and Lachlan at the forge with work she wanted done. Often, she passed Ewan's eldest daughter coming to collect broth for old Tom. Eventually, when she couldn't put it off any longer, she walked back to the cotts with her. She had avoided facing Cath, robbed of a father for her baby.

'He was a brave man, who died courageously,' she told the young mother. Cath had moved herself and her baby son into Ewan's cott, taking responsibility for his sick father and his two young daughters. It was warm but gloomy as ever inside, with light only from the peat fire. The baby tried to find its feet, pulling itself up on anything to hand, falling over and chuckling. The girls kept him away from the hearth.

'I know what they did to him,' Cath said. 'Aeneas told me.'

'Aeneas?'

'He brought the word himself, with Ewan's plaid and dirk, choked up when he told me how they'd tortured him. Cut to the bone, he was, with the whip. But he told them nothing.'

Anne stared down at the dirt floor. It was because of her that Ewan died tormented. It was her he'd protected.

'I'm so sorry, Cath,' she said.

'If he died serving you, he died proud.' Cath picked up the baby, which was climbing over her to get at the breast, and pulled down her dress to suckle him. 'You tried to save Calum. They tell me Ewan paid the *Sasannaich* well for him and Seonag.'

'He did, and Meg has made it her personal quest to get the English lieutenant.'

'I know.' Cath smiled in the firelight. 'Even when you beat them and call the peace, she'll not stop till she finds him. She has her new man warned of that. Look –' she stretched out her feet '– he's been making shoes for all of us.'

Anne walked back from the cotts, pensive. A future, that's what the people needed, shoes on their feet, stone houses with windows to let in the light, the means to sustain themselves, enough food to go round. They didn't need taxes that bled them dry or laws that destroyed their way of life, their customs and habits, the mutual support, their occupation and use of the land, the equal say in their own affairs, removed by a nation that believed in ownership of people, land, resources, wealth.

Around her were trees, hills, rivers, lochs. No one could own these, nor the fish, beasts or birds that lived in them, no more than own the rain, the sea, the sky or another person. Each thing owned itself. Aeneas knew that. He couldn't be Highland and not know that. As chief, everything was given him by his people, not for who he was, he was a man as any other, but for what he represented, the clan, the one in whom they invested the preservation of who and what they were, a free people, choosing to live freely together for the good of all. He had cried for Ewan, for Ewan's pain and loss, not for his own. Maybe her sister was right, she should be magnanimous.

When he and Elizabeth returned from their walk that afternoon, Anne was busy with correspondence, but she watched him come in, take her sister's cloak, hang it. He didn't have the look of a man who was afraid to lose. He looked at ease in his own skin, vital and dangerous still, fearful of nothing. As he turned towards her, heading for the stairs, she dropped her eyes back to her papers. When he was close enough, about to step on to the bottom step, she spoke.

'Would you like to eat with us tonight?'

She had not looked up. When there was no answer, she did. He was half-turned towards her, looking at her, dark hair flopping over his forehead, his peat-brown eyes a deeper darkness than the pool under the waterfall at Invercauld, looking right at her. Her stomach twisted. She dropped her eyes quickly.

'No matter, if you don't care to.'

The letters in front of her blurred, didn't make sense.

'No, I'd like to,' he said. '*Tapadh leat.* Thank you.' He went on up the stairs. She stared at the incomprehensible writing, hearing every footfall. Then Elizabeth rushed over and planked herself down opposite, delighted.

'Well, where did that come from? How clever of you!'

'Clever?' A sense of shock had overcome her. 'I don't know what I was thinking of. I'll never be able to sit through supper.'

'You will, you will. I'll be there. You know me, I can talk for Scotland. I'll let Jessie know, then we'll go up and I'll help you get ready.' Elizabeth hurried to the kitchens, grinning. It was four weeks since Aeneas had been foisted on them.

Upstairs in the main bedroom, Anne sat at the dressing table while Elizabeth painted her face and décolletage for her with creamy-soft white, then rubbed carmine into her cheekbones and lips. She had moved back into the room when MacGillivray left, staking her claim over Aeneas as master of the house. Behind them, her marriage bed seemed to take up more space than before, its covers slightly crumpled.

'I don't see why we're making all this fuss,' Anne complained. Her innards were churning. Elizabeth dressed her hair, making little curls fall by her ears on to her cheeks.

'Pistols and broadswords don't capture hearts and minds,' Elizabeth said. 'You want to win him over.'

'I don't want his heart, and if he had a mind, he would be at my side.'

'He wants you still, to lie with you.'

'Does he?' That was pleasing. It meant she had some power over him.

'Watches you all the time, coming in, going up the stairs. He's a fish with his mouth open, waiting to be hooked. You're too busy ignoring him to notice.'

'He doesn't imagine I want him?' The knot in her gut tightened. Why did she feel so threatened?

Elizabeth grinned and laid down the curling tongs.

'No man ever knows what a woman wants. Not till he finds himself in her bed or out on her doorstep. Even then, he'll believe what suits him. Now, what dress?' She began rifling through the wardrobe. 'Not white, we don't want to be confrontational. Blue, what do you think?' She held up the gown.

'I'll wear white,' Anne said. The Jacobite colour would strengthen her nerve. The rose water on the dressing table was perfumed with the white rose of June. She rubbed some on her hands, patting it round her throat.

'Maybe you're right.' Elizabeth pursed her lips. 'Make him remember your wedding day,' she grinned, 'and night.'

'That's not why!' Anne protested.

'It'll do one thing for you, another for him.' Elizabeth made her selection and held the dress for Anne to step into.

As her sister fastened her into it, Anne looked down at her bosom. Her breasts were exposed, almost naked.

'I can't wear this,' she said. 'I might as well be undressed!'

'Stop thinking like a soldier,' Elizabeth said, stepping round to look. 'You want him to see the error of his ways.'

'You've laced me too tight. My nipples are barely covered.'

'A little titillation, that's all,' Elizabeth grinned, then she slapped Anne's hand away. '*Sguir dheth!* Don't pull it up. If you must think like a warrior, imagine this is a campaign to cause him regret.'

'You mean he has no remorse?' Anne frowned.

'Of course he does,' Elizabeth hastened to reassure her. 'But he's a man, so he doesn't know it yet.'

'Then he'd better soon discover it!' Anne flounced out of the bedroom, her sweeping white skirts trailing as she swept down the stairs. Elizabeth hurried behind.

Aeneas was already in the dining room, studying an opened bottle of wine as if he considered it of great interest. He looked up when they came in.

'Colonel,' he said, 'you're incredible.' His eyes raked Anne from head to foot. Then that familiar, half-mocking smile twitched his lip. 'Incredible,' he repeated. 'I'm honoured.'

'And I'm hungry,' Anne said, going straight to her seat and sitting down. He needn't think she could be flattered and, whatever he might say, he had made an effort to be presentable himself. His long black hair still shone damp against his shirt. He wore a lace jabot at his throat and, though no weapons were allowed him, his belt buckle and the brooch which pinned his plaid were both silver.

Elizabeth, minding everybody of their manners, waited till Aeneas drew her chair before she sat. Anne saw the nagging glance her sister cast at her but ignored it. Other things were not so easily put out of mind. When Aeneas walked round behind her to pour wine into her glass, his plaid brushed her shoulder and she could feel the warmth of his body next her as he leant forward. There was a brief hesitation before he tilted the bottle. Was it her perfume he'd noticed, or her closeness?

She kept her head down, knowing he, too, would remember there was a time when she would have looked up and he would have bent down to kiss her, his mouth on hers, his tongue teasing her own, a time when they might have made love there and then instead of eating. He was her prisoner, she reminded herself, but when he sat down opposite, smiled across the table and raised his glass for a toast, she wondered who imprisoned whom.

'The rebels,' he said. If he was mocking, he would find no satisfaction in her response.

'Victory,' she replied, returning the smile. '*Slàinte.*'

Jessie had outshone herself with the food. The main meal, dinner, was taken at midday, when visitors and workers often joined them. Supper was a light meal, but not this night. Oysters – whatever was Jessie thinking? Will must have been sent specially, Anne supposed. A haunch of venison, greylag goose, cottar cheese and half a dozen sweet preserves with oatcake and sugared shortbread. The conversation was strange, too many subjects to avoid: the war, the clan, Anne's running of the estate. Their whole lives were bound up in enmity. They took refuge in the weather but avoided what would happen when it improved. They talked about the health of the stock but ignored its reduction to feed troops. They discussed Jessie and Will's expected baby but not why the young couple were at odds. Elizabeth filled the gaps, prattling on about food, fashion and her mother's recently discovered liking for snuff.

Though Aeneas could have little interest in her topics, he appeared fascinated, asking questions, making good-natured jokes and ensuring their wine glasses were kept brimming. Any time Anne looked in his direction, he seemed to be watching her and she looked away, affecting disinterest, but with her face flushed. Towards the end of the meal, when he stood next her yet again, filling her glass, she had an overwhelming urge to turn her head towards him and bury her face in his midriff, just to feel the tautness of his abdomen against her cheek, to push aside his plaid and shirt and press her mouth against his skin, to know again the warmth and scent of him.

'No, thank you.' Elizabeth put her hand over her glass as he came round to replenish it. 'I've had quite enough.' She stood. 'If you'll both excuse me, I'm off to bed.' With a swish of her skirts, she was gone. A click and the door shut tight behind her.

Now there was just Aeneas. Anne felt a rush of terror. She could barely look him in the eye, though she could feel his close attention on her. The best thing, the only thing, to do was to get out of here before something irrevocable happened and weakened her position.

'The oysters were a welcome surprise,' he said.

'The naval blockade of the coast doesn't affect the warmth of our hospitality,' she replied, grasping politeness as a lifeline, staring at the ruby wine in her glass and the reflected candlelight trapped within it. She sensed him lean forward over the table and looked up into his dark, shining eyes.

'I thought you might feed them to me with your fingers,' he said slowly, his gaze hypnotic, 'then from your mouth, with your tongue guiding them into mine, the salt of them crazing our lips for each other's sex.'

'Aeneas!' Had he really said what she heard?

He threw his chair back and stood, coming round beside her.

'Did you think I wouldn't notice your sister's blatant manipulation?' He pushed his fingers into the top of her dress, between her breasts, caught the cloth and pulled her to her feet so her own chair fell backwards as she rose. 'Wife, if this is all the husband you want, you can have him. Here, now. I don't need the wine of our wedding, the scent of roses, or the food of our first love-making to want you.' His arms were round her, his body pushed her back against the table edge. 'My hunger for you, after all these months, is beyond appetite.'

His mouth came down on hers, hard, as desperate as he said. She fought against the kiss, the brutality of it, but as his impulse yielded to urgent desire, hers did likewise. This was the husband she knew and remembered, the mouth she wanted on hers, the body she ached for pressed against hers, the man she'd missed. They kissed each other's faces, throats, mouths again, moved their hands over each other, touching, caressing, renewing the geography of their marriage, desperate to confirm it, murmuring each other's names and those half-spoken meaningless words of desire. When he gripped her buttocks and raised her on to the table, she pulled the front of her skirts up, blindly eager for the consummation of this force between them, that he would give himself to her, lose himself into her in that sensate heat of passion and become hers again.

It did not come. He didn't push his kilt aside. Instead he held her tight, close so she could barely breathe, his cheek pressed hot against her own, his body hard and tense, so tense he trembled with his own need.

'Aeneas?'

There was only the sound of great deep breaths in her ear, his chest moving against hers with each of them.

'Aeneas, what's wrong?' She kissed his ear lobe. 'I want you so.'

'I know,' he said, his voice rough, his breath moving her hair. He leant back, still holding her, his hips still pressed between her thighs. 'But I don't care to satisfy my need –' his eyes were black as moonless night '– with another man's leftovers.'

It took a short second for what he said to fully register. With both hands on his shoulders, she thrust him back, away from her and swung her arm to smack a stinging slap across his face. The force of it jerked his head to the side. Her palm tingled, fiery.

'Jessie!' she screamed, jumping down off the table to her feet. 'Will, Donald!'

Donald Fraser, on house guard that evening, was first in, pistol in one hand, sword in the other. Jessie and Will were close behind.

'I saw no one,' Fraser said, alarmed. 'Where are they?'

'I want Captain M<sup>c</sup>Intosh locked up!' Anne demanded. 'This minute!'

'Dè, the chief?'

'The prisoner,' Anne snapped. She couldn't look at Aeneas, sensed he was smiling that infuriating half-smile. If she saw it, the humiliation would force her to shoot him. 'Put him in the cellar,' she ordered, 'in the wine cellar, where he might drink himself to death!'

# TWENTY-NINE

When Elizabeth bounded down the stairs next morning, Anne was already in the hall, dressed to go out, sword and dirk buckled at her sides.

'What's all this,' she grinned. 'Are you fighting him off?'

Anne wasn't amused.

'I'm going to Inverness. I've given Jessie and the guard instructions. Yours are that there will be no more walks.'

'Hold on,' Elizabeth said. 'I must've missed something.' She glanced around. 'Where's Aeneas?' Then she laughed. 'Still asleep? Worn out, is he?'

'Very comical,' Anne said. 'He was toying with us, Elizabeth, with both of us. He's locked in the cellar, and in the cellar is where he'll stay.' She reached for her cloak.

'No, wait,' Elizabeth said. 'I'll come with you.' She dashed back upstairs to change into outdoor travelling clothes.

While Anne waited, she had Will unsaddle Pibroch and prepare a carriage and horse instead. There was some fresh snow, wet and slushy. The carriage would be cosier for her sister in such chilly weather. Outwardly controlled and in charge, Anne seethed inside. A woman might refuse her husband, if he was brutish, drunk, unclean or annoying or because she simply didn't want him, but this was unheard of. Men honoured their wives. That was all there was to it. He couldn't change things to suit his peevishness.

By the time Elizabeth came down and joined her in the coach, Anne had worked herself back into the fury which had kept her awake half the night. She pushed the bag of fresh cockades for the troops behind the seats and set off at a cracking pace. After five minutes of skelping through slush, bouncing over ruts and stones, Elizabeth unclenched her jaw.

'Anne,' she said, her teeth rattling as she spoke, 'could we maybe not drive so fast and you could tell me what happened?'

Mortified, Anne eased off slapping the rein and pulled back on it. She had been driving the horse too fast, dangerously so, and risking her sister as well as herself on the bends.

'But he can't do that!' Elizabeth exclaimed when she heard Anne's explanation. They both wracked their brains, but neither could think of a single occasion when it was said a man had refused his wife on purpose, from choice. Failure was as common as *uisge beatha* was popular, the one leading to the other as sure as night followed day, but that was an inescapable result of drink and ageing. A frustrated wife would normally take a lover if her husband's over-imbibing left him unfit to please her.

'That's it!' Elizabeth squealed, frightening the horse so it shied and nearly had the coach over anyway before Anne calmed it down.

'That's what?' Anne asked once they were safely steady on the road again.

'He said you'd made a mockery of his manhood.'

'Aeneas is far from impotent,' Anne snorted. 'I think I can tell by now what's going on under a man's plaid.'

'No, but he's angry that he'd seem to be. Other folk will believe he can't keep his wife content.'

'So he punishes me?'

'You took a lover.'

'I'm entitled to have my needs met and Aeneas wasn't there.' Anne's hackles rose. 'He abandoned me, remember!'

'I know, I know.' Elizabeth tried to calm her. 'But that's not how he sees it.'

'There's another way to see it?'

'Anne, just keep a tight rein for a minute. He thinks you left him, that you didn't give him a hearing. You just rode off to war and didn't come back.'

Anne frowned. There was some truth in that. She'd meant to return, several times. It hadn't worked out that way for reasons that made sense at the time, reasons he couldn't know.

241

'You see?' Elizabeth pushed the point home. 'He couldn't be a husband to you if you weren't there.'

Male pride was tricky terrain. She'd taken his leadership of the clan. MacGillivray had taken him prisoner. Between them, they'd neutered his manhood. He'd lost chieftainship, his primacy as warrior, and, without any truth in it, his reputation in bed. Aeneas would hate being thought incapable.

'No wonder he was cruel,' she realized. 'Spite is all he has left.'

There was a considerable buzz of excitement in and around Inverness. March had gone out like the proverbial lamb and, despite the changeable damp chill, everyone knew the next battle, perhaps even the last battle, would come some time in April. There was a gaping hole where the hated Fort George had been. Finishing what the townspeople started, the Jacobites had blown it up. They found MacGillivray directing men to billets around the square. Elizabeth jumped out of the carriage and ran to him.

'MacGillivray!' she called, gaining his attention and his open arms when he saw who it was. 'We've missed you.' And into his ear. 'I missed you, at any rate.' She had her arms round his neck, kissing his cheek, his mouth, but then he saw Anne, hanging back, waiting, and there was no point to any more hugs or kisses. The two of them stood looking at each other as Elizabeth unwound her arms from around MacGillivray and stepped back.

'Would you take that note to the Dowager?' Anne asked her sister.

'But I want to stay here.'

'And I want to have a private conversation with my commander-in-chief.'

'Military?' Elizabeth persisted.

'Just take the carriage and go,' Anne said.

When Elizabeth flounced off, Anne appraised MacGillivray. He had stood to attention and wouldn't look at her now.

'You can't just walk away from me, Alexander.'

'I'll serve you till I die, you know that, but I owe Aeneas.'

'You can't owe him me. I own myself.'

'My life, I owe him my life.'

'I don't understand. You took him prisoner.'

Now he looked down into her eyes, wanting to make her understand.

'He could have killed me, if he'd wanted to.'

She looked at his arm. He'd winced that day, the day he brought Aeneas to her, from a wound.

'He blooded you?'

'It's healed now. He tried to make me kill him first.'

'Did he ask for your life?'

'He asked nothing. I offered. He wouldn't take it.'

Anne's temper exploded. 'So he humiliates us both!'

'Dying would've been better,' MacGillivray agreed, but he couldn't resist smiling. Aeneas could no more have killed him than he could have killed Aeneas. Things were straight between them now. Anne would have to sort the rest out.

'I should keep him in the cellar till he rots.'

'He's in the wine cellar?' MacGillivray shook his head, grinning. 'That's a terrible punishment for a man to endure.'

Anne laughed. There was no staying angry with MacGillivray, and she knew he was at least relieved Aeneas wasn't in her bed.

'I'll have him chained when I go back.' She grew serious again. 'We can't be in the same room. When the war is won, I might go home to Invercauld.'

Hope flared in MacGillivray as if she'd breathed on dying embers.

'If you leave, come to Dunmaglas.'

She couldn't promise that. Last night had proved the passion between her and Aeneas was still powerful, strong enough to break them both. They'd be tied together until there was no anger left.

'It's not over,' she said. 'I can't come to you unless it's finished. Not again.'

Watching the hope die in him, she would have ripped this thing out of her if she could, if she knew what it was and how to end it. She had a joyous, untarnished love for MacGillivray with none of the unfathomable currents that eddied around Aeneas. He did not deserve the grief she gave him.

'He said you'd never be mine while he lived.'

'I don't mean to do this to you.' She put her hand on his chest. 'Find someone else to love.'

He covered her hand with his, threading his fingers between each of her own. 'I don't even wish that was a choice. My heart has a mind of its own, as yours has. All we can do is follow, until it beats a different tune.'

She reached up and kissed him.

'I'm so glad of you, Alexander. Never mistake that. You're right, and we should leave the future where it is. But be certain my world is brighter with you in it.'

'Better watch my back then,' he smiled.

'I'll do that,' she promised. 'We're not done with this adventure yet.'

They discussed tactics. The Prince had asked the McIntosh regiment to hold Inverness. The other regiments were stationed at Ruthven or further afield in order to supply themselves. Several were already holding other parts of the country. They'd be called back when Cumberland moved out from Aberdeen. Weather permitting, it might all be over in a few weeks.

'We will be up to strength?' Anne frowned, none too happy about the geographical spread of their army if conditions prevented a rapid return. Cluny's Macphersons were still at Atholl. Kept in Inverness, her depleted Clan Chatton forces would be the front line.

'The regiments in Perth and the north will need time but we can avoid Cumberland till then. George is no fool. He'll choose the right time and place.'

Reassured that everything was in good order, she took her leave.

'I'll be back when I'm needed,' she assured him.

'When the time comes, I'll send word.'

Now that her relationship with MacGillivray was settled, the confidence and excitement in the liberated town was infectious. As she walked along the streets towards the Dowager's house, people waved and called or stopped to talk to her. She was still their heroine, the anticipation of victory heightened by how easily she'd routed the hated government troops from Moy, causing them to flee Inverness. It had been her intention to ask the Prince to remove Aeneas from her custody, but here, away from the oppressiveness of the house, that became inconsequential. She wasn't disappointed to find their royal leader was out inspecting troops with O'Sullivan. Even Elizabeth's huff that she'd been dispatched on an errand like a child couldn't dampen her mood.

'And how is Aeneas?' the Dowager asked, giving her a delighted hug.

'Well, and out of harm's way,' Anne answered.

'Good,' the Dowager said. 'My house is full of argument between the Prince and George, and I wouldn't wish a disagreeable home on anyone. It's good to have a day when they're both out. Now come through and eat with us.'

A dinner party had been hastily arranged in Anne's honour, the dining room full of old and new friends. The provost and dignitaries of Inverness showered her with plaudits and invitations, that she sit on the town council, join this guild and that. The French officers of the *Écossais Royaux* flirted, declaring her *magnifique* and *notre guerrière héroïque*. Margaret Johnstone and David Ogilvie were there with Greta Fergusson and Sir John, and Robert Nairn, her companion from the Edinburgh parole sessions.

'You were so right, Anne,' Robert said happily as he greeted her. 'Better here in the wild and generous Highlands than down among those dour, hidebound *Sasannaich*.'

'So who's the lucky man, Robert?' Anne laughed, glancing round the room, trying to guess which of those present had his favour.

'I am,' he assured her. 'The place is crawling with muscular warriors, and a wee politician or two doesn't go amiss for afters.'

'Don't you ever fall in love?'

'Every five minutes.' His face became serious then. 'I am in love, don't you know that? But, for the moment, he prefers a touch of the blarney.'

Anne was mystified. Then she remembered the Prince, drunk

and petulant at Stirling, giving ear only to O'Sullivan, enduring no other companion, allowing no other advice.

Robert grinned at her again. 'If you can't have whoever you love, love whoever you can. Isn't that what we both do?'

Returning home in the dusk, a light slushy snow falling, full of wine and fond wishes from good friends, with Elizabeth cuddled in beside her for warmth, Anne thought about that. Did she love Aeneas? If love could be measured by the degree of anger it could generate when thwarted, then she did. What bound them seemed hard as iron, inescapable, welded with fury. Shouldn't love be kind, tender and joyful, as it was with MacGillivray, without challenge or confrontation? Aeneas didn't accept or forgive, he demanded the absolute of their union. Her mind, body and soul committed to him. He could go hang. Twice, he'd held MacGillivray's life in the palm of his hand, on the battlefield at Prestonpans, believing they were lovers, and when he was captured, knowing they were, and had given his life back to him. Yet he gave her nothing.

The carriage rattled over another rut. Elizabeth bumped sleepily against her. Anne looked down at her sister's pretty young face. She loved her and she didn't doubt Elizabeth returned that love. But it wasn't the same as that shared by Aeneas and MacGillivray. Loyalty was a fair-weather companion between women, trustworthy only until it conflicted with other desires. The close bond between men was enviably more noble and selfless. They made no demands, didn't judge and never turned away from each other. Even Robert Nairn, who loved and wanted the Prince, could serve without rancour, love without expectation.

Perhaps with a child, she might love so unconditionally, but not with a man. Aeneas had it quite the wrong way round. It didn't matter if she loved him. It mattered that he should love her.

# THIRTY

'Can't we at least torture him?'

'*Isd!* Shh!' Behind the scrub, Anne ducked her head lower and steadied her aim.

'It would be more fun than this.' Elizabeth lowered her voice to almost soundless.

Anne's musket cracked off the shot. Elizabeth's followed.

'*Siuthad!* Go!' Anne ordered the dog beside her. The black-and-tan setter streaked off into the darkening waters of the loch to retrieve the kill. 'We got both,' she told her sister. 'You're a good shot.'

'Well, guess who taught me.' Elizabeth extricated herself from the scrub.

'I thought you'd forgotten. Why don't you hunt more often?'

'Because –' her sister picked leaves and twigs from her clothes and hair '– I don't like doing boy things. I like doing girl things.'

Anne laughed, and took the first goose from the setter's mouth. 'Oh, yes,' she said. 'Girl things like torturing prisoners?' She held out the heavy bird by its limp, slippery neck.

Elizabeth screwed up her face in disgust as she took it. 'Girl things like not getting blood, dribble, mud and sodden feathers all over me. Why didn't we bring Will or Lachlan to do this?'

'They're busy.' Anne took the second bird from the dog, and the trio set off back towards the house.

'Torture would at least be a change,' Elizabeth said. 'He's been down there more than a week. It must be freezing.'

'Has he apologized yet?'

'To what, the wall?'

'He could tell Jessie,' Anne insisted. 'Three times a day she takes him food. I'm sure they talk.'

'We're not plucking these, are we?' Elizabeth got no response.

'Oh, come on, Anne.' Still nothing. 'All right, Jessie's busy, but there are plenty other folk on the estate.'

'It's their party. The whole point is they don't do the work.'

'There must be somebody who's not going off to fight,' Elizabeth persisted, 'somebody who's not invited?'

'There is,' Anne said. 'He's in the cellar.'

'I think I'll join him.'

They walked on, the dog panting along beside, its tongue lolling from its mouth, every now and then stopping to shake water from its coat, spattering them.

'Wait a minute.' Elizabeth halted. 'I'm not gutting this.' Anne didn't stop. 'I'm not,' Elizabeth insisted. 'Anne!'

Fifteen minutes later she grimaced at the soft, squelching sound as she pulled the warm innards out of the carcass before carefully separating the gizzard, heart and liver to be cooked later. The rest of the slimy, bloody mass of intestine was taken out to the dog, which waited patiently outside the kitchen door. This was its reward, a change from its usual diet of porridge, and gobbled up quickly before it took itself back to the stable where it lived and slept.

'Your mother would be proud of you,' Anne said, washing out the inside of her own gutted bird before stringing its legs to hang on the pantry hook.

'I should write and tell her how much fun I'm having,' Elizabeth said, pulling a face. 'I thought we were plucking too?'

'Tomorrow. They could do with hanging longer, but needs must.'

'Something to look forward to,' Elizabeth groaned. 'Sore hands, aching fingers, feathers up my nose and down my back.'

'More good stuffing for pillows,' Anne said. 'If you want to be a wife, you must think like one. Waste not, want not.'

'I'm trying,' Elizabeth retorted. 'Can't have good stuffing go to waste, not to mention a deal of wanting, or a spare husband.'

Anne sighed. There just was no stopping this sister of hers. 'I can't make him give himself to me.'

'I know. It's not fair. We get the appetite, men get the means of satisfying it. Are the gods perverse, or what?'

'Mischievous,' Anne said. 'A woman loved wants loved again. Men want sleep. If we could just take our pleasure, they'd die of exhaustion in a week.'

'*Gu sealladh orm!*' Elizabeth exclaimed. 'You know one who'd last a week?'

They both laughed. Anne poured two tankards of ale. 'Anyway,' she said, more seriously, 'Aeneas has the desire, if he'd submit to it. He's just being spiteful. So he'll stay in the cellar until his humour improves.'

'A little bit of torture might help it along,' Elizabeth suggested again.

The party was two days later, two days of cooking, baking, rendering, steaming. Sheep turned on the spit, the geese were plucked, stuffed with sweet chestnuts and oatmeal then cooked, the larder and kitchen gardens raided, a plentiful supply of ale and pipers laid on. It was a send-off to those who'd billeted with them and would return to their own units the following day, and for their own warriors who'd been needed at home but would now rejoin MacGillivray.

Everybody who could walk, and some who had to be carried, came. Moy Hall throbbed with life. Braziers stood round the yard, filled with glowing peats. Singing, dancing, drinking, eating and telling tall tales was the order of the day. Anne and Elizabeth donned aprons and served. Jessie was supposed to have the time off as a guest, but she refused, armed herself with a tray and helped. Will, despite Jessie's constant cold-shouldering of him, carved the mutton. He was a quiet lad who said little and Anne ached for him in his youthful devotion.

'Just give her time,' she told him when she caught him gawping at the girl again. 'When the baby's nearer, she'll want someone to lean on.'

'A man is what she'll want,' he said sorrowfully. 'Not me.'

Old Meg had her new man with her. The *Sasannach* shoemaker, Duff, had settled into Highland life fine, as good a hand at the dancing now as any.

'Didnae ken what ma feet were for afore,' he told Anne as she filled his tankard for him. Or other parts, Anne thought, smiling to herself at the spring he'd put in Meg's step. Somewhere between sixty and seventy years old, Meg had lost her husband and two sons in the last rising thirty years ago. Ewan had taken the place of those sons. She had a lot to pay back, had Meg. It was a joy to see her find warmer feelings in her heart too.

Anne refilled her own tankard of ale and went to speak with MacBean and his wife. Their cottage was up on Drumossie, near Culloden House, and she wanted to know if they still had need of the extra grazing rights.

'Not during winter,' the old man said. 'We sold some beasts into army supplies.'

'I sold them,' the old woman corrected. 'They were too much for me while he's gadding about pretending to be a young blood again.'

'The blood is always young,' MacBean said, winking at Anne. 'It's muscle that wastes if it's not put to good use.'

His wife elbowed him in the ribs. 'I saw that wink,' she said, then she caught Anne's arm. 'He's more talk than action these days. Don't let him be fooling you.' Then she turned on MacBean again. 'If you've spirit for fighting and winking, you'll have spirit for dancing,' she said.

The two of them spun off to kick up their heels among the other dancers. The drums beat, the pipes skirled, feet stamped. Smoke from the braziers drifted through the whirling bodies. A boy with one arm birled about, hooching loudly as he turned the reel. It was Howling Robbie. Anne cut in to speak with him.

'Robbie,' she cried, delighted to see him so well. 'You're a fine dancer still.'

'Not so good with the Highland fling,' he said cheerfully, 'but I can do most things without falling over. It's a laugh when I forget and put up the wrong arm to catch something, or to open a door and end up walking into it because there's nothing there to push with.'

'Has Shameless been back?'

'Can't come back, can he?' A sadness clouded Robbie's otherwise cheerful face. 'Gave me his parole, and he's away with Lord Louden and them English folks.'

Anne swung him around and then gave him a hug. 'Never mind,' she reassured him. 'It'll maybe be over before long and then he'll come home.'

'I'll show him I can write my name again,' the boy grinned. 'With my wrong hand.'

Anne swung him on to partner Cath and went back to serving. Donald Fraser and Lachlan came to find her.

'My boy wants to come with me this time,' Fraser said.

'I owe you, for getting me off the field,' Lachlan added.

'It was your father that saved you at Prestonpans,' Anne reminded him. 'And he did it as a father, not as a warrior. You know I don't want two from one family, and I won't risk both my smiths.'

'My back is healed fine well,' Lachlan said, stubbornly. 'And my mother says I'm to go.'

Anne considered. It was Màiri's right to say if her men fought or didn't.

'Then you'll stay here till the pipes and drums call us, and you'll come back after the first battle. If there's more fighting needed then, it'll be one or other of you. Right?'

'Right.' The boy shook her hand as if he thanked her for treasure. 'And I'll look out for my dad this time.'

'I won't forget this.' Fraser shook her hand too. 'It'll be fine to line up with him instead of against him.'

The party lasted all the afternoon and into the evening, when the celebratory mood changed to one of leave-taking, and the singing started. Old MacBean's wife, with the finest clear voice despite her age, led the songs. They ended with a rousing chorus of the rebel anthem, 'The Auld Stuarts back Again', before rag torches were lit at the dying braziers and they all began to find their various ways home.

Anne chased Jessie off to her bed with strict instruction to leave all clearing up till morning, asked Will to do the first spell of house guard and went in to relax by the fireside. She was slightly tipsy from the ale she'd been drinking all day, but the bottle of wine opened by the fire was a welcome sight. Elizabeth being thoughtful, goblets ready and waiting. Of her sister, there was no sign. Anne poured her own goblet full, stuck the poker in the fire and, when it glowed hot, drew it out and thrust it into the ruby wine till it sizzled. Then she sat, with her feet up on the footstool, to sip it. It had been a good day, a great party, a fine send-off.

Elizabeth appeared from the hallway, papers in hand, when Anne was half-way through her second drink.

'Oh,' she said, startled. 'I thought you'd still be seeing them off.'

'All gone,' Anne said. 'Wine?'

'I'll get it.' Elizabeth put the papers she held on the table and came over to sit by the fire.

'What's the paper?' Anne asked. 'Where were you anyway?' Then she realized the direction her sister had come from. 'Were you in the cellar? Elizabeth –' she tried to be serious, though her tongue proved tricky in getting it round the words without slurring them '– have you been torturing my husband?'

'I tried.' Elizabeth made an apologetic face. 'But he wasn't having any.'

'Well, we know that!' Anne squealed, swaying a little.

'Actually, I took him some food. Jessie was busy with the guests.'

'You're so kind, 'Lizabeth. That's why I love you.' She leant forwards and spoke slowly. 'How is he?'

'Merry enough,' Elizabeth said. 'It's the wine cellar, remember.' She filled her own wine goblet and topped up Anne's. 'I also tried to persuade him to sign a parole bond.'

'Why?'

'Because then he could come up and join us. He wouldn't be a prisoner any more.'

'And what did he say to that?' Anne swayed, curious.

'He said he wouldn't give you the satisfaction.'

Anne shouted with laughter. 'We know that too!' She got, unsteadily, to her feet. 'Right, tell him to come up to my room.'

'Why, what are you going to do?'

'I'm going to do some of that torturing you suggest.' She picked up her goblet, and the bottle. 'I'm going to demand satisfaction.'

'Fight him?' Elizabeth was alarmed.

'No, no, no.' Anne shook her head. 'I will make him satisfy me.'

'Anne, you know you can't.'

'I'll tell him it's his duty. His honour as a husband and a man is at stake. I'll tell him, if he doesn't please me, I'll take two lovers tomorrow and put him out to grass.'

'I don't think this is a good idea.'

Anne was not listening. Her mind was decided.

'My pistols are beside my bed,' she said. 'Will can sit down here. Give him the cellar key when you've sent Aeneas up. If he doesn't please me, Will can put him back.' She went carefully up the stairs, managing to trip twice but without spilling her wine.

Elizabeth watched her go, challenged by her conscience. Anne would never have suggested this sober. It could all go horribly wrong. Perhaps, if she just sat, drank her own wine and waited, her sister would forget and fall asleep. But then again, didn't drink give permission where sense would not? This might be the best chance, maybe the only chance, to get those two together, properly together, before the end of the war allowed them to part. A chance for MacGillivray to find out he needn't wait any longer for a woman who'd never fully be his. He'd be sad, of course, but she would comfort him. It would be a sweetened sorrow. The thought of comforting MacGillivray was enough. Elizabeth took a deep swallow of wine, stood, removed the key from her pocket, smoothed her skirts and headed back to the cellar.

# THIRTY-ONE

The bedroom was warm from the peat fire. Though her hand was a little unsteady and the spill wavered, Anne managed to light the candles. Unfastening her dress and removing her stays was quite a struggle but she was in her shift, standing by her dressing table, when the knock came at the door. She picked up her goblet of wine and swallowed a mouthful.

'Come in,' she called, as calmly as she was able.

The door opened and Aeneas stepped into the room. If he was surprised at her state of undress, he didn't show it. Nor did he look half as merry as Elizabeth had suggested.

'Your sister said you wanted me,' he said.

'I do.' She faced him, holding tight to her goblet. 'Close the door.'

Her head was a little woozy, but she was all too conscious of his physicality, the tense, muscular maleness of him. It was as if an animal presence had come into the room, the different scent, shape and energy creating a frisson of fear. Like any wild creature, he might do something unexpected, dangerous, something she might be unable to deal with. Those who thought men and women were the same kind of beast were quite wrong. No woman could alarm her the way this man did.

'So what did you want?' he prompted now the door was shut.

She blinked to help her concentrate on getting her tongue around the words. He was not going to take charge here, not this time. She would tell him.

'You are my husband, and my prisoner,' she said.

He tilted his head, a touch of amusement lighting his eyes. So he realized she was a little drunk. It would make no difference. He would please her or he would leave this room impotently cast aside.

'You're also a captain,' she reminded him.

'Are you about to pull rank on me?' His eyes grew more amused.

'I'm simply pointing out that you are duty bound to me, in several ways.'

'That's true.'

'And if I make a request, you must comply.' Did he realize how attractive he was when he looked so seriously at her, how sensuously his hair fell against his face, how weak her legs had become?

'You only have to ask,' he said, his voice darkening a tone.

'Then I insist that you pleasure me.' There, she'd said it. 'Now,' she added, for good measure.

Perhaps there was the tiniest flicker in his eyes, but his gaze did not waver. Instead, he moved towards her, stopped in front of her, took the goblet of wine from her hand and set it down on the dressing table. A tremor of fright ran through her, parting her lips, the intake of breath faster. How vulnerable she suddenly was, to mockery. He put his hands up to her shoulders, tugged loose the ribbons that tied her shift. With the slightest of sighs, it slid over her body to the floor around her feet. Now he broke the contact with her eyes, glancing down at her naked breasts, her belly, her thighs. It seemed a long time before he returned her gaze again. When he did, and his eyes met hers, he unbuckled his belt and let his plaid fall away with its own weight so he stood before her equally naked but for his long linen shirt.

'The pleasure, Colonel,' he said, 'will be mine.'

He swung her up into his arms then and lifted her, as easily and gently as if she were a butterfly, round on to the bed. Almost before she was aware of the cold silk cover warming under her own skin heat, he had pulled off his shirt and straddled her, the sudden weight of him on the bed, his arms either side of her shoulders. She was pinned between those arms, the blood heat of him against her. His chest pressed on to her breasts, his mouth covered her own, his tongue sought hers.

The risk of rejection fled. This was her marriage bed, and all the intimacy it had held returned, familiar, erotic, secure. How desperately she wanted him now, arching up against his strength and hardness, returning his kisses, the murmured words of love and longing. Her hands sought the taut muscles in his arms, his back, his buttocks, just to know him again. She kissed his mouth, his eyes, his ears, the round curve of his shoulder, breathed in the musky scent of him, buried her face in the warmth of his neck.

His deep, dark voice in her ear spoke of love and desire and the ache of wanting, breath hot against her skin, his mouth and hands touching and caressing her face, arms, breasts. When she reached for, touched and stroked his erection, he moved away to pleasure her first, so she gave herself up to sensation. If there was one part of her he didn't touch or stroke or kiss or nip lightly with his teeth, she couldn't have said which it was. It was a learning re-learned, an agony of love and strange to be this passive in it, to allow adoration, the worship of a man for his woman. She moved when he moved her, turned when he turned her, parted her thighs when he put the slightest pressure between.

He slid his fingers into her, stroking till she was so wet with desire she thought she might come just from wanting, but then he moved his head closer between her thighs, tasting her with his tongue, teasing her so gently. Effortlessly, he held her tormented, breaking off to kiss her belly, to lick and stroke her thighs, then coming back, time and again, with his tongue caressing her so tenderly till she was half-crazed, more than half-crazed, become mindless, and the tide of sensate tension burst down through her, shuddering and flooding her trembling flesh, as she cried out for him, over and over and over, falling off the edge of the world to that place where nothing was but feeling. He had moved to hold her, his face pressed into her belly, his arms holding her tight, tightly.

'Anne, *a ghràidh*,' she heard him murmur, as her chest heaved and her breath came back into deep slowing gasps, the awareness of skin and flesh and limbs returning and with it, the ache of desire in her cunt, to be full of him, now, more than ever, to be joined with him, a wife ready to be husbanded. He moved back up the bed to lie on his side next her, running the warm palm of his hand lightly over her tingling skin as if to smooth out the fading tremors from her flesh.

'Now that you are pleasured,' he said, his voice soft, heavy, his eyes deep, dark and serious in the candlelight, 'I have something to ask.'

How could he think asking was required when she ached to have him inside her, his hard maleness thrusting into her, to own him as husband as he gave himself wholly up to her just as she had lost herself to him. Reaching up, she put her hand behind his neck, to pull him down to her.

'Oh, my love,' she said, pressing closer, her mouth at his shoulder, 'whatever you want of me.' She slid her hand across his chest, down against the shudder that ran up through his abdomen, letting her fingers find his hard, swollen cock. If he wanted surrender to her touch, fucking could wait. Exciting him first would be a deeper pleasure. 'However you want loved.' Her lips brushed his heated skin. 'I would do anything to please you.'

He swung himself off the bed, stood and pulled his shirt on over his head.

'Then, if you will,' he said, brisk and emotionless, 'I left some letters in my study that I'd like to get back to.'

She was sure her mouth fell open. For sure she stared at him in disbelief, then she leapt off the bed, dragged the quilted silk round her body to cover her nakedness and barged past him to the door, which she flung wide open.

'Will! Will!' she screamed down the stairs, then she spun round, glaring at her husband, who stood watching her with that infuriating half-smile on his face. 'How dare you!'

'You're as good as your word then?' he said, raising an eyebrow.

Will barged in through the door. 'Is everything all right?' he asked, seeing only the two of them.

'No, everything is not all right!' Anne spat out. 'Take the captain back to the cellar. Now!'

Will stared, bemused. Anne couldn't contain herself. She barged past Aeneas again, going for the pistols in her bedside drawer.

'No, don't bother,' she shouted. 'I'll shoot him here.' She grabbed one pistol and spun round.

'I think we'd better go now, Chief,' Will said, hauling Aeneas by the shirt. Aeneas ducked and scooped up his plaid as they left.

Anne had the pistol aimed as they vanished out the door, her hand shaking, knowing if she fired, she might hit the wrong man. She ran back to the door.

'And bring Donald,' she shouted after them. 'Get him out of bed, and bring him here to me at once!' She slammed the door shut, threw the pistol on the bed and herself after it, and wept.

Elizabeth arrived before Donald, wakened by the shouting. She wrapped her arms round her sister, trying to comfort.

'He humiliates me,' Anne sobbed through her tears and frustration. 'He just humiliates me.'

Alone in the cellar, Aeneas wrapped his plaid around him and sat down heavily on the bunk he'd been sleeping in. He put his head in his hands and groaned. His testicles ached but his heart ached worse. What the hell had he done? He wrapped his arms round himself to keep out the cold and rocked to ease the pain in his groin. What a bloody fool he was, to let pride carry that through, when it was the last thing his body or his feelings wanted to do. Twice now, twice, he'd been driven to create pain where love should have been restored.

He got up and paced about. If he wasn't so wildly crazy with love for her, if he didn't want her half so much, it would have been so easy just to fuck and forget all the rest. So he wanted her to know what it was to be rejected, what it meant to be torn apart in the heart of marriage, what it felt like to have your union turned into the common currency of lust. What an arsehole, he was. He kicked the wine rack, yelling as the bottles rattled, his toe stubbed. Now he hobbled back and forth, wincing more. What an absolute fool.

The door opened above him. Light and feet descended the stair. He hoped it was Anne. He hoped he'd have time to say sorry before she shot him. She shouldn't have to live not knowing he'd take it back if he could, that if he could live those minutes again, he'd do things quite differently. He hoped she'd shoot him in the head, blow his brains out. It was Donald who came down, carrying a lantern and laden with tools.

'I'm to chain you,' he said. 'Long enough so you can reach the chamber pot. Short enough so you can't get the wine.' He put the tools and lantern down. 'Sorry, Chief,' he said. 'Not my idea. I'm sure she'll come round, given time.'

'I've got it! I've got it!'

Cumberland put down his knife, wiped his chin with a napkin and turned to glare at the interruption. It was General Hawley who barged in through the tent flap.

'If it's the clap from camp followers,' the Duke snarled, 'you should think better than interrupt my breakfast with it.' They had moved out of Aberdeen, advancing towards Inverness.

'No, no.' Hawley was too excited to take the hint. 'What you've been looking for.' He unrolled the map he carried on the table, pushing Cumberland's plate aside in his eagerness. 'There,' he said, jabbing a finger.

Cumberland frowned and peered down at the cartography.

'It's moorland, quite high.'

'Yes!' Hawley agreed, stabbing his finger again. 'Boxed in with these walls, here and here. And wet. Boggy, in fact, across this part.'

'So,' Cumberland said, seeing the intent, 'if we set up here –' he pointed '– is it firm enough for the guns? We need the artillery.'

'Dry across there.' Hawley swept his hand over the area. A one-handed beggar from Aberdeen's cruel streets provided the information. The man, Dùghall, had dribbled hatred for the clan whose lands bordered the site. 'And the best part, right on the witch's doorstep. Their Colonel Anne,' he spat out, 'will have a ringside view.'

'You got this from the turn of a screw?' Cumberland stared at him, certain he heard the rattle of bones from the general's skinny frame. The man was more obnoxious gleeful than he was spiteful.

'Oiled with gold,' Hawley leered, 'the currency of deceit.' The beggar had cost little. But his new informer commanded a high price. He stabbed the indicated wetland. 'They won't charge through that. My life on it.'

Cumberland pulled the napkin from his collar, threw it on the table.

'I believe you,' he said. 'They certainly won't.' His voice rose angrily. 'Nor will George Murray be fool enough to set his forces up like sitting ducks with their wings plucked just so we can shoot them down!'

'Ah,' said Hawley, rocking back on his heels, his mouth spreading in a smile that was like a slash wounding his bony face, 'that's where it gets better, and better.'


'Have you lost your mind, sir?' George Murray glared at the Prince. 'This ground is useless for Highland warriors.' They had moved out of Inverness the day before, knowing Cumberland was not far off, and taken residence in Culloden House. The old judge, Forbes, who owned it, had fled Inverness with Lord Louden.

'It's flat, open, and we are protected on both flanks by these walls, here and here,' the Prince said, indicating the dry-stone enclosures on the map.

'But wet in winter.' MacGillivray frowned. 'There will be no purchase underfoot.'

'Not at this height above the sea,' O'Sullivan disagreed.

'We could throw down those dry-stone walls first,' Lovat offered.

'Open it up.' Balmerino nodded.

'And expose our flanks?' O'Sullivan questioned.

'Better exposed than boxed in,' Lord George snapped at him. 'Sir –' he turned to the Prince '– I advise that you forgo this field. Our forces in the north need more time to get here. Cross the Nairn. The ground will suit us better and another day's delay will let Cluny's force rejoin us from the south.'

'Always you counsel for delay, Lord George,' the Prince smiled. 'Your last cost us London. We will not trust you in this. I will command our next engagement. O'Sullivan chose the ground, and I agree.'

A ripple of shock ran round the war council.

'Lord George gave us Prestonpans and Falkirk,' Margaret Johnstone said.

'*Mais oui* – ' the Prince gazed at her '– the counsel of women. Well, Lady Ogilvie, this should appeal to your female sensibilities. My cousin celebrates his birthday today. Let him party while he may. Tomorrow, he will have our belated gift.' He stabbed the map with his forefinger. 'Here is where we fight.' He scanned the group. 'If I am to be alone and unsupported by my troops, so be it. But, tomorrow, we make our stand.'

'And an end to a bad affair!' George Murray declared.

# THIRTY-TWO

Elizabeth sat alone in the dining room, eating dinner. The food, leftovers from the party, seemed tasteless. Whatever Aeneas intended, he had ruined everything for her. She had tried to prise the key from Jessie, to go down to the cellar and berate him, but Jessie would not give it up this time. Before finally falling asleep, Anne had ordered no visitors and short rations for her husband. She was still asleep, exhausted from the long day and its disturbing, emotional ending.

There were raised voices from the kitchen now, Will and Jessie, then another man's. The door from the kitchens opened. Jessie ushered in the stranger. It was the boy with one arm who'd danced for most of yesterday.

'Sure Robbie can't see Anne?' Jessie asked.

'I have to,' the boy said. 'MacGillivray said I had to.' He drew a note from inside his plaid. 'I'm to give her this.'

'I'll deal with it, Jessie,' Elizabeth said. 'Go make a pot of tea. I'll take it up shortly.' When Jessie was out of the room and the door shut, she looked at the lad. 'Let me see the note.'

'I'm to give it personal to Colonel Anne,' he resisted.

'She's not well,' Elizabeth assured him. 'I'm her sister, and very close to Chief MacGillivray. If you give it to me, I'll take it up.'

Robbie handed it over, though he hovered.

'They're gathering on the moor,' he said. 'That's where I saw them.'

'Have you to go back?' MacGillivray might expect a reply.

'No, miss, I'm not much for fighting now. I'll go tomorrow to watch, when the English come. My Shameless might be there.'

Tomorrow? The situation was urgent then.

'I'll see she gets this,' she told Robbie. 'Off you go.' As soon as he was gone, she tore open the note and scanned the brief lines.

MacGillivray wanted Anne to join him on Drumossie. It was war business, mainly concern about Anne's cousin being relieved of command. It meant nothing to Elizabeth – the Murrays were no relation to her – apart from the undying devotion expressed at the end. What was it Anne had that men found so easy to love?

When Jessie brought the tea in, Elizabeth put the note in her pocket, took the tray and went upstairs. Anne would go to MacGillivray today as he asked, and, with her and Aeneas so at odds, would likely stay with him. It would be the end of her sister's marriage, the end of Elizabeth's hopes for her own. There was nothing left that she could do to turn events, and MacGillivray's attention, in her favour. It was too late.

Anne was not asleep. She was awake, washed and dressed, and she was packing.

'Oh, tea,' she said when Elizabeth came in. 'That's probably just the thing.'

Elizabeth set the tray down and poured a cup. 'What are you doing?'

'Leaving,' her sister said. 'There's nothing for me here. If I stay now, I'll become bitter and vindictive.'

'Aeneas well deserves that,' Elizabeth assured her.

'But I don't,' Anne said. 'I've been a fool, making a fool's choice. Love isn't hard and unforgiving. It's generous and kind. Alexander showed me that.'

'You're going to him.' It wasn't a question.

Anne nodded. 'Tomorrow, my things can go to Dunmaglas. I'll rejoin my troops.' She put her teacup down and gave Elizabeth a hug. 'Don't be disappointed,' she said. 'There will be someone for you but it never was him.'

'He likes me well enough. This isn't fair. You don't love him.'

'I do, and with an easier love than I have for Aeneas. Alexander gives me nothing but goodness. More than that, he welcomes my love of him.' Aeneas shut her out now, did not allow. A man who wouldn't be loved, who could not be vulnerable, who would even control intimacy, was a man who couldn't love. She rubbed Elizabeth's arm. 'You and I are both suffering desire for men who won't care for us. That's too hard a bed to lie in for long.' She looked around the room. 'All these things. It will take till bedtime to have them ready.' She opened the door and called Jessie up.

Elizabeth wandered over to the window and looked out towards the moor. She could see nothing at this distance. The note taunted from her pocket. Why had she not given it up? It could make no difference now if Anne left today or tomorrow.

'Jessie,' Anne said, when the girl came in, 'I need Will to ride to Inverness, and back before night. He'll have a cart to load in the morning.'

Jessie's face crumpled. Her hands worked at her apron, now stretched tight over her swelling stomach.

'He's gone,' she said. 'He's gone to fight.'

'But Will's no warrior,' Anne said.

'I know. I told him.' Jessie started to cry. 'He said he'd show me he was man enough.'

'Oh, dear.' Anne pulled the girl to her in a hug. 'Don't cry. I'll find him tomorrow and send him back.'

'Will you?' Jessie brightened up.

'I will,' Anne nodded. 'That baby of yours will not grow up without its father. Now, let's all have a cup of tea. Then we'll be ready to pack.'

'What did you need from Inverness?' Elizabeth asked. Her heart had clenched in her chest. The moor was on the way there.

'It can wait,' Anne said, pouring more tea. 'The Dowager needs to be told she'll be mistress here again, at least until Aeneas finds himself a woman he can live with, if any can live with him.'

'You're leaving us?' Jessie asked.

'I am,' Anne said, 'and no tears, for I've run out.'

'I'll go to Inverness,' Elizabeth said. 'I don't mind and, tell the truth, I'd be glad to be out.'

'You'd ride all that way and back before night?'

'If it helps.'

Anne threw her arms round her sister and kissed her cheek. 'You're such a blessing to me,' she said. 'But I can't let you do that. Not on your own. You're nineteen,' she smiled. 'And there's a war on.'

'I'll be fine,' Elizabeth insisted. 'The road goes there so I can't get lost.'

And that was it settled. She would let the Dowager know Moy Hall would be short of a mistress come morning. Jessie and Anne would pack. Tomorrow, when the cart was loaded, Elizabeth would go with it to Dunmaglas, then on home to Invercauld. Anne would return to the army. It was all quite simple, except Elizabeth had no intention of going to Inverness. There was one night left, one night in which she might finally persuade MacGillivray his future didn't lie with Anne but with her. It was a slim chance, but the only one she had. She would go to Drumossie to find him, and maybe change both their lives.

He wasn't difficult to find. Among thousands of men being moved about and settled down, his stature and that blaze of red-gold hair picked him out, standing near a supply tent. His face lit up when she rode towards him, for a moment thinking she was Anne. When he saw she was not, his expression became concerned.

'*Ciod e?* Is Anne not coming?' he asked before she was even off the horse.

Elizabeth held out her arms to be helped down. Maybe it was her turn to play the fool. His first thought was always for her sister, not even manners to greet her.

'Tomorrow,' she said when she stood beside him, looking up into his frowning face. He should worry for her, abroad among armies of strangers.

'Then she's happy with this?'

'Why would she not be?'

'I thought she might want us to stand down.' He looked around, shaking his head. 'This is not good ground, and with Lord George relieved of command –' His thought faded away into silence.

'But she expects you to fight for this idiot Prince.'

He spun round, looking intensely at her. 'Is that what she said?'

Elizabeth had only meant to point out how little Anne cared for his survival.

'She doesn't call the Prince an idiot,' she corrected. 'That's my opinion.'

'But she intends we should fight?'

'Of course she does.' Elizabeth put her hand against his chest. 'That's all she wants you for, isn't it? Aeneas wouldn't do it.' How could her sister risk such a man? He should be a lover not a warrior. 'If you'd listen to me instead, I'd take you off this field right now, to a warmer, better place.'

'You could make that offer once too often,' he warned, smiling.

Elizabeth's stomach turned over. This was the MacGillivray she wanted, the one who laughed and joked and flirted, the man who looked at her with such naked cheek.

'Then take me up on it,' she suggested, glancing flirtatiously at him.

But he'd become serious again. 'A better place is what we're fighting for,' he said. 'To be a free people living as we choose.' He put his hands on her shoulders, smiling again. 'So that spirited women like you can offer loving to men like me, and be safe to do so.' He tilted her chin, bent down and kissed her mouth lightly.

Every thought and word scattered from Elizabeth's head. He could be hers if Anne wasn't always in the way.

'Are you chasing after both my sisters?' a voice interrupted, none too happy. It was James, her brother. She'd forgotten he'd be here too. Baron Bàn, her cousin Francis, strode over with him.

'It was just thanks,' MacGillivray answered. 'She came to wish us well.'

'That could be timely,' Francis said, greeting Elizabeth with another kiss. 'Lord George has suggested we attack Cumberland in his camp after dark.'

'I thought George was out of favour,' MacGillivray said.

'Then he's hoping to win it back before tomorrow,' Francis answered. 'The Prince has agreed. He likes the idea of delivering defeat for the royal birthday, and while they're in their cups celebrating it. O'Sullivan is none too pleased.'

'That's good enough for me,' MacGillivray said. 'We'll lead the way.' He called Donald Fraser over and gave him instructions to ready the regiment.

'You should be in Invercauld,' James said to Elizabeth. 'It's safer there.'

'I'm going home tomorrow,' she told him, but she made a face at his back as he walked off with Francis to get the Farquharsons ready for the night raid.

'That's good advice,' MacGillivray said. 'Cumberland is only ten miles from here. If his army is broken up, you don't want to contend with fleeing soldiers.'

'So you'd care what happens to me?' Elizabeth tilted her head, coquettishly, looking into his eyes as she ran her hand up his arm.

'Of course I care.'

That was all she needed to hear. She slid her arms round his waist, pushing his weapons and sporran round from between them, her face against his chest.

'Then stay with me.' She spoke softly, her voice heavy, stretching up, lips brushing his throat. 'Let the rest of them go play at war.' Her hips pressed against him, moved against him. 'I can love you better than you imagine.'

'I would only be taking advantage.'

'Who can that hurt?' Under his plaid, he was becoming aroused. 'We're both free to fuck whoever we please.' She put her hand down to raise the hem of his kilt. He really wanted her.

'Come, trobhad.' He pulled her into the supply tent and ordered the startled storesman out.

As soon as they were safely and privately enclosed by the canvas, Elizabeth wrapped herself against MacGillivray again, reaching up to kiss his mouth, pulling his kilt out of the way with her other hand so she could touch him. He caught hold of her arms, gentle but firm, pushed her away.

'Can you not be let down easy?' he asked.

'But you want me.'

'My body's an instrument of desire and wants ease,' he said.

'But put a rope round my neck, make me fear or want to hurt, you might get the same response.'

'Is that why you brought me in here, to say no?'

'I wouldn't embarrass you before everyone,' he said quietly, then he gave a little smile. 'Would you have your brother fight to make me fuck with you?' He stepped closer to her again, put out his hand, stroked her hair. 'Elizabeth, I love your sister. Understand what that means.'

She pushed his hand away, angry tears welling in her eyes. 'Well, she doesn't love you!' she shouted at him. 'That's why she's not here, she's too busy fucking with her husband!'

He flinched then. There was at least some satisfaction in knowing she had hurt him. But when he looked up at her again, the bleakness in his eyes made her want to take it back.

'Then everything's as it should be.' He swallowed, hard, as if something was stuck in his throat. 'Were you sent to console me?'

She dropped her gaze, staring down at the muddy grass round their feet, feeling shame, hot shame, and shook her head.

'Anne doesn't know I'm here.'

He took a step towards the doorway and stopped level with her. 'Go home, Elizabeth,' he said, his voice rough, breaking. 'And before you take a husband –' he cleared his throat '– learn that men are more than soulless fucks.' The tent flap slapped behind him as he went out.

Anne was fastening the strap around the last kist when she heard Elizabeth come running up the stairs, go into her own room and shut the door. She wondered if she should go to her but decided not. It would be kinder to let her sister think she hadn't guessed, kinder not to make her confess MacGillivray's rejection. Had it been otherwise, her sister would have bounced into Anne's room to announce she had just bedded Alexander. Poor Elizabeth, as if she'd ride to Inverness to serve anyone except herself.

Anne stood and looked around the room. Apart from her riding clothes, ready for tomorrow, everything was packed. She didn't blame her sister. She'd been the same, wanting to change the world so it fitted instead of fitting into it. Downstairs were other boxes. Everything she'd brought with her when she married was going. Next day, when Aeneas was released from the cellar, nothing of her would remain. She went downstairs. With Will gone, Elizabeth's horse would need stripped, rubbed down and fed. It was growing dark out and a wet April snow had just begun to fall.

# THIRTY-THREE

On the morning of that day, Anne woke to the grey light of driving sleet. She had left the shutters open so the sky would wake her early, but the dullness meant it was already later than it seemed. Icy rain streaked across the window like thin, sharp blades. She lay and watched it for some time, the hypnotic shafts, the flakes of iced snow in it running down the panes, gathering white then washing away. There was no triumph in what she was about to do, only grim determination. The weather suited. Relief would come when everything was done and cleared away. Spring would follow this last spit of winter. It would bring new life with it, as it should.

In the wine cellar, Aeneas turned uneasily in a half-sleep; the shadow of wine racks and barrels made tricky companions. Donald Fraser had shackled one chain to his right ankle, another to his left wrist, the workmanship solid. He'd need a smith to get out of them. Strong enough to hold him, not heavy enough to weigh him down, they rattled as he turned, moved or stood. Chains put on him by his wife. How long would they keep this up? He thought himself done with his own anger. When Jessie came with breakfast, he'd ask for Anne, apologize, admit himself wrong. She had bested him, not because she chained him but because she did no worse. Anne was true to herself. Even when that angered him most, he admired it. At the top of the cellar, a fanlight window at ground level let in a thin, grey light. It was early yet.

It was not so early, the light cheating. In the sparse woods and rough buildings around Culloden House, thousands of exhausted Highlanders slept in whatever cover they could find. Bodies crammed supply tents, lay under wagons and the few light cannon.

Those with nothing to keep the sleet off huddled together under plaids. MacGillivray had chosen to be outside, near his men. Knowing the terrain, they had led the march to Nairn last night, to within two miles of Cumberland's sleeping camp. Unbelievably, the tail of their forces had not kept up. Constantly, he stopped with Lord George, waiting for the Prince and O'Sullivan to bring up the rear. The delay meant it was too late to go on and attack before daylight. They turned around, marched back again. Sleep hadn't come till dawn. Now, feet hurried past. A Cameron hand shook him awake.

'They're coming! They're coming!' the man said, then ran on into Culloden House. MacGillivray was on his feet, calling his men awake. The pipes and drums began sounding the call to arms. It was eleven o'clock.

In a cottage at the edge of the moor, MacBean's wife kneaded bread. Her husband hovered at her back, belting on his sheathed sword. When she'd had enough of his dodging about, she spun round, grabbed him by the plaid and planked a warm, wet kiss on his mouth.

'Now, get on. Go if you must,' she grumbled, turning back to the dough so she wouldn't see the love in his watery eyes. Old fool. 'Give me peace to my baking.' The door opened behind her, letting wind and rain blow into the warmth. 'You'll be wanting fed –' the door shut behind him '– when you get back.'

At breakfast, Anne looked up from her porridge and listened. It wasn't weather for clear sound, everything muffled by the curtain of driving sleet. She strained to hear – drums, pipes, she was sure, here then gone. They must be gathering, leaving Inverness. Her decision to go was timely. MacGillivray would send for her soon. Elizabeth came in, dressed but half-slept by the look of her. Anne wished she could speak to her sister about last night, and about her ride to Inverness that stormy night in February, but it was better not, better left to Elizabeth to confess.

'Are you looking forward to going home?' she asked instead.

'I am now,' Elizabeth said, miserably, 'with you gone.'

Anne poured tea, but her sister wrinkled her nose, preferring ale with her porridge. When Jessie brought it in, thick, steaming hot, she told Anne that she'd found an old man – a crofter – and a young lad to ride the cart to Dunmaglas and then escort Elizabeth on to Invercauld.

'They'll be along shortly,' Jessie said. In Highland time, that could mean several hours.

'Did you hear the pipes and drums?' Anne asked. 'My ears were maybe playing tricks.'

'Aye, started a half-hour ago,' Jessie said. 'Stopped now. They're gathering on the moor. That's where Will went.'

So she was right enough, gathering. They wouldn't fight on Drumossie, unless they wanted to lose. George would bring them over the Nairn, to this side of the water, where the ground was dry, hilly and rough. If she waited till they crossed, she wouldn't have so far to ride, a half-hour trot instead of twice that. But she wanted away, wanted to be with them. The army was more her home now than here. She went out and hitched the wagon, brought it to the door. When Elizabeth had eaten, they started to bring down the kists and boxes from upstairs. Jessie was excused heavy lifting, packing food for the journey instead.

Up on Drumossie, driving sleet blew into the faces of the warriors. Visibility was poor. They'd been lined and blocked in battle formation for an hour or more, tired, hungry and growing chilled because of that. Among the tufts of rough moorland grass, crusts of icy white collected.

'Did you send for Anne?' Donald Fraser, on MacGillivray's left, asked.

'I did,' MacGillivray answered, face grim. 'Maybe Aeneas keeps her back.'

'If she's trying to unchain him, he will,' Fraser laughed. 'For I doubt he'll be out of that cellar till me or Lachlan get back.'

'You have him chained?'

'Last thing I did before coming up here,' Fraser said. 'He's so far the wrong side of Anne now, I doubt there's any right side to be found any more.'

MacGillivray was puzzled. However Anne treated her husband was for her to decide. He couldn't guess what Aeneas might have done to merit chains. A smile flitted across his face. Disagreeing with Anne was probably enough. But it was strange, all the same. Not quite the situation described by Elizabeth. For the first time he wondered about the note he'd sent. Anne would not have ignored it. Yet it had been delivered; Elizabeth knew where to come.

'I think her sister has my note,' he told Fraser. 'I doubt Anne ever saw it.' She wouldn't abandon them or let him down.

He squinted against the sleet, across the field. Lord George and his Atholl men were lined up on the right, leaving the Prince with O'Sullivan to command from the rear. George had let loyalty to their cause win the day, against his judgement. They were going to fight. It was as well Anne didn't come. This would be a hard-won victory, if they could do it. Better she found out afterwards. It would be a bloody field to watch.

Despite the weather, there were watchers. Crowds of folk from Inverness stood a good way off. A bunch of older boys who should have been in school settled on a ridge. The warriors' womenfolk and children were well behind the lines, out of harm's way on this flat ground, apart from a group of commanders' wives led by Margaret and Greta, who stayed near the Prince. Will McIntosh pushed up between MacGillivray and Fraser.

'Can I stand with Donald?' the stable-boy asked, looking strangely at odds with the weapons belted at his side.

'No, you can't,' MacGillivray said. 'You have to earn your place at the front.' MacBean was on his right. Age and experience went first into battle, to inspire the young behind to bravery and courage. 'Get on back,' he told Will, 'behind Lachlan, where you were put.' As the boy dodged off, MacGillivray walked along Clan Chatton's lines, from the McIntoshes to the Farquharsons. Commander-in-chief of Clan Chatton, he had charge of both, and would have a word with their captains, Anne's brother and cousin, before the enemy arrived. While he was talking with James and Francis, they heard the drums. Peering forward into the sleet and rain, MacGillivray saw the first flash of red coats in the distance.

In her room, Anne laid out her riding habit, the blue velvet trimmed with tartan that she'd worn to raise the clan the first time she'd ridden away from Aeneas. She would change when everything was loaded up. It seemed right to wear it the last time she'd ride away from him. She pinned a fresh white cockade to her blue bonnet, ready to pull on. There would be no coming back, not again. Behind her, their marriage bed was made up with clean linen sheets and fresh covers. Not even the scent of her would linger. Aeneas would have it to himself as soon as she was gone. He could move his own clothes back from the boxroom. Jessie had Donald's tools. They could work it out between them or wait till the blacksmith returned.

The old crofter and the boy had arrived to load the cart. The last things were taken down from her bedroom. Everything to be loaded was downstairs. Anne checked the room, opening cupboards and drawers, wanting to leave no trace behind. In the bottom of the wardrobe, only the box with Aeneas's private documents remained. She had forgotten their marriage lines, as much hers as his. She lifted the box on to the dressing table and opened it. The papers on top were new. Curious, she opened them and read.

Aeneas stood up, chains rattling, when the cellar door opened at the top of the steps. Feet came down, Anne's feet, white skirts skimming the stairs. Now he could tell her, ask forgiveness, make his peace.

'Anne,' he said, as soon as he could see her face, 'thank God. Jessie said you were leaving. I thought you might go without letting me speak.'

'I haven't come to let you speak,' she snapped. She was furious. 'I've come to tell you what I think of you.' In her hand she had papers, the debt waiver with the deeds of Moy Hall and their clan grounds. She shook with rage as she held it out. 'You sold us out!

You sold our cause, sold out your clan, and you sold out our marriage, for this! For stone walls and a bit of ground! Now I know why you went to the Watch, why you stood against us for this government!'

'I didn't ask for that, or expect it.'

'It has your name on it! It makes you owner of Moy, which you never were and cannot be. It is the clan's land!'

'Woman, will you ever let me speak!' The anger he thought would not be roused by her again rushed through him. 'It has my name on it because that's how they work. You know that! Ownership is what you fight against.'

'Because they create it to control us!'

'I know. Forbes held the loss of Moy over my head. But he drew that up, after Prestonpans, when he thought we were defeated. He gave it to let me go!'

'What, he gives a gift of what is not his to give nor yours to take!' She was scathing. 'And, having got it, did you go home to your clan, to your wife? I think not!'

Aeneas glowered at her.

'My wife was in the arms of another man.'

'Not then. Not till I thought you hanged Ewan. Not till after Falkirk.' She moved closer to him. 'But I'm going to him now. You can stick this in your sporran.' She threw the papers at his feet. 'See if it can keep your sex roused from now on!'

There was a crack of thunder, a loud boom. Both Aeneas and Anne looked up at the small window high above them. The boom became a volley of cannon fire, distant but unmistakable. Elizabeth appeared at the top of the stairs.

'Anne, do you hear?' she shouted, coming down a few steps till she could see her sister, her face fearful.

'That's up on the moor.' Aeneas turned back to Anne.

'It can't be.' She looked from him to Elizabeth. 'MacGillivray would've sent for me.'

Elizabeth was in tears, slumping down on to the stair.

'He did, yesterday morning,' she cried. 'I didn't mean any harm. He said you wouldn't want them to fight there.'

275

Anne ran up to her. The noise of the big guns, almost seven miles away, was like rolling thunder.

'You let him think I wouldn't come?'

'Anne, get me out of here.' Aeneas pulled against his chains. 'I'll come with you!'

'It's too late for that!' she screamed at him. She dragged Elizabeth to her feet, up the last few stairs and out of the cellar. The door slammed shut and locked.

# THIRTY-FOUR

Thick smoke surrounded MacGillivray, standing at the front of his men, while round-shot from government cannon whistled overhead and grenades from the Coehorn mortars exploded among the Jacobite lines. Further back the ranks, horses squealed, men cried out as the missiles tore into their targets.

'Close up, close up,' he heard the captains in the rear yell to their troops to fill the gaps left by the onslaught. Ten minutes of this they had stood, waiting the command to charge. Lord George had left his post, gone back to seek the order to attack from the Prince. Grim-faced, MacGillivray waited, flinching as a low ball tore into his own line, not turning to see who had been taken down, just hearing the thud, the sickening thump of bursting flesh and cracking bone. Whoever it was, dead already, did not cry out.

'Close up, close up,' Donald Fraser yelled behind him.

Anne galloped Pibroch past the end of Loch Moy and on to the hills, urging the horse faster than she dared. Even at the gallop, Drumossie was twenty minutes away. However well she navigated the slopes and streams, there was hill and bog to cross, the Nairn to ford. All would slow her down. The booming cannon grew louder with every stride, the thump and crack of mortars. Would she hear the war cries over the barrage, the answering musket-fire? If MacGillivray was already away, cutting into the enemy, she couldn't stop them, could only hope to make her presence known, to let them see she hadn't abandoned them to fight while she sat safe at home. 'Don't go,' she prayed, 'not yet.' Again, she urged the white horse on to greater effort.

'We have to take down the wall on our right,' Lord George shouted at O'Sullivan. 'We're being outflanked behind it!'

O'Sullivan kept his eyes front, ignored him. Lord George swung round to the Prince.

'*Pour la pitié*, will you order the charge,' he urged, 'or will we just die out there?'

The Prince turned on his horse, looked at him, indecision in his eyes.

'The enemy should advance first,' he said.

'And if they don't?' Lord George was chilled by the look of the man. The Prince had no idea how to command, despite assuming it. 'Highlanders charge,' he prompted again, stating the obvious. 'That's their strength.'

The government cannon boomed. A ball thudded into Lord Elcho's horse regiment, dangerously close to the Prince. O'Sullivan leant over to speak in his ear.

'Let the guns do their work,' he said. 'Then they'll advance.'

'Ours are near silent,' Lord George raged. 'The only work is done by theirs!'

'We can wait,' the Prince assured him. '*Noblesse oblige.*' But he looked to O'Sullivan for agreement. The adjutant nodded and indicated the command party should retire further back, behind their French reserves, out of range. Already there was slaughter, limbs, bodies, the smell of blood and death, in the rear ranks.

Lord George gave up, swung his horse round and headed forward again.

Up front, MacGillivray clenched his jaw tighter. Twenty minutes now they had stood and still no order came. The government artillery thundered on. Shot whistled past, cutting swathes into their ranks. Men screamed from the back of his own lines.

'Close up, close up,' Fraser yelled again behind him. The order was echoed from further back as the living moved forward to fill the places of the dead.

'No more,' MacGillivray muttered. They had taken all they would take. He scrugged his bonnet, raised his hands behind his head and drew the great-sword from its scabbard on his back.

'Claymore!' he roared.

Relief swept along the M<sup>c</sup>Intosh and Clan Chatton lines. Embattled men pulled their bonnets down, drew their pistols. MacGillivray thrust his claymore forward.

'Loch Moy!' he bellowed, the war cry taken up by the men behind, and then they charged, racing down the field towards a tightly formed red-coated enemy.

Hearing them come, the government guns changed to grape-shot, loading the cannon with bags of nail, shards of metal, the angle lowered to cover the field in front. Seeing MacGillivray go, Lochiel drew his own sword and roared his Cameron men on to battle. Lord George, arriving back at his Atholl brigade, saw the decision had been taken from the Prince's hands by the M<sup>c</sup>Intosh regiment and gave the command to charge.

Half-way down the field, the first grape-shot cut into MacGillivray's men as they stopped to fire off their pistols. Bodies fell but the shot went off, pistols were dropped, and the great searing slash of steel sounded as broadswords, axes and dirks were drawn. The front line of government foot fired into them and dropped to their knees to load. The second line took aim.

'Loch Moy!' MacGillivray roared again, and charged on.

Skirting the lower braes, head down over Pibroch's neck, Anne had heard the change in the sound of the cannonshot. Not knowing the cause, she hoped it meant some of the bigger guns had been silenced. Now, she heard musket fire, rapid, repeating volleys from massed guns. She was too late. The charge had begun. Her men would be racing into that, M<sup>c</sup>Intosh and Clan Chatton men she had raised for the cause, Farquharson and Atholl men she'd known all her life, men she cared for, men she loved, all three of her families, her mother's, father's, and her married family, charging side by side. She prayed to all the forces known to humankind to keep them safe together and strong. More than half-way to the river Nairn, she drove her horse on, leaning low to urge it with her voice, faster, as its hooves drummed over the grassland.

★

MacGillivray thudded across the moor, setting the pace, grape-shot whistling past his head. Ahead, he saw bog in front of him. If his charging warriors ran into that they'd come to a stop. He veered right to skirt it, losing momentum as the whole line following did likewise. Exposed to crossfire of their flank, several men behind the dozen leaders fell, making a gap in the charging ranks.

Behind them, racing Camerons and Atholl men saw their route to the enemy narrowed by the drift of M<sup>c</sup>Intoshes into their path, forcing them tighter against the walls on their right. Behind those walls, General Hawley commanded his troops to throw down the stones and fire at the Atholl flank. At the Jacobite front line, Francis of Monaltrie drew his claymore and roared the Farquharsons into the attack, Anne's paternal clan following her husband's towards the massed government ranks. Behind him, her brother, James, waited to lead the second line. On the left, Lord Drummond urged the MacDonalds to join the charge, but they would not go, angry to have been usurped from their place on the right of the field by Lord George coming forward. They stood, stoic and stern, weapons sheathed and shouldered, as a hail of grape-shot tore into them, a third of their force already dead around their feet.

Plunging into the enemy, MacGillivray swung his claymore, down and across, beheading the nearest foot soldier in one swipe. Around him, his men crashed through the front government lines, slashing, hacking, trying to force the break that would weaken the wall of enemy guns. He swung again, splitting a redcoat's head open down to the neck. As the man dropped, MacGillivray glanced around. Only a dozen of his men had got through with him. The government lines closed at their backs, still firing at the oncoming warriors. Beside him, MacBean and Donald Fraser parried bayonets with their targes, cut and hacked with their swords. Behind him, the shoemaker, Duff, speared his sword through a redcoat's throat but took a bayonet in his gut from the next man down and dropped to the ground.

Will, who had run fast to be as near Fraser as he could, dropped the targe he had little idea how to use and swung wildly, cutting one man to the ground, slashing another across the face. An officer pulled a sword, raked it across Will's arm, then his throat. As the boy fell, MacGillivray brought his claymore down, bringing off the officer's sword and hand both. Fending back the foot soldiers, he dragged Will nearer to him and stood over the boy as his remaining men drew tighter to their chief. Fraser, seeing the protective move, turned to cover MacGillivray's back. A bayonet stabbed into the blacksmith's ribs. As he staggered on the point of it, a sword glanced off his face and he went down. The heavy weight of another Highlander collapsed on top of him.

MacGillivray dropped his claymore, drew his broadsword and targe, dirk behind the shield. He thrust his sword into the throat of the nearest soldier and swung his dirk back to cut another on his left. On his right, a bayonet stabbed forward. He felt it go into his side, shuddered as it was withdrawn. With one stroke, MacBean cut the arm from the man who wounded his chief. A raised musket took aim, fired. The ball tore into MacBean's chest. He fell, twitching, blood pumping out of his back. MacGillivray was on his knees, in a red mess of blood, his side weeping fluid, breath coming in great gasps. An English lieutenant stepped up behind him, raised and thrust his sword down between the wounded chief's shoulders. It was James Ray. As MacGillivray pitched forward, Ray put his foot on the Highlander's broad back and withdrew his blade.

Half a mile away, at the Jacobite rear, O'Sullivan reached over to the Prince's horse, took hold of the reins and turned them both away from the decimated field. Lord Elcho cantered up, his horse's rump and legs spattered red. Like Lord George, he, too, had begged for the order to charge, his cavalry brutally torn to shreds by the cannon as they waited, unused.

'Will you order retreat?' he shouted at the Prince.

His royal commander looked at him, tears running down his cheeks. 'Let every man save himself who can,' the Prince cried out. 'We are defeated. *Nous sommes défaits.*'

'You snivelling, pampered coward,' Elcho snarled. 'Run away. Go back across the water. It was a better day for Scotland had you never come!' He yanked his horse round, seeking a drummer boy still alive and able to beat retreat. As the Irish Brigade and the *Écossais Royaux* moved forward to provide cover for it, the command party set off, O'Sullivan escorting the Prince, at a fast gallop, away from the battlefield.

Anne urged Pibroch into the water of Nairn. The horse shied. She kicked it on, the water shallow over the pebbled bottom. Two steps, the horse tried to turn. She dragged the reins tight, wouldn't let its head come round. They were close enough now to hear the screams of men and beasts, the roar of cannon, the repeated rounds of musket-fire.

'Come on, Pibroch,' she urged, kicking her heels into its sides. *'Siuthad, a-nis!'* The horse went forward four more steps, threw its head back, whinnied, stopped.

The squall of sleety rain had passed, the cloud gone as if it had never been. Face flat on the wet ground, MacGillivray stared ahead at the surrounding soldiers' feet as they moved past, re-forming their ranks, ignoring the group of dying men in their midst. He could feel nothing except a cold, chilling calm. His breath staggered, came again. Blood from his chest leaked into a small moorland stream running past his shoulder. Beside him, Will's cut throat still seeped. Ahead of him, MacBean struggled on the ground, inched towards MacGillivray, trying to reach his chief, to cover him with his body. He reached out, fingers almost making it, his hand dropping into the spring, blood running the length of his arm. MacGillivray, staring through stained, dank grass, watched the narrow flow of brackish water run red.

Anne jumped off, keeping a tight grip of the rein. Landing ankle deep in the water, she pulled the horse forward by its head. It wouldn't budge. She stared ahead, looking for deep water, a drop the animal could sense but she could not see. Nothing, just pebbles, water rippling over, becoming murky. She looked up at the opposite bank. Shafts of warm April sun probed down through overhanging trees to where sleet still crusted white in the clumps of grass, lapped by the river, staining red. She looked down to Pibroch's white legs. Red crept up from the horse's fetlocks. Glancing at her wet white skirts, trailing in the water, she saw the stain creep up, red on to white, white into red. She, and her mount, stood in a river of blood.

A gasp shuddered through MacGillivray's chest. The green blades in front of his eyes, smudged crimson, were thick as a forest. He could see Anne on the ridge, on her white horse, snow falling round her shoulders, that smile men would die to be the cause of on her lips. He hoped she would be proud, not sad. The cold chill passed. There was no ridge, or snow, just white light, the sharp sound of battle.

'Eyes front, soldier,' a voice said. 'Ignore 'em, they're no harm to us now.'

He was dying. No more hurt could come. Peace flooded his bones. The old myths were right. Death was the last love a man lay down with. A well of it rose up to receive him, filling all the emptiness that life had hollowed out, bringing him in.

Emptiness filled Anne's ears, the roar of nothing. She tore her gaze away from the bloody water to Pibroch's wild eyes. The reins, twisted round her hands, burned as the horse pulled against her. The racket of cannon and guns had ceased. A strange mockery of silence fell, filled more fully by shrieks and calls from way beyond the far bank, up on the moorland. She raised her eyes to the sound. A pall of yellow smoke drifted above the riverbank trees.

Up on the moor, Cumberland had ordered fire to cease. His men had done a fine job. Following Highland form, he'd put his Flanders veterans to the fore, men who would not shirk, turn, run or break rank. His front lines stared through the rising yellow clouds of smoke, clouds eerily lit more yellow by the sunlight behind the impenetrable smoke. The field before them moved, writhed, groaned, shrieked and whimpered, bodies piled on bodies. Hardened soldiers, never had they seen such a field of slaughter. The

Highlanders had kept charging, wave on ferocious wave of them, even when knee-deep in their wounded, over piles four bodies high, before being shot down. Few had reached their lines, even fewer had breached them. They had held their ground.

Cumberland rode forward, the Earl of Louden beside him. Trotting his horse past the rubble of the walls he'd ordered taken down to attack the Atholl flanks, Hawley came to join them. Among a group of fallen Highlanders behind the lines, a bulky older warrior retched bile and blood.

'Dispatch that man,' Cumberland ordered Lord Louden.

The Scot glanced sideways at his commander. 'You can have my commission, sir,' he said, 'but not my honour.'

Hawley pulled his pistol, aimed, fired. The Highlander's body jerked, lay still.

'Clear the mess up, Hawley,' Cumberland said. 'Dispatch the wounded. Round up any living officers who can walk. Give no quarter to the rest.'

# THIRTY-FIVE

Anne turned from staring at the pall of smoke, incongruous now against clear blue sky, back to Pibroch, gripped the bridle with both hands and pulled. She had to get there, had to get this stubborn beast across the river.

'Come on, Pibroch. *Siuthad!*'

Behind her, feet slithered down the riverbank, splashed through the water. A hand grabbed her shoulder. She spun round. It was old Meg, pitchfork in her other hand, face alarmed with fear.

'Run.' She tugged Anne's arm. 'They're killing everybody.'

The bank was now alive with folk, women and children, running for their lives. Upstream, warriors crashed through the trees, Highlanders fleeing the battlefield.

'Come away,' Meg urged, pulling Anne towards the other side.

Pibroch strained to turn, hooves stamping backwards towards the far bank. Anne held tight to the halter.

'I have to go on!' She struggled against the older woman's iron grip.

'There's nothing you can do,' Meg argued, tugging her wrist.

'That one's alive!' From high above, the thin voice sounded. Hooves stamped on sodden grass. The lifeless weight on Donald Fraser's chest crushed down on him. His eyes flickered open. Another man's arm half-covered his face. In the space where sky was, an English general, a shadow on a black horse, leant forward, pointed. A body in dark tartan stepped into the space, a face loomed. It was Shameless, peering down. Recognition lit his eyes, a brief smile. Then the McIntosh lad raised his musket, drew it back, plunged down with his bayonet, into the dead weight that lay across Fraser's chest.

'Dead now, sir,' Shameless called over his shoulder.

★

Pibroch was out of the water, backwards, feet gaining purchase on the grass. Tugged along by horse and Meg, Anne was pulled clear of the Nairn. They were surrounded by fleeing women. Those who passed close by urged Anne to run, hide, get away. A woman splashed out of the river, half-dragging a boy about seven or eight. They stumbled and fell. The mother grabbed the child by his plaid, hauled him up, tried to lift and carry him. The weight of water in the sodden woollen cloth slowed her down. Anne got up into the saddle, bent down to the frightened woman and pulled the child up in front of her.

'Get up behind,' she told the mother. She rode them on a mile or so, dropped them at a cottage and went back to pick up another woman trailing a youngster. Sometimes, it was the child who hauled the parent, fearful of staying, afraid to go on alone. Latterly, it was an older woman, her ankle turned and swollen, limping along as the others vanished over the hills. Each time, they were further from the river. On her last journey back, the distant bank swarmed with government troops. Meg had vanished. The women and children had all disappeared. No warriors were visible on the surrounding hills.

In the cottage on the edge of Drumossie, with a clean towel spread between her hands, MacBean's wife drew a second loaf out of her oven and set it to cool on the table, next to the first. Bread kept her busy. The noise of battle had ended half an hour ago. Someone was coming now. The cottage door burst open, letting in the cold air. James Ray stalked in with two redcoats who searched quickly round the one room.

'There's no one here,' the old woman said.

Ray raised his sword, drew it across at shoulder height. Blood spurted on the cooling bread. The old woman slumped into the hearth.

'No one now,' Ray said, and stalked out.

As the redcoats splashed through the river, Anne swung her tired horse back round towards Moy. It was warm now, the sun startling in a blue and white spring sky. The bright flash of tartan under a nearby tree caught her eye. She rode over. It was Lachlan, wounded, his young face cut, a gash on his thigh bleeding badly; he had struggled this far before he collapsed. She jumped down beside him.

'Can you stand?'

The boy shook his head.

'No, go on. I'll do fine here awhile.' He grimaced. 'Nine lives, I have.' It was a saying of those belonging to the clan of the cat.

'They're hunting people down,' Anne said. The soldiers had fanned out but were closing and would find him easily, as she had. 'Come on, I'll get you home.' She hauled the lad to his feet, his arm round her neck, his injured leg dragging, got him up and on to Pibroch's back. A shot from behind threw him forward over the horse's neck.

Anne spun round. The redcoat who'd fired was several hundred yards away, well ahead of the rest, running towards them. She grabbed her pistol from the saddle bow, turned and fired. The man's face exploded with the shot. Anne hoisted herself behind Lachlan, gripped the boy's plaid to stop him sliding to the ground and kicked the horse away. Tired though he was, Pibroch leapt forward and cantered half a mile before slowing to a trot. There was no life in her passenger but Anne could not let the body slip to the ground. She held on grimly until she reached the forge, called Màiri out and delivered the dead son into his mother's distraught arms.

As he crawled over moorland grass, head split and bleeding, Robert Nairn heard heavy breath beside him. He looked towards the sound. No one was there. The breathing ceased. He lurched on. His right arm, almost severed, dragged behind. The breathing rasped again. It was his own, gasping roughly in his chest. His head bumped against stone. Painfully slow, he turned over, rolled his back against the shelter of the dyke. His head lolled, eyes closed.

★

287

Heavy-hearted and weary, Anne walked the tired horse on to Moy, letting it take itself into the stable. She'd strip and rub it down later. The loaded wagon was at the door. Nothing had changed since she left.

Inside, Elizabeth and Jessie both jumped, startled when Anne came in, relief lighting their faces as they rushed to her side.

'Are you hurt?' Her sister stared at the blood staining her clothes.

Anne shook her head. 'We're defeated,' she said.

'Will, did you see Will?' Jessie asked.

Again, Anne shook her head. 'I didn't reach the field,' she explained. 'Lachlan's dead. I brought him home. He's the only one I know about.' She turned to Elizabeth. 'You should be away to Invercauld.'

'I couldn't go, not till I knew. We can go together now.'

'I have to stay.' Anne started to peel off her bloodied dress. 'Our men need to know where to find me, when things settle. I won't have them think I ran away.' Tears came then, hard, sore.

Elizabeth took her in her arms, held her tight. 'Don't cry, please don't cry.' She rubbed Anne's back, rocked her. 'How will we cope if you cry?'

A row of drummers marched before Cumberland into Inverness. He rode beside Cope, red uniforms pristine, brass buttons shining. The regiment that marched with him cheered, encouraging the few folk on the streets to do the same.

'All we have to do now, Johnny,' he said, 'is allow no respite. We'll clear the rats out while they're on the run, every single one of them.'

Lord Boyd rode up from scouting ahead. 'The best lodging is the house their Pretender occupied,' he said.

'If it suited my cousin, it will suit me well,' Cumberland nodded.

When they reached the house, the Dowager Lady McIntosh stood outside waiting to welcome him into her home. He drew her a look of contempt. Highland men were uncouth, savage and not to be trusted. Their women were worse.

'Throw that woman in jail,' he said.

Washed, dressed in her clean riding habit, the only clothes not packed, Anne stood by the fire, a tankard of ale in her hands. Her belongings were back inside, piled upstairs, the man and boy sent home. Hope was not gone. Hundreds of warriors ran off that field. Others would have fled in different directions. The Prince had sought engagement far too soon. Half their army was still on its way. They would regroup. One battle was lost, not the war.

'George will gather them together,' she said. Her cousin would not easily give up.

'If he survives,' Elizabeth answered. 'And they won't gather here. We should've gone home. What are you waiting for?'

Anne watched her sister pace about. She should know why. 'MacGillivray,' she said. It wasn't hope or expectation; simply the truth. She should have been with him. She wasn't. Now she would wait. It was a necessary vigil, like a penance. He would come to her, or word of him would. She could not go till then.

Elizabeth stopped pacing, reached into her pocket, withdrew a sheet of paper and held it out.

'His note,' she said, shame colouring her face.

Cottars ran from their homes. Soldiers on horseback fired into them. Those on foot chased after, cutting them down. Old Meg's cott burst into flame. The torch-bearers moved to the next. Cath, her baby clutched desperately to her breast, ran from Ewan's cott. Inside, old Tom lay on his bracken pallet, coughing. Ewan's two young daughters cowered behind. The cott door was yanked shut. Outside, a soldier thrust a spar of wood through the handle, across the frame. Another put a burning torch to the turf roof. Cath scrambled up the slope, grabbing at heather to pull against. Two redcoats ran behind. The nearest raised his musket, crashed the butt down on the back of her head. Stunned, she dropped. He yanked the screaming baby from her, tossed it to his companion, turned her over, ripped her skirts up, spread her legs. The second soldier rammed his musket into the rocks, bayonet pointing skywards, raised the struggling, howling baby above his head and brought its body down, sharp. The crying squealed to a thin stop.

Jessie ran in from the kitchens. Elizabeth stopped pacing. Anne looked up from the note.

'*Isd!* Do you hear guns?' Jessie asked.

All three of them listened. Faintly, there was the crack and echo of sporadic fire.

'It'll be groups of soldiers fighting some of our own,' Anne reassured them. 'We'd do the same, trying to take as many prisoners as possible.'

Frightened, Elizabeth turned on her. 'Why are you involved in this?' she wailed.

'I was feeding thin soup to people who need meat. Poverty is all we can expect in this Union. They only use us!'

'And killing us is better?'

'Elizabeth –' Anne caught hold of her sister's hand, wanting her to understand '– the English make slaves of their women. They have no rights, no power, no names. Their bodies, children and homes are owned by the men. If we don't win, we'll become like them.'

'That's nonsense,' Elizabeth retorted. 'No man could stop me being who I am, or from doing what I want.'

The front door was flung open. They all turned towards it. Anne pushed MacGillivray's note down the front of her dress. Donald Fraser, bloody and torn, carrying a crumpled plaid, stumbled in.

'Fetch water and towels, Jessie.' Anne went to help the blacksmith.

'There's no time,' Fraser said, as she and Elizabeth got him to a chair. 'They're on the estate.'

'*Dè?*' Elizabeth asked. 'Who?'

'The *Sasannaich.*'

'We heard the guns,' Anne said. 'Have you been home?'

'No, they're hunting us, killing the wounded. Shameless got me away.' He stopped to cough up a little blood. 'I came to warn you, they're coming here.' He broke off, coughing again.

Jessie hurried back, a bowl of water splashing in her arm. Fraser shook his head, pushing away the help.

'I can't stay. If they find me, you'd all be shot.'

'Did you see Will?' Jessie asked.

Fraser got unsteadily to his feet, held out the ragged, stained plaid over his arm.

'His belt was cut. It fell.' He shook his head. 'He ran up front, with me. Killed five or six of them before . . .' his voice broke. 'Him that couldn't fight.' He slumped as Anne caught hold of him.

'He can't go back outside,' Elizabeth said. 'They'll catch him.'

Chained in the cellar, Aeneas strained to hear. There had been gunfire on Moy land, near the northwest cotts, he was sure. The key was put in the lock. He stood, chains rattling, to watch the stair. The lock turned, the door opened, lamplight lit the steps. Two pairs of feet came down, others behind.

'Anne!' The relief he felt changed quickly to concern as he saw the wounded blacksmith being helped down. 'Donald!'

Elizabeth, with lamp and basin, followed at their backs.

'We have to hide him here,' Anne said. 'Careful,' to Fraser as they reached the bottom step. She guided him to Aeneas's bunk.

'I can help,' Aeneas insisted, gripping her arm, 'if you get these chains off.'

'There's no time.' Anne reached round and took the towels and bowl of water from Elizabeth. 'Here.' She thrust them in his arms, then followed Elizabeth, hurrying back up the stairs. Half-way up, she stopped, turned round. 'Whatever you hear, keep quiet, or they'll find him.' The cellar door shut, the key turned in the lock again.

Jessie had not moved from the spot where they'd left her. She stood, holding Will's tattered plaid over her swollen belly, sobbing. The sound of horses' hooves could be heard outside. Anne slid the key back into Jessie's pocket.

'Don't let on you have that,' she said. 'Not to anyone.'

The front door pushed open. James Ray stalked in, two redcoats beside him, half a dozen armed Black Watch behind. He looked Anne up and down, smiled.

'Colonel Anne,' he said, clicking his heels.

'Do you not have manners to knock, Lieutenant?' Anne asked.

'Arrest her,' Ray said, casually nodding his head towards her.

Two Black Watch soldiers rushed forwards to either side of her, the others swarmed the house, searching. Anne glared round at them.

'Will you have your men treat my home with respect?' she said to Ray.

One of his redcoat guards stepped forward and thumped his musket butt into her chest. Anne winced. The Black Watch lad on her right side raised his gun, pointed it at the redcoat.

'Don't touch that lady again,' he said, threateningly.

Anne looked at him properly. She knew that voice, that face.

'Shameless!'

'We won this time,' he grinned. 'I can come home again.'

'Yes, you can.' There was no point explaining he should not have left.

'And that will do for the pleasantries,' Ray snapped. 'Attention!'

Both Shameless and her other guard jumped to it. A shadow moved at the door, a thin man in black, followed by two more redcoats, stepped through the doorway. It was General Hawley, sword swinging casually in his hand.

'Well, well,' he sneered. 'The viper's nest.'

'My apologies, General,' Anne said. 'I should have asked you to dinner.'

'We're far from Falkirk now –' Hawley pushed his face close to hers '– and from Miss Forbes.' His thin smile returned, more alarming than his ire.

'You have a warrant to be in my house?' Anne fought to keep her voice calm and steady.

'Very amusing.' He withdrew an order paper from inside his coat, a smirk on his skinny lips. 'For your arrest,' he said. 'Signed by His Royal Highness, Prince William, the Duke of Cumberland, no less.' He put the warrant back in his jacket and considered Elizabeth. 'You're Elizabeth Farquharson, yes?'

Elizabeth nodded. Hawley snapped his fingers to the two guards at his side.

'Take her out,' he ordered.

The redcoats moved forward and took hold of Elizabeth.

'She's done nothing!' Anne protested. 'It's me you want. My sister is loyal to the government!'

'On the contrary,' Hawley corrected. 'She rode from here to Inverness, the night of February sixteenth, to spring a trap you had set for Lord Louden's troops.'

Elizabeth grabbed Anne's arm.

'I didn't mean to hurt you. I wanted MacGillivray, that's all.'

'I know. It's all right, I know.'

'So,' Hawley leered, 'a catfight over the red-haired savage.'

'Do you have him?' Anne asked.

'You'll see him soon enough,' he said, turning back to Elizabeth's guards. 'She wants a man,' he smiled. 'So give her to the men.'

The two guards tore the terrified girl away from Anne.

'No,' Anne shouted, trying to catch hold of her sister again. 'It was me she betrayed, not you!'

Hawley placed the point of his sword at Anne's throat to stop her moving as Elizabeth was dragged, struggling and pleading, outside. Shameless and the other soldier swung their muskets in to lie, crossed over, in front of Anne. The move might have been for restraint, or protection. Hawley's eyes flicked up from one Highlander to the other. Both of them stared straight ahead. The other Black Watch soldiers clattered back downstairs and out from other rooms. Hawley lowered his sword, turned to James Ray.

'Your Captain McIntosh is a prisoner somewhere in this house,' he said. 'Find him, and return his liberty to him, after we're gone.' He scrutinized Anne again. 'I'm told you're a fine dancer, Mistress McIntosh.'

'Farquharson,' Anne said. 'Colonel Anne Farquharson, the Lady M<sup>c</sup>Intosh.'

'Whichever alias you use, Colonel,' he sneered. 'I will see you dance, at the end of a rope.' He stood aside, indicating that she should precede him.

From outside, a slow drumbeat set up, the dead beat, the march of those going to the grave. Anne drew a deep breath, straightened her shoulders and walked out through the door.

# THIRTY-SIX

A bright, afternoon sun hung over Loch Moy, its warmth lingering. Four drummer-boys stood in pairs on opposite sides of the steps, drumming the dead beat. Pibroch had been saddled up. The horse snickered gently as she approached. She stopped, hearing rude calls, grunts and squeals from near the stable. As she turned, a hand grabbed the back of her hair, twisted her head round.

'You want to watch?' Hawley spat into her face. 'Is that why you've stopped?'

'No, let her go, please.'

'Mount your horse or I'll have you stand over your sister till every man here has done with her!'

He let go. Head down, blinking back tears, Anne put her foot in the stirrup and got herself into the saddle. A redcoat held the reins. Two more, weapons carried abreast, stood ready either side of the horse's head. The four drummers formed in their pairs at each side, still sounding the slow beat. Shameless and the other Black Watch fell in behind. Hawley took the lead, intense satisfaction written on his face. Anne did not look towards the grunting, scuffling group near the stable. Men were given strength to protect women and children, not for this. Not for this. A cold horror spread inside her. She could not speak, cry out, weep, could only sit, erect, back stiffly straight, eyes front. There was some compassion in shock, the human mind put up barriers of disbelief against what could not be borne.

James Ray stood watching Jessie as he listened to the sound of horse and drums move off. The girl slumped against the wall, clutching a bloody, tattered plaid in her arms. He waited while the beat faded out of earshot until the only audible sound was the pregnant girl whimpering and the fainter hooting yells from the redcoats still outside. Then he waited again, till it came.

'Anne!' The shout, muffled, repeated.

Ray smiled, walked along the hall until he came to the door. He turned the handle. It wouldn't open. He walked back to Jessie.

'Where is the key?' There was no answer. He studied the plaid she grasped over her swollen abdomen. That explained the snivelling. 'I suppose he fathered your brat,' he said, sliding his hand under the tattered cloth and spreading his fingers over the bulge of her belly. There was something wholly disgusting about this young woman with her puffy eyes, snotty face, the shuddering breasts. Like a rutting sow, that was it. Animal, barely human. He clenched his fist, drew his arm back, punched into her abdomen as hard as he could. She doubled forward, the filthy plaid falling to the floor, the grunted squeal just like a pig's.

'Where is the key?' he repeated. Didn't she understand English? Maybe not. Most of these barbarians didn't. He reached down to search her pockets, and she reared up, fists flailing, smashing into his face. He grabbed her arms. She spat in his face. He punched her belly again, harder, and again. As she went down, he swung his boot into her gut. Hunkering down, he raked in her pockets, turning her roughly as she retched, his hand closing on the key. He pulled it out. This would be the one.

Crouched astride her bare trembling legs, he glanced at her naked thighs, tugged her skirt up higher to expose her buttocks. They were at it all the time, these Highlanders. That's what accounted for their dress, male and female, barely decent. Rumour had it the heather was alive with moaning, thrusting couplings come May Day, and this one had certainly already had a man in her. No ring on her hands either, nobody's property. He was near bursting out of his trousers, had never rutted with a pregnant sow before, and if she still had some fight in her, it would be livelier than his wife's dutiful submission. Subduing the natives, that's what he was paid to do. They had to learn who was master. He slid the cellar key into his own pocket. The captain would keep a while longer.

*

Hawley did not take the road to Inverness. He led his captive on the older paths through the estate. Two scouts went in front to keep them on the route he wanted followed. Anne stared straight ahead, the drumbeat thudding in her ears, saw drifts of dark smoke in the sky, and nearer, through the trees. They slowed going past two burning cottages. The old crofter and the boy who'd packed then unpacked her belongings earlier lived in one of those. She turned her eyes away from the charred heap lying in one smouldering doorway. They were heading for the north-west cotts.

Reaching them, the general slowed the procession, winding in and out among the shot and torn bodies. He wanted to ensure she saw everything. Cath, raped and shot dead, lay half-way up the slope. Her baby hung, still spiked on a nearby bayonet. Ewan's cott smouldered, roofless. Old Tom would be inside, what was left of him. The other dwellings burned still, even Meg's. Had she been home? Acrid smoke stung Anne's nostrils, a roast-pig smell of charred and burnt flesh. Hawley said nothing to her, though he watched as, blow on blow, she was hammered down, numbed. She stared at the white hair blowing between Pibroch's ears, knowing she was now in hell with no way out.

On they went, drums tolling their beat, winding through the hills, down the slopes, past the tree where she'd picked up Lachlan. At the Nairn, higher upstream than she had tried to cross, she wondered if the horse would refuse again, but he didn't, following Hawley's mount across, led by the English redcoat's hand on the reins. The smell reached them first, a cloying metallic sweetness, then the buzz, the buzzing of millions of flies busy in congealing blood and open wounds, laying eggs in dead eyes, crawling into split intestines. If what had gone before was a taste of hell, this was its banquet. The field fluttered here and there with crows. Now and then, a body shifted, a limb moved, a voice moaned. Government soldiers searched the two thousand dead, checking. Dull thuds echoed as they clubbed a wounded survivor to death. A shot fired off into another, scattering the crows.

Anne was guided through the carnage from what must have been the rear of the Jacobite lines. At the moorland edge, several young boys sprawled together, shot where they stood. Nearby, a kilted lad lay face down, a hole in his back, his right arm gone. Pibroch's hooves squelched in gore. There was no respite. If she closed her eyes, the procession stopped and waited, letting the fetid smell, the cawing and the buzz jerk her back to awareness. For relief from torn limbs, ruined bodies, gaping eyes, she looked skywards until the circling crows dizzied her. She tried to keep her grip then. This was her punishment, duly meted out. The dead merited her respectful attention. Ahead of her, triangular mounds peaked out of the ground, unfathomable until, closer, she saw they were bodies heaped on bodies. More, they were her clans. Knowing the line-up, she knew where each would fall. Only the MacDonalds were out of place, on the left, but her own were where she expected.

Unable to turn away, she scoured the Farquharson corpses for signs of her brother or Francis, not seeing them but sometimes catching sight of a face she recognized: Dauvit, the diviner; little Catríona's father; a shepherd she last saw tying a bloodied fleece to an orphaned lamb. The dead were difficult to know, with life gone, features torn or crusted with dried blood. It seared her that she might look on her brother, James, the quiet gentle one, and not know him. Now the M<sup>c</sup>Intoshes. Would she know MacGillivray in death? How deep the pain drove home. All these men who once had lived and loved, marched and fought with such hope, gone. Hawley ensured she saw them all, winding in and out of pile and pile of dead. Among the Atholl Murrays, she could not tell if George lay with them, nor any of her uncles or other cousins. She was beyond begging to be taken from here.

Finally, the heaps were behind them, there were fewer scattered dead, then almost none. The bodies here were government soldiers, redcoats being collected on to a cart for burial. Hawley led his horse past one group and stopped, turned in his saddle to watch her. These were not redcoats. She would not look, she would not, yet she did. They were M<sup>c</sup>Intosh men who'd died crowding together among the enemy, the shoemaker, Duff, at the edge of them. Further in, there was MacBean, arm reaching out, to Will, poor, dear Will, and, oh dear life, to . . . She couldn't look, turned her head, saw Hawley staring at her face.

'Have you no mercy to beg?' he asked. 'No forgiveness to plead?'

Her throat closed. Her eyes ached, sore with tears that would not come. Could she not be blessed by blindness, not even by the release of tears?

Nor could she go without seeing him. She turned back round, gazed down at his red-gold hair lying in the mud and gore, that brave, strong body she had loved broken like a great tree torn down by storm. If only he could see she'd come, know she'd been here. With no more thought than the desire to close his dead eyes from the crows and stroke his face, she shifted in the saddle. Hawley barked a command. The two soldiers at her sides gripped her legs. She would not be allowed to dismount. She was not to be allowed any grief, any relief.

The sharpness of her own nails bit into her palms, blood trickled from her hands. Hawley swung back round in his saddle and led them on, picking up the pace.

Ignoring his bleeding wrists, Aeneas prised the last chain free with Fraser's dirk, shook off the shackle and ran up the stairs. Just as he reached the top, the key turned in the lock, the door swung open. James Ray jumped back, surprised.

'Captain,' he saluted.

Aeneas shoved him backwards, glanced around the hall. Jessie lay between the wall and the chairs. A slight movement told him she was still alive. He raised the dirk to slash Ray's throat.

'Not me, Captain,' Ray raised his hands, protested. 'I just let you out.'

'Where's Anne?' Aeneas yelled.

'Hawley took her.' Ray pointed to the door.

Aeneas tossed the dirk to his left hand, grabbed Ray's sword from its sheath with the other and ran. Ray ran after him. Aeneas flung open the front door, leapt down the steps, looked around. A group of men in red coats with yellow facings hung around the stables, watching something on the ground. It took a second to register what they watched before Aeneas heard the grunt, the sniggering, recognized the jerking movement, saw the woman's skirts. A great, raging bellow roared out of him, and he raced towards them. All the men's heads, bar the busy one, turned towards him.

There were ten of them, one of him. Three turned and ran. One, their sergeant, drew a pistol from his belt. The others dived for muskets that stood against the wall. Aeneas swung at the sergeant, a poor stroke. It hit the gun, sent it flying, took the man's thumb off. The others tried to aim their muskets, but Aeneas was on them and in his stride now. He swung the sword, hard, fast, cutting two to the ground, one near headless. The dirk slashed in the opposite direction, opening one man's gut.

Clutching his bleeding hand, the injured sergeant ran off after the others. The man on the ground leapt to his feet, his organ still jutting erect. Aeneas chopped the sword down, castrated him, then pinned the dirk through his neck. A musket fired, the shot tore his right arm. It was the last thing that soldier did as his breath stopped, his windpipe severed. The sixth man thrust his bayonet. Aeneas chopped down on it. The spear stabbed bluntly through his plaid, catching his thigh. The soldier ran. Aeneas threw the dirk. It speared the runner between his shoulder blades. Aeneas looked down at the woman on the ground. It was Elizabeth.

'Oh, lass.' He bent down to her grey face. Her head was turned awkwardly to the side. Semen trickled out her mouth. She was dead, suffocated. He threw her skirts down to cover her body, stood and let out a terrible howl. Behind him a horse galloped away, James Ray on its back. Aeneas ran over to the sixth man, drew the dirk from his back, kicked the man over and cut his throat.

'Chief!' It was a half-shrieked gasp. He looked back at the house. Jessie was in the doorway, doubled over, hanging on to the doorframe. He thrust the weapons into his belt, limped back to Elizabeth's body and, gently as he could, lifted and carried her to the house. When he got near to Jessie, he saw blood round her feet. It trickled down her legs.

*

On the outskirts of Inverness, Hawley slowed his company down again, to match the dead beat of the drum. Hearing the death march, people peered out their windows, came out to the street. Seeing Anne, their chatter fell to silence as she was paraded past them. Their heroine was taken, the drums proclaiming she was going to her end. Everyone who watched strained to see till she was out of sight. A few fell in behind the soldiers, others followed. Hearing the tramp of feet multiply, Hawley looked round. He wondered if they expected a hanging this late in the day. The sun was low. They would be disappointed.

Cumberland had taken over a downstairs room in the Dowager's house as his command centre. Seated at the table, he drank wine, good wine, from her cellar. His chefs were busy in her kitchens, cooking a special dinner. He looked forward to it. It would be a celebration. Lord Boyd had just presented him with a list of the ranked prisoners. There were a few names still missing but, for a day's work, it was most satisfactory.

'General Hawley is here,' Lord Boyd announced.

Cumberland did not think he'd ever adapt to a delighted Hawley. The hollow-cheeked bony face was most disconcerting when pleased.

'I have the rebel bitch, Anne M<sup>c</sup>Intosh,' Hawley announced. 'A crowd followed up the street, looking for a hanging, I suspect.'

Cumberland went to the window, peered out. Several hundred silent townspeople thronged the doorway and beyond, hats in hands.

'Not a hanging, I think,' he said grimly and addressed Lord Boyd. 'Disperse that crowd, with fire if you have to.' He walked back to his seat, settled himself. This would be interesting. 'Well, Henry, bring in your prisoner.'

She was not at all what he expected, a young slip of a woman, extremely pretty, who walked in with that strange dignity he'd noticed in these Highland folk. Even though he knew she was a few years younger than himself, he had still envisaged someone mature, more solid, and not this ethereal, graceful girl. She stopped in front of his desk, staring straight ahead rather than at him, her face pale but calm, as if she felt and feared nothing.

'I brought her across Moy and Culloden,' Hawley said, 'rubbed her nose in the dirt she'd made. But I doubt she sees the error of her ways.'

'Does she speak English?'

'I do,' Anne answered as Hawley nodded, looking down at him for the first time. Her eyes were clear, blue but empty of emotion.

'Then you will understand you are a prisoner of the Crown,' he said. 'Charged with treason and fomenting rebellion, the penalty for which is death. Have you anything to say?'

She had not taken her eyes off him as he spoke, nor had she shown any reaction. Now, she drew a deep, audible breath and stood even taller.

'You have made a sad slaughter of my regiment,' she said. 'It will be my honour and privilege to join them.'

# THIRTY-SEVEN

Aeneas carried Jessie carefully to the kitchen as the water from her womb washed out of her. It was warm here, and there was fire, water, ale, towels. He laid her into the box bed, fetched extra pillows from the linen store and propped them behind her head. He'd have gone then, to find a woman who'd borne children to help with this, but Jessie's birth pains already wracked her and, though it could be a long night, she was too distressed to be alone. Elizabeth's body lay in the hall. Donald Fraser was still in the cellar, asleep, unconscious or dead. Aeneas had washed and dressed the blacksmith's wounds before he'd freed himself. That would have to serve until Jessie's need of him was done.

He did as much as he knew, and what seemed right to do, washing her face with cool water, rubbing a warm, wet towel over her belly and thighs. Growing up in a cott, he'd seen babies born, though he'd never delivered one. Grown men were chased from birthing mothers by the other women. The horse, cattle and sheep were his practice ground for this. It couldn't be much different. While she groaned and writhed, he rubbed her back, talked soothingly, as he would to any scared beast. When it was time to push, he held her hand, arm round her shoulder, gave encouragement.

Will's baby daughter was born just before dawn. Her tiny form fitted one of Aeneas's hands. He held her so that Jessie could see. The baby's arms moved, her legs stretched, her head turned. Awed, they both watched. Jessie, propped up in the kitchen box-bed, stroked her child gently with one finger. The little mouth opened, closed, but the breath of life could not be drawn in, the child born too soon, her movements only those left over from the womb. When they stopped, Jessie kissed the small dead face. Aeneas laid the body in the bucket waiting by the bed.

'You see,' he said to the tired young mother. 'You made a perfect child. She just wasn't ready for this world.' He held the cup of ale to her lips, let her swallow a mouthful. 'You have more to do.'

'I can't.'

'You will,' he said, 'because you're going to live.' He put his hand on her belly. 'I'll give what help I can but you must push it out.'

She was seventeen, brave and strong, and the demands of nature brought the courage to bear them. When the pain came, she gritted her teeth and did what was required.

'As hard as you can, Jessie,' he urged, pressing his hand down behind the muscle in her abdomen to help. 'Then it's finished.' The afterbirth slid out of her, far easier than either had expected. Jessie dropped back on the pillows, worn out. Aeneas cleaned up, adding the mass to the bucket, wiping Jessie clean, washing her face. He gave her another mouthful of ale then and let her fall asleep. By the time he had the bucket outside, the contents buried down by the loch, he was weary, worn out. He rolled on to Will's pallet by the fire and shut his eyes.

It was Donald Fraser who shook him awake.

'I thought you were dead yourself,' he said when Aeneas jumped and stared at him, 'the state you're in.'

'Jessie?' Aeneas looked over at the box bed.

'Sleeping.' Donald winced. Fresh blood seeped through his shirt from the chest wound.

'You get on here,' Aeneas insisted, getting himself up and Fraser on the pallet in his place. 'That's deep and you've already bled too much. I'll fetch Màiri over.'

Ignoring the redcoat bodies outside the stable, he saddled a horse and rode down to the forge. There had been smoke to the north when he'd chased the soldiers yesterday, but there was no sign of disturbance near the smithy. The troops had not gone beyond Moy Hall. It was his wife they'd wanted.

Màiri stared in horror as he went in, at the bloodied state of him, then got to her feet. She had been sitting next to Lachlan, laid out for burial on his bed.

'Have you come to pay your respects,' she asked, 'or do you bring word of my Donald?'

Aeneas took his bonnet off, stepped over to the bed. The lad had come back from the dead once. This time he'd taken a shot in the head. Aeneas pulled the cover back over and turned to Màiri. He was father to his people, age no matter. That was his role and how he felt.

'I'm sorry for your loss. He was a fine son, to yourself, his chief and his clan.' He put his bonnet back on. 'Donald is alive, at Moy. Good care will keep him so. I came to fetch you there.'

Màiri's grief fell to one side as her fear turned to hope. She fetched her daughters and they all returned to Moy. When they arrived, Shameless was there. He had seen a body he thought was Howling Robbie, dead at the edge of the battlefield, and gone back to check. It was. He'd taken his friend home then come on.

'I'll not go back,' he said stubbornly. 'Not after what they done to Robbie and at the cotts. *Gonadh!*' he swore. 'They're bad people.'

The cotts were in the direction of the smoke Aeneas had seen.

'You've no duty to go back,' he told Shameless. 'You're under my command and I need you here.' They packed some food, saddled a second horse and left for the cotts.

The scene was desperate. Of the thirty cottars and their children, only six survived. The least injured had begun laying out the bodies. Aeneas and Shameless dug the long grave near where Seonag and Calum had been laid. Even in her burnt-out cott there was no sign of old Meg, no remains. The dead were put to rest, Cath's baby on her breast, old Tom with his granddaughter. Somehow, the older girl had survived the burning, her face and body painfully scarred. One of the two cottar women tended her. She'd bide with them. Clan children were raised by whoever was able, if blood parents could not. The child of one was the child of all.

The redcoats had taken their livestock, looted the grainstore, burnt or smashed their tools, fired their homes. A tumbled milking pail was all they had to fetch water. The ruined cotts were beyond repair, but a rough shelter could be made of the one least affected by the burning. The able-bodied pushed off the still-smouldering turfs from the roof, brought water to throw on the rest. It would be roofed tomorrow. That night, they all slept outside. Next day, when the cott was habitable and all that could be done for the injured was done, Aeneas and Shameless rode on up to Culloden, seeking survivors.

The battlefield was guarded. Troops still moved about, checking and dispatching any injured. The heady stench of blood had faded. The stink of decay had not begun. A slight sweetness hung in the air. All across the moor, scattered bodies lay, grey, lifeless, strangely twisted, like heaps of broken things that had been thrown away.

'Why didn't they cross the Nairn?' Aeneas asked, expecting no answer except the shrug of incomprehension Shameless gave. This was his clan's territory, land familiar as his own body. Drumossie was the worst possible site for Highlanders to fight on. He would have taken them across the river, if he'd been there. The other chiefs would have followed his territorial lead. It was senseless slaughter, easily avoided, had he been here.

They were not allowed to walk among the dead. A gruff English officer and his squad turned them back at gunpoint. Returning to Moy, they passed two burnt-out cottages. Corpses were being removed by others from the estate. Both men got down to lend a hand. By the time he reached home, Aeneas was bereft of strength or comfort.

Before going in, he tore off his ruined, filthy clothes and plunged into the loch, scrubbing and washing himself clean of blood and death and dirt and smoke. The greylag geese were gone. The ducks would soon return. His people would not. They had stood against oppression. He had not stood with them. He dived below the surface, came up, rubbed his hair roughly, dived again. The graze of the musket ball on his arm nipped. The cut on his thigh stung. But his body was whole and would heal. It was his heart and soul that were scarred.

With Màiri and her girls in the kitchen, the house was almost normal, if it could ever be normal again. The fires were seen to, food cooked, the sick cleaned and cared for. Even Elizabeth's body was washed, dressed and shrouded in the hall. Tomorrow, after he buried the soldiers outside, he would take her home to Invercauld. Tonight, he was hollowed out, haunted by images of brutality and slaughter. Dead faces, broken bodies, his clan decimated, his wife in prison. A deep and terrible emptiness yawned inside him. What had he done?

Inverness jail was full. Anne sat in her small, walled cell, staring at the straw-covered floor. When night came, she lay on the hard bench, watching the moon and stars pass overhead through the tiny barred window high above. Inside her dress, MacGillivray's note still pressed against her breast. She had not shed one tear. Around her, the prison whispered. A group of schoolboys, gone to watch the battle, had been deliberately slaughtered. Watching townsfolk were also killed. Voices asked who lived, who died, who was imprisoned, until sleep or sorrow silenced them.

In the morning, the jailers dished out water in metal cups. Anne was given a basket of bread, sent in by friends, the guard said. The only food available in prison was supplied from outside. Anne passed the loaves through the bars to outstretched hands on either side of her. The bread passed from hand to hand, the pieces becoming smaller as it went, cell to cell, round the room.

'Few folk know we're here yet,' the woman in the cell on her right said.

'Margaret?' Anne knew that voice. 'Is that you?'

'Yes,' puzzled, then the realization: 'Anne!' All the questions came next, the where and how of capture. Margaret had been taken at the battlefield. She had no word of her husband, David, Lord Ogilvie, if he was alive or dead.

The other prisoners identified themselves. The Dowager Lady McIntosh, still mystified by her arrest, was incarcerated four cells down, between Lady Gordon and Lady Kinloch. Next door, among the men, Lady Kinloch's husband, Lords Lovat, Balmerino and Sir

John Murray of Broughton were imprisoned. No one knew the whereabouts of Sir John's glamorous wife, Greta Fergusson. No mention was made of Anne's brother, James, or her cousin, Francis. At night, even in sleep, it seemed, the names of the dead turned over and over in her head, like stones in a pocket.

Each day, food came for her – bread, meat, a flagon of ale – and was shared around. Notes arrived too, often from strangers or people she barely knew, brought by a guard or pushed through her cell window, falling to her feet like snow. They offered sympathy and hopes, words she knew were well meant, and they gave news, venting anger over it. The army allowed no one near the battle site. No parents, wives or children could identify their dead. No bodies were released for burial. The wounded who had fled were hunted down, imprisoned if they were officers, shot if they were not. Rough treatment was meted out to any who harboured or helped them, goods and animals stolen, homes looted then burnt down around their heads. Then word came of Moy. Elizabeth was dead. Anne sat and stared, unseeing, for days after that, but still she could not cry.

At the end of the second week, with no evidence against her, the Dowager was released. Her young niece, the pregnant Lady Gordon, went with her, freed for the imminent birth. The Dowager returned next day, to visit Anne, furious to be barred from her own home by Cumberland's occupation of it.

'I've had to impose on friends for a bed to sleep in,' she complained, before confiding the troubles of others. Lady Gordon's release had been bait to trap her husband, with troops waiting at her mother's house where their child would be born, a trap still to be sprung. 'So it was not kindness,' she said, bitterly. From among the prisoners, Lovat, Balmerino, Sir John Murray, Lady Kinloch and her husband, had all been taken away. Sent to England for trial, the guards said.

Anne listened without emotion, her expression bleak as barren moorland. Neither woman expected the courts to be more merciful than the murdering, victorious army. Culloden, the English had named the battle, after Forbes's house on the moor.

'Don't give up,' the Dowager urged, gripping Anne's cold fingers. 'They might kill your body, but don't let your spirit die of grief.' Then, keeping her voice low so the guards wouldn't hear, 'I have news of Lord George.'

'He lives?' There was relief in the question but no vigour.

'Yes,' the Dowager nodded. 'He and the other officers who escaped gathered the army at Ruthven, three thousand of them, with more on the way.'

'Then they'll fight on.' She couldn't understand why they'd fought when half their army was elsewhere. Culloden. The puzzle of it wearied her.

'No,' the Dowager corrected. 'The Prince sent a letter, ordering them to disperse. Let each man save himself who can, he said.' She was bitterly angry. 'Whose side is he on?'

'His own,' Anne said.

In the Dowager's house, Cumberland sat back in his chair and studied his visitor. It was night. Informers preferred the dark.

'General Hawley has been generous with our funds,' he said, 'and our promises.'

'I delivered. You have your victory, and the dispersal of the rest.'

'Yet your countrymen protected the Highlanders' retreat before they surrendered. I have more to round up than I hoped.'

'Well, you can't buy the whole flock, and you'll be remembering, as King Louis's mercenaries, they're prisoners of war not traitors.'

'They ship for France tomorrow,' Cumberland confirmed. 'Your reward goes with them. I hope you trust the bearers.'

'With my life.'

'Now you hope to secure your own safe passage, with your master?'

'That was part of the price.'

Cumberland stood up and paced the room. If he was to do as intended, eradicate this barbaric race and bring their nation to its knees, the threat must remain.

'The problem is,' he said, 'there are already faint hearts bleating on about mercy. Those voices will grow if he's gone. I can't have him leave this land until my job is done.'

'If you're after catching him, you'd make a martyr, and a prisoner folk could rally to. France and Spain'll not sit back and let him be cut down.'

'Don't tell me my business,' Cumberland snapped. 'A Prince in the Tower is not something my father relishes, nor parliament either. But nor is one left free and troublesome overseas where this rebellion can simmer and explode again.'

'My influence –'

'Will not last for ever,' Cumberland cut him off, 'might not last long when other flattery takes over. No, he cannot go until I say the time is right. Until every traitorous noble's head is off its shoulders, every rebel hanged, their supporters transported and those who fund them broken and impoverished.' He sat down again and explained what would happen next. The Prince would flee from place to place. On the pretext of pursuit, the army would come behind and clear out sympathizers. 'There are more rats yet to be flushed out.' When the Highlands and islands of Scotland were finally subdued, then, and only then, would passage back to France occur. 'Do you understand?'

There was no answer. Living rough among barbarians for what might be some time clearly did not appeal. Cumberland leant forward again.

'A quiet execution can be arranged,' he said. 'In the barren northern hills, a few anonymous graves would never be found.' He sat back. 'Now do you understand?'

The man nodded.

'Then our business is concluded. You'll receive our instruction from time to time, on the area we would like to attend to next.' He poured a glass of wine.

His guest turned for the door.

'A moment,' Cumberland called. 'I'm curious. England's triumph would not be King Louis's wish.'

'Neither was Scotland for the Scots.'

'But he wouldn't be averse.'

'We could have had London, and Britain's Crown, but the Highlanders wouldn't give it. I wouldn't give them Scotland then.'

'So it was revenge,' Cumberland nodded. That made sense. 'Now you can watch me exact it.'

The door closed behind the nocturnal visitor. After a few minutes, Hawley returned from seeing the informer out, discreetly.

'He doesn't look pleased.'

'He ought to,' Cumberland smiled. 'He's about to enjoy the luck of the Irish. Always one step ahead.'

Better news began to filter into the prison, about some who survived. Cluny castle was burnt down but Macpherson had escaped. The French *Écossais Royaux*, treated as prisoners of war, had been shipped home. The Irish mercenary Wild Geese, also sent by King Louis, went with them. Between them, they'd provided cover for the Highlanders' retreat from the battlefield, brave action that had saved many Scots lives. There was relief that they, at least, had been spared.

Greta Fergusson surfaced, at least in gossip, safe with friends, also pregnant and hiding out in Edinburgh, it was said. Her husband, Sir John Murray, had been taken to London. To save himself, he offered evidence against Lord Lovat, buying his own life with an old grudge for Lovat's rape of his kinswoman. With Lord Balmerino, Lovat was held in the Tower. Lord Kilmarnock, sent down from Edinburgh, had joined them.

But many had escaped abroad. Thwarting the trap set for him, Sir William Gordon fled without seeing his firstborn. Lochiel, Lord Elcho and Margaret Johnstone's husband, Lord Ogilvie, had gone to France. Under the Auld Alliance, citizens of each country were citizens of both. They would be safe there. Late that night, Anne heard Margaret crying in her cell, weeping with relief that her husband was alive and for the loneliness of facing the last few days of her life without him. Other women wept too, frightened for their lives or grieving. Anne's own cell seemed all the more oppressive. She lay, listening to the sobbing through the walls, and she ached for the release that death would bring.

When the Dowager visited again, she hurried in, barely able to contain herself.

'Anne, Anne –' she took hold of the younger woman's arms, her face alight '– your brother and your cousin are alive!'

Anne stared. After weeks of mourning them, the words did not make sense.

'James, and Francis, they're free?'

'No.' The Dowager's face fell. 'They were taken on the field, injured. Not seriously,' she assured. 'But they're being nursed, that's why they're not in jail. Their wounds are almost healed and . . .' her voice trailed away '. . . they will be shipped south soon.'

The joy that had begun to surge inside Anne fell away. What kind of pain was this, to have them back from the dead to lose again? Her sweet, gentle brother. Her strong, self-assured cousin. Both of them would rather have suffered a quick death in battle than the indignity of trial and the ignominy of a traitor's end. She slumped back on her bunk.

The Dowager sighed. These were brutal days when good news only brought more sorrow in its wake.

'I've had two kings' sons under my roof,' she said, her voice breaking. 'I hope to never see another.'

While her home remained occupied by Cumberland, she had decided to go to Moy. A young McIntosh girl waited outside the cell, carrying a jug and basin. The Dowager called her in.

'Morag says she'll come every day and see to your needs,' she explained. 'She'll dress your hair, bring clean clothes and help with your toilet. It's shameful that they keep people like this. Animals are better treated.' She tried again to rouse Anne from her grief. 'They're alive,' she insisted. 'While there's life, there is hope.'

'Hope of what?' Anne asked. The trials had begun.

In the cold stone dungeon of Carlisle Castle, the prisoners were processed in small groups, the English Jacobites first. Each day, lots were drawn. Whoever drew the short straw went for trial.

The others were transported to the colonies to be sold as indentured slaves. Then they started on the Scots.

'My faither cannae draw lots,' Clementina objected. 'He's no weel!'

The prisoner who had the job of making the draw held out the straws.

'We all have to do it,' he said.

Clementina drew first, then her father, then the others of their group, men and women.

'I've got the short wan,' the girl shouted.

'You broke it,' her father said. All the others agreed, she had broken hers on purpose. Her father held the short straw. Somehow it was always a man who went to trial, never a woman or a child.

'Tell them ye were made tae fight,' she cried, holding on to him. 'Tell them ye were forced. That's what awbody else is saying.'

Most prisoners denied raising arms against king and country. Expecting to be understood, some said their wives had sent them out, others that their chief had. To the English judges, from a nation where women had no power and the obligation of the clan system was a mystery, their excuses meant nothing. Many said whatever might spare them. That they were forced to fight on pain of death, by threats to their families, of their homes being burnt. Few pleaded guilty. Guilt meant being hanged, taken down half dead, castrated, their intestines drawn out and burnt before their eyes. Hearts were ripped out, sometimes still beating, to be held up to the crowd. Heads were picketed outside town gates, warning of the fate that awaited traitors. In the northern towns of England where most trials were held, newly erected gallows worked daily, three at a time. Rarely was a prisoner judged innocent. Clemency, when given, meant not being castrated, drawn and quartered, just hanged by the neck till dead.

When Clementina's father kissed her goodbye, it was final. He went to the gallows, she to the boats. In the ship's crowded hold, she wished she could go up on deck, under the creaking sail, just

313

to see the shores they left behind. They were going to a foreign land from which they'd never return. A Highland woman, her husband hanged, sat rocking to the rhythm of the swell and sang softly, as if she sang herself a lullaby.

> When I'm lonely, dear white heart;
> Black the night and wild the sea;
> By love's light, my foot finds;
> The old pathway to thee.

# THIRTY-EIGHT

When Morag brought Anne a pillow, she slept with MacGillivray's note under it. In the mornings, washed and changed into clean clothes, she tucked the note back into the top of her dress, where it nestled against her breast. She would go to her grave with it. Knowing her life would end soon was all that kept her sane.

Cells emptied and refilled. Hundreds were sent to England for trial, Anne's brother and cousin among them. Others were tried and executed where they were caught. Thousands were transported. In the West Indies, they would be sold to the highest bidder, to labour till the end of their days. Even those with shorter sentences would never obtain the means to return home. The banishment to slavery was permanent.

Margaret's brother and sister arrived in Inverness to provide care for her. Anne's visitors increased. The situation was not without its ironies. Young Morag fetched a tray of morning tea, complete with china cups, so incongruous in that grim place.

'You'll want to take tea with your visitors,' the girl said. It seemed there were many who wanted to see her.

The first day with tea, her earliest visitor was James, Lord Boyd, the young man despondent but still capable of blushing when his eyes met hers.

'I'm glad to see you,' Anne said. 'How is your mother?'

'Distressed for my father,' he answered, seating himself. Lord Kilmarnock was to be executed, with Lords Lovat and Balmerino, on Tower Hill.

'No clemency then?'

'Only that it will be quick.' Scotland's Jacobite lords would be beheaded, an easier death than the hanging meted out to those without title.

'I can't sympathize with Lovat,' Anne said. 'Nor will many.' Fifty years earlier, he'd fled a death sentence passed by the Scottish courts for the rape of his brother's widow, the Marquess of Atholl's daughter. 'His end is long overdue. But I'm pained for your father. He is a kind, gentle man.' She poured tea, barely able to recall a time when conversation was of life and love, births and farming matters.

'I leave next week to attend,' Lord Boyd said, 'but I wanted to see you first.'

'There is something I can do?'

'No, but I thought you'd like to hear about a friend of yours, Robert Nairn?'

'You know Robert?' Anne was jolted. Memories of their weeks in Edinburgh flooded back, weeks when they were so full of life. 'Is he well?'

'Severely injured. I found him two days after the battle and brought him in.'

'That was kind of you. From what I hear, others would have finished him off.'

'I didn't know then he could expect to hang.' Lord Boyd struggled with his place on the side of such brutality. 'He's being nursed by someone you also know, a woman from Skye, name of Nan MacKay.'

'Yes, I do know her. She held my horse for me once, in her kitchen. Her husband came over to fight. Is he safe?'

'There has been no word since the battle. She hopes. Today they began digging long pits at Culloden for the burials. I think she hopes in vain.'

Anne stirred her tea. MacGillivray would go in those great pits, dumped like a rotted carcass, he and so many others, nameless in a mass grave. Nothing became easier as each day passed.

'But Robert is here, in Inverness, and still alive?'

'For now.' Lord Boyd leant forward, earnestly. 'You have many friends, Lady Anne. They are doing what they can.'

The activities of those friends caused the Duke of Cumberland some annoyance. Petitions for release piled on his desk. Now it was Forbes of Culloden, Lord President of the Court of Session, rankled that his family seat had been chosen to name the battle, angry that the law was usurped.

'The Act of Union states Scots should be tried in Scottish courts, not in England.'

'So you can set them loose again?' Cumberland snapped.

'She's a slip of a girl,' the old judge protested.

'A dangerous one. Look at this.' The Duke scattered the pile. 'We're pursuing warriors. Must we chase every pen as well?'

General Cope, seated beside General Hawley, put down his glass of port. 'They only want to honour a woman they see as a hero,' he said calmly.

'Damn the bitch,' Hawley snarled, getting to his feet and pacing. 'I'll honour her, with mahogany gallows and a silken cord!'

'She has to be tried first,' Cope said. 'If she had bested me I would be less eager for the world to know.'

Cumberland considered him. Colonel Anne would certainly attract attention.

'We do ourselves no favour by pursuing people quite so hard,' Forbes said. 'Our troops are brutal. They murder men, rape women, slaughter them and their children. The old are dragged from their beds, their homes burnt to the ground.'

'To prevent the rebels re-forming,' Cumberland explained.

'And breed more hatred?' Forbes asked. 'What have we become?'

'Without women and brats, they can't breed,' Cumberland said. 'They're a vicious race of savages who'll rise again if they're not wiped out.'

'You can't mean to achieve that.' The elderly judge's face paled.

'Don't talk like a whining old woman, Forbes.'

'Rather that than the butcher of a people.' Forbes was shaken. 'I'll write to the king and to parliament about this.'

'Write,' Cumberland said, grabbing a handful of the petitions about Anne and waving them in Forbes's face. 'You'll not be the only one. But don't expect sympathy. I'm charged to destroy these Scots, to ensure this cause can never be revived!'

★

A few days after Lord Boyd's visit, Anne received a more unexpected visitor, Lieutenant James Ray's wife.

'Anne.' Helen took hold of both her hands. 'My dear, I am so sorry. To think my husband had anything to do with this.'

'He was doing his duty,' Anne said.

'Relishing it,' Helen said. 'Of that, I'm certain. It's so awful. I could weep. They say you'll hang.'

'Don't be upset. I'm content. Others have suffered so much worse.'

'You, content?' Helen was taken aback. 'We can't have that. My dear, you've been an inspiration. I've written to all my friends. You've been mentioned at court.'

'I'm sure they celebrate our defeat, and mine, as their enemy.'

'Pish tush, enemy nothing. Don't believe everything you hear. The papers like a good stir-up, that's all. Oh, there were fireworks and all that hoo-ha after Culloden, but not now. Do you know, after just three days of watching strong young men die so painfully on the gallows, the people of Carlisle turned their backs and walked away.'

'They don't have the stomach for what they do?'

'Not for atrocities.' Helen sat down on Anne's narrow bunk and spread her skirts. 'The English people are more kind-hearted than you think. We're not all like Butcher Cumberland.'

'Helen, be careful.' Anne glanced around to see if any guard would overhear.

'It's all right,' Helen reassured her. 'They're at the gate, and I know when to hold my tongue. Something you could learn.'

'I doubt it,' Anne smiled. It was the first smile for many weeks. 'Mine will be silenced for me.'

'Maybe, maybe not. There is no need. The Union is saved.' She paused, looking pleased. 'I have to say I'm glad of that. Why, you Scottish women have titles of your own, position, property, homes and land. And you can divorce your husbands! England has a lot to learn from you. I have, since I've been here. But –' she patted Anne's hand, conspiratorially '– I must teach you how to handle Englishmen. They like to be humoured. It allows them to feel strong and smart if women are docile and weak. Once you learn how, you can twist them round your little finger.' She looked round as Morag brought a tray of tea in. 'I'm glad they're civilized enough to allow you a servant.'

Anne frowned, puzzled.

'Morag's not a servant,' she said. 'She's a McIntosh, one of the family, the clan.' Her visitor still looked mystified. 'She gives her help because she chooses. We don't have servants, or slaves. The clan provides everything we need.'

'How very kind,' Helen said. 'But don't they need to help themselves?'

'We're all obliged to help each other,' Anne explained. 'No one goes hungry or without shelter, or care if they need it. We all do our part.'

'I see,' Helen said, though she clearly didn't. 'Well, we do too. One of my friends visits with your cousin, Francis, in Southwark jail. She's taken quite a shine to him. A fine, handsome man, she says. I think romance blossoms.'

'But he's been sentenced to hang.'

'Not if Elizabeth can help it.'

'Elizabeth?' A shiver had run down Anne's back, hearing her sister's given name.

'Elizabeth Eyre,' Helen confirmed. 'She's from a wealthy family, and a fighter. She has written to the king's mistress pleading for your cousin's life.'

'Not the king?' Anne was surprised. Weren't Englishwomen powerless?

'No, no, no,' Helen smiled. 'You've not been listening. Ask a man for something and he'll refuse, just because he can. So we get round them. If the Countess of Suffolk decides your cousin should be pardoned, the king will find himself thinking it's been his idea all along.'

'Isn't that deceitful?'

'Does it matter, if it works? Look what your directness gets you.'

Later that week, Helen joined Cumberland's evening dinner party. Her husband had been reassigned to the Duke's staff while Lord Boyd was absent for the executions. This dinner would be the last before the young Scottish equerry left for London.

Lord Louden was the only other Scot present. Forbes was well out of favour and would not have wanted the invitation any longer. The talk was of the Pretender Prince and his evasion of their pursuing forces. The army had searched Aberdeenshire and the Mearns, shooting rebels, pillaging and laying waste to the counties as they went. Now, their intelligence had it the Pretender and his companions fled north to the Hebrides.

'You must hope to catch him soon,' Helen said.

'I'm in no hurry,' Cumberland smiled. 'He leads us to supporters we might never have suspected, if he but knew it.'

'I took tea with the Lady McIntosh the other day,' Lord Boyd said. 'She really is a very pretty woman. It's a pity she's a rebel.'

'Not for much longer,' Hawley said. 'She goes for trial next week.'

'Tea?' Cumberland frowned. 'She's in prison, not holding court.'

'But she has many visitors,' Cope intervened. 'They queue up outside, several of our own officers among them.'

'And their wives.' Helen smiled and turned coyly to the Duke. 'My Lord Cumberland,' she said, 'I would ask your permission to attend that trial.'

'You can speak against her?'

'Why no,' Helen said, innocently, 'but what a story she must have to tell. My friends in London are agog for news of her.'

'Are they, indeed?' Cumberland was not pleased.

'She raised her own husband's clan and fought against him. Then –' Helen laughed merrily '– she kept him prisoner under his own roof. It's most amusing.'

Cumberland glared at James Ray. Ray, himself, stared coldly at his wife.

'There would be far fewer rebel wives,' Ray snapped, 'if their Hanoverian husbands kept them under better control.'

'Do we know this man, her husband?' Cumberland asked.

'One of my captains, sir,' Lord Louden replied. 'Brave and loyal. He fought at Prestonpans, saving the small number of our troops who escaped, and was at my side when we attempted to take the Pretender from his own home at Moy, which his wife, Colonel Anne, thwarted. He was captured in the wake of that.'

'The Pretender placed him in his wife's custody,' Ray added. 'When we arrested her, I found him locked in the cellar, where he'd been chained.'

'There must be no love lost there then,' Cumberland pondered. 'I don't recall a petition from him. Will he speak against her?'

'He knows little of her actions, bar hearsay,' Louden said. 'They were apart. General Hawley has more damning evidence, of her role in his defeat at Falkirk.'

'I hope you'll give evidence, General,' Lord Boyd urged Hawley. 'No one else has come forward, though we've held her now for six weeks. She made fools of us all, especially the high command.'

Cumberland frowned. Hawley did not appear to relish the task. Cope filled up his glass with claret.

'Courage, Henry,' he said. 'Your reputation will recover, I'm sure.'

'There is no need for witnesses,' Helen said. 'She intends to confess, the whole story from start to finish. Oh, I am so looking forward to hearing it.'

'Does she want to hang?' Cumberland asked. 'All the other traitors lie about their involvement. Listen to them and we fought no one, least of all those bloodthirsty, murderous savages who charged into our fire. They showed no discernible reluctance then to die for a cause they now disclaim.'

'She doesn't seem to mind death, sir,' Lord Boyd said. 'She is quite calm, as if she has found peace within herself.'

Cumberland had not forgotten that pale but pretty face, the quiet dignity.

'Like Joan of Arc!' Helen exclaimed. 'Imagine –' she gazed, awestruck, at the Duke '– you could make a great Scottish hero of her when she dies.'

# THIRTY-NINE

It was the first day of June. The wide River Ness sparkled in the warm summer sun. The red field of Culloden began to turn green. There might have been peace, except there was none. No birds sang above the site of the slaughter. Wounds healed slowly in those seven weeks, keeping the injured from trial and sentencing. In towns and cities, the creak of the gibbets slowed but had not stilled. The Prince was chased north and back again. Army units trawled his wake, raiding homes, raping and murdering occupants. As the flow of warriors reduced and known sympathizers became a trickle, arrests were made for a word overheard, the wearing of white, an expression of sympathy for the condemned.

Cumberland received a letter from his father, commending him for securing the realm and his united kingdoms. 'But we are concerned to make no martyrs,' it read, 'especially from the fairer sex whose influence should not be spread.' Female rebels, however high-ranking, should be tried in Scotland then sent south for sentence, their actions considered too shocking for the citizens of England to hear. The king's letter confirmed the course of action the Duke had decided on. Lord Louden stood waiting for the order. Hawley was not a happy man.

'This is the paper you will serve on Aeneas, Chief of M<sup>c</sup>Intosh and Clan Chatton,' Cumberland said, dipping the quill in the ink and scrawling his signature. 'It will turn the tables neatly.'

'But is hardly fair punishment!' Hawley complained.

'Your hanging would give her glory and influence,' Cumberland responded. 'A death she seems to seek. This –' he blotted the ink dry '– will remove her from our history.' He handed the paper to Louden. 'Soon, she'll be forgotten. I doubt she will have peace now.' As Louden left to carry out the order, Cumberland smiled. He had a fitting answer to the problem of Colonel Anne Farquharson, the

Lady M<sup>c</sup>Intosh, and his cousin, the Pretender, to thank for it. Justice was done.

Bright in the sunlight, the blade of the axe flashed as it was raised. The crowd on Tower Hill gasped audibly, in an intake of breath, and held it. On his knees, Lord Kilmarnock felt the hard wood of the block press against his throat. The blade flashed down.

The minister in Anne's cell had come to give comfort in her last days.

'Whither thou goest I will go,' he read. 'And where thou lodgest, I will lodge, thy people shall be my people, and thy God, my God. Where thou diest, will I die, and there will I be buried.'

Anne stared up at the cell window. Margaret's trial had begun that morning. Soon, they would come for her. She was afraid of dying but not of death. All the pain and grief would go. In the grave, there could be no more torment. The trial would relieve her guilt. She would confess it there, make her peace. She hoped she could walk calmly to the scaffold. Others, whom she knew to be brave souls, had been unable to give life up with ease. From the jail, their screams and struggles could be heard. She'd think of Ewan, the suffering she'd been spared. Let her stay numb to life. Let her not dishonour the dead with the body's desire to live. Let her not fail at the last.

A key was put in her cell door and turned, clattering. The minister's voice faded away to silence. This must be the moment. She closed her eyes briefly, drew a deep breath, turned round. Lord Louden stood in the doorway.

'*Trobhad*, you are to come with me,' he said.

Coming out of the prison, Anne was blinded by the light. How dull and dingy it had been inside. But even with her eyes shielded, she recognized the hooves, fetlocks, legs and body of the horse she was led to. It was her own Pibroch. She was helped into the saddle, to the familiar shape and warmth of the beast. She might have broken then. How cruel they were. She could have walked more easily to the court. But Louden did not lead her and her escort there. They rode on through the town. Folk stopped to watch then talk as she passed by.

They took the road towards the port. Ships sailed south from there, taking those for trial in England to Berwick or to London. Some had said they were afraid to try her in the Highlands, afraid of public riot, others that they were afraid to let her speak at all. Those being transported also left from there, sailing to the colonies and a life enslaved. Was that the intent, to tear her from her homeland, make her live, far away and silent?

She asked the soldiers at her sides but got no answer. Lord Louden, up ahead, did not turn round. At the crossroads, they did not take the coast road, but turned south. So, there would be no trial, just sudden death. As had happened to so many, she would be taken to some quiet place and shot. At least that would be quick. Poor boys, she glanced at the escort, so young, most of them, to be made do such desperate things.

She tried not to think of what would come. Instead, eyes adjusted to the light, she took in all the shades of green, the dark heather, bright trees, the birdsong. Pibroch's strong back was under her, his muscles worked against her legs. Up above the sky was blue, streaked with thin, white cloud. Larks sang, soaring out of sight. The warm, light wind brushed her skin, teased her hair. Out here, there was no judgement, just the earth doing what it did. The cruelty of being in it stung. This world would be hard to leave.

On Tower Hill, Lord Balmerino stopped the executioner's apology.

'Friend, you need not ask me forgiveness, the execution of your duty is commendable.' He gave the man three guineas, all he had, took off his coat and waistcoat and laid them on the waiting coffin. 'There are some who may think my behaviour bold,' he said, 'but I tell you, it arises from a confidence in God, and a clear conscience.' He knelt, put his head in the block, and called the executioner to strike.

The blade of the axe flashed in the sunlight as it swung back. Aeneas was with Donald Fraser and Shameless, out on the slope above Loch Moy. The blacksmith had healed well but must still be careful not to tear his wound open again. It was Aeneas who wielded the axe. Shameless chopped branches from the fallen trees. Fraser stacked them. They were felling wood to re-roof the burnt-out cottages. The cottars who had lost their homes would move in once the repairs were done. Stone buildings provided better shelter than the turf cotts had. Again, the blade of the axe flashed as it swung forward. The whack as it hit the wood echoed through the glen. White chips flew out of the cut. Aeneas pulled the axe out, swung again.

'Chief,' Fraser called over, 'look.' He nodded towards the road from Inverness, distant across the loch. Foot soldiers and riders could be seen, travelling in their direction.

Instantly, Aeneas turned and ran for the house. Fraser and Shameless crashed along through the trees behind him. He burst into the hall, startling the Dowager, who sat by the window, reading.

'What on earth is happening, *ciod e?*' she asked, as he hurried to arm himself with sword, dirk, pistol. Shameless and Fraser followed him in, doing likewise.

'There are troops coming,' he said, strapping on his sword.

Hearing the fuss, Jessie came in from the kitchen and picked up the axe.

'Has there not been enough killing?' the Dowager asked, though she lifted the poker from the hearth as the sound of horses clattered into the yard outside.

'They've done all they will do here,' Aeneas retorted, grimly turning for the door, sword in his right hand, pistol in his left, the dirk pushed in his belt, and backed by the equally armed blacksmith and M<sup>c</sup>Intosh lad.

The door was knocked and opened. The three men spaced themselves in the wide hall. Lord Louden strode in.

'Aeneas,' he smiled. 'Good day to you.' He took in the guns and blades all aimed at him. 'Are you expecting trouble?'

'That depends if you bring any,' Aeneas answered.

'I have an order for you, and a prisoner,' Louden answered. 'You can decide for yourself how much trouble that is.' He called to the men outside. 'Bring her in.'

Anne was escorted into the hall. There was a stunned silence, broken first by the sound of the Dowager's poker falling to the hearth.

'Anne!' she cried out, rushing to her.

As his aunt threw her arms round his wife, and the others sheathed their weapons, Aeneas stared, frozen with disbelief that she was here. She looked pale but well. How could she look so well? Louden held the order paper out.

'Lady McIntosh is to remain in your custody until she learns the error of her ways and is reformed,' he paraphrased.

'My prisoner?' Aeneas said, belting his pistol and sheathing his sword to take the paper and read.

'Aye, Captain,' Louden grinned. 'The Duke has turned the tables rather more pleasantly this time.' He nodded to the Dowager and left, his men following him out.

Aeneas scanned the document, barely able to take it in. Anne was to remain his captive until such time as she demonstrated proper, modest behaviour befitting a wife subject to her husband, the law and the Crown. She would not espouse any cause bar that acceptable to him and he was charged to ensure the denial of her previous unlawful activities at all times, present or future. He looked up at her. She had not moved, nor responded to the Dowager's warmth, but stood tense and unapproachable, eyes downcast, barely present.

'Are you all right?' the Dowager asked, worried.

'I'm well, thank you,' Anne replied. Her quiet politeness was chilling. She might have been a stranger in a strange place.

For seven weeks, from the moment Shameless told him she was taken, alive and unharmed, to Inverness, Aeneas had been unable to think of her without becoming enraged by his impotence to act. Now she was here. His aunt had petitioned for her release, as had many others. He had not, could not, without further jeopardizing his beleaguered people. His role in the British army was all that

326

protected any of them now, a role that shamed him. There was nothing he could say to her.

'Would you take Anne up to her rooms?' he asked Jessie.

Anne's head came up. Her eyes met his, alarmed.

'Don't worry, my lady,' he said, tersely. 'I'll confine myself elsewhere.'

Immediately, she dropped her gaze but not before he saw her relief.

'As you wish,' she murmured.

'As I wish?' he burst out. 'There is not one single thing in this whole sad and sorry situation that is as I wish!'

The others, standing around, gasped. Anne flinched, but she kept her head down.

'I didn't choose this,' she said.

He snorted; even gratitude was beyond her if it meant she must bear his presence.

'Neither of us has any choice now,' he snapped, turning his back as Jessie took Anne upstairs. When the door closed at the top, the Dowager came over to him.

'Aeneas, have pity. She's alive.'

'Barely, since she obviously would rather be dead than here.'

'Isd, no! That's shock. She was prepared to hang. Can you not be kinder?'

Aeneas unbuckled his sword and threw it down. 'I have trees to fell,' he said, snatching up the axe Jessie had left against the wall. 'There are homes to build.' He went out. Fraser and Shameless exchanged a look and followed behind.

The axe glinted as it rose. On the block, Lord Lovat pulled the cloth that would catch his head closer to it. The crowding folk on Tower Hill held their breath, waited. Some said this old man should have hanged five times over for past crimes. Now he met his match. The axe flashed down.

There had been a point on the road when Anne realized where

they headed. Before she could form the thought of execution at her home, Lord Louden turned in the saddle.

'Moy will be glad to have you back,' he said.

Weakness hit her. This was all wrong. Hope was a bitter thing, unwanted and undeserved. At the door of Moy Hall, white roses, their fat buds about to burst, mocked her return. The sickening echo of a scuffle by the stable rose in her memory. Inside, they all stood, like accusations: Jessie without her child, Donald without his son, Shameless without Robbie, Aeneas with hundreds from his clans gone.

Now, upstairs, Jessie talked as if some good had come.

'I unpacked your things,' she said. 'Even when we thought you were gone for ever, I hoped you would come back.'

'How could you want that, Jessie?' Anne sat down, heavily, on the bed. 'Look what I caused.'

'Not you.' Jessie crouched down on the floor in front of her, looking earnestly into her eyes. 'We all did our own choosing. I tell myself my baby did too, that she'd rather be with her father, where the heroes are, than here, where we are now.' Tears filled her eyes. 'Even Will . . .'

Anne put her fingers to the girl's mouth. The mention of the lad's name brought his face in front of her, lying in the gore. Visions of them all, cut and torn, swam up.

'*Isd*, wheesht,' she said, fighting for control. 'I have them all inside me, but if I speak of them or cry for them, they will all come out for me, as they did before.'

'But you can't hold them. Not so many.'

'I can. I have to.'

Jessie got up, sat beside her on the bed and put an arm round her.

'We can't live without hurt.'

'I am so sorry, Jessie.'

'Now you *wheesht*,' the girl echoed her, 'or you'll have me crying again. Your life is saved. There will be something you are meant to do with it.'

The Dowager came in then, with a tray of wine and glasses.

'You'll be needing a drink,' she said. 'And if you're not, I am.'

'And a bath,' Jessie said, jumping up to go and prepare one. 'I bet they don't have baths in the jail.'

'Would it be all right,' Anne asked, 'if I had paper, pen and ink?'

Jessie and the Dowager exchanged a glance.

'I don't see why not,' the Dowager said.

'I'll fetch some up,' Jessie said, brightly, 'when I come to take you for your bath.'

As she went out, the Dowager poured wine and put a glass in Anne's hand.

'What is it you would write?' she asked, casually.

Anne stared at the red liquid. The windows were wide open. In the summer warmth, the scent of the opening roses below already filled the room.

'Whatever I can,' she said, her voice a whisper, 'to stop others following them.'

# FORTY

'I can't let you send these.' Aeneas laid the letters down carefully on the table and looked up at Anne. 'You're not allowed to talk or write about the things you did, not even to get someone else released.'

It was almost two weeks since she'd been returned to them and still he could not get used to her demeanour. She stood, hands folded in front of her, head bowed, staring at the floor, not looking at him.

'Anne –' he tried to speak more gently '– saying your brother and cousins only did as you asked isn't an excuse, even if it was true. The English don't understand clan law.'

'Then what can I write?' Even her words didn't seem like her. Anne usually just said what she would do. She sounded lost.

'Plead for mercy. Say they were misguided. Point out what their loss will mean to others. If you can throw doubt on the Crown's witnesses, do that. Blame a chieftain only if that chief is dead or safe abroad, and make sure you explain clan obligation.'

'So I can try?' Briefly, she looked at him.

'Yes,' he nodded. 'Margaret Johnstone –' He paused. Now he couldn't look at her. 'Lady Ogilvie has been sentenced to death. You might want to appeal for clemency.'

Anne turned and left the room. The Dowager, seated by the open window reading, had heard the whole exchange.

'What's going on?' he asked her.

'In what way?'

'The way she speaks, as if there was no one inside her who could decide anything. Even her friend's sentence provoked no reaction. She wears acquiescence like a shroud.'

'She's a prisoner.'

'Oh, come on. The Anne I know would rage about that.'

'Then why don't you ask her?' The Dowager looked over her magazine at him.

He couldn't, that was the answer. Subservience was a foreign attitude, not one Highlanders wore. Pride was usually their problem. Guilt was his.

'Is it me, what I've done, what I do?'

'You just read her mail.'

'I have to.' He put the sheets of paper in the cold hearth and set light to them. 'She'll get us all hanged.'

'He's a clever man, the Duke. We're Scots, but now you live by English rules, your wife under your thumb.'

'Which doesn't alter the fact they'd hang me first, take over Moy and –' he couldn't resist it '– leave you without a wine cellar to raid.'

'You really need to re-stock.' The Dowager didn't bat an eyelid. 'Things have been let slide. Your uncle must be turning in his grave.'

A few days later, at breakfast, he approved the letters Anne had written.

'These are very good.' The people she wrote to plead for included her brother, her cousin, Margaret Johnstone and Jenny Cameron, but she had also written on behalf of those who would have few champions left, their chiefs either dead, fled overseas or among those in prison. Every word made him more ashamed. 'I hope they bring results.'

Across the table, Anne kept her head down, ate her porridge and said nothing.

'I'll have Shameless take them to the post,' Aeneas added.

'Can I do that?' she asked, still not looking at him.

'What, go into Inverness?'

'Please,' she begged. 'Margaret will be gone soon. Can't I see her one last time? Jessie could come with me.' She glanced at the girl, who was pouring her tea, then dropped her eyes back to the table. 'If she likes.'

'I'd like that fine,' Jessie said. 'I haven't been out since, well, for months.'

'Not three months, Jessie,' Aeneas corrected. 'I don't want you risking your recovery.'

'I have an easy time,' she assured him, 'now Morag's come to do the cleaning.'

'She'll be fine,' the Dowager added. 'If she's well enough to cook, she can sit in a carriage. Let Anne say her goodbyes.'

So it was settled. Shameless hitched up the carriage. He wasn't the natural with horses that Will had been, but he was willing. In the kitchen, out of earshot, Anne helped Jessie prepare a couple of food baskets for the prisoners.

'You don't have to do this for me, Jessie,' she said. 'It could be dangerous.'

'I'm doing it for me,' Jessie said. 'I've scores of my own to settle with the *Sasannaich*. A life for a life seems a fine way.'

Aeneas insisted Shameless drive them, for protection. So that he could carry weapons with impunity, the lad wore his Black Watch uniform. Aeneas gave him a brief written order detailing his escort of the two women in case they were questioned. He wasn't convinced the trip was wise but he hoped it might help Anne. He would rather face her anger with him than be treated to this pitiful subjection. It was at least a fine day they drove off into, Jessie jaunty in a fresh white cap and apron, Anne wearing her favourite blue summer dress. He didn't realize until they left that he was afraid they might not drive back.

On the outskirts of Inverness, the first stop was at the house where Anne had left Pibroch on the day she'd witnessed Ewan's death. The guard on the door checked the basket of food Jessie carried before he let them in. The Skye woman, Nan MacKay, had nursed several wounded Jacobites back to health and on to face trial. Now she only had one patient left, the paymaster, Robert Nairn.

'Anne, *a ghràidh!*' he exclaimed from his sick bed when she came in. '*Fàilte!* I heard you were released. You must be fond of Inverness to come back so soon.'

'Fond of the folk in it,' Anne said. 'How are you?'

'Healing too fast, with the gallows waiting.' He smiled, his face lop-sided with the livid scar across his cheek. 'This arm's near useless, though it's a miracle I still have it, and Nan to thank for that. But I've lost my good looks.'

'Not a bit of it,' Anne insisted. 'You look –' she paused to consider '– interesting and wicked.'

'Then you should see the rest of me,' Robert grinned. 'I have the most interesting body a man could wish, and no chance to be wicked with it.'

'So your vital parts are still intact?' Anne smiled. It was so easy to be with him, where no guilt weighed her down. With Aeneas, she was cowed by shame, deep shame. 'How long till they decide you're fit to travel?'

'A month, maybe longer. Nan says she'll keep me sick as long as she can. I think she plans a fever to set in, but it's the filleting knife I least like the look of.'

They talked till it was well gone midday, about who was here, who was gone, who was going. Robert remembered Shameless and would like to see him, but another time, maybe. Despite his bravado, he was still in great pain, his internal injuries severe. Anne left him with a bottle of whisky, a kiss and the promise she'd visit again. On the way out, she stopped to talk with Nan in the kitchen, shooing her two children to play elsewhere. Outside, Jessie chatted with the guard.

The prison was the next stop. Again, the basket Jessie carried was checked. The guard recognized Anne. As he unlocked the main gate to let them in, he joked that her old room could be made available if she wanted it. He didn't follow them through. Margaret's cell was already opened for other visitors, her brother, Tom, and sister, Susan. They were all upset. Margaret would be sent south for execution in two days' time. Unlike Anne, she had acted with her husband and could safely die for it. Since Lord Ogilvie had escaped, her death was a way to punish them both.

'I doubt she'll be pardoned,' Tom Johnstone said. 'They're determined to make her an example.'

'Having chosen not to with me,' Anne said.

'Aeneas made the difference,' Tom said, embarrassed, 'his loyalty to the Union.'

'Not just that,' Susan added. 'Your story wasn't one they relished in open court. Bad enough to go against the king, but to go against your husband? Every man in England would be threatened by that.'

'To think I envied you David,' Anne told Margaret.

'At least he's free,' Margaret said. 'In court, my lawyer blamed him for my involvement, but I persuaded him to fight. I earned the loss of my head myself.'

'Well, let's not lose it yet if we can help,' Anne said. 'Jessie?'

Jessie, standing waiting in the corner of the cell, untied her apron, unfastened her dress and let it fall. She was still fully dressed, complete with a second apron and frock under the first, another cap still on her head. Anne explained what they'd do next.

'What do you think?' she asked the bemused trio when she finished.

'I've nothing to lose,' Margaret said, 'but what about the rest of you?'

'You'll be flogged, or worse, if you're caught,' Tom told Jessie.

'I've a strong back,' the girl said.

'And we'll be fined or thrown in jail,' Susan said. 'But none of us will have our heads chopped off, so let's do it.'

While Margaret changed, Tom distributed the food in the basket around the other cells. Anne and Jessie rolled up the bunk's thin mattress and pulled the cover over it. In the gloomy cell, laid with the pillow carefully arranged, it almost passed for someone lying asleep. Susan did Margaret's hair in Jessie's style, cap pinned on top. Dirt was rubbed into her face and hands to darken the pale skin which had not seen daylight for ten weeks. Anne had chosen well, asking Jessie. The two were reasonably alike in height and hair colour. When her brother came back in, they all studied the result.

'Maybe,' he said slowly, 'if nobody looks too closely at her.'

'Then let's find out,' Anne said.

Jessie hid in the corner of the cell so as not to be seen through

334

the door. Susan pulled her chair in front of the bed and sat, talking to the mattress while screening it from view. Anne and Tom walked to the main gate, Margaret close behind, head down. The guard unlocked the gate and held it open.

'Her sister not coming?' he asked as they walked through.

'She wants to visit a while longer,' Anne said, certain he must hear her heart thumping and discover them. 'I have other things to do.'

'All of them better'n hanging,' the guard joked as he locked up again at their backs. He barely glanced at the serving girl on the far side of the man. She'd come in with Anne. She left with Anne. Had he looked in her basket, he would have discovered a fine lady's dress, but there was no reason to check what people took out of prison.

Once in the street, the trio did not take time to congratulate themselves on how easy it had been. Hands still shaking, Anne kissed her trembling friend goodbye.

'Now get away to France and David.'

Tom helped his sister into his carriage and they were off, heading for the coast to seek safe passage. Anne walked back to where Shameless waited.

'Jessie found a friend to visit,' Anne told him. 'I said she could have an hour.'

Though Shameless didn't know it, they waited for the guard to change at six o'clock. Serving girls came and went without attention. Even if the new guard looked at Jessie, he would not suspect her of being other than herself.

Shameless wandered off to talk to old acquaintances. The time came and went. The guard changed. Anne fretted. What was taking so long? Then the two women appeared, Jessie hurrying down the street to the carriage. Margaret's sister came too and gave Anne an excited hug.

'It couldn't have worked better,' she said, quietly but ecstatic. 'I chatted on as if she was still there. When we left, I told the guard she wasn't feeling well and had gone to sleep. He hardly looked in the cell as he locked it. By morning, she'll be far away.'

Susan left then, to walk back to her lodgings. Seeing Jessie with Anne, Shameless came back to drive them home. Sitting behind him in the coach, the two women grinned conspiratorially at each other. The plan had worked perfectly. Both their hearts began to slow to normal speed. Anne felt better than she had since Culloden. One saved.

The following night, in the middle of supper, Lord Louden paid Moy a visit.

'I'm sorry to interrupt, Aeneas,' he apologized, 'but I have an order to search your home.' While the troops he'd brought rattled through the rooms, checking, he explained. Margaret Johnstone, the Lady Ogilvie, had escaped from prison some time during the night. 'From a locked cell, apparently.'

'And what has this to do with Moy?' Aeneas asked, quite deliberately not looking over at his wife, though he noticed that the Dowager did.

'Probably nothing,' Louden said. 'Anne visited her yesterday, but she had other visitors after that and was there when the guard locked up, or so it appeared.' He had orders to search places where Margaret might take refuge.

'And I'm suspect?' Aeneas asked, angrily.

'Not at all,' Louden reassured him. 'But she and Anne were friends.' He turned to Anne, sitting, head bowed, at the table. 'Did she mention her plans?'

Anne looked up at him and shook her head. 'Margaret wouldn't compromise me,' she said. 'I didn't stay long. She talked of her execution. We said goodbye on parting and didn't expect to see each other again.'

'Much the same as her sister said.' Louden seemed satisfied. 'Her brother has disappeared. I suspect he bribed the guards.' As his men returned from their fruitless search, he repeated his apologies and left.

'Well, there's a turn-up,' the Dowager said, holding out her empty wine glass to be filled.

'In a moment,' Aeneas said. 'I think we can expect Jessie.'

The door from the kitchens opened. Jessie hurried in, her eyes seeking out Anne. The relief on her face was as obvious as it was fleeting, quickly suppressed as she lifted up the wine bottle to fill the Dowager's glass.

'Leave that, Jessie,' Aeneas said, 'and wait here.' He leant forward towards Anne, chillingly calm. 'You didn't stay long,' he repeated. 'Yet that was your reason for going, and you must have spent several hours with your friend.' He had counted those hours, wanting them safe back home.

'We visited others,' Anne murmured, not looking at him.

'She didn't stay long in the jail,' Jessie defended her. 'An hour maybe.'

'Would you lie to me now, as well, Jessie?' Aeneas asked.

The girl shook her head, miserable. 'That wasn't a lie,' she said.

'Then perhaps I should ask you for the whole story?'

'Jessie's not at fault,' Anne protested.

Aeneas threw his chair back as he stood. It clattered to the floor.

'So,' he thundered. 'Does my wife hide inside that submissive shroud after all? And still does not care whose life she risks! *Taigh na Galla ort!* Jessie, of all people?' He stormed round the table as he raged. 'With Will and her baby dead, her body raped, and you –' he stood over Anne '– you involve her in your schemes!'

'I chose to do it,' Jessie insisted, tears in her eyes.

'I'm sorry,' Anne whispered, staring at her hands clasped in her lap.

'Sorry?' Aeneas was only more enraged. 'Get up, get on your feet!' He dragged the chair from under her as she stood, throwing it backwards to crash across the room.

'Aeneas!' The Dowager got up. 'Calm yourself.'

'I'm calm,' he bellowed, glaring at Anne, standing, hands clenched at her sides, head down, staring at the floor between them. 'Look at me!'

Anne's head came up. If she'd been a man he would have hit her.

'So you can look at me,' he thundered. 'As you looked at Louden. To lie!' He stared at her, chest rising and falling as he fought to control himself. 'I had a wife who could look any man in the eye and speak fearlessly. But you? You hide, pretend, deceive. I don't know who or what you are now.'

Anne lowered her eyes again. 'Your wife,' she whispered.

Her response only enraged Aeneas further. He swept the dirk out of his belt and, while the others gasped, tilted Anne's chin with the tip of the blade.

'Show me,' he said when her eyes met his again. 'Show me if they sent back the wife I know. Take off your dress.'

'No, Chief, *sguir dheth*,' Jessie objected. 'Don't.'

'Do it,' Aeneas ordered, not taking his attention off Anne, his voice dangerously quiet now. 'Let's see how obedient you really are. Take it off.'

Anne reached behind and untied the ribbons round her waist, then she began to undo the hooks at the front, from the top down. When they were all undone, she paused, still looking at him, her expression unreadable.

'Aeneas,' the Dowager said, 'stop this.'

He ignored her, watching his wife's face intently. Now he wanted to know when she would stop, when she would reveal the spirit she'd been pretending was cowed since she'd come home. Disturbingly aroused by the tantalizing ease with which she could be naked with him, he also wished they were alone upstairs, to push her dress aside, touch the warmth of her skin, make her his wife again. But he was not about to break the tension of the moment. Lightly, he traced the tip of the dirk down the length of the gap in the front of her dress to her navel.

'Go on,' he prompted.

She seemed as fixed in the moment as he was, her eyes holding his. Her left hand rose to her right shoulder, eased the straps off. As the material peeled away from her skin and began to slip down, she raised her other hand and pushed the straps off her left shoulder. The blue silk began to slide to the floor. A scrap of paper fell out from against her breast where it had been lodged.

Anne gasped and tried to catch it, but he was quicker. He had the note in his hand as she clutched her dress to stop it falling round her feet. She stood, half-naked, holding the crumpled cloth against her with one hand, reaching out with the other. Now he could tell what was in her eyes. They were pleading. He pushed the dirk back in his belt, unfolded the paper, looked down and read.

# FORTY-ONE

Colonel, *mo luaidh*,

The time is come. We are on Drumossie, where we might engage tomorrow. Lord George has been stood down from command. I need your advice before this day ends.

In my heart, yours ever,

MacGillivray.

Aeneas rocked back, punched in his own heart by the hand, and the signature.

'Please,' Anne begged, holding out her hand.

He put the note into it.

'Cover yourself,' he said, his voice rough, hoarse. 'And get out. All of you, get out of here!'

Jessie rushed to Anne, to help raise her dress and get her out of the room. The Dowager lifted the wine bottle and her glass and followed. The door shut behind them. Aeneas collapsed into the nearest chair, swept his arm across the table, clearing the space in front of him with a clatter of dishes, put his head on his folded arms and wept, his body wracked with the grief he had held back for weeks, grief for the torment of his people, for the deaths of his *clann*, his family, for their losses and his own, and for the loss of MacGillivray, his bright, brave friend and brother chief, and for the pain of having lost the woman who was not his wife now and never could be again, a woman who loved a dead man.

The next day, as soon as he knew she was up, he went to Anne's room, the room they had once shared and which he'd been unable to occupy even in her absence. She was seated at the dressing table but jumped up, as if she was afraid, when he came in.

'Anne, don't.' He couldn't deal with this or the gulf it put between them. 'I did wrong to you last night.'

She only bowed her head.

'If I could send you home to Invercauld, I would. But until the order of constraint is lifted, you must stay here.'

'I know,' she whispered.

'Can't you understand? There is no escape. I hope Margaret lives. But, in Angus, the Ogilvie lands are forfeit, like the Camerons' and MacGregors', like Monaltrie and Dunmaglas. The people are driven off by new English landlords. Invercauld survives only because Forbes supported your stepmother. Isabel –' he stopped. Isabel Haldane was not young, pregnant with her fourth child when she was raped, her home dismantled, the looted shell torched before her eyes, she and her children turned out of doors, left to give birth alone in a barn. He was too harsh, driven by his own guilt, wanting to protect. When he spoke again it was with sorrow. 'Ardsheil came out because Isabel insisted. Now she and the Appin Stewarts have no home. Is that what you want here?'

'I'm sorry.' Her voice was so quiet he could barely hear. 'I didn't think.'

He ached to take her in his arms, to give and receive forgiveness, but couldn't bear to have her flinch from him again.

'Anne, you can only help if you co-operate. Confine yourself to the estate. Write your letters. If you save one chief, lawfully, you might save a clan.'

Even as he said it, he didn't believe. This British government would not be appeased. Loyal clans also felt their wrath. A life here and there, a home, a piece of land, those might be saved. Moy would go on, but changed. He might keep Anne safe but had failed his people. There was no reward in having made his point. All he could do was leave the room. Outside, in a white drift, the last petals fell around Moy Hall from the white rose of Scotland.

Aeneas spent the weeks of summer occupied with moving the cottars, changing their status to tenant farmers, allocating land. It would be hard, with so many gone. The skills lost with them would need to be bought from strangers. They could not survive as a reciprocal family group any more. From now on they would sell produce and pay rents, be self-sufficient – if they could with their cattle stolen, tools burnt, their grain stores looted. But currency, not kinship, would matter now. Survival would depend on wealth, not warriors. The old ways were gone, dead on that moor with more than half their men.

Anne wrote her letters. When Shameless took the mail to Inverness, she sent Morag with food for the prisoners. Letters began to arrive back. Jenny Cameron was released, without trial, from Edinburgh, where she'd been held for months. Without a husband to blame, her story was too like Anne's to bear exposure in court. Women who thought for themselves, who bore arms and led troops to fight for freedom, were too threatening to the stability of England, where everyone knew their place and women's was not in the lead. Her friends had carefully hinted as much. It paid off. Jenny's life, like Anne's, was exchanged for silence, her part in the rebellion erased.

Anne's brother, James, wrote to say his death sentence was reduced to banishment beyond the shores of Britain. He would go to France, travelling with the Kinlochs, who were also banished, and hope some day to be pardoned and return. Her cousin, Francis, also reprieved, was released into the care of Miss Elizabeth Eyre, whom he hoped to marry, but banned from return to Scotland. The tone of Anne's petitions changed, from pleading for clemency to seeking pardons.

But, with each letter, there was less to do. By August, and a fine summer almost over, normal concerns began to clamour for attention. Anne walked Pibroch down to the forge. Outside, in the filtered sunlight under the trees, Donald Fraser taught his eldest daughter how to shoe a horse. Old habits died hard.

'Get a firm grip,' he told her as the girl bent to lift Pibroch's hoof. 'And dig in. You're getting a shoe off, not tickling the beast.'

'She's doing well,' Anne said.

'Aye,' Fraser said, proudly. 'Wants to, what's more. It was her asked me.'

'Rather this than work in the house,' the girl said.

'She's no housekeeper.' Fraser watched his daughter pull off the last shoe. 'She'll not be agreeing with everything a husband says, either. Not like those young Edinburgh women, picking up new-fangled ideas from the English *Sasannaich*.'

'My dad says men need women who'll argue with them to keep their wits sharp,' the girl added, 'until you argue with him, of course.'

'My wits are sharp enough,' Fraser grinned.

'You did a fine job on the cottages,' Anne said. 'I walked past yesterday. Ewan's daughter was out washing the windows. The novelty will wear off, I expect.'

'Aeneas did most of the work. I just banged the nails in.'

Anne dropped her head at the mention of her husband. Aeneas suffered her because he had to. He'd made that clear enough.

'Do you know what I wish most, Donald? I wish I'd been on the field that day, at MacGillivray's side.'

'Surely not. You have your life. He'd have wanted that.'

'A life I can't bear,' she said. 'He sent for me and I didn't come.' She looked up into the blacksmith's eyes. 'I've let everybody down. Even he died thinking that of me.'

'I don't see how.' Fraser scratched his head. 'He knew your sister had the note he sent, that you didn't.'

'*Dè bha siud?*' Anne's legs weakened under her. 'He knew?'

'Aye, and he was right glad you wouldn't see the mess we were in.'

'Then he didn't believe I failed him?' She felt light-headed.

'As if you could.' Fraser took hold of her arm, seeing she had gone pale. 'As if you ever would.' He led her over to a bench and called for Màiri to bring ale.

While she drank it, Fraser told her as much as he could remember, about Elizabeth's visit to the field the day before, about their point-less march to Nairn and back that night, and the morning of the battle.

'Lord George stayed, so we did,' he said. 'The will of the majority. We knew it would be bloody, but if the Prince had ordered the charge, we'd have gone sooner and could've broken through to their cannon. MacGillivray did all he could, but we'd no chance with our numbers down and grape-shot chewing up our flanks.'

'I was coming to take you off the field.' Tears filled her eyes. 'It was too late.'

'*Isd*, don't torment yourself. There's nothing you've done that needs forgiven.'

He got up then to check the shoeing, gave each new one a cursory tap lest his daughter think she'd done too good a job. Anne wiped the tears from her eyes. Grief was a luxury she couldn't afford, her guilt was greater than that. She had put freedom and independence before life and led them out in the first place.

She rode Pibroch back to Moy, leaving him with Shameless to strip down and put out to the grass with the other horses. Aeneas and the Dowager were already at dinner. A letter lay beside Anne's place.

'Aren't you going to open it?' Aeneas prompted. 'It might be more good news.'

She shook her head. The hand was familiar. She'd wait for privacy.

'I have good news of my own,' the Dowager announced. 'The Duke of Cumberland has vacated my house and gone back to London.'

'Pity he didn't take his troops with him,' Aeneas commented.

'I expect we'll live with them a while yet, with a prince hiding under every stone,' the Dowager said. 'But at least I can leave you to your home now.'

'What,' Aeneas smiled, 'while my cellar still has stock in it?'

'This afternoon,' the Dowager said, archly, then, with a wicked grin, 'before you check the cellar.'

She was eager to get off, to find out what state her house had been left in. Aeneas offered to change his plans and accompany her, but she wouldn't hear of it.

344

'Shameless can take me,' she insisted.

Anne's mind was on the letter in front of her. As soon as she could escape, she took it upstairs to her room, opening it by the window in the sunlight. It was from Robert Nairn. The military doctor had pronounced him fit to be moved.

Some sea air will be just the thing. Several of those we paroled
in Edinburgh apparently remember me well enough to testify.
That'll teach me to flirt with the enemy. I will, hopefully, be the
last man in Scotland to hang for it!

The rest was his good wishes to her, thanking her for help and friendship, and for the good food she'd sent during his convalescence. She was not to think it had contributed to his well-being, in case she tormented herself, but it had made the days lying in bed more palatable. He was being removed to a ship tomorrow for transport to his trial in Berwick.

I expect to renew my acquaintance with a certain dour minister
of the Kirk. No doubt he has a front seat blessed and set up
ready. Live well and love well, Anne, there is nothing else.
Yours, sadly in health,
Robert.

She let her hand drop and stared out the open window. All these months to heal and for what? He was the Jacobite paymaster. Despite his joke, it wouldn't take paroled prisoners to hang him. There would be enough evidence to string him up a hundred times. Beyond the loch, she could see Aeneas ride away through the trees. Down in the yard, Shameless hitched up the carriage. The Dowager would be in her room, packing.

Anne laid the letter down on her dressing table, went out the door and hurried quietly along the corridor to the rooms Aeneas had been using. Her heart began to thump in her chest. His bed was made, but something of his presence in it hung about, the slight untidiness. On his dresser a bottle of whisky, three quarters full, sat beside a glass. The air smelled of maleness, so close she'd turn round and he'd be there. It was terrifying. Feeling criminal, she searched his wardrobes. He would never miss what she was looking for. Once she had it, she turned to leave. The whisky bottle caught her eye again. She grabbed it too and left.

Later, downstairs, Jessie eyed the covered basket.

'Why did you take it upstairs first?'

'I was putting a surprise in it,' Anne answered, filling food through the opening in the cloth cover. 'Have you any potted hough?'

'There's nobody sick at the cottages,' Jessie said, fetching a small pot of it.

'I know. But I should take something when I visit.'

Shameless carried the Dowager's kist through the kitchen at their backs. He wasn't dressed for town.

'Aren't you driving?' Jessie asked him.

'No, the chief asked me to but the Dowager changed her mind. You know what she's like.'

'Women,' Anne tutted, sympathizing.

Outside, the Dowager waited in the sunshine for Shameless to load the kist behind the carriage seat.

'I should come with you,' he grumbled.

'I drove myself around before you were born,' the Dowager told him. 'And the English troops don't trouble Moy. So *isd* and let me be.'

Anne stood waiting, the covered basket at her feet.

'Can I say goodbye and thank you,' she said, giving the older woman a hug. *'Tapadh leat.'* That done, she picked up the basket and set off towards the cottages while the Dowager took her leave of Jessie and Morag.

Ten minutes later, a mile up the road, the Dowager pulled the carriage under some trees and waited. It wasn't long till Anne appeared through the wood. She put the basket beside the kist and climbed up into the seat.

# FORTY-TWO

'Better folk are treated worse,' the guard complained, seeing the whisky in the basket.

'That's not for him,' Anne smiled. 'It's for Nan. She's done such a good job getting him well enough to hang. Maybe she'll share a dram with you, if you'd like that.'

'After dark, tell her,' the guard said, 'when I won't get caught.'

Inside, sensing trouble, Nan's smaller child hid under the table. The older one peered out from the curtained box bed. Nan was upset to be losing her patient. Robert sat at the table, trying to convince her she'd done a fine job and it was his own fault, not hers, that the government would soon undo it. But, when Anne emptied the basket, it was the whisky he reached for not the food.

'*Uisge beatha*,' he said, 'the water of life.'

'I hope it will be,' Anne said. 'But that's for Nan. The food is for the children. This –' she pulled the cloth from inside the bottom of the basket '– is yours.' Underneath, neatly folded, was a linen frock coat and a rather squashed hat. 'Aeneas never wears them.' She made a face. 'Maybe they're from his misguided youth, from France?'

'The French have more style,' Robert joked. 'I should think they'd hang me for that alone.'

'You're not going to hang,' Anne said, reaching under her skirts. 'You're going to walk out of here, wearing them.' She pulled down the matching breeches she had worn underneath her dress. 'They'll be looking for a kilted warrior.'

'Fetching,' Robert grinned. 'I'm glad they match at least.'

'I have some stiff white linen,' Nan said. 'I could be making a collar to pass you for a minister.'

The plan was simple. Just before the ten o'clock curfew, as soon as it was dark enough, Nan would distract the guard by drinking whisky with him while Robert slipped out the door. Once in the street, nobody would pay him any attention. Anne would wait on the edge of town with the carriage and drive him out of Inverness overnight to Portsoy where he might get a boat for France.

'Overnight? But you'll be missed.'

'Not till it's too late,' Anne assured him. 'And Aeneas won't turn me in.'

'Love's young dream,' Robert sighed.

'Not quite,' Anne said, wryly. 'But he won't. He has too much to lose now.'

The hours waiting would be hard. Anne went back to the Dowager's. The older woman had carried an *arasaid* and her pistols out of Moy for her, in the kist. They spent the time removing all traces of the recent occupation from her home.

In his room, preparing for supper, Aeneas saw the bottle of whisky was absent from his dresser. His aunt was incorrigible but she might, at least, have left him his nightcap dram. Downstairs, the dining room was empty. While he waited for Anne, he read the day's mail. The first was from Forbes, to include a copy of the Disarming Act recently passed by parliament. The old judge did not approve: 'Scots law is for Scotland to decide,' he wrote. 'This is a travesty of the Union.'

The act was worse than Aeneas had expected. Every Highland weapon was named and banned: 'Broad Sword or Target, Poignard, Whinger, or Durk, Side Pistol, Gun, or other warlike Weapon.' North of the River Clyde, all arms were to be collected and destroyed. Men or women keeping, bearing or using any were subject to prison until heavy fines were paid. Men who could not pay would be sent to fight for the British army in the Americas. Women would be jailed for six months. A second offence by either sex meant transportation to the colonies for seven years' servitude. The act went on to ban Highland clothes, bagpipes and tartan, except within the armed forces, and to compel all school teachers to swear oaths of loyalty to the Crown. The penalties were the same. It was crushing. Their culture would be eradicated and, between the lines, their children would be taught lies, their language put down.

His impotence beat down on him. He had helped this come about. They had all seen it happening, a creeping domination that, since the Union, had bit by bit eaten away at their tribal lives. He had tried to save what he could. Anne had fought to stop it. She'd been right. He wished she would come down. At least if she was roused to anger, they would talk with honesty. He glanced at the second letter. It was on fine headed paper, from the English royal court. He and his wife were ordered to London to attend a celebration ball to mark the restoration of peace.

'*Taigh na Galla ort!*' he swore. 'First destroy us then make us dance!' He threw it down, called Jessie and sent her up to find out if Anne meant to eat with him. The girl was back in minutes.

'She's not there.'

'Did she go out?'

'After dinner, when the Dowager left. She was going to the cottages.'

'But you saw her come back?'

Jessie shook her head. 'I didn't think anything of it. She could have come in while I was busy. But she wouldn't be all this time. It's near dark out.'

'Ask Shameless to saddle up a fresh horse for me.' He ran upstairs to Anne's room, a bad feeling in his gut. The letter she'd received that day lay on her dressing table. He squinted at it in the fading light. His brow furrowed as he read, seriously doubting, now, that his wife had met with any mishap on the road. He yanked open the drawer where she kept her pistols. They were gone. Hurrying back to his own room, he changed into his kilted Black Watch uniform, strapped on his sword, thrust a pistol in his belt, ran back downstairs and out to his horse.

Outside her house, Nan MacKay poured another dram for the guard and topped up her own glass. She had positioned herself beyond him so his back was to the open door. Flirting was not her usual style and, with him English and her speaking only Gaelic, it was difficult. But Robert had shown her how, and she did the best she could, with smiles and shrugs, glancing into his eyes, asking questions and answering though he couldn't understand, nor she him. It seemed to please the man, at any rate. As he laughed heartily at what she supposed was his own joke, Robert keeked out the doorway. Nan joined in the laughter, as if she knew what was funny. Robert slipped out and away down the street, vanishing quickly into the darkness. Nan splashed more whisky into the guard's tin, drank a toast with him and, as the curfew sounded, went back inside.

On the edge of town, Anne sat in the carriage, waiting. She wrapped the *arasaid* tighter round her to keep out the evening chill and tucked the pistols more securely in its folds. Ten o'clock, they'd said. It was past that now and dangerous to be out. But then Robert was there, climbing up beside her, looking every inch the cleric he most definitely wasn't. She grinned at him, clicked the reins and drove off sedately. It was hard to be restrained, not to gallop, but that would draw attention. As soon as they were out of earshot of the houses, she urged the horse up to a fast trot, heading east for the coast.

'We made it!' Robert exclaimed.

'We did,' she grinned.

'Colonel Anne, you're a hero.'

'Not me,' she said. 'Nan took the real risk.'

'They can't prove she helped me, can they?'

'No. She'll be questioned. But she's too poor to have bought you clothes or paid your transport. So long as she keeps quiet, they'll have to let her go.'

'My family will see she never wants for anything again.' His scarred face grew sombre in the moonlight. 'I'll never forget this. Hope, hope of living.' His eyes filled with tears. 'I didn't realize what it is to lose something so normal.'

'Don't cry,' Anne said, slowing the horse down so she could put an arm round him. 'If you get me started, I might never stop.'

The sound of a galloping horse behind interrupted them. Anne grabbed the reins.

'Don't speed up,' Robert hissed. 'It looks guilty. Just let whoever it is go past.'

The rider didn't go past. He rode up level to their horse, slowing as he came, reached out and grabbed the halter. Anne drew a pistol from her *arasaid* as he pulled their horse to a halt. She aimed at his back just as he turned around. It was Aeneas.

'*Plus ça change,*' he said, raising an eyebrow. 'Nothing changes, except this time I won't walk away. You'll have to shoot.'

She lowered the gun.

'Please, Aeneas,' she begged. 'He'll die if I don't get him away.'

'Is this your husband?' Robert asked.

'I am,' Aeneas answered, his voice hard. 'And since she's compromised, why should I care if you die?'

'Your wife's honour is in no danger from me.'

Aeneas held up a hand to quiet him as he listened to a sound from the road ahead. 'But her life is,' he snapped.

Anne and Robert could hear it too, feet on the road, marching towards them.

Aeneas stepped from the saddle into the carriage, looping his horse's rein over the whip spur. 'Get down behind the seat, quickly!'

Robert was bundled over the seat and down behind it. Aeneas pushed Anne along into his vacated place, sat down, pulled her into his arms and put his mouth on hers.

The sudden closeness startled Anne, the body heat, arms holding her, his face so close, the pressure of his mouth, his breath against her cheek. Aeneas stopped the kiss, moved his mouth close to her ear.

'Push the pistol out of sight,' he murmured, 'then try to act like you want to do this.'

She pushed the gun into the folds of cloth and, as his mouth found hers again, wrapped her arms round his neck. The warmth of his lips moved against hers, and a familiar desire rose like

351

memory in her to a desperate wanting. His body moved closer, pressed hard to her, his right arm round her, holding her tight to him. Between them, his left hand moved up to the pistol at his waist. The marching feet, more than two pairs, were close now. Maybe they would go on past.

'Halt!' The feet stopped. 'Oi, you!' the same voice called.

Aeneas broke off the kiss. In the dark, his eyes shone as he looked into hers.

'Just when life gets interesting,' he said, that almost-forgotten half-smile on his mouth. He looked round, keeping her held against him, his right arm still across their bodies, masking his gun, hand holding her waist, towards the speaker.

Anne turned too. The man who spoke was a sergeant, musket in his hands. Three redcoat privates were with him, weapons shouldered. One stood behind the sergeant who'd come forward beside the horse, facing Aeneas. The other two hung back near the carriage horse's head. They were from Wolfe's regiment, red coats with yellow facings, a watch patrol heading back to town. They all seemed amused. Against her side, she could feel Aeneas's left hand tighten on his pistol. He couldn't draw and shoot before the sergeant fired. She slid her own hands into the folds of the *arasaid*, gripped both her guns.

'Captain, is it?' the sergeant said, noting Aeneas's uniform. 'Then you'll have a name, and orders to be out at this time.'

His men sniggered, clearly thinking the clandestine meeting on this quiet road was exactly as it appeared, an adulterous tryst.

'Couldn't you spare the lady's blushes, Sergeant,' Aeneas answered, letting go of Anne, 'and just go on your way?'

There was more tittering from the three privates. The sergeant grinned, as if he shared the joke. He shifted the musket a fraction. There was no thumb on his right hand.

'We'll take care of the lady,' he snorted as crude laughter spluttered behind him. 'You worry about yourself.'

Anne fired through the tartan cloth. The shot made a round hole in the sergeant's forehead. Aeneas drew his pistol, aimed and fired in one smooth move, dropping the private behind. As he leapt to the ground, drawing his sword, Anne pulled her other pistol out, aimed and fired at the third redcoat. Aeneas swung his sword across the throat of the fourth. Their bodies crumpled to the road.

There was a scuffle from behind the seat. Robert's head appeared, peering over. He gaped at the four bodies lying twisted as they'd landed, on either side of the carriage horse, then he let out a low whistle.

'I'm glad we're all on the same side.'

'I've met these men before.' Aeneas sheathed his sword and dragged the thumbless sergeant's body away from the horse. 'This one, for certain. They were overdue for death.'

'We should move fast,' Anne said, 'in case the shots were heard.'

'Can you ride?' Aeneas asked Robert.

He nodded, getting himself out of the carriage.

'Take my horse.' Aeneas held out the reins. 'Go on through Nairn to Elgin. The farrier there will give you money for him and put you on a fishing boat at Lossiemouth.'

'You two will be all right?'

'If we get away without being seen,' Aeneas said. 'But you'll have a reputation as a warrior when your escape's discovered and this lot are found.'

Robert rode the horse round to Anne, leant over and kissed her.

'If you're ever done with him,' he winked, 'send him my way.'

'Go safely, Robert,' she urged as Aeneas got back into the seat beside her. 'Good speed.' For some inexplicable reason her eyes filled with tears.

The young paymaster swung the horse round, kicked it away and rode off, fast, into the night. Aeneas lifted the reins, snapping them as he gave a curt command to the horse, and they were off. Tears blinded Anne, no matter how she dashed them away. A lump swelled in her throat. She buried her face in the *arasaid*'s warm woollen cloth and sobbed, broken-hearted, as the carriage picked up speed, taking them through the night, back to Moy, and home safe.

She was still weeping, great, deep, agonizing sobs that shook her whole body, when they pulled up in the yard. Aeneas shouted to Shameless to see to the horse, then he lifted her out of the seat, carried her into the house and up the stairs. In her room, he laid her on the bed, and she turned her face into the pillow, body heaving. Jessie was not long behind them, bringing ale and wine.

'I'll brew tea as well,' she said. Glancing at the bed, she saw the hole burnt through the *arasaid*. 'Is Anne hurt, is she shot?'

'No.' Aeneas shook his head. 'Hurting, not hurt. Don't fret for the tea.'

'She has a lot to grieve for,' Jessie said. 'Crying will help.' She left them to it.

All that night, Aeneas lay beside Anne, holding her, stroking her hair, murmuring words of love and comfort. Gradually, her crying slowed and ceased. Worn out, she fell asleep, still in his arms. He lay a long time, his cheek resting on her head, taking in the sleeping scent of her, his woman. Even when she'd thought her rescue was threatened by him, she didn't shoot, couldn't. She asked for his help instead. He hadn't lost her. It was she who got the first shot off, to save his life, and left herself exposed, relying on his support. Relying on him? No, he hadn't lost her, he had thrown her away. For hours, he lay, tormented by his own guilt. Eventually, he fell asleep. When he woke, she was gone.

# FORTY-THREE

Anne walked Pibroch across the battlefield. In the morning sun, it was quiet, so quiet, and peaceful. Coarse moorland grass sprouted green hummocks among the clumps of purple heather. Even the long graves had almost blended in, nature taking life back to its heartland. She walked along them, slowly, knowing he was there and there was no telling where. But it was the last moment of life and not dead bones she looked for. She wasn't certain she could find the right spot till she saw the stone.

*Well of the Dead*, it read. *Here the Chief of the MacGillivrays fell.*

On her knees in front of it, she drew her dirk, pushed the blade into the ground and opened up the soil. Reaching into her dress, she took out his note and looked again at the written hand. He was present in it, such a personal stamp, part of him, his own writing of his name. For a long time, she sat, just holding it in her hands. Then she pressed it to her lips, folded it and pushed the paper into the slot in the earth.

'So you know I came,' she whispered.

With the handle of her dirk, she pushed the edges of soil together, closing the wounded earth back over it. She cleaned the blade on the grass, pushed it back in her belt and leant forward, tracing the writing on the stone with her fingertips.

'*Slàn leat, mo luaidh,*' she said. 'Goodbye, my love.'

She rose, took Pibroch's reins and turned. Several yards away, Aeneas stood beside his horse, watching her. On the spongy ground, she had not heard feet or hooves approach. She walked over to him, stopped close enough to reach out and touch, looking up into his eyes.

'It's a fine stone,' she said, knowing he had put it there.

'I loved him too.'

'I know.' Last night, he stood beside her, risking his own life for a man he didn't know, to save her. It was what he'd always done, tried to protect those he cared for. 'I am so sorry,' she said. 'I gave you a world of great pain and loss.'

He closed his eyes for a moment, from hurt or relief she couldn't tell, then he put his hands on her shoulders.

'No, Anne, 's mis' a tha duilich,' he said. 'It's me who is sorry, and ashamed. If we'd been together in this, it would not have ended here, or like this. My place was with you.'

She slid her arms round his waist and drew close to him, resting her head on his chest, hearing his heart beat strongly inside him. The fight had gone out of her. Her spirit was spent. She'd done all she could, but it would never be enough. There was no way back to what was lost, and she couldn't imagine the future.

'Has it ended?'

'No.' He looked down at her. 'We're only defeated if we give up. There will be other ways.'

She wasn't sure what question he answered, or which she had asked. They were irretrievably bound together because others had made it so. She was his prisoner. Could they truly choose each other when they couldn't choose otherwise? She put her hand in his and they walked the horses to the edge of the moor.

'Last night,' she said, 'you knew an escape route.'

'It was for us. If they'd tried to hang you, or take you to the boats, we'd be in France now. Moy would belong to an Englishman.'

He would have given it up, put her before himself, before clan and country. All those long weeks in jail, she hadn't been alone. He'd watched over her. The food that came, Morag's care, an escape arranged. He chose her even then, as he had from the first and through everything that parted them, just as he'd vowed; his sword and clan in her defence, for only death would part them now. No, the future couldn't be imagined, only that she wanted to live it with this man.

'Let's go home,' she said.

★

356

After breakfast, James Ray and his wife set off in their packed carriage, heading south out of Inverness. With his tour of duty done, they, too, were going home.

'Can we stop at Moy Hall on the way?' Helen asked. 'It would be nice to say goodbye to your captain and his wife.'

'No.' Ray was blunt. 'The sooner I get you back to civilization the better. I haven't been at all happy with your behaviour since we came here.'

'We could have gone by boat,' she said, looking the other way. Her husband suffered seasickness. He didn't like reminding of it. 'Oh, look.' She pointed. They were passing a group of ruined turf cotts, only one of which remained whole. Smoke drifted through its roof. 'Aren't those the turf houses we came past on our way here, where we first met Colonel Anne? I wonder what happened to them.'

'Be quiet!' Ray pulled the coach to a stop. He was looking the opposite way, up the gentle slope on the other side of the road. Half-way up, the figure of a woman crouched near a cow, milking it. There was something familiar about her. He got down, drew his sword and started up the slope.

The old woman bent over beside the cow worked its udders rhythmically. Pale, creamy milk scooshed into the wooden pail. Her head was tucked into the beast's rump, turned to one side. In the corner of her eye, she saw the man creep closer, drawing his pistol as he came.

'You there!' he called when he was near enough.

She did not respond, though her eye went down to the wooden shaft lying in the long grass beside her. The man was right behind her.

'Are you deaf?' he shouted.

She jumped, snatched the shaft up, turned and thrust. The pitch-fork dug deep into the man's gut. She jerked it upwards, grinned a maniacal gap-toothed grin.

Ray shuddered on the end of the prongs. His head jolted, his eyes widened. The sword dropped from his hand. His mouth opened. Blood dribbled from it. He tried to bring the pistol round.

'*Danns, a Shasannaich!*' Meg snarled, twisting the fork again and again, up into his rib cage. 'Dance!'

The pistol fired, uselessly. Blood spurted from Ray's open mouth. He was still upright, impaled on the pitchfork, but his life was ended.

Hearing the shot, Helen stood up in the carriage, looking up the slope. Her husband was still there, jumping about angrily in front of the woman. She sat back down and waited.

Up on the hill, the old woman let the Englishman's body drop, stabbed her pitchfork in the soil to clean it, gathered up her pail and hurried off.

A culture was dying. Almost overnight, tartan vanished from the land. Yarn-dyers emptied vats of bright colours. Looms clacked busily with browns and greys. Bonnets, belts and brooches were put aside, bagpipes burnt. Dancing ceased. The old songs died away. Men put on the unmanly Lowland clothes, cursing the inconvenient discomfort as they did. Women turned their *arasaidean* to blankets, their tongues to learning new words. The Gaelic slunk behind locked doors as English stumbled on to the streets. Weapons were delivered up for destruction. The British army began a systematic search of every house for any arms that were not surrendered, looting and brutalizing again as they went.

At Moy, Aeneas took on the task of clearing weapons himself. There would be no more raids on his people. As August mellowed into September, he and Shameless drove the cart around the farms and cottars, thanking men and women for their co-operation, trying not to notice their shame.

'Swords into ploughshares,' Donald said, sorrowfully, as they delivered them to the forge for breaking, 'as the good book says.' But none of them believed good could come with dishonour.

Anne began the work of teaching the adults the language of the English. Their children helped them, since the school teachers would now not allow a word of their native tongue to pass their lips in class and the young were quicker learners. It wasn't joyful work, except that she learnt more Gaelic curses in that first fortnight than she'd heard in her whole life before. The interruption of their royal invitation was almost a relief.

'You can't really want to go.' Aeneas watched Anne pack the last few things into the kist sitting on their bed.

'I do,' she said. 'I want to see these people who tell us how to dress and speak and live. And I want them to see us. Besides –' she motioned him to sit on the lid of the kist so she could strap it down '– we have no choice.'

Aeneas wore his Black Watch kilt. Military was the only use of tartan not proscribed. He would have resigned his commission, but to do so would have meant no plaid or weapon, going naked in a world that was under duress. People were still hauled to prison from the straths and glens, and now there were additional reasons for punishment.

'I feel like a traitor, wearing this.'

'One of us should be armed for travel,' Anne said, pulling the leather strap tight round the kist. 'It will be safer.'

'Are you expecting trouble?'

'Not at all,' she smiled, planting a light kiss on his lips as she moved around him to the second strap.

'I'd feel a lot happier if you didn't smile when you said that. You'll have to behave down there.'

'I'll behave perfectly,' she assured him, buckling the strap. 'I have a duke to impress.' The constraint against her would not be lifted until Cumberland agreed.

'You're smiling again.' He pulled her in front of him, wrapped his arms round her waist.

'Did I miss that bit?' she asked. 'There will be no smiling. Any Scot found smiling north of Stirling will be shot on sight.'

He rolled her over the kist on to the bed and pinned her down.

'You need something to smile about,' he grinned, pulling her dress up.

'Now you're doing it,' she giggled, 'smiling for no reason.'

'Oh, I have reason enough,' he said, kissing her throat, 'and a cure, temporary though it is.' His fingers stroked her thigh. 'And when I'm done –' his lips brushed her mouth '– I'll know why you're smiling.'

The bedroom door opened. Jessie came in.

'Could you two save that for the carriage?' she said, seeing them on the bed.

'Now there's an idea,' Aeneas winked at Anne, straightening her skirts as he got to his feet. 'Did you interrupt just to suggest it?'

'No, I did not,' Jessie objected. 'But there's a boat to catch and I thought you'd want to know Nan MacKay was arrested three days ago. They won't let her eat, sleep or even sit down till she says who helped Robert Nairn escape.'

'Three days?' Anne was shocked. She'd assumed that Nan, too poor to provide means of escape herself, would not be suspected. 'Why did no one let us know?'

'The Dowager just found out and sent word.'

Aeneas threw the window open and called Shameless up to help with the kist. Anne ran downstairs and grabbed her cloak.

'Don't forget,' Aeneas reminded Jessie as they headed for the door. 'Speak English while we're away.'

'What, to myself?' She put her tongue out at their backs but, that being the part she might lose, quickly withdrew it. There had been stories of people's tongues cut out and nailed to public doorways as warning. 'Gonadh!' she swore, then glanced guiltily around the empty hall.

In the carriage, on the way to Inverness, Anne fretted. 'It was my idea. I can't let Nan be punished for it.'

'Your confession won't stop that.'

'It would stop the interrogation.'

'And put you back on the scaffold, with me alongside.'

'No,' she insisted. 'I'll keep you out of it.'

'You can't.' Aeneas drove home his advantage. 'Even if I'd let you say I took no part, you're my prisoner. I'm responsible for what you do now.'

Anne was staggered. In their home, the order against her had begun to seem no more than irksome. But out in the world, the incapacity inflicted by Cumberland was exposed. She was rendered helpless, a burden not a companion, an unequal being, powerless to act or to take responsibility for her actions, like a small child or a miscreant dog. If she spoke or acted out of turn, Aeneas would suffer and, through him, their suffering people. Even as her spirit began to rise and the desire to fight back returned, it was quashed. The constraint against her struck deep. She was not free. It was crushing.

'Then what can we do?'

'They want victims, not justice,' Aeneas said, taking a hand off the reins to take hold of hers. 'One of the clan will confess, if need be. It will only be a prison sentence.'

'And if it's not?'

'One step at a time. We can play it by ear. Just, please, don't say anything unless we're agreed.'

At the prison, they were allowed into the interrogation room only because Aeneas was an army captain. Five minutes, the guard said. Nan MacKay was in a bad way. The Skye woman's legs were swollen and puffy from standing for so long. She was black with bruises where they'd struck her to keep her awake.

'*Uisge,*' she begged through cracked lips.

Anne fetched her a little water from the pail. She bit back the warning against speaking Gaelic. There was no point. Like most Highland and Island women, Nan knew no English. She still had her tongue only because they wanted her to speak.

'We'll get you out of here,' she promised as Nan gulped from the tin mug.

'I'll not be saying,' Nan whispered. 'Whatever they do.'

'You're not abandoned,' Aeneas told her. 'Don't think it. We'll get this stopped.'

Forbes was with the Earl of Louden in his offices. The judge had grown old and disillusioned since the victory. To support the government, he'd bribed chieftains and funded Black Watch companies from his own coffers, yet no reparation had been made. Now his courts were bypassed. Parliament passed repressive

361

legislation against his beloved Highlands. Tribal people pushed off the forfeited estates fled to the cities. Others left of their own accord, unable to bear the changes forced on them. Ships sailed for America every day, crowded with disenfranchised clans.

'Soon there will be nothing here but cattle and sheep,' he complained. Hardest of all, the name of his home would live in history as the site of that bloody slaughter, as the start of a bloodier pacification, the ruination of a people, and not as the seat of a reputable justice. Culloden. Cumberland, amused by Forbes's protestations, had thought it apt.

The Dowager Lady McIntosh had petitioned the judge as soon as she heard of Nan MacKay's torture. Now he harangued Lord Louden. When Anne and Aeneas came in, the beleaguered earl threw up his hands.

'I suppose you've come to confess?'

'Of course not,' Aeneas said.

'I have,' Anne said.

'My wife was with me when Robert Nairn escaped,' Aeneas glared at her.

'If you'd let me finish,' she protested, 'I was about to add, if it will stop her torment.'

'Oh, come now, Aeneas,' Louden urged. 'Don't be left out.' The commander was clearly under pressure. 'I take it you know your aunt has already confessed to supplying whisky, clothes and transport to aid the rebel's escape.'

'She has?'

'Along with every single member of her household,' Louden fumed, 'one after another. I'm just about to take Forbes's confession, and his staff's, no doubt. Perhaps you'd like to get in line.'

'Eh, no,' Aeneas declined. 'We've a boat to catch.'

'Then catch it. I've just sent an order to the prison that the torture of Nan MacKay ceases forthwith. But she'll stay in prison till her sentence is carried out.'

'I came to protest at her treatment,' Forbes growled, 'not confess. I'll also lodge appeal against that sentence. Eight hundred lashes is an execution. She's not military, they have no right to try or punish her.'

'Eight hundred lashes?' Anne grabbed Aeneas's arm for support.

'I spoke to the woman,' he said. 'She did nothing wrong.'

'They all say that,' Louden pointed out. 'The guard insists she distracted him. I agree the sentence is excessive, but I can't overrule the verdict.'

'The Duke of Cumberland can,' Forbes suggested.

'Then we'll ask him,' Aeneas said. 'When will the sentence be carried out?'

'The end of next month,' Louden answered. 'Go to London. I'll see she comes to no harm till you get back.'

With that settled, they all shared a dram. Forbes resumed his criticism of the punitive legislation. Yet another act was being drawn up, to end the heritable jurisdictions. The clan chiefs would have no authority over their people when it was passed.

'You'll be relegated to landlords,' he told Aeneas, 'nothing more. The clans are finished.'

'They can't prevent you being chief, can they?' Anne asked. 'The people chose you. Only they can take that away.'

Aeneas shook his head. This was a blow, perhaps the hardest to their culture than any. It removed the bond between clansmen, took away their choice of leadership.

'Without the power to settle disputes, what will a chief be? The people will turn to the law, to the state. The reason to have and uphold a chief will be gone.'

Louden poured the old judge another whisky and saw Anne and Aeneas out to catch their boat.

'Did you hear your lieutenant was killed?' he asked as they reached the door. 'We shipped his body south last week, with his wife. Just outside of Moy, it was.'

'Was there a skirmish?' Aeneas frowned.

'No.' Louden sounded weary. 'The work of a solitary villain. Usual story, nobody saw anything. He left his wife in the carriage on the road and went to speak with an old woman. Never came back. Stabbed twice, bayonet the surgeon thinks.' He paused. 'I saw the wounds. Strange thing is, I'd swear it was a pitchfork. So much for banned weapons, eh?' He bid them safe journey and shut the door.

Anne and Aeneas stared at each other. The old woman had not been seen since the cotts were raided. They'd assumed she was dead.

'Meg,' they both said at the same time.

# FORTY-FOUR

London was startling. Street after street after street of tall buildings, relieved only by the river running through it. Even that waterway seemed to be alive with people, throbbing with boats and barges, the many bridges constantly criss-crossed by horse-drawn carriages and sedan chairs. Grandiose stone mansions filled elegant squares, chained off with iron padlocked gates. Hovels huddled incongruously between them. Beggars, traders and hawkers crowded the pavements. Political pamphleteers and way-side preachers bawled their different furies on every corner. Smells of smoke, street food and bakeries mixed with the fumes of sugar-processing and textile trades, the stench of breweries, distilleries, the stink of fleshers and sewer ditches running open through the streets from overflowing cesspits under houses. It was altogether both grander than Edinburgh and more squalid.

'Are you all right?' Aeneas asked, coming over to the window where Anne watched the throng below.

'They're very small,' she said.

'But plentiful,' he said, wryly, looking down. 'Like ants.'

'I can meet the men's eyes without tilting my head, and the women only reach my nose.' She glanced up at him. 'You must feel like a giant.'

'I feel out of place,' he smiled. 'You didn't answer my question. Pensive doesn't suit you.'

'I think I'm afraid.'

'Of what?'

'For Nan. Bad comes of everything I do.' Her brows furrowed over clouded eyes. 'Will Cumberland see you?'

'I've sent a request, and he's hosting the ball tomorrow. We can talk to him there.'

'You can.' Anne turned back to the window. 'Helen says I should only speak to my superiors when spoken to.'

Aeneas turned her round to face him.

'There will be none there,' he said, 'for there are none. Don't accept this. At home, you speak with stable-lads, cottars and blacksmiths, or with princes, earls and dukes, and you are the same with each as they are the same with you. That's who we are. If the opportunity arises to speak with Cumberland, take it.'

Unconvinced, she nodded. They were in Helen Ray's home. The Englishwoman had insisted, despite her recent bereavement, and tutored Anne in the manners expected at court. Aeneas was a lost cause. He refused to entertain courtly bowing. A brief nod to humour Cumberland was all he would agree to, and that only because Nan's life might depend on it.

'It's Highlanders they want, it's Highlanders they will get,' he insisted.

Helen fluttered back into the room, clearly excited. 'You have visitors,' she announced.

Behind her, a tall, blond man in city clothes ducked his head as he came through the doorway and then stopped just inside. Behind him, a dainty, younger woman hovered.

'Francis!' Anne breathed out his name in a whisper of disbelief, then rushed across the room into her cousin's arms calling it. 'Francis!'

'Anne, Anne.' Farquharson of Monaltrie lifted her off her feet and crushed her in his arms. 'It's been so long. I feared we'd never meet again.'

Aeneas crossed the room to join in the welcome. 'If you'd put my wife down,' he said, 'I'd like to shake your hand.' There was much back-slapping, hugs and teasing about the unfamiliar London garb. Francis, Baron Bàn, was a man back from the dead, his sentence commuted from hanging to banishment from Scotland for ever.

'And, along with your petitions, my new wife to thank for my life,' Francis said, introducing her. 'Mistress Elizabeth Eyre, the Lady Monaltrie.'

As Aeneas took Elizabeth's hand to shake it, she dipped a curtsey.

'Oops,' he said, catching her arms, then realized she hadn't tripped but was doing that strange thing women here did at such moments. They all laughed together.

'I've asked them to stay and dine with us,' Helen beamed. 'You'll want time to catch up with each other.'

Anne's first concern was for news of her brother, now exiled in France.

'Did you see James before he sailed?'

'Went with him to the boat,' Francis nodded. 'That's where I would have gone too, but for Elizabeth. It was you he thanked for his life. Didn't he write to say so?'

'Yes, of course, but you know how mean he is with words. Was he well?'

'He has a slight limp, but his health is good. His heart is another matter.'

'We'll keep trying for a pardon,' Aeneas promised, 'to bring him home, and yourself.'

'Francis talks all the time of his beloved Highlands,' Elizabeth said. 'I expect poor Helen feels a bit of that too, now her home is lost.'

'Oh, it's not the same,' Helen said. 'My brother offered me a home. At least I'll still be in London. That doesn't compare with banishment.'

'Then you won't stay here?' Anne asked.

'I can't,' Helen explained. 'My father gave me this house but, of course, it became my husband's when we married. Now it will pass to his nephew.' From her time spent among them, she expected the shock among the Highlanders. 'It's not so bad,' she added. 'The homes of your chiefs also pass to the next heir.'

'But no other woman would lose hers, wife or no,' Aeneas said, 'and a chief's widow is given a new home of her own, with an income to keep her for life. I hope your nephew means to provide for you.'

'That's not the way of things here,' Helen said. 'But,' she added, brightly, 'I will probably marry again. I'm young enough and still have my looks.'

While that was undoubtedly true, an embarrassed silence struck the three Highlanders. To criticize their host's way of life was an affront to hospitality. But marriage which stripped women of their belongings was surely theft. As the solution for enforced poverty, it made whores of women, whoremongers of men.

'Tell them about Lady Broughton,' Elizabeth prompted her husband, tactfully changing the subject.

'My wife should tell you this story herself,' Francis chuckled, 'since it fascinates her.' But Elizabeth ducked her head, shy again, and so he continued. With the help of several friends, Greta Fergusson had hidden out in Edinburgh after Culloden. It was there she delivered her baby, but the child, born too soon, had died. Twice, her attempts to sail for France from Leith had failed, so she travelled south, trying at several points to gain passage overseas. Finally, she fetched up in London.

'But there's still a warrant out for her,' Anne worried. 'Is she captured?'

'No,' Elizabeth answered, forgetting her shyness. 'But only because Francis persuaded her not to seek out her husband.'

'John Murray would surely help his wife,' Aeneas said. 'He certainly proved capable of helping himself.' Sir John had turned king's evidence, betraying the despised Lord Lovat to save his own life.

'I doubt it,' Francis disagreed. 'With his title and estates restored, he wouldn't jeopardize them again, not for Greta. After his release, he took up with a Quaker schoolgirl and passes her off as the Lady Broughton.'

'But the real Lady Broughton is safe,' Elizabeth finished triumphantly. 'My father knew a ship's captain who'd help, and she sailed for France the very next day.'

'How exciting!' Helen exclaimed. 'I really don't know why they must still hound people. After all, it's over. That's what we're celebrating tomorrow.'

'It wasn't an invitation we could refuse,' Aeneas pointed out.

'Not when your wife is the guest of honour,' Elizabeth said, then she caught the look which passed between him and Anne. 'Didn't you know?'

Anne shook her head. The reminder that she faced the scrutiny of England's courtiers the next night did nothing to lessen her anxiety. Knowing the attention would centre on her deepened it considerably.

'I doubt the Duke of Cumberland had honouring me in mind.'

'Forget him,' Helen said. 'He struts like a conquering hero, yet that victory was a fluke. He never won a battle before, and we'd all be very surprised if he ever does again.'

'England is safe from invasion because of its navy,' Francis said, 'not because of its army. I doubt they'll hold the New World territories against the French and Spanish.'

'They will if the clans make up that army,' Aeneas said, 'and these prohibitions are designed to do that. It's the only way our dress and martial skills can survive. This ball is probably the carrot to that stick.'

'You're very suspicious, Aeneas,' Helen chided. 'It's a celebration, of peace.'

'To which the enemy is invited?'

'The defeated enemy,' Anne added.

'It's not like that,' Elizabeth said. 'People clamoured for your presence. Now that they feel safe, everyone wants to meet the fierce warrior woman they were so afraid of.'

Anne glanced down at the table. That woman was long gone. Whatever they expected, she couldn't provide it.

'Do they hope a show of wealth and power will pass for courage and keep us cowed?' Aeneas asked.

'Some do,' Francis replied. 'Others feel amends are due for the purges. But most are just curious.' He looked thoughtfully at Anne. 'You've nothing to prove. They've invested you with an exotic glamour, that's all. And I'm thankful for it,' he grinned. 'It means I can wear proper clothes again.'

A long, convivial evening followed, the inevitable sorrows tempered by more immediate joys. As it wore on, Anne lapsed into silence. Despite Helen's dismissal of him, Cumberland still had control of her and, through her, Aeneas, their home and people.

It was his response tomorrow night that mattered, not the gossiping crowd.

The palace buzzed with lords, ladies and excitement. Powdered periwigs were primped. Embroidered satin skirts were draped with finest silk. French lace and fans were in abundance. Even the government ministers wore new frock coats and matching breeches. Everyone who was anyone was there, grasping their sought-after invitations.

Anne and Aeneas stood in line, waiting for their introduction before they could descend the broad, curving stairs to the ballroom. The few Highlanders available in London made up the final pairs. As guests of honour, the M<sup>c</sup>Intoshes would be last.

'It will be fine,' Aeneas said in Anne's ear.

'*Tha mi an dòchas,*' she said. 'I hope so.'

'We should speak English.'

She bowed her head, stung.

'I know when to hold my tongue,' she muttered.

He could have bitten his own. The proscriptions only applied north of Stirling.

'There will be a lot of that.' He cast a nod at her outfit. 'But your dress speaks for you.'

She wore the rebel white, a sweeping low-cut gown of silk and lawn, with a blue sash at her waist. In her dark, coiled hair was one perfect white rose. Not the Jacobite rose, it was the wrong time of year, but the closest to it she could get in mid-September London. A white lace fan and dance card dangled at her wrist.

'I'm giving them what they expect,' she said. 'As you are.'

He stood beside her in his full kilted chief's attire, complete with feathers, bonnet and silver brooch and, with official permission sought and granted, his silver-handled broadsword. That dispensation was due to his military status and loyalty during the conflict. Francis had already escorted Elizabeth down to the ballroom, equally resplendent but, as a constrained enemy, with his scabbard empty.

Anne's stomach churned. They were there as curiosities, wild rebel Highlanders from a land that had now been safely pacified. Though Aeneas seemed as quietly dignified as she strove to appear, she knew he, too, was nervous. Whatever else happened, they had to win Nan's reprieve from the Duke.

Down below, England's chattering, courtly crowd nudged each other, whispered and stared, trying to glimpse them behind the few in front still waiting to descend. At the wide doors, the major-domo thumped his cane twice on the floor.

'Sir John Murray of Broughton, and Lady Broughton.'

Anne studied the plain young girl beside the erstwhile Prince's secretary. Greta would have loved this. Glamorous always, feathers flouncing in her hair, she would have swept elegantly down the stairs on her husband's arm, head high. Defeat or subjection would not have entered her mind or her soul. She would do well in France. Aeneas grabbed the pencil from Anne's dance card and scribbled on their invitation.

'What are you doing?' she hissed.

'You'll see,' he winked.

Thump, thump went the cane.

'The Right Honourable, the Lord Boyd.'

James glanced round briefly at Anne and nodded good luck, his face colouring as it always did in her company, then he, too, set off down the sweeping stairs. For all his loyalty to this government, three of the four titles he would have inherited were forfeit and his father executed. She wondered if he flushed now from shyness or from shame. Aeneas handed their invitation to the major-domo, then turned to her.

'If it's to be the last time,' he said, 'they should get it right.'

Thump, thump, the cane went again.

'The Much Honoured, Captain Aeneas M<sup>c</sup>Intosh of M<sup>c</sup>Intosh, Chief of Clan Chatton and –' there was the tiniest of hesitations '– Colonel Anne Farquharson, the Lady M<sup>c</sup>Intosh.'

'Aeneas!' Anne protested. Her rank and the Scottish form of naming might be construed as confrontation.

'Be who you are,' he said, placing her hand on his arm.

Every head in the ballroom had turned at the announcement.

371

A whisper like the sea rushing to the shore swelled round the room, rising to meet them.

'That's her.'

'She's here.'

'It's them.'

'Pretty little thing.'

'So slender.'

'That girl, I don't believe it.'

'Hardly savage.'

'So that's the heavenly Lady M<sup>c</sup>Intosh.'

The comments multiplied, washing back and forth, behind fans or hands or openly, as Aeneas led Anne down the flight of steps. Behind them the cane thumped again, ignored, announcing latecomers. All eyes watched the Highland couple come down and walk the length of the room to pay their respects to the host, the Duke of Cumberland. Anne's fingers dug into Aeneas's arm.

'I feel like a freak,' she muttered.

'There's one over there.' He nodded in the direction of a foppish courtier.

Anne spluttered with laughter.

'In fact,' Aeneas added, leaning down to speak in her ear, 'we're surrounded. Take your pick. I'll deal with those you leave.'

She flipped her fan up, giggling and snorting behind it.

'Oh dear,' a woman they were passing said, 'I think she's overcome.'

A man stepped out in front of them. 'M<sup>c</sup>Intosh.' He nodded the greeting. 'Is it true this genteel little wife of yours led those savages into battle?'

'Aye,' Aeneas said, 'and ate the dead afterwards.'

Annoyed, the man stepped back to join his friends, all clamouring to know what the Highlander had said.

'Anne!' A woman dressed in black waved. It was Helen, fanning herself excitedly. She was announced as Mistress Helen Ray, her first name restored to indicate her widowhood.

Watching them come down the hall, Cumberland was quietly

pleased. He turned to General Hawley, who stood behind him, simmering still at being thwarted.

'You see? Tonight they'll meet a reformed, submissive woman. One so amenable and boring that, tomorrow, they'll move on to other tittle-tattle. She'll be forgotten.'

Henrietta Howard, the Countess of Suffolk, swept up to his other side.

'William, my dear,' she said, 'you must introduce me to your little rebel. I'm told she's bedded more men than I have. We could compare notes.'

Cumberland's distaste for the countess equalled his feelings for Hawley. His bulbous eyes glinted. It seemed the evening offered many rewards.

'I think you'll find, Henrietta,' his jowl quivered, 'that she does it for pleasure.'

'Really?'

'I gather these Scotswomen do.'

Lady Suffolk turned from appraising the approaching couple to consider him. 'What a waste of currency,' she said coolly.

Arriving in front of the Duke, Aeneas nodded curtly. Anne did as Helen had taught she must and sank into a deep, elegant curtsey.

'McIntosh,' Cumberland nodded. 'Lady McIntosh.' He waved a hand towards the woman at his side. 'Allow me to present the Countess of Suffolk.'

'Well, McIntosh,' Lady Suffolk smiled. 'You certainly look the part. And your wife –' she glanced at Anne '– is extremely charming.'

'Thank you,' he said, as smoothly as if he always spoke for his wife and wincing as Anne's nails dug into his arm, a wince he quickly covered with a smile. Helen's education of them at least prevented surprise. They could never have guessed that people would address a husband about his wife as if she were absent while present, nor that Anne should not speak unless spoken to. The countess was a powerful woman, the king's eyes and ears. She'd gained that power the only way Englishwomen could, through powerful men. Now she was the king's mistress, having worked her way up.

'Rather boringly,' Cumberland said, 'it falls to me to begin the dancing.' He turned to Aeneas. 'As my guest of honour, I'm sure you won't mind if I ask your lady wife.'

'Not at all,' Aeneas said, covering the wince quicker this time. If Anne kept this up, his arm would be scarred for life.

The Duke escorted Anne to the middle of the floor. When he was happy with their position, at arm's length, he turned to face her. As if on cue, the band struck up.

'A very suitable start, I think,' he said, smiling.

The tune was his Scottish war song, 'Ye Jacobites by Name', written to sing his praises and laud their defeat. An audible gasp ran round the hall. Aeneas stiffened.

'My, my,' Lady Suffolk said. 'He does mean to rub it in.'

Francis stood with his wife's family, his hand automatically going to his empty scabbard. Anne would surely walk off the floor.

She didn't. Instead, she kept her eyes on her partner's face, her expression bland, as if the tune meant nothing to her. Cumberland held out his hand, a question in his eyes. Without any hesitation, Anne raised hers and laid it lightly on his. Together, as the singer launched into the lyrics, they began to step out the dance.

> You Jacobites by name, now give ear, now give ear.
> You Jacobites by name, now give ear.
> You Jacobites by name, your faults I will proclaim,
> Your doctrines I will blame, you shall hear.

Stunned by the humiliation being visited on their Highland guest, it was a few minutes before the crowd responded.

'They must have her on laudanum,' Helen whispered to her friends.

'Perhaps we should join them,' Lady Suffolk suggested to Aeneas.

Dancing to the Duke's victory music was the last thing Aeneas wanted to do but, if Anne could do it, he could. He offered his arm, and they took the floor. As soon as they did, other dancers crowded on, most of them trying to get nearer the central couple, desperate to overhear the exchanges between them.

'You're as fine a dancer as they say,' Cumberland complimented Anne as he turned her.

'As are you, sir,' she smiled, sweeping out from him and back.

'Your husband has done a fine job,' he approved. 'I must congratulate him.'

'You're most kind,' Anne dipped her head.

Helen Ray danced behind them with her brother. 'It's awful that he'd torment her like this.'

'I'm sure he just wants her to know her place.'

An air of disappointment and let-down hung over the hall, though no one could have said what they'd expected. This mild-mannered young woman acquiescing to the Duke's superiority wouldn't make the good story they'd hoped to tell those poor, eager folk who'd been left off the guest list.

Anne shut her ears against the lyrics as the singer sang of Popery and cast the Prince as the son of a robber and a thief. She had one thing to do here. Aeneas had said any opportunity should be grasped. Affecting the coquettishness she had seen Helen use when speaking to men, she smiled coyly at Cumberland as they turned around each other.

'There is a woman in Inverness jail,' she said, lightly, 'Nan MacKay.'

'The riff-raff doesn't concern me,' Cumberland responded.

'She's to be given eight hundred lashes.'

'I doubt it. Few could live beyond five.'

Nearby, the lord who had enquired about Anne's battle record bent to his partner's ear.

'Hardly the bloodthirsty warrior.'

Aeneas had given up trying to overhear what Anne and Cumberland talked about, giving his full attention to his dance partner.

'I'm told your wife killed a dozen men at Culloden,' Lady Suffolk said.

'My wife wasn't even there. She was at home, with me.'

'How perfectly boring.'

'Life with my wife is many things,' Aeneas said. 'Boring isn't one of them.'

'And you, McIntosh –' she stroked his cheek with her fan as they made a pass '– is life with you boring?'

'You can ask my wife about that,' he suggested.

The singer sang on:

When Duke William does command, you must go, you must go;
When Duke William does command, you must go;
When Duke William does command,
Then you must leave the land,
Your conscience in your hand like a crow.

Ignoring thoughts of her beloved brother, and all the others driven from home, Anne concentrated on her purpose. She and Cumberland stepped forward and back, then passed around each other again.

'Then I can't prevail on you to intervene?' She returned to her plea for mercy.

'Don't have me revise my opinion,' Cumberland warned. 'I'm sure McIntosh can deal with any concerns.'

'And I will be suitably grateful,' she smiled, certain her face would crack.

'I hope so.' Cumberland turned her around him. 'Politics is a male province, not for you to worry about. A wife is an adornment, Lady McIntosh. Stick to dancing.'

The dance was coming to an end. The singer drove home the last words.

They ought to hang on high for the same.

It was a long time since Anne heard old MacBean's voice, but she remembered it now. Death should come with honour, he'd said. Nan was ready for it, as Anne had once been ready and could be again. Without honour and the dignity of it, a person was nothing. She executed one last pass with Cumberland. The music ceased. The Duke bowed, Anne curtsied. Everyone applauded. Cumberland offered his arm to escort her off the floor.

Instead of taking it, she stood, motionless, facing him. Acting like an Englishwoman meant being treated like one. An image flickered in her memory, of a small child thrashing on the ground, fighting its shadow. This time she was glad to lose the battle, glad frustration won. The applause frittered away. Nobody moved. No one could until the Duke left the floor. He indicated again that Anne should take his arm. She didn't. Be who you are, Aeneas had said. There was no one else she could be. She raised her chin a little, looked Cumberland in the eye.

'Sir,' she said, her voice steady and clear as a bell in the silence, 'I have danced to your tune. Now will you dance to mine?'

# FORTY-FIVE

Aeneas flinched. Automatically, his hand went to his sword. Lady Suffolk put her hand on his wrist, gave a brief shake of her head. Francis, with his empty scabbard, marked the nearest guard whose weapon could be purloined and drew his wife close. This might be a short marriage. Like most in the room, Helen's mouth gaped like a dead fish. Nobody breathed, no one dared in case they missed the Duke's response.

The Duke hesitated – it was only a moment but one of the longest moments the court could recall – then he bowed his head, acceding politely to the request. Anne turned towards the musicians.

'Can you play "The Auld Stuarts back Again"?' she asked.

A collective intake of breath surged from the mass of people in the hall. She had asked for the rebel song. Several women swooned and had to be caught by their partners. Helen was near delirious with delight. Lord Boyd smiled and shook his head, flushed with admiration. Elizabeth's hand went to her mouth. Realizing now what was happening, she gazed at Francis, tears starting in her eyes. Sir John Murray, shamed by his own cowardice, stared, uneasily, at the floor.

The musical conductor nodded. It might be the last time he would have a head to nod but he couldn't seem to stop nodding it.

'Yes, my lady,' he answered Anne. 'We can, we can.'

'Then play it,' she said calmly and turned back to the Duke, dropping the deepest curtsey as the first chord was struck. She placed his hand around her waist and showed him how to skip out the first steps. Everyone quickly joined in. This was faster, wilder and, from time to time, required a partner to be held close to execute the steps well. Even those around the edges of the floor found their feet tapping, legs twitching, their hands clapping. Lady Suffolk squeezed Aeneas's wrist. They hadn't moved, though bodies whirled around them.

'You see, McIntosh,' she said, 'there was no danger. Manners are everything at court. The Duke could not refuse.'

Aeneas grinned, broadly. It felt good. He might be ordered to kill his wife when he got her home, if he got her home, but right now pride swelled in him and all he could do to celebrate was dance. He pulled the countess into his arms, tight against him.

'My goodness,' she said, 'my hair will come down.'

'Then let it,' Aeneas said as he spun her round.

For a rather stiff and bulky young man, Cumberland was light on his feet and a fast learner, quickly taking over the lead as soon as he'd mastered the pattern of steps and movements. Scottish dancing was easy to do. Mistakes simply looked like innovation. By the half-way point, he was expert. Anne spun back into his arms, put her cheek against his and spoke into his ear.

'Have Englishmen always been afraid of women?' she asked.

'I don't know any who are,' he answered.

She leant back as they turned so that she could see his face.

'Then why do they control them?'

They danced forward and back, out, clapped and back into each other's arms.

'Women are the weaker sex, Lady McIntosh. They need guidance.'

'Eight hundred lashes, half of which will be administered to a corpse? That sounds more like fear than guidance to me.'

'You're tenacious, I'll give you that.'

Needing breath for the dance, they swung on in silence until, with a final flourish, the ladies were spun, skirts billowing, as the music came to a close. Bows and curtsies were exchanged. The Duke offered his arm.

'If your husband attends me in the morning,' he said as she took it, 'he'll be issued with an order remitting that sentence to a short period in prison.' He led her off the floor, both of them a little breathless. 'I admit to a grudging admiration that McIntosh would choose to be married to you. But that caper, Colonel Anne, will be your last. Do we understand each other?'

'Yes,' Anne smiled. 'Yes, sir, we do.'

On the west coast of Scotland a full moon hung over Loch nan Uamh, lighting a path across the water. A small boat put out from Borrowdale. In the bow, a prince sat with his retainers. Rocking gently on the tide in deeper water, two French privateers waited, flying the false colours of British men-of-war. Several Highland chiefs were already aboard, men who could not return home, their clan lands, and their lives, forfeit. Wood creaked, thudding into wood, as the small boat came alongside. Feet ascended the narrow ladder. Anchor chains rattled, rolling up. Sails unfurled, billowing as they caught the wind that would carry them out to sea. The ships lurched forward into the swell. Behind them, the land lay etched in the moonlight, sharply shadowed in shades of grey.

In Inverness jail, Nan MacKay lay on the bunk in her cell watching thin shafts of late October sunlight fan in through the small window high above. The swelling in her legs was gone, the bruises faded to yellow stains. Food arrived for her every day, so she did not hunger or thirst. She was a patient woman, had waited patiently for her husband to return long after she knew he never would. She had tended Robert Nairn patiently, believing for many weeks he'd leave her house a corpse before realizing she'd saved him for the gallows to claim. She was patient again now, waiting for Anne and Aeneas to return. Fate had a dark face and a light one, and you never knew which would turn towards you. She kept herself patient by conjuring images of Skye, of returning to the island with her children, hurrying up from the harbour with their few belongings as rain hissed down on shining cobbles, to the home she had been born in. As she imagined, she murmured old, forbidden words, softly chanted words that could draw a dream closer to being.

The lock on her cell clanked as the key turned. She jerked upright as the door swung open. But it was not Anne or Aeneas. It was the Dowager Lady McIntosh, with a package which she pulled from her cloak and unwrapped as soon as the jailer was gone. Inside was a bottle of gleaming straw-gold liquid.

'*Uisge beatha?*' Nan frowned.

'Whisky, Nan.' The Dowager shed her cloak, took up Nan's mug and poured. 'We must get you speaking the English.'

'Should I be troubling with it now? It's bearers of bad news that bring whisky.'

Anne and Aeneas were late. Their boat should have docked seven days since. Whatever news they had would be bad news if it didn't arrive soon.

'There is no news.' The Dowager handed Nan the mug. 'They're not back.'

'There's only the one cup I have.'

'The bottle will do fine for me. We can sit till it's gone.'

'They wouldn't be having storms at sea, not in harvest month.'

'No, the lack of wind, most likely.'

'If the *Sasannaich* let them go.'

'Robert Nairn's family put someone to see to your children.' The Dowager avoided the implication. 'When all's done, they've promised transport to Skye and a pension for –' she hesitated to say 'life', for that might be short, nor could she say 'till they're grown', for that implied they'd be motherless '– for as long as it's needed.' She settled herself on the bunk, clinked the bottle against Nan's tin mug. '*Slàinte mhòr,*' she said, and drank.

In his offices, Lord Louden studied the plans spread out on the table in front of him. The new Fort George would spread across the whole of the Ardersier promontory that jutted into the Moray Firth. It would replace the old fort in town, dismantled by the inhabitants when the Jacobites arrived. In resentment of it housing a government garrison since the Union, as if they were a conquered people, they had torn it down with bare hands. Now they were a conquered people, and the magnificence of the new fort would stand for centuries to remind them of that. It would be the mightiest artillery fortification in Britain. How he coveted command of it.

The guard outside tapped on the door and opened it. 'Captain M<sup>c</sup>Intosh and the Lady M<sup>c</sup>Intosh, sir,' he said.

'Show them in, man. Show them in.'

It was late in the evening when Anne and Aeneas drove back to Moy. In the dusk, a squawking flight of geese arrowed overhead towards the loch, the first greylags arriving for winter. The journey home had been nerve-wracking, even after a fair wind filled the sails north of Berwick, for fear it would drop again. But the order remitting Nan's sentence was delivered. They stopped at the prison to tell her she would be free in another month's time. At the Dowager's, they had supper, caught up on the news Louden had already sketched in and collected their carriage. Now, as greylags cross-stitched the faded purple sky, dropping out of formation to land, Aeneas guided the horse easily around familiar curves and through known shadows.

Returning home should have been joyful. After the ball, Anne was the toast of London, envied, admired and sought after. But, as the carriage wheels spun through the dust, dancers whirled again in her head. All that bowing and scraping instead of simple courtesy, women flirting and wheedling to manipulate men because they were powerless without them. Even Helen, desperate to regain some status, had simpered with suitable swains. That could be Scotland's future, always the cowed and beggared spouse in a mis-matched union. Those customs and habits would increasingly impinge on Scottish society, changing it until the people forgot who they were, what they had been.

Anne had not expected to bring it home with her. Her innards knotted. Anger flickered and grew. Her own situation had been forgotten. Aeneas had complete power over her. Like those English wives in thrall to their husbands, she was still his prisoner.

He pulled the carriage to a halt in the yard, jumped out and came round to help her down.

'I can get myself down,' she snapped.

'Hey!' He stepped back as if stung. 'Where did that come from?'

'Don't patronize me.' She struggled with her skirts, stumbling to the ground.

'It's late,' he said. 'Go on up; I'll bring wine.'

'To soften me up, is that it?'

He caught her arm, drew her back against the side of the carriage. 'What are you talking about?'

'I said once I was no English wife to be owned and ordered. But listen to you. Behave yourself. Don't speak. Speak English. Be yourself. Go to bed.'

'That's not how —'

'No doubt you want to fuck with me as well!'

'No, of course not.'

'I'm no man's pet,' she raged. 'Even the miserable Calvinist kirk says husband and wife are equal between the sheets. So do not come to my bed until we are. I will not be the spoils of war!' She pushed past, stormed off inside.

Aeneas turned, hand raised, mouth open to call her back. The door slammed shut. He let his arm fall to his side, expelled a long breath. His mouth twitched. He shook his head. Chuckling, he turned to see to the horse.

Up in her room, Anne banged the bedroom door behind her, touched a spill to the peat glowing in the fireplace, lit the candles, threw off her clothes, put on a wrap and sat at her dressing table to unfasten her hair. As it tumbled loose about her shoulders, she brushed it out. As she brushed, holding the length of it up to tug tangles from the ends, her fury calmed to indignation. They both spoke with Cumberland. She sought Nan's freedom. Aeneas hadn't even thought about his wife's. Let him work it out. He could sleep in his study until he had. She knew how to be alone now. Her nation might go cap in hand to its lord and master, begging favours, learning shame. She would not.

The bedroom door clicked open and he came in. He had removed his weapons and plaid, was dressed only in his shirt and kilt. In his hand he held the scrolled order which consigned her to his custody.

'Anne, I will never be equal to you,' he said.

'And that will be the truth of it,' she snapped.

'I made a mistake.'

'A big mistake,' she agreed.

'The answer is yes,' he said.

'Yes what?'

'Yes, I want to fuck with you.' He shut the door, walked over to her.

Involuntarily, she stood. No piece of paper would allow him to dominate her. If he wanted a fight, he could have it.

'But, as you are my wife –' that infuriating half-smile played on his mouth '– and my prisoner –' he loosed the tie that held her wrap '– and I am your chief –'

He couldn't do this to her. She couldn't do this.

'Are you pulling rank on me?'

His eyes shone, reflecting the candlelight. '– I'll settle for you pleasuring me instead,' he finished.

'Aeneas,' she groaned.

'You invented this game, my lady.' He stroked her neck with the edge of the scroll, parted the front of her wrap with it. 'And, as I remember, when it was in your favour, I served you well.'

She remembered. A wave of desire rushed through her body as it remembered. He drew the scroll lightly down to trace the line of her breast.

'When I saw the Duke, he passed the progress of this order to me.'

'Why didn't you tell me?'

'I wanted to be here, in our home. That's what the wine was for, to celebrate.' He moved closer, his body almost touching hers. 'So,' he offered, the glint of fire deepening the darkness in his eyes, serious now, 'if you please me well enough tonight, you can burn this in the morning.'

She could hit him. She might snatch the order from his hand, throw it on the fire. But it meant nothing to him. He offered himself, vulnerable. She could refuse, mock him, belittle or berate him, have her revenge. She did none of those. Something deeper would be honoured here. Tilting her head, she raised her chin a little. A smile curved her mouth.

'The pleasure, husband,' she said, 'will be mine.'

Outside, the moon rose high above the loch. Greylag geese settled themselves on the water. Slender shadows of roe deer moved through the woods. Up on the scree of the higher slopes, a wildcat hunted alone. Above the trees, wings beating like breath, an owl hovered. Over among the ruins of the north-west cotts, a peat glowed in the one remaining hearth as old Meg turned in her sleep on the pallet beside the fire. In the stone cottages, the scarred side of her face against the pillow, Ewan's daughter slept, dreaming of tomorrow. On the horse-hair mattress of the kitchen box-bed, reassured now her chief and his wife were safe home from the heathen south, Jessie drew the cover round her shoulders and settled for the night. There would be work to do come morning.

Long before morning, grey ashes crumbled in the grate in the master bedroom at Moy. The last flame flickered from the parchment. Anne and Aeneas lay in each other's arms, talking softly, caressing, making plans. She could feel her heart beat against him, steady as a drum. So many of those they cared for were gone, but not all. The way of life they valued was lost, yet love remained. The delicious irony of the Duke dancing to the rebel tune did not constitute a victory. But it raised hope, hope that there was still a spark to be lit that might blaze into tomorrow. A nation did not die while its spirit lived. She had won small concessions. In them, the tide turned. Life would not be stopped. Laws could be repealed, new ways found to live. Freedom was an idea. It could not be destroyed.

# Author's Postscript

'Woman is half the world'

*Margaret Oliphant, 1828–97*

Colonel Anne Farquharson, the Lady McIntosh, transferred her political activities to civic life. In 1763, she was elected as a burgess freewoman and guildsister of the burgh of Inverness. When her husband died in 1770, she moved to Leith, Edinburgh. On her death, in 1787, she was buried in St Ninian's churchyard on Coburg Street, where a plaque, erected in 2001, commemorates her contribution to the Rising of 1745. Beside it, a rose bush is planted, the white rose of Scotland – the Jacobite rose.

*White Rose Rebel* is a work of fiction. Only tantalizing scraps of Anne's story survive. I found the first in Rennie McOwan's *Stories of the Clans* and searched out more from Maggie Craig's *Damn' Rebel Bitches*, in first-hand accounts and from the many other histories. Rising out of the reduction of later opinion was a recognizable woman, an historical character who sounded like most Scotswomen, a bonny fechter, a genuine ancestor. History generates a myth that men make the world and women suffer for it, patently false and a disservice to both genders. Men and women make history together, co-operating with each other to uphold whatever society they create. The women of the '45 were not victims but perpetrators, active participants in a British civil war which was ended by genocide. To tell that story meant simplifying it. Time is compressed at the beginning and end, the campaign condensed to main events, secondary characters merged. *White Rose Rebel* takes a Jacobite stance, but the actions of Anne, and others, echo those ascribed to them by the government at the time. The need for self-preservation combined with British guilt over brutal acts of pacification meant involvement was soon rewritten. Period accounts and later histories are all contradictory. But the Duke of Cumberland reports Anne's capture, naming her among 'four of their principal Ladies'. Colonel Anne, *la belle rebelle*, the heroine, a very pretty woman, the heavenly Lady M<sup>c</sup>Intosh, that bloody rebel, a masculine spirit, traitor, a damn' rebel bitch – she was all that, a hero of the '45.

In 1747 an amnesty was passed. Monaltrie was pardoned after twenty years. Some never were. The proscription against Highland clothes was lifted in 1782. Acts abolishing the bearing of arms and heritable jurisdictions remained. The clan system was destroyed, replaced by capitalism. The status of women was reduced, the Highlands emptied, the people scattered.

In 1997 Scotland voted overwhelmingly to regain its own parliament, which sat in 1999 for the first time since 1707. Perhaps the nation might also recover its own history.

*Janet Paisley*
*August 2006*

# Glossary

## Gaelic

*Ach*: But, except

*arasaid*: two yards of tartan or plaid worn pleated and belted over women's clothing

*Bàn*: fair-haired

*Bheir me ò, horo bhan o; o;*
*Bheir me ò, horo bhan i*
*Bheir me ò, o horo ho*: chorus vocables from the 'Eriskay Love Lilt'
    *... o cruit mo chridh'*: O harp of my heart

*Cha dèan iad sin*: They won't do that.

*Chan eil! Chan eil idir!*: It is not! Not at all!

*Ciod e?*: What is it?

*clann*: family, children, clan

*co-dhiù*: anyway, at any rate, whatever

*Creag Dhubh!*: Black Rock!

*Danns, a Shasannaich!*: Dance, Sassenach!

*Dè?*: What?

*Dè bha siud?*: What was that?

*fàilte*: welcome

*fàilte oirbh*: welcome (plural/formal)

*fuirich*: wait, stay

*Greas ort*: Hurry up

*Gonadh!*: Damn!

*Gu dearbh, fhèin, chan fhuirich!*: It will not wait, it certainly will not!

*Gu sealladh orm!*: My goodness!

*Isd!*: Hush!

*Isd, a ghràidh*: Hush, my dear.

*Isd, no!*: No, not at all! (literally, 'Quiet, no!')

*mo chridhe*: my heart

*mo ghaoil*: my dearest, my love

*Na can sin!*: Don't say that!

*Nì sinn dannsa, a Shasannaich*: We dance, Sassenach

*Och*: interjection of annoyance

*O mo chreach*: Oh, dear

*Peighinn rìoghail*: Pennyroyal, a species of mint

*Pòg mo thòn*: Kiss my arse

*Rinn mi a' chùis!*: I did it!

*Sasannach*: Southern

*Sasannaich*: Southerners, Southerner's

*'S coma leam*: I don't care.

*Seachdnar!*: Seven men!

*seadh*: just so, yes

*Seadh, a-nis*: So, indeed

*sgian dhubh*: small black-handled knife

*Sguir dheth!*: Stop it!

*Siuthad!*: Go!/On you go!

*slàiinte*: Your health! (used as a toast)

*Slàinte mhòr!*: Your very good health!

*Slàn leat, mo luaidh*: Goodbye, my beloved

*'S mis' a tha duilich*: It's me who is sorry.

*Taigh na Galla ort!*: Go to Hell/ Damn you!

*tapadh leat*: thank you (informal)

*tapadh leibh*: thank you (formal)

*Tha e crùbach*: It's lame.

*Tha mi an dòchas*: I hope so.

*Tha mi sgìth*: I'm tired.

*Tha mi uamhasach duilich*: I'm so sorry.

*torr-sgian*: a spade for cutting peat

*trobhad*: come

*trobhad an-seo*: come here

*uisge beatha*: whisky (literally, 'water of life')

*uisge*: water

## Scots

*bailie*: town magistrate and burgh councillor

*birl*: whirl around, revolve rapidly

*bonnie*: lovely

*brae*: steep slope

*burn*: stream or river

*carse*: extensive flat, alluvial land along a riverbank

*close*: alley

*diddle*: singing without words, usually to imitate dance music ('diddle-di-di-di', etc.)

*dunted*: nudged, struck

*fash*: fret

*fechter*: fighter

*firth*: estuary

*glen*: valley

*guddle*: to fish with the hands, a mess

*guid-dochters*: daughters-in-law

*keek*: to peep, glance

*kist*: chest, trunk, large box

*loch*: lake

*provost*: civic head of burgh council and chief magistrate, mayor

*scaffies*: street sweepers, refuse collectors

*scoosh*: to squirt liquid, a rush of liquid

*scrug*: to tug (cap or bonnet) forward over the brow

*skelp*: slap, hurry

*snip*: to be short with

*spate*: flood

*strath*: river valley, esp. broad and flat

*thrawnness*: perverseness, contrariness, obstinacy

*wheen*: lot, several

*wheesht*: hush, be quiet